# SMOKE

# SEASON

T0281895

## ALSO BY AMY HAGSTROM

*The Wild Between Us*

# SMOKE SEASON

*A novel*

## AMY HAGSTROM

LAKE UNION
PUBLISHING

Text copyright © 2024 by Amy Hagstrom
All rights reserved.

Published by Lake Union Publishing, Seattle

www.apub.com

Amazon, the Amazon logo, and Lake Union Publishing are trademarks of Amazon.com, Inc., or its affiliates.

ISBN-13: 9781662518294 (paperback)
ISBN-13: 9781662518287 (digital)

Cover design by Caroline Teagle Johnson
Cover image: ©Magdalena Wasicek / ArcAngel; ©reklamlar / Getty

Printed in the United States of America

*For my three sons, Nate, Calvin, and Tobias, born and raised in fire country.*

# The Spark

# CHAPTER 1

Kristina Truitt doubted anyone in Carbon, Oregon, would forget where they had been and what they'd been doing at a quarter after five the evening of July 10, 2018. True herself had just pulled onto the sand at Fern Creek after a full day on the Outlaw River, urging her river-rafting clients, a mother-and-child duo from Marin County, California, to pitch their tent quick. A hot summer rain would be upon them in minutes; if she looked to the east, it already approached in a solid wall.

"Don't forget the rainfly!" True called after them, her voice drowned out by the first crack of thunder. They scurried like sand crabs up the embankment to the tree line, Vivian Wu clutching their shiny new Big Agnes tent under one arm like a football and young Emmett Wu looking wildly upward at the darkening sky as he chased after his mom.

"And avoid widow-makers, like we talked about!" she added. It was only day one of five they would spend together, after all, and fifteen years of river-guide experience told True the wind she'd rowed against for the last five miles would only intensify with the rain. Any standing dead trees posed a high risk of toppling onto the unsuspecting ER nurse from San Rafael and her kid.

True wrestled with the heavy-duty polypropylene straps securing their gear to the oar raft, her fingers feeling thick from the oppressive humidity of the afternoon. A flash of light lit up the overcast sky—the bow of the oar raft momentarily glowed bright red—and then another crack of thunder sounded, this one so close True could have sworn she felt the rumble's reverberation in the metal clasps of the straps.

Shit, they'd gotten off the water just in time. At least no rain was falling yet, she thought as she freed the Wus' dry bags of clothing and her two largest metal ammo boxes. She'd picked up the military-issued boxes years ago at the Army Navy store after discovering their usefulness for storing first-aid supplies, her repair kit, her sat phone, and their five-day supply of TP.

She hauled all of it out onto the sand and climbed back into the boat for one more box, a smaller, even more banged-up container she eyed warily before carting it up with the rest, tucking it amid her personal duffel and waterproof Paco Pad. Like it or not, it was best to keep this particular cargo close.

Next, she freed her own dry bag and tent, the camp table, and her stove. She debated getting out the canvas tarpaulin she used for shade but decided this wind would whip it down the Outlaw like an oversize kite faster than she could count thunderclaps. She left it behind, along with the gargantuan Yeti cooler containing dinner. They'd need to wait out this storm before getting the grill going.

"True? Can I help?" Emmett called from halfway up the sandy bank.

He jumped as another bolt of lightning lit up the sky but made a noticeable effort not to cower at the angry answer of thunder. True threw him a grateful smile as she held up his family's dry bags for him to retrieve. "Thanks!"

She appreciated how willing he was to give this camping and rafting thing a go, knowing the trip had been his mom's idea. "Emmett's pronouns are *he*, *him*, and *his*," Vivian Wu had informed True before booking. "I won't raft with anyone who won't respect that." She'd paused. "It's why I felt most comfortable booking with an LGBTQ-owned guide company."

Company of one, but still, True had felt honored. Her sympathy was acute for young Emmett, who'd apparently had a hell of a school year after finally finding the courage, just shy of his twelfth birthday, to whisper to his mom that he was not, and never had been, the *she* he had been known as for the first eleven years of life. Clearly, True decided as she tied up the raft and followed Emmett up the embankment, Vivian Wu had done her research.

She made her way up the bank loaded down with steel boxes and bags, staggering for a step or two when her feet sank hard into the sand. The Wus had celebrated snagging such a beachy campsite all to themselves, though True knew this had more to do with rafting-company pecking order than any stroke of river luck.

Her solo operation always departed a day or two after the big weekend groups with their gear boats and kayaks trailing behind, and though she never minded the quieter water, she sometimes missed having an extra pair of hands. So when Emmett offered to unburden her of a sleeping bag and duffel at the top, she accepted, dropping the rest in one unceremonious heap where the sand flattened up. Once this crazy weather subsided, this would serve as their camp-kitchen headquarters for the night.

"Take your mom's bag to her," she told Emmett while trying to secure her hair—at least the long, sun-bleached side; the other side she'd shorn close to the skull—up under her Patagonia cap. "And dig out your rain jacket!"

Emmett decided to obey this second order first, and so was still standing there, clawing through his bag, when the next lightning strike—*the* lightning strike, the one to start it all—cut through the air, this time so close the fine hair on True's arms stood on end. She glanced up in time to see the bolt shoot straight down toward the tree line on Flatiron Peak, at her ten o'clock to the northeast.

Directly toward the base of the mountain and the town of Carbon.

As True watched, the long, crooked finger of electricity made contact, setting the tip of the tallest tree on the peak's plateaued flattop aflame as effortlessly as a Bic igniting the wick of a birthday candle.

It was so beautiful, she actually gasped.

Emmett cried out. He pointed at the distant trees, gesticulating crazily, like maybe True hadn't seen the strike. "What do we do? True!" He yanked on her arm. "What do we *do*?"

"Nothing," she assured him, though the word left her lungs in a somewhat shaky exhale. A forest fire, no matter how inconsequential, was the last thing she needed on this trip. Emmett's mother had already complicated it for True enough, bursting into her warehouse in Carbon for their pre-trip debriefing yesterday in a blaze of mama-bear glory. True's precise type of kryptonite. True turned to lay her hands on Emmett's shoulders, still warm from the sun that had shone fiercely all day, right up until the clouds had rolled in, and told them both what they needed to hear. "It's okay. Emmett. It'll be fine."

"But! I mean . . ." He pointed again, speechless, and True nodded, watching the flame grow with him, just a tiny orange dot against the ridge of Flatiron, smoke beginning to billow in one thin upward coil like vapor from a cigar in a cartoon.

"Happens all the time," True assured him, even while eyeing the location with more scrutiny than she'd care to admit, calculating the distance between the strike and town. As the crow flies, what? Five miles? Ten? She thought first of her best friends, Sam and Melissa Bishop—Sam residing in Carbon with their kids, Melissa undoubtedly called to this blaze as Carbon Rural's battalion chief—and then of her own place, tucked off the grid just a few miles upstream.

Her acreage on this very river was carpeted with sage, its branches the color of barrel-aged bourbon, and poison oak that turned fiery under the summer sun and blackberry bushes that bit back if you tried to squeeze between branches to pluck their fruit. A feisty place, her Outsider, as True had christened the land and yurt she'd ordered and erected from Outside Enterprises in Bozeman. Feisty as well as thirsty, these days. It might be only July, but Carbon had already recorded its tenth hundred-degree day.

"You know the insurance will be through the roof, Truitt," Paul Jackson, Carbon's poor excuse for a State Farm agent, had said after she'd bought the property last year, pushing the paperwork back toward her across his desk.

"We can't choose our neighbors, Paul," she'd countered. Last she'd checked, she wasn't responsible for the grow site next door, even if it *was* considered to be on the shady side.

Which was precisely why she needed the Outsider insured to the rafters. That and the fact that Mother Nature seemed to have a fiery temper these days.

"That's why we have fire lookouts," she told Emmett now, setting her jaw as she deliberately looked away from the smoke now spiraling lazily upward from the mountain. "Remember the one I pointed out this morning?"

They'd checked it out from the shore after a midmorning snack on the bank of the Outlaw just a stone's throw from the Outsider, the Wus peering upward at the stilted watchtower, built back in the Civilian Conservation Corps days, on the top of the nearest mountainside. True had used the opportunity to take care of a little errand of her own, liberating the same small ammo box she now carried from its hiding spot behind a thick patch of blackberry bushes straddling the property line by the river. She hadn't had any trouble, though she hadn't been able to resist a glance behind her to ensure the Wus were still engrossed in CCC history, stepping directly into the berry patch in the process. No matter: the scrapes True received from the blackberry thorns always felt like a fair tradeoff for the relief that flooded her each time the box was still there, week after week, waiting for her.

At least the end was in sight. The river gods willing, this trip would mark the last time she jumped like a jackrabbit at the sight of her own shadow whenever she handled the thing.

Looking back at her young charge, she reminded Emmett of the height of the lookout they'd seen this morning, the expansive views its steward must be afforded from its glass walls, and he nodded, though he didn't look entirely convinced. "But who will put out the fire, after they spot it?"

*Melissa, most likely.* The thought brought with it another quick kick of worry, even as True laid what she hoped was a comforting hand on the crown of Emmett's precisely shorn head, a recent haircut she knew he took pride in. But then she smiled, turning her palms upward to catch the first of the smattering of drops to hit their skin. Finally, the rain was upon them. An ironic sign of clear skies ahead? "Mother Nature will."

Emmett glanced up, an experimental smile on his face. "Oh hey, yeah! Good."

True glanced back to where Vivian Wu had managed to erect their tent. "It's gonna pour, kid. Go give your mom her coat."

Emmett ran off, his gait lighter somehow than it had been all trip, the careful posture True had observed in his body giving way to a loosening of limbs as he loped up the slope. True hoped Vivian saw the unwinding within him that she did.

She dug her own rain jacket out of her bag and pulled her hood up over her hat as she went about putting up the table and her own tent and fly. The heavy, hot drops felt good on her bare thighs as she worked. They ran off the bill of her hat to splash onto her cheeks, soaked her board shorts, and ran down her legs to cause her feet to squish in her Chacos. By the time she had the table set up, the rain was coming down hard enough to leave sudden puddles in the divots of the sand.

But before she could move to higher ground, it stopped almost as quickly as it had come on. Emmett popped back out of his tent, followed by his mother, who sported an Arc'teryx rain shell that True knew for a fact cost more than her entire wardrobe of river wear. Emmett's was identical to his mother's, though his petite build swam in a men's extra small. Instead of seeming over-the-top, however, the detail struck True as touching. The care Vivian had taken to follow the packing list to the letter, buying only the best, served to remind True how important this trip was to her.

"It didn't rain for long!" Vivian called over now.

No, it hadn't. It hadn't rained nearly long enough. True glanced back toward the ridgeline of Flatiron Peak. Through the haze of the moisture still clinging to the air, she felt pretty sure she could still make out the glow of the blaze taking shape, its smoke now a cloud, dense against the damp sky.

# CHAPTER 2

The sudden rain was already letting up when Melissa Bishop closed the automatic vehicle-bay door of Carbon Rural Fire District 1 and made her way into the break room, Mother Nature saving her the task of the customary post-shift vehicle hose-down.

"Looks like you're gonna have to wash that rig after all, Chief." Rookie volunteer Deklan Jones smirked over the rim of his Diet Coke can as what had been furious pounding just moments ago gave way to a light patter.

"Yeah? Think fast." Mel tossed the keys, which Deklan caught on instinct, in midair. "Guess *you've* got the job now, newbie."

"Wait . . . what the . . . ?!" Deklan's face flushed practically the color of his ginger hair in indignation. He threw a cursory glance around the room, as if in hope that someone outranking Mel would come to his rescue. Dave Lewis, captain of their station? Not likely, Mel thought. He stared at his phone with a disgruntled frown, obsessed with some game his teenage kid had told him he'd never beat. The big boss, Fire Chief Gabe Hernandez, was still stuck in the city of Outlaw for the day, at one of the interminable meetings that made him curse his position at the top of the station ladder, and Doug White, Mel's assistant chief, was mercifully already in the process of clocking out, which meant that he'd decided to take a night off from questioning her overtime hours for a change. As a single mom—even if the title still felt unnatural less than one full year into her separation—and the primary breadwinner in her family, she'd take what she could, thank you very much, and she'd save any apologies for her daughters, eight-year-old Astor and five-year-old Annie.

The thought of her kids brought the usual double punch of guilt for being here and guilt for wishing herself anywhere else, and she was glad to turn her focus to young Deklan.

"Eighteen years old and totally clueless. I keep telling you, kid, you gotta learn some respect for your superiors." She flicked a fry Deklan's way for good measure before scooping up the remaining wrappers from her crew's takeout order and disposing of them in the garbage can at the end of the galley kitchen.

"For my *elders*, more like," Deklan grumbled. "What are you, like, forty?" He said this like he meant seventy.

"Thirty-eight, for the record," Mel told him cheerfully, already headed toward the door. "I know, I know, that sounds ancient to a kid fresh out of Carbon High. And speaking of kids . . . I'm ready to see mine." With any luck, she just might escape the station with time to catch up with their father before the customary kid handoff. Her feelings for Sam Bishop were every bit as conflicted as her feelings for her work, but she *did* owe him a drink at the bar and grill they still owned together. He'd bought the last round, and lord knew they had plenty to talk about. She waved a farewell, mentally halfway to the River Eddy.

Naturally, the fire gods couldn't let *that* happen. The phone buzzed on the wall, catching Mel up short in the doorway, like a woman snagged abruptly on a line. A low curse escaped her lips. A call on the landline, instead of across their comms network, could only mean one thing: an interagency request. She listened as Deklan answered—anything to get out of washing the truck, Mel figured—while reluctantly fishing her cell phone out of her pocket. She didn't relish having to call Sam to let him know she'd be late for pickup. Again. It would trigger their usual argument, or at least one of their top ten, and they were already tangoing to a one-step-forward, two-steps-back beat.

She'd just hung up when Deklan called out to Lewis. "Hey, BM? It's a Red Book request for us."

This got Lewis's attention—the request, not the nickname, which Deklan swore, in all innocence, stood for Big Man, despite Lew ranking below Mel's battalion-chief standing. He looked up from his phone screen with a groan.

"Red Book?" he confirmed, while Mel bade a silent goodbye to any evening at all at home, let alone an early one. The girls would be disappointed. Or at least Annie would be. Astor might turn one of her newly discovered, post-parent-separation surly looks in Mel's direction.

Deklan nodded. "Outlaw National Forest Service has a blaze sighted on Flatiron."

The operating manual commonly referred to as the Red Book outlined the policy of cooperation between municipal fire stations like Carbon Rural and wildland stations run by the United States Forest Service and Oregon Wildfire Response and Recovery, promising first response from whoever stood closest to any fire. In this day and age of brittle-dry forests, deadly pine-beetle infestations, climate change, and increased urban development, teamwork and swift action proved any community's best defense. And Flatiron was close—damned close—to Carbon, where Mel's kids called home. Where Sam still tried to eke out a profit at the River Eddy. As Lewis listened on the old landline, Mel stood in the doorway, her head craned upward toward the distinct topography of Flatiron Peak. Its oddly flattened top had been formed by volcanic action some ten thousand years ago. Mel had heard the spiel of its geological history just last month, when Astor had brought a collection of lava rocks home from her second-grade field trip, lightweight enough to float in the bathtub like a misshapen Navy fleet. She'd shown Mel her science trick in an increasingly rare moment of childhood levity. Was it the looming divorce that seemed to be robbing Mel's eldest daughter of her childhood, or had that ball been rolling since her baby sister's birth? No *I'm a Big Sister* T-shirt should come with a life-threatening heart condition for the younger sibling attached, but here they all were.

She squinted into the haze lingering after the electric storm, scanning the sea of evergreen carpeting the slope of the mountain, but couldn't pick out the start of a fire.

"Uh-huh," she heard Lewis say into the phone as some Forest Service interagency supervisor got him up to speed. "Eight miles south of here? Gimme the coordinates."

Lewis waved his thumb and forefinger in the air toward Deklan, indicating his need for a pen, then wrote the GPS coordinates given to him onto the legal pad that hung by the door. "Yep. Sure."

While Lewis's attention remained on the call, Mel continued to scan the mountain, searching, searching, and then *there!* She saw it . . . a fine but distinct plume of smoke, almost but not quite blending into the sky still thick gray with rain clouds. Below it, the telltale blur of orange glowed, fuzzy and ill-defined as a smudge on one of the heat maps she'd studied back in her first days as a novice, ground-pounding in Colorado. "Hey, Lew?" she called, leaning back toward the hallway. "I've got eyes on it."

Mel instructed Deklan to make the initial callouts to the rest of the Carbon Rural volunteer crew—"What am I, a secretary?"—while White, Mel's superior only in title, as Sam had been known to say, trudged back in to ready the rest of the team, his face set in stony resignation. For once, Mel couldn't fault him for his mood. Like her, he'd had one foot out the door.

Most of their skeleton crew of paid firefighters were still chilling in the break room after a call to the Carbon Happy Daze trailer park for some sort of electrical short. "So listen up," White told them. "We're on monitor status."

"Wait . . . we don't even get to *do* anything?" Deklan said, listening in instead of making his calls.

"We're ordered to stand by and assess only," White barked, so Mel threw the kid a bone.

"But we're the first responders, so we'll still have to yellow up."

This earned her a grunt of satisfaction; even a newbie like Deklan knew that donning the mustard-yellow wildland-issue fire-retardant wear meant action *could* be required, even if his captain and chief couldn't promise anything. Carbon Rural's lieutenant, Janet Stillwater, got everyone up and off the couches, her straight ebony hair sashaying in its long ponytail as she opened lockers to make sure every team member had the required wear.

"Carbon Rural is closest," she added, "so Carbon Rural goes."

This assignment might not be as sexy as Deklan would like, but protocol was protocol, with their station situated so close to the wildland-urban interface. Even if it *did* keep them all from their families, Mel tried to dispel the resentment that could fester if she let it.

Back out in the vehicle bay, driver engineer José Juarez had already fired up the tactical engine, easing his ample girth behind the wheel. The vehicle rumbled reliably as Mel climbed back into her truck, its dirt now streaked with rainwater, and turned over the engine. Janet hopped in beside her, along with Deklan and his rookie partner, Ryan Sloan, fresh from his day job at Carbon Grocery. Lewis and White followed in Lew's assistant-chief vehicle.

Ten minutes from the time of the phone call, they rolled out as a team of twenty: eight staff and twelve volunteers ranging in age from eighteen to seventy-two. The three trucks and two chief vehicles eased down Main Street toward the state highway that led to the network of Forest Service roads crisscrossing Flatiron. Despite her reluctance to load up this evening, the rush of adrenaline that was probably responsible for Mel getting into this profession in the first place made itself known. She leaned forward in her seat, letting it carry her forward, away from her family, away from Carbon. It wasn't until they'd turned up FS 7312, Mel's Dodge Ram bouncing through the ruts like a raft over rapids, that she realized she'd forgotten to update Sam with her new ETA. Not that she knew one.

"Sam knows this comes with the territory," Janet reminded her, her trademark practicality always a welcome contribution to the team. "He'll assume he's on call until further updated."

She was right, of course, but Janet, mom of four, should understand: working mothers had to go the extra mile, which meant that, by very definition, you never fully caught up. Mel had already missed Astor's end-of-year school picnic and Annie's five-year-old doctor checkup, which had been more extensive than her sister's. Mel's inner critic gnawed at her relentlessly, grating at the back of her mind like the serrated edge of her standard-issue pilot knife. *You'll never do enough for Annie,* it told her, *no matter how many medical articles you read. You'll never set the perfect example for Astor, no matter how high up the ranks you climb.*

She exhaled hard, refocusing her concentration on the road as they eased their way up the switchbacks of Flatiron, sticking to the main FS 7312. While the Ram trucks and the smaller of the engines could have detoured to take a more direct route up a lesser-used, more deeply rutted logging road, they were only collectively as strong as their weakest—or, in this case, largest-axled—link.

They got as close as they could, Janet consulting Mel's handheld GPS units as they drove, then pulled up short when the grade of the road finally got too iffy. They piled out of the vehicles, making their way up the rest of the slope on foot. Ryan and the older volunteers all hiked silently, but Deklan talked a mile a minute, mostly about the boots he'd neglected to break in.

"Such a rookie," José muttered under his breath with a chuckle. "Should have swapped those brand-new kicks out for those Sasquatch slippers I bequeathed him. He'd be better off." Mel and Janet both laughed; José was infamous for his practical jokes, most of which were directed toward Deklan these days, who appreciated them most.

Only Janet exhibited some mercy. "Hey, kid!" she called. "Find me later for moleskin."

At the tree line, they finally got their first unobstructed view of the fire. They all paused, a hush settling around them despite the persistent presence of the wind, even Deklan falling mercifully silent. As expected, the blaze wasn't large, not by wildland standards, but Mel didn't care if a forest fire burned a quarter acre or five thousand, ten thousand, even a hundred thousand acres . . . This undulating, licking, *living* thing deserved their respect. The fire danced far above them on the ridge, one moment like a flag waving lightly in the wind, the next like a ship rocking gently on a sea, mesmerizing to watch. A few tall pines burned like torches, adding to the dramatic flair. They were responsible for most of the smoke that now billowed in a mushroom cloud that migrated west, but the vast majority of the blaze was, in a word, underwhelming. It consumed the dry undergrowth in a slow, meticulous crawl, fanning out in thin spots to lap at the denser stands of trees that proved more formidable foes. It was what Mel had been taught to call a "shallow" blaze, just skimming the surface of the forest . . . a trickle rather than a rushing river.

"Hell," Deklan said, his voice flat with defeat, "it's about as tame as a campfire."

"All we're missing are the s'mores," Ryan agreed.

Mel smiled, pausing to secure her long hair in an elastic band she found in her pocket. It felt good to get it off the back of her neck. Sweat already beaded on her skin, and it was only going to get hotter. In this post–Smokey the Bear era, forestry professionals realized the folly of putting out every fire in the American West, which meant this one would burn, unless specialized wildland crews decided otherwise. "Our job as Carbon Rural?" she reminded the rookies. "Containment." As frustrating as that was when her kids needed her. While Sam waited to debrief with her.

Deklan mumbled something about signing up to be a fire*fighter*, not a fire babysitter, which sent Mel's thoughts back to her girls.

"No one expects you to win mother of the year," her best friend, True, pointed out once, when Mel's Wonder Woman act had shown signs of wear. She had winced, trying not to let that sting. As far as Mel was concerned, she'd been out of the running for that particular distinction since the moment Annie was born with a heart defect she'd been powerless to fix.

But thinking of True would only cause Mel to worry further, her thoughts splintering in yet another unwelcome direction, so she refocused on the conversation at hand.

"Don't worry," Lewis reassured Deklan and Ryan now. "You'll still be putting some calluses on those pretty hands of yours tomorrow, carving out firebreaks with the Forest Service. In the meantime," he added, much to Deklan's delight, "stomp out any hot spots to your heart's content."

Mel joined them, but her heart wasn't in it. It had snagged on the word *tomorrow*. Lewis was right. Tonight, her crew would need to stage indefinitely, monitoring the fire from the safety of the lower tree line until the wildland ground crew could get on scene. Which meant that though she'd now find time for a quick call, she wouldn't be heading back to Carbon and her girls anytime soon.

# CHAPTER 3

In the wake of the sudden deluge that had split the sky, Sam Bishop stood at the window of the River Eddy Bar and Grill, watching his kids scurry around like chipmunks on the now soaked back deck, picking up windblown napkins-turned-pulp and throwing them at each other. However, what should have been a common enough show of childhood antics was anything but; little Annie lacked the stamina to play in earnest. Sam knew there was no need to go outside to referee the situation; soon enough, his eldest, Astor, would either lose interest or scoop Annie up in a bear hug to cart her around under her big-sister steam.

Even eight years into fatherhood, Sam heaved a quiet little sigh of wonder at this, such a startling contrast to his own growing-up years filled with sucker punches and spitting contests. His onetime best friend and pseudo brother Chris Fallows had shown no such mercy, but even so, while the sight of Astor coddling her sister should have filled Sam's chest with pride, an odd sort of remorse lingered there instead. He wasn't sure whether he mourned Astor's childhood, on a fast track since her sibling's birth, or Annie's, destined to lag behind. Probably both.

He contemplated closing up early, but a handful of patrons had weathered the storm and still sat at the bar, mostly seasonal workers off shift from grow sites along the river valley. Though they could use a shower, these young crews always had cash burning in their pockets, cash Sam had no qualms about parting them from. Besides, his long-time server, Kim Murphy, needed the hours. He was about to duck into the kitchen to get a jump on the grease coating the fryer before Mel turned up to collect the girls when the Eddy door swung open again, cutting a swath of summer light across the polished wood-plank floor. One glance at the entrance had all thought of abandoning his post eradicated from Sam's mind.

*Speak of the devil, and his father will appear.* "Out," he said immediately. Every town had a resident lowlife, but John Fallows, the owner and operator of the biggest grow in the valley, took it to a new level. And he knew damned well he wasn't welcome here. That went the same for Chris these days, much as it pained Sam to think it.

Kim blanched and beat a hasty retreat toward the deck, corralling the girls en route, as Fallows crossed the threshold of the Eddy. And who could blame her? If Sam was still fuming over the Fallowses' mistreatment of her nephew Zack, Kim must be positively sick to her stomach.

"Isn't there anything we can do?" she had begged Sam the night young Zack had been arrested on the Oregon-California border of I-5, baffled by the thick wad of Saran-wrapped cash and handful of pills found stashed in one of the boxes of grow lights he was transporting for Fallows. "He thought he was only making a supply run, trying to make enough money to enroll at Oregon State next semester. You know he's a good kid."

Sam did know, which was one of many reasons he wanted nothing to do with the man who'd just darkened his door. Sam raised his voice. "Get lost, Fallows." He flung one arm in the direction of the door. "I've warned you enough times."

John Fallows approached the bar anyway. "C'mon now, Bishop. Why you gotta pretend like we ain't family?"

"Because we're not." Just because Sam's old man had been plastered to Fallows's side back in the day, not to mention just plastered, didn't mean Sam had to put up with this shit now. And just because he and Chris had no one but each other then didn't make it true now. Sam planted his feet firmly, shoulders square, channeling his years in the military as best he could. You didn't forget boot-camp training in a hurry, and he was no longer the kid who'd grown up in Carbon with no choice but to cower under this family's bullying. "I'm not kidding. Leave my bar."

Fallows held up a lazy arm. "Keep your panties on, Bishop. We're just here to talk to my guys. Those DEA pricks have been all over my shit."

Not that the Feds would find anything, unfortunately, no matter how suspicious they got. Ever since marijuana had been legalized in the state, Fallows made sure to stay squeaky-clean, at least in the eyes of the law. Licenses all in order, storefront on Main Street, even a line of CBD lotion. An LLC and everything. That way, Fallows could carry on with the much more lucrative side of his operations unfettered and unchecked.

"I can't believe I have to pay some overeducated, pansy-assed, fragile-as-a-snowflake chemistry PhD in Salem to tell me what I already know about my own goddamned weed," Fallows griped now to his crew. "Goddamned worst idea ever, this fucking blue state voting to make my shit legal." Some of the guys at the bar agreed with Fallows with a nod, but most kept their eyes on their beers.

Sam just continued to see red on behalf of young Zack, who now sported a record instead of a college ID. Along with all the other pawns who'd found their way into Fallows's path.

Sam could have easily been one of them, a statistic instead of an entrepreneur. He still had plenty to lose, his reputation in this town first and foremost, just by association. Which was precisely why Fallows was in no hurry to vacate the bar.

He slid Sam a slow smile. "Want a sample? On the house. It might chill you the hell out, man."

"Get. The fuck. Out of my bar," Sam repeated, the crew members' heads now on swivels, following the confrontation like spectators at a tennis match.

Fallows threw his hands up in the air. "Good thing your old man can't see what a pussy you've become."

"My old man in federal prison? The one *you* put there? That one?"

"Whatever, man. I'm out." Fallows turned on his heel, like it was his goddamned idea in the first place, leaving Sam, per usual, fuming.

Heart pounding in his chest, he told Fallows's crew to follow suit; he was closing up early after all.

A half hour later, he stood in the galley kitchen of his two-room apartment over the River Eddy, his hands still a bit shaky as he reached for his phone. Mel's face graced the screen, a sight that still caused a little uptick of his heart. But they weren't together anymore, no matter how much Sam wished it could be different, and their days of impromptu calls signaling *good* things were over.

"Don't tell me bad news," he entreated with a sigh. "I've had a day."

"Look out your kitchen window, toward Flatiron."

He clocked the thin plume of smoke in an instant. "Shit. All right, your day trumps mine."

"Well, maybe," Mel agreed, "given that mine appears to just be starting."

She sounded tired. Sam knew she'd rather be with the girls than on the job, and he also knew she couldn't turn down the hours. A familiar shame-resentment cocktail rose up like bile. Sam swallowed it back down. It wasn't Mel's problem that running the Eddy didn't provide Sam's full share of the money that was always in such desperately short supply with a medically fragile child, but it *would* be his problem to tell Astor and Annie that their mom wouldn't be coming to get them tonight.

He changed the subject. "You think it's going to turn into anything, this fire?" It wasn't like they didn't see them all the time at this time of year.

"Nah, just a little lightning strike." Mel paused. "I'll come get the kids first thing in the morning, all right?"

Sam agreed and disconnected the call with his customary "Stay safe," because old habits died hard, already reaching for one of the boxes of Kraft mac and cheese he kept handy on the counter. Maneuvering in the tight space to retrieve a trio of bowls from the sole cabinet, he thought wistfully of the spacious farm kitchen sitting empty in his two-story home on Highline Road overlooking town before remembering that that space, too, was still in a state of upheaval. Just like it had been for the entirety of his childhood.

"You don't have to renovate the *whole* house," Mel had said—more like begged—for the duration of the half decade she'd lived there, when they'd still been a family of four. "This isn't the hill you have to die on."

Sam always brushed her off or made a joke. Because he just *might* die on that hill. He'd been born on it, after all, into a life of poverty, to Shelley and Mark Bishop, the former of whom hadn't stuck around long. Ever since he'd taken over the place, remodeling it from the foundation up had felt more like an essential obligation than a choice.

"You're nothing like your dad," Mel promised time and again. She knew how hard it had been for Sam to reinvent himself in a small town with a long memory, but talking about home improvements had led to talking about money, and talking about money had been their downfall.

Or at least one of them.

After their marriage had imploded, he'd retreated to the Eddy apartment to lick his wounds. Sharing custody was easier if he was in town, he'd reasoned, though really, he'd just hoped to keep the constant reminders of their former life together at bay.

"We were happy," he'd tell True, usually after one too many once the bar was closed. "Right?"

It always came out as a question, which was probably half the problem. He knew Mel had eventually grown weary of convincing him he was good enough, man enough, all the enoughs.

But the thing was, he hadn't been. Not for Annie.

"That kind of thinking isn't healthy," True always told him with a firm shake of her head. And if he pushed back, wallowed even, she gave him shit, for which Sam was downright thankful. True could have chosen sides. More specifically, she could have chosen Mel. Sam wouldn't have blamed her, even if True and Sam *had* been friends first.

"You're stuck with me, and so is she," True said instead. "Sorry not sorry."

He made a mental note to try to touch base with True tonight—she, too, was out in the field tonight in her own right—then called out to the kids. The three of them might as well eat while the cheesy goo still bubbled. His stint as a firefighter's husband had taught him not to wait on dinner, even back when Mel's presence had graced their table, making it complete.

He pushed this memory back as Astor immediately ran into the kitchen from the couch, Annie attempting to keep up in a rare but gallant show of energy.

"Astor! Slow down!" Sam chided as Annie predictably gave up the race at the doorway, the short sprint leaving her gasping. "You know how important it is that your sister not overexert herself until she's cleared at her pre-op."

Mention of impending heart surgery tended to alter the tone of a room, and Sam was immediately sorry when Astor's expression clouded. It wasn't the first time she'd felt the gloom of this particular storm gathering, but Sam reminded himself that according to Annie's surgeon, it could be the last. Annie only had one more pediatric surgery to go.

"What? I just came when you called," Astor quipped, her expression guileless. But something flickered behind her eyes as she added, "And I don't know why we're in a rush. It's not like Mom's on her way." She glanced up at Sam, testing his reaction. "Right?"

So the sudden attitude had less to do with her sister and more to do with her mother. It came and went with Astor, righteous anger at the fate of her family flashing one moment, gone the next, disappearing under the serene surface of her steady personality like the elusive rainbow trout in the shallows of the Outlaw outside the Eddy door.

"She got called out on a fire out by Flatiron," he told her, and he was sorry as hell about it, but he couldn't let Astor walk all over him as a result. He gave her a pointed look until she reached out and helped her sister up onto her seat at the counter.

Annie accepted the proffered hand eagerly, and, watching how instantly she forgave and forgot, Sam knew he should press the issue with Astor, but the truth was, it heartened him to see Astor treating Annie more like an equal than the invalid everyone else saw. It allowed her to experience having an annoying kid sister for a change, not the sick little girl with the congenital heart condition that ran as a headline in everyone else's mind.

Annie took inventory of the kitchen. "Mac and cheese! Yay!" she exclaimed, just as Astor reached around her to snag a bite from the stirring spoon on the stove, then let out a squawk when the hot cheese hit her tongue.

"That's karma, kid, for a few minutes ago."

Sam dished them up, and Annie was three halfhearted bites into her bright-yellow noodles before noting with a disgruntled little sigh, "Mom promised we'd play Sorry!"

"You hate that game anyway," Astor told her, though whether in solidarity or to cause more friction, Sam couldn't say. "You never get to Safety."

"Do too!"

His phone rang, and Sam fished it out of his back pocket, shushing the girls while wiping off his palms on the already dirty dish towel. "This might be her again," he told them.

He was greeted instead by the voice of his longtime neighbor, Claude, who, after retiring from forty years of medical practice, still lived next door to Sam's house on Highline. Though "next door" was a relative term. Claude's place, where he and his late wife had raised their kids, lay almost a quarter mile across a shared field.

"Looks like the lightning storm lit up Flatiron," Claude said.

Sam nodded. "Yep, Mel took the call."

"Well, shoot. I know that's tough," Claude said.

Tough to be parenting solo again, or tough knowing the woman he loves—yes, present tense, unfortunately for Sam—and the mother of his children was out on the line? Both. Definitely both.

"Anyhow, I'll have a front-row seat to Mother Nature's fire show tonight, I'd wager," Claude continued as Sam smiled to himself. Claude managed to see the beauty in everything. He pictured the old man craning his neck out his kitchen window toward his unobstructed view of Flatiron Peak. Even perched a full ridgeline away, their houses sat in its shadow.

"We can see it here, too," Sam told him, reaching across the stove-top to push the pot to the back burner, out of the girls' reach, before stepping out onto the narrow back deck, where the lingering humidity from the electrical storm greeted him in an unwelcome embrace. It prickled the scruff along his neck; as Kim was always quick to point out, he'd fallen a bit out of the habit of shaving in the months since he'd semi-returned to bachelorhood. "I'll keep you posted if I get any news."

Astor followed him, asking, "Is that Uncle Claude?"

"Hi, Uncle Claude!" Annie chimed in, trailing after.

Astor squinted into the distance, eyeing the small plume of smoke as Claude returned the girls' greeting with a chuckle. Sam switched the phone to speaker in time to hear "You kids gonna be good for your papa now?"

"Never!" they both chorused, just as Claude had taught them, Astor adding, "You see the fire up there, too, Claude?"

"No bigger than a Bic flame, kiddo," Claude answered, and Sam told him, "She doesn't know what a Bic lighter is, Claude."

But Astor cooed, "Coool."

"Sam?" Claude added, "you still got that John Deere in your side yard? Got it juiced up?"

"Think so." They'd saved it from repossession the last time Annie's hospital bills had ballooned out of control, Sam able to claim it in some roundabout way for work.

"I thought I'd go ahead and mow the back acre," Claude said, "between the houses, just in case."

Sam felt a lurch of regret. He'd been meaning to get back up there to mow—standard fire-deterrent practice for any homeowner out here on the wildland-urban line—but had kept putting it off. Seeing the house that had once embodied so much hope always pressed on the still-tender parts of his heart. "I can't ask you to do that, Claude."

Why hadn't he just mowed it last month, instead of spending his free evenings trying to find elusive profits in the columns of numbers in the Eddy business ledgers, or worse, on halfhearted nights out with True, who was ill-equipped to cheer him up, seeing as she was nearly as gutted about his family situation as he was? "I've been meaning to get that done," he said lamely.

Claude pshaw-ed. "You gotta give an old guy something to do in his retirement years, or else he starts feeling less useful. Anyway, you've got your hands full."

Claude was being kind. What he didn't say: *You have enough on your mind, working your own business, raising two kids, and trying not to drown under medical bills in sums bigger than any of us will ever see in a lifetime, let alone pay off in a year.*

"Relief is in sight," Mel kept saying, though Sam couldn't see how. Sure, her making chief had taken the edge off, enabling them to pay a few of the bigger bills to their Portland pediatric clinic and the cardiological-specialist group, but still left Sam playing his least-favorite guessing game: pay the electric bill or home oxygen delivery? Car payment or echocardiogram? And there was still a pile of unpaid invoices as long as his arm, all with overdue notices stamped in red ink.

He sighed into the phone, imagining seventy-five-year-old Claude making the turns up and down the field in this heat, struggling with his old mower. "I'll come up and do it myself first thing in the morning, Claude," he promised. "I just don't want to leave the girls here alone." Even if he asked Kim to come by and babysit, he didn't trust the likes of Fallows to keep to his own lane, not after turning up today. The very thought of him interacting with his kids made Sam's blood boil all over again.

"I got it, Bishop," Claude insisted. "You just take care of that little one of yours. Unless her big sis has already worked you out of a job." He chuckled.

"You sure?"

"Absolutely. Where I come from, neighbors take care of one another."

Sam smiled, knowing that, while Claude might have grown up outside of Munich, Germany, he considered himself an Oregonian through and through. "We sure do," he agreed, ending the call as gratitude replaced the stress his earlier confrontation had placed on his heart.

An hour later, he'd settled the girls into bed on the pull-out sofa and retreated to the River Eddy deck one story below, PBR in hand. He liked to come out here on summer evenings to watch the sun set over the river, but tonight he faced the opposite direction, staring up at Flatiron. Claude was right: they certainly had a nature show to watch. Even here in town, he could glimpse the flames undulating like a well-choreographed dance just one ridge over.

*Carbon's seen fires before,* he told himself firmly. The Bear Creek Fire of '92, the Pine Flat Fire of '05 . . . both worse than this. And Mel had handled those just fine, hadn't she? By late summer, it wasn't uncommon for over a dozen fires to burn across the state. But early July? Smoke season had come early. Sam figured he'd better make peace with losing his view, as well as his out-of-town customers.

If the air quality got bad enough, he'd have to keep Annie indoors tomorrow, and the next day, and the day after that, where medical-grade air purifiers hummed day and night in both the Eddy apartment and in Mel's place across town. Painfully unfair for a kid on summer break, and especially for Annie, who'd already been robbed of too much of her childhood.

The doctor and midwife had known something was wrong the moment she'd been born by C-section at Carbon General. Though their faces had remained professionally neutral, it had been the heavy silence throughout the sterile room that gave them away, punctuated by Annie's weak cry after far too long a delay. Later, Mel would liken that moment to the silence right before the *pop* signifying a combustion fire . . . when all the air seemed to go still before being sucked right out of the room.

Sam scrubbed his hands across his face, trying, unsuccessfully, to rub out the memory. No dice. It rushed right back in like a back draft in the gas line on the Eddy grill, same as always.

Annie's diagnosis after a barrage of tests: tetralogy of Fallot. Tet, for short. Sam had never even heard of the condition, and no wonder. Only four hundred out of every million babies were born with the complex congenital heart condition that left baby Annie weak, winded, and hypoxemic.

The first thing you think, after being informed you have a child with intense medical needs: *Just tell me how to meet them. Let's go, what's it gonna take, time's a-wasting,* all that. He and Mel, they'd been a dream team, getting second opinions, meeting with experts, finding time, even in the thick of it, for a hand squeeze here, a bracing hug there, even a lingering kiss or two in the sanctuary of the half-remodeled Highline house, Mel's arms around him enough to keep him together. Back then, the pillars of the life they'd constructed had seemed load-bearing. The foundation solid. Sam had thought they'd weather it, he really had. But he hadn't seen the wolf at the door.

First the insurance advocates had called—their tones always clipped but friendly—then the doctors—still helpful—and clinics and registered pediatric RNs—more businesslike. Then the collectors. Who had proved to be worse bloodsucking bastards than the drug runners and car thieves Sam had grown up around.

Sam and Mel had burned through their savings first, though that hadn't taken long. Then the credit-card debt began to pile up. Mel had reluctantly turned to her parents and True, but lord knew Sam's dad, his only family, had nothing to give.

"Contact John if you need some cash flow," Mark Bishop had said, on one of Sam's last visits to see his old man in the state penitentiary at Pendleton. "He owes this family big time."

Wasn't *that* rich. Sam had pushed back from the table between them like it was on fire, the legs of his folding chair screeching across the linoleum of the visitation room.

"That would require us to be a *family* in the first place," he'd shot at his father. Sam and Mark Bishop were anything but, in no small part due to Fallows's intrusion in their lives.

"Just let me know when you're ready to swallow your pride," Mark had called after him, the clatter of metal echoing in Sam's ears.

He'd tried to rent out the rooms over the garage at Highline instead, had even tried to convert the garage itself, but couldn't get past the red tape of the Airbnb contract. Too many code violations while he finished the wiring and the drywall in the kitchen. Too hard to ensure the space met ADA requirements. Things had been tense before, but to hear that Sam couldn't even manage to wire his own house well enough to run a small business tipped the scales. He was a failure. He had let down his family.

"No one said anything of the sort," Mel had argued, exasperation lacing the exhaustion and fear in her voice. "Certainly not me." And of course she hadn't, not in so many words, but Sam was more than capable of filling in the blanks.

The arguments turned into days of silence, then outright absence as Mel poured herself into work and childcare, her embrace reserved only for her children now. To be fair, that might have been all she had to give after the hours she put in at the station. At the hospital. At the heart center. In a last-ditch effort to salvage what he could of his marriage and their finances, Sam had put the Eddy on the market, with no luck on either count. No one else in economically depressed Carbon wanted to take it on. And Mel, even knowing what it had cost Sam emotionally to list it, had not been moved.

So here he was, still at the rail of the deck, a.k.a. the helm of his sinking ship. At least he had gotten Fallows the hell out of his bar. He exhaled long and hard, the way he'd been taught by the meditation app he'd downloaded to help calm his nerves. It had come in handy just tonight, as he played one of the sleep stories for the girls. Astor had had a hard time settling down; she was prone to nightmares when Mel was out in the field. Hell, so was Sam. He stared back at the fire, trying to read it, wondering what Mel saw in it from where she stood right now.

Thinking of her in the field, his mind hopped from Mel to True with a guilty pang. It was probably too late to try her on her sat phone by now. Did she have a view of this fire tonight, too? She sure wouldn't welcome it, this early in the summer. The rafting season got shorter and shorter in Oregon every year, it seemed, as the watershed got drier and the rivers got lower.

It was a hell of a way to make a living.

For all of them. Without the rafters and anglers, Sam's bar would be empty all August, Carbon a ghost town. Even his Highline house, sitting as close as it did to the urban-wildland line, had depreciated in value in today's ecological climate.

And then what he feared the most in his darkest moments would come true, if it wasn't already: he'd turn out to be no better a provider than his father. According to the Army psychologist he'd been required to see before each deployment, a childhood of neglect with regular, healthy servings of verbal abuse would do that to a person.

He knew better than to let his past dictate his future, but it was easier said than done. The ending of his marriage still felt more abstract than real. Mel had initiated it but hadn't yet followed through on the formalities of a legal divorce. On good days, this gave Sam hope. It had to mean something, didn't it, that Mel hadn't signed on the dotted line? But then on bad days:

"It's not like we need the extra paperwork," Mel would quip as they sifted through medical forms. Their finances were complicated enough as it was, she said.

Should Sam have taken Fallows's money, had it been offered those years ago? It was probably a moot point: Fallows, like Mark, never owned up to responsibility, at least not without the threat of a bat to his knees.

He envisioned his half-finished house perched on the ridge, still fighting the tight feeling in his throat that always arose with this kind of self-talk. Memory of his father's mockery echoing through the tinny payphone at Pendleton seeped through the cracks. *What? You think if you build it, they will come . . . back?* His laugh had crackled from the connection, splintering as it hit Sam's ears.

It hurt because it held a ring of truth. Wasn't that what they said? No, that wasn't it. It was *funny* because it was true. Sam bit back his own bitter laugh. Somewhere in the back of his mind, did he really hold out hope that if he finally made the house on Highline into the sanctuary he envisioned, he and his young family could break generations of toxic patterns?

Sure. And a fairy godmother would wave a wand and Annie's heart would magically heal, too.

How pathetic.

Thank goodness for True, who'd practically adopted the Bishop girls from birth.

*At least there's one man of the house around for your kids.*

Another of Mark Bishop's observations. He'd told his father to shut the fuck up, though he might as well have saved his breath; offensive statements were one of Mark's favorite ways to get under Sam's skin. He pushed the memory aside now, determined not to let his old man hijack his brain for one more second.

True was the girls' godmother. Astor looked up to her and Annie adored her, always pressing in close to True when she came over for their weekly dinners together, perching herself on True's knee like she was some sort of river-goddess Santa Claus. Which she was, Sam conceded, in her faded board shorts and worn sandals, always bearing gifts . . . beaded things she'd made the girls at camp in the evenings, whitewashed river rocks shaped like hearts and stars, welded sculptures of wolves and river otters made from scrap metal in her shop on that acreage she had by the river.

Up on Flatiron, the fire gave a little spurt of a flare-up as it consumed one of the tallest ponderosa pines near the ridgeline, and Sam sat up straighter, swallowing his beer in a quick gulp. *Shit.* That edginess was back. Should he worry, like, *seriously* worry, about Mel? And what about Annie? Nothing, not even smoke, could be allowed to compromise her health right now. He went inside the Eddy to retrieve the portable radio he kept on the bar, turning the dial to 93.2, the station that alerted him to every snow day, every delayed start at Carbon Elementary, and every traffic incident. If he needed to know anything about this fire that Mel couldn't tell him, this local channel would deliver the news.

*Every summer brings forest fires,* he reminded himself again as he returned to the deck rail to study the pulsing line of heat in the distance. This one was close, sure, but it was tiny, and Mel's whole team was out there somewhere, on the job. He finished off his PBR in one last, long swallow and turned to go inside, leaving the orange glow of the spot fire at his back.

# CHAPTER 4

From the crew camp, Mel thought she'd try to connect with Sam again to say goodnight to the girls, only to realize it was already far too late. And now she'd been staring at her blank screen for at least thirty seconds. Sam had told her she'd seemed distracted of late, and with Annie's surgery looming, was it any wonder?

Mel frowned as she made her way back toward camp, where her team loitered in "wait and see" mode until further instructions came down. She noted Lewis's eager anticipation as he opened a case of MREs to dole out to the crew—that man could eat—and the cocky smile on José's face as he slid discreetly behind Deklan to photobomb his selfie in front of the shallow blaze. She laughed, despite herself. If she couldn't be with her kids tonight, she had to admit there was no place she'd rather be than with her team.

"We're a team, too," Sam always insisted. "You don't have to come up with every solution yourself."

*Easy for you to say,* she tended to think when ugly resentment rose within her. But she managed to bite this back, because first of all, he was right. It was her choice to take so much on, and Sam contributed what he could from each day's profits at the Eddy. But second of all? There was a reason Mel didn't lean on Sam more; at times, his self-doubt could be crushing. If Mel wasn't careful, she'd get caught under the weight of it herself.

She had tried to keep the faith, she really had. In the early days, when she and Sam had been able to leverage this and loan that to pay for medical expenses, she'd been right there with him, trying to keep their heads above water. But they'd still been paying off Annie's first surgery, at six months, when the cardiologist ordered the next, and, well, once a ball started rolling, it only gained speed, didn't it?

Did Sam think it didn't sting—no, sear—to know they'd made it this far, with only this final surgery for Annie to go, before they were bowled over? Annie's presurgical protocols included a list of prescription meds longer than Mel's arm, none of which Blue Cross covered in full. Add a surgical-center down payment higher than with most mortgages in Carbon, and, well, all Mel could say was she'd never felt helpless a day in her life until she'd become the mother of a child with tet.

By the time they both realized they were at an impasse, financially and maritally, even filing bankruptcy, which Sam absolutely refused to do anyway, wouldn't have helped. He had his reasons, but that didn't mean Mel had to forgive him for it.

"You didn't fix this when you could have," Mel had whispered, gutted the day she left him. He could have tried to sell the house, even in this economic and ecological climate. He could have filed for Chapter 11.

Sam's voice had sounded every bit as heart-wrenched as her own. "You never asked me to."

How could Mel have? She loved him. She'd seen him claw his way up in this community, finally able to hold his head high after who knew how many generations of Bishops had dragged the name through the mud. To Sam, admitting to financial ruin was akin to admitting failure as a father, as a business owner. As a human. Of *course* Mel had shuffled asking this of him to last-resort status.

She'd barely made it a day before he'd asked her to come home. And she'd wanted to. She'd wanted to from the moment she drove away down Highline. But to Mel, it had been too late. Mel had Annie to think about, her job to do, Astor to parent . . . She'd simply been too tired, too bone-weary exhausted, to fight for Sam, too.

*But now you have a plan,* she reminded herself as she took her ration of dinner and settled on the bumper of her rig, watching the fire continue to lick the hill. Maybe physical space from Sam had been required for her to make her way to it, but the plan would work. It *had* to. *Someone* had to ensure Annie got the care she needed, and for all his promises, that someone just wasn't going to be Sam. It still broke Mel's heart every damn day to admit it, but this summer, her real partnership lay with True. There was no other way.

God bless her best friend, who at this very minute carried out the weekly task that had become standard operating procedure all summer. Working for John Fallows was easy enough, Mel reminded herself, as long as they didn't overcomplicate it. Step one: pick up the ammo box of cash at the grow site on the river. Step two: float it down to the end of the line. Step three: hand it off. Step four: get paid their cut, earmarked for Annie's meds that kept her healthy enough for surgery.

*Step five,* their circumspect employer had growled, his breath hot on the back of Mel's neck, *ask no questions, make no enemies, and make damned sure nothing goes sideways.*

Mel swallowed hard at the memory as she washed down the god-awful freeze-dried food with a swig of water from her bottle. Shaking out her sleep kit from her pack, she fought a sudden trepidation. What exactly might breaking step five lead to? Drug traffickers, even small-time backwoods ones, weren't exactly the reasonable type. Just ask poor Zack Murphy.

His arrest last spring had given Mel the idea in the first place.

"My Zack knew Fallows was trouble," Kim had insisted between sobs, confiding in Mel outside the Eddy. "But he was no drug mule. It was why he was about to quit. 'I won't work for some wannabe cartel boss,' he said."

Mel had just nodded in sympathy. Cartels, drug-trafficking operations . . . She'd heard the rumors, too. Black-market distributors and investors were always looking for grow sites to leech from. The ones with property owners who didn't shy away from the shady side of the law were their favorite partners. Who fit the bill better than Fallows?

Kim looked up, her face still tear-streaked. "The cops, they implied that Zack should have known, should have at least suspected that, going south, over state lines, he was carrying contraband of *some* kind, given who he worked for, but you know Fallows! He never gets his hands dirty enough to leave his own prints. They interrogated Zack for hours, but he simply didn't know the answers to their questions. Didn't *want* to know."

"Of course not."

"It's why Fallows planted the fentanyl, along with the cash Zack was found with. Insurance. No way was Zack *not* going down for this."

Mel had sworn under her breath. She knew Fallows was a first-rate asshole, but *fentanyl?*

Kim wiped her eyes. "At least Fallows can't make any other Carbon kids his scapegoat. Not with the Feds still watching I-5 so closely."

Mel had laid a hand on Kim's shoulder in comfort, thinking of poor Zack. Thinking, too, of young Sam, tormented by this man when he was too small to have any agency. *Maybe it's time Fallows picked on someone his own size.* The thought sprang into Mel's mind from nowhere, but once there, it proved impossible to banish. With the troopers aware of the I-5 distribution route, Fallows would need a new way to transport his monthly tithe to his black-market investors, or whomever he was paying off. And Mel had one.

"Are you crazy?" True had blurted when Mel had cornered her for a clandestine meeting the very next day. "You want *me* to float *product* for John *Fallows* down the Outlaw *River?*" She'd said each word slowly, like Mel did to Astor when she wanted to be sure Astor had heard her own outlandish suggestions.

"Not product," Mel had said swiftly. "What he needs moved is money. Payoffs." And with True's help, right under the noses of the Feds, without using a single road.

"All you have to do is take the cash, weekly, from Fallows's place next to your property downriver to Temple Bar," Mel had said. "Just that one quick stop along the river route. That's it. And then you hand it off to one of Fallows's guys at Temple." She'd spoken in a breathy rush, afraid True would cut her off. "Everyone knows he fishes the bar every Friday with his favorite crew members. Everyone knows about his weekend cabin down there. No one will think a thing of it."

She wasn't proud of this idea—it turned her stomach, actually, and she couldn't allow herself to think about Sam at all as she weighed it in her mind, but Annie's surgeon's office had called just the day before to prescribe the latest batch of presurgical meds, the sum of which had exceeded Mel's monthly car payment. With Mel's bank account at $97.42 and her savings nonexistent, with Sam heartbroken and both of them close to giving up, what else could she do? She pictured Annie, listless on the couch in Mel's rented apartment, her heart failing her at age five. Each beat pumping blood throughout her little body was the tick of a clock. Where would Annie be at age six? Seven? Mel knew where . . . the doctors told her. In her head, she recited the litany of medications currently monopolizing all their combined income: morphine, beta-blockers, inhalers, oxygen, sodium bicarbonate. And the list went on.

True had narrowed her eyes. "What does Sam say?"

Mel had dropped her gaze. "Sam won't come within spitting distance of Fallows, and you know it."

"But you will?" True had sounded incredulous.

Mel had lifted her head. "I'll do whatever it takes!"

And because they both knew this was true, True had sworn loudly. "Fuck, I hate this." She'd paced for a moment, wrestling, Mel knew, to justify this against her loyalty to Sam, same as Mel had, coming ultimately to the same conclusion. "Sam can't know," she'd whispered.

"No." On that, True and Mel agreed. She and True were on their own.

Did she have eyes on this blaze from where she camped tonight on the Outlaw? As her team rolled out their own bags and settled into a restless night of semi-sleep around her, Mel decided she had better call True, too, though on the sat phone instead of her cell, and make sure she was still on course.

True lay stretched out on the floor of her oar raft, back braced against her Paco Pad, her long lean legs resting on the front inflated tube that had served as Emmett Wu's seat all day, after beating his mom to "shotgun" after every dip in the river.

There was a time she'd stare up at the stars in wonder on clear nights like this, after her clients had turned in. This summer she'd mostly just stared blankly, worrying about the damned ammo box and the money inside it. Tonight, however, her gaze remained on the shadowy outline of the Wus' tent, her mind still abuzz, her body still energized by the electrical storm. Campfire circles lent themselves to deep conversation in short order, and even though they had skipped the ritual tonight, she had learned a lot about Vivian as they'd lounged in their camp chairs after dinner, sipping wine and hot cocoa.

"I bet you're underestimated all the time," True had mused after they'd compared professional careers. "When you're not being hit on by guys," she'd thrown in as a test of sorts, just to be sure, after Emmett had embarked on a mission to unearth the Hershey's bars in the cooler. True's instincts could not always be trusted, and falling for straight women was a cliché she was tired of falling prey to.

But Vivian had shaken her head, gesturing toward Emmett, now carefully building a s'more to roast on the stovetop. "Single mom, remember? It's the ideal male deterrent. Female, too, for that matter."

True's eyes had shot to hers, and Vivian had held her gaze, the confidence in that look saying volumes. Speaking True's language.

Which left True wrestling with cliché number two: sabotaging potential happiness out of the fear of being burned. Again, as it happened. And so, despite the chance of more rain—Mother Nature willing—she'd left her one-person tent empty tonight, too, needing a bit more space. The storm clouds that had come in hot and heavy this afternoon had all but burned off, leaving the mountain air as thin and brittle as usual for southern Oregon in July, as poor a buffer as always against the heat of the night that absorbed into every pore of her bare arms and legs.

She lay back, finding the Big Dipper and Lyra and making a mental note to show them to Emmett tomorrow night, after their campfire . . . assuming the smoke hadn't caught up with them.

But if that was Lyra, where the hell had Aquila gone? She peered into the darkness, trying to spot the less prominent constellations in the gathering haze. It had been Sam who'd taught True how to find all these stars years ago, during her short stint on a trail-maintenance crew with the Forest Service and National Guard. She and the young Army vet fresh from Operation Enduring Freedom had bonded over a shared love of the outdoors and lack of tolerance for incompetency and general inaptitude among their peers, both of which had been in ample supply that summer. They'd been besties ever since. The only time True and Sam's friendship had been tested—before now, she amended—had been the spring he'd met Mel.

*Show her the ropes,* Sam had said, when his new girlfriend had landed on True's crew back when she'd guided for Paddle, Inc. *It will be fun,* he'd said. And was it ever. Mel had been twenty to True's twenty-four, emerging from the bright-yellow Paddle bus with the other college employees as toned and tomboyishly athletic as a model stepping out of the pages of a Title IX catalog.

The moment True had laid eyes on her, she'd been a goner.

She'd fought it, of course, for Sam's sake. She'd pretended the sight of Mel emerging from her sleeping bag each morning, hair tousled, smile radiant, didn't warm every cell of True's body. She'd tried to convince herself there was nothing to adore about Mel's earnestness to learn and her natural leadership style that drew people to her instead of setting them against her.

But throughout that one beautiful season they'd guided together, True had taken Mel under her wing. Sam had asked her to, hadn't he? She'd started by showing her how to leverage a thousand-pound raft out of literal metric tons of rapidly flowing water with only the muscle of a woman's forearms. "Forget diamonds," True had told Mel, high-fiving her after a successful training exercise. "A Rapid Ditch Bag is a girl's *true* best friend."

She'd taught her the best line to navigate for every square inch of this river, had taught her how to put fretful clients at ease, had taught her the art of baking her famous blueberry breakfast scones in a Dutch oven over the fire (the trick was to reserve the bacon grease from the loaded baked potatoes the night before). And whenever they'd had a layover day in Boise or Bend for Paddle, Inc., restocks, she liked to think she'd taught Mel how to have a little fun, too.

"Ladies' choice," True had always said, smiling, half enjoying Mel's uncertain expression, half not, when they planned their evenings out. She knew her reputation preceded her, suspected the other rafting guides had warned Mel about her, jokingly, of course. *Careful, Mel, she's a woman-eater.* The ones who grew up in Carbon had fun ribbing Sam, too, by proxy. *Bishop must feel pretty damned secure, letting you out on the town with Truitt.*

"'*Letting*' me? Please," Mel answered, and True had known right then and there: for better or worse, whether it about killed her or not, Mel would join Sam's ranks, becoming True's best friend for life.

During their nights under the stars, they'd confided their hopes for the future like middle schoolers at a slumber party, whispering to one another from their Paco Pads: True's dream of having her own rafting charter, Mel's envisioned life with Sam. She would have a river-rock fireplace one day to hang their future children's Christmas stockings on the mantel. An herb garden in a shady patch of the yard. True had closed her eyes and pictured it with her: home, hearth, family. Did she want these things, too? The way Mel wove it for her, she thought she just might.

True was a realist, however, so whenever she suffered from predictable surges of self-pity, she soothed herself with the only salve she knew: other women. Other women in bars; other women at whitewater-certification clinics or art shows, where True displayed the mosaic and metal sculptures she created from river glass and old mining scrap metal she found on the shores of the Outlaw; other women in her bed. Pretty women, beautiful women even, as toned and fit and sun-kissed from the river as she was. But never women she was serious about. What if another one tripped her up? True had seen Mel coming a mile away and had still fallen under her spell. She wasn't eager to make the same mistake twice.

She gave up identifying the stars with a sigh, watching the faint orange smudge of fire on Flatiron slowly gain size instead. Usually, the rocking of the boat underneath her soothed her to sleep, but right now she felt tense. She thought of the metal ammo box of cash once again tucked into the boat, and then of Mel again, somewhere out in the wilderness by Flatiron, undoubtedly at the scene of this blaze.

They weren't going to have a problem, were they? Fallows expected his handoff every Friday like clockwork, no exceptions. True would like to think acts of God might be exempt, but she doubted it. The Fallowses—John and his son, Chris—were shady motherfuckers, and she should know. One got to know one's neighbors, after all, even if one didn't want to. Chris had shit for brains, but his father was another matter.

She calculated the distance between where she lounged in her raft on the Outlaw and the fire, holding her thumb out in front of her face, measuring it against the forest of trees blanketing the peak . . . At least five air miles from town. Which meant at least fifteen from where she and the Wus now camped on the shore of the river. She toyed with the dial of her sat phone, wondering belatedly if she should call Mel, then tried to laugh at her own paranoia. Like she'd told Emmett, the local lookout attendant had undoubtedly spotted this fire early. Mel's crew was almost certainly on scene already, and it would be put out without much fanfare, same as all the ones that would follow in the coming weeks. If she wanted to worry about something, it should be about the poor air quality an early smoke season would produce. Two weeks from surgery D-Day, Annie couldn't risk respiratory compromise.

Undoubtedly, the Bishop kids were with Sam right now. How was Annie managing in the rooms above the Eddy? True pictured Annie's little smile—a spitting image of her mother's—and bit her lip. She adored Astor for her gumption and, yes, even her sassiness of late. Mel wouldn't admit it, but this, too, came from her maternal genes.

But Annie captured True's heart in a different way. A way that made her wonder sometimes: What would having a child of her own, of being part of a family—not just as a beloved aunt-godmother but an actual, bona fide member—feel like?

Her mind was still snagged in this particular eddy when the sat phone buzzed to life in her hands, and True nearly dropped it in her sudden jonesing for an update. She chastised herself under her breath as she depressed the talk button. Usually, True was known for the ice water that ran through her veins.

"You got True."

"True, it's me."

"Mel." The single syllable escaped on a sigh as relief flooded her. She savored the feeling, closing her eyes tightly now that reassurance was on the other end of the line. Yeah, she *was* going soft. "You looking at Flatiron?"

"Yeah, we're staged near midmountain. So you can see the fire from where you are?"

"Saw it strike." True gave her the coordinates. "Everyone okay in town? The girls are good?"

Mel paused, which automatically made True's stomach tighten with . . . not alarm, not quite that. Just trepidation. "I got called out before I could see the girls and Sam," she admitted, "but this spot fire's still a good ways from town."

"Let's just hope it stays that way." And what about the smoke? "Maybe they should move up to Sam's house on Highline." The views across the Cascades were enviable from the castle he still seemed determined to erect from the wreckage of his childhood home, even after he and Mel had called it quits. Which meant the air quality was better, too.

Mel answered in the negative, but most of her words were cut out, thanks to static. Par for the course, when using the sat phone. All True got was "town" and "for now."

"If you're sure," True said slowly. Sam was a great guy, but he had a hell of a blind spot when it came to that house. The result of a childhood that, to hear him tell it, had basically been feral. "But *is* it just a spot fire, Mel?" She studied the blaze again from her vantage point on the boat; did it already seem bigger than just a few minutes before?

"You know as well as I do that's what it is until it isn't," Mel said. She sounded testy. No, tired, True amended, as she heard her exhale. "Carbon Rural did a preliminary tonight, and trust me, True, this thing's just a baby. We'll start cutting a containment line in the morning."

"They're gonna let it burn?"

Mel paused again, or maybe they were experiencing another delay in their connection. "Yeah," she said eventually, "so listen, True. It's bound to get smoky out there, on the river. Wind's going west. What if your clients panic and want to cut the trip short? The bigger operations probably will."

True frowned. "They'll be off the river by then, anyway." She didn't need the reminder that she and the Wus would soon be alone out here, or that, with the authorities on John Fallows like stink on shit—his words, ironically—it was crucial that she stick to her itinerary. Nothing new about that. What *was* new? She felt a surge of unexpected loyalty rise up within her, and not for Mel for a change. "This trip is really important to the Wus," she heard herself say. "And they don't scare easily." After all, standing one's ground—hell, just daring to exist—as a transgender kid and that trans kid's parent and advocate was no walk in the park.

But Mel wasn't privy to any of this. "What day are you supposed to hit Quartz?" she asked.

Quartz Canyon, the highlight of the trip, and by far the most technical Class IV rapids True tackled, still sat a good distance west, two days' float from where they camped tonight. Quartz required a scouting trip to survey the rapids and give guests a preview of the whitewater to come. Boats tended to bottleneck there . . . a river traffic jam of sorts, and even though True's river colleagues should be through by now, it was imperative she hit the canyon at the right time to ensure they stayed on schedule.

"We're not supposed to run Quartz until Thursday," she said slowly. She had intended to take the Wus only as far as the Nugget, an old historical landmark halfway along their course, before camping again for the night. "So that we end at Temple Bar on Friday, per usual." She always disembarked at Temple on Fridays. Not a day earlier. Not a day later.

No exceptions. It robbed her of half the joy of being on the river, letting the current guide her, but True could mourn that later, when Annie was post-surgery. Mel needed the cash from only one more river run to refill the prescriptions that ensured Annie's eligibility to go under the knife, which meant this nightmare summer project was just about over.

"If your clients spook," Mel pressed, "you may not have until Thursday."

*They won't spook,* True wanted to shout, but Mel's paranoia had ballooned in her own chest, expanding there, holding her words captive. God, she hated this shit.

Mel carried right on, making contingency plans. "Worst-case scenario? You talk them into stopping over at Wonderland. Get relief from the smoke, stage a full day. Then you can still end on Friday, on schedule." Or at least that was what True thought Mel said . . . She had begun to cut out again, her familiar voice crackling with static.

But Wonderland Lodge sat below Quartz Canyon, and it wasn't open to unexpected smoke refugees. The longtime owners of the isolated and rustic smattering of cabins and aging outbuildings weren't exactly the warm and fuzzy type. Henry and Sue Martin regarded rafting guides as the unwashed and unwanted, True perhaps the worst among them, for no more reason than perhaps her "unconventional" hairstyle (that would be Sue) and "bossy ways" (True preferred "leadership style," thank you).

"That's a crapshoot at best," she reminded Mel now. "Anyway, we can't rush the canyon. My clients aren't ready." There was that protective tug for the Wus again, but this time, True had logic on her side. They would need at least another day on the water before Vivian and Emmett felt comfortable enough to tackle such a technically difficult slot canyon. And it was crucial they *were* ready, because if anything went wrong, if they failed to navigate between the narrow rocks and True missed the deadline with Fallows . . . She swallowed hard, the idea of being caught between a rock and a hard place taking on secondary meaning.

"Like I said, you might not have a choice," Mel pressed, her voice still tight with stress despite her assurances that they were dealing with a "baby" fire. "Be proactive. Push to Wonderland. Stage twenty-four hours."

True frowned into the receiver. It never sat well with her when Mel gave orders. *Save that for the station,* she usually told her. Tonight, she remained quiet, prompting Mel to fill the silence. "I'm sorry to ask this of you," she said. "I'm sorry to ask any of it."

True shuffled through several retorts in her mind, but bit back all of them. Yes, Mel had the ability to press an unfair advantage, but what mother wouldn't do anything to protect her kid? Besides, True was a big girl, and she'd made her own choices.

"I know," she assured her, pinching her eyes shut tightly to ward off another swell of nerves. "I just hate this, Mel. It wasn't supposed to be like this. This complicated."

"What's that?" Mel said. "You're cutting out."

*I hate feeling edgy all the time. This is supposed to be my safe space, where my life is simplified to just the flow of the current, without distributaries channeling me toward unrequited feelings I cannot entertain in families I cannot have.* "Nothing," True answered. "I'll keep them on the river. Whatever it takes."

She swallowed the hard lump of misgiving that arose in her throat, one hand resting on her stomach as if to calm the butterflies that danced there practically all the time these days. She went to switch off the sat phone—it was pointless prolonging a call with a bad connection—then hesitated. "But Mel? Try Sam one more time, will you? Just . . . I'll feel better, knowing the kids are okay."

A long pause, while the connection seemed to cut and paste on itself in repeated spurts of the same gravelly white noise. "Yep," Mel's voice sounded eventually. A delay, this time upward of ten seconds. "Feel better," she added, which let True know she'd misheard her. She said something more, her voice warbling in and out like a country-western singer on an old radio program.

"I can't . . . I can't hear you," True answered, frustration rising, causing her voice to rise pathetically. "Bye, Mel," she managed. "Stay safe."

*Please.*

# The Smoke

# CHAPTER 5

*July 11*
*5:15 a.m.*

After a restless night, Mel awoke on the side of Flatiron to a whole new world. On either side of her, crew members stirred in their sleeping bags, coughing and shifting as an eerily intense warmth in the air awoke them. They arose one by one as Mel had, sitting up with exclamations of alarm at the ash that covered their bags, hair, and skin. She scrambled out of her bag, kicking at it as it clung to her boots, which she was now glad she'd worn to bed. Shaking a dusting of ash from her long hair, she weaved her way between sprawled sleeping bags and hastened up the slope from their impromptu camp, José on her heels.

As they crested the edge of the plateau at the tree line, the sight of the blaze met them through the smoke.

"Shit!" Mel staggered back, one hand rising to shield her face. She knew now that they should have taken things more seriously last night; the docile spot fire of the evening before was now an angry, pulsating wall distinguishable even at this distance. The heat of it hit her like she'd just opened an oven door to check on the progress of a batch of cookies, and she skidded out in the shale, holding up a fist toward José, ordering him to stop where he stood a few yards back. "It's rolling!" she shouted.

José froze, hands on his head in dismay, tears from the heat and the smoke already forming in his eyes. "How the *fuck* did this happen so fucking fast?"

Mel shook her head. So much for the campfire they'd hoped to stomp out. The wall of flame before them contradicted everything Mel had learned in her years of fire science. Sam had seen something like this, she remembered suddenly, during his first tour in Afghanistan, when the chemical fires would barrel down the narrow streets of Ghazni City. But here in the wilderness, the flames should have decreased, not increased, in the cooler night temperatures. Not act like lava as it consumed the dead, highly flammable undergrowth on the forest floor, gulping oxygen as it progressed. Suddenly tackling this blaze felt like more than babysitting, and she swallowed a swell of actual worry. The heat of this fire was sufficient to tinge Mel's skin, standing this close. Which meant the smoke of it just might reach Annie's lungs.

Just before dawn, True dreamed of snow. It was one of those early-morning dreams in which she lay just on the cusp of wakefulness, reality almost but not quite in reach. Usually, her dreams these days involved wads of cash and raging river currents; snow in July was a fresh take on preconscious anxiety. And while possible, it wasn't remotely likely. Not while she lay sprawled out with her down sleeping bag only half-zipped, the air hitting her skin lacking even the tiniest bite. Then she opened her eyes and did a double take: wispy flakes indeed floated lazily from the sky, a layer already accumulating on her bag.

But not a layer of snow. Of ash.

True blinked, trying to make out the shape and scope of the soot that had been falling on her face as she'd slept, but the sky was virtually the same color as the falling soot . . . a pale, almost translucent gray. The morning light looked flat and dull, as two-dimensional as the monotoned joke postcard she'd once received from a rafting buddy on vacation in Central America: *Costa Rica in the fog.*

She scrambled to stand up, steadying herself in the now rocking oar raft as she shook out her sleeping bag, eyes squinting as she surveyed first the mountain, then their camp from the shoreline. Camp looked quiet enough, though a thin sheen of ash covered everything, from the cooler to the foldable kitchen table and chairs to the Wus' tent, where they continued to sleep. *Good.* True could use a few minutes to get her bearings.

Because Mel had been right. Flatiron wasn't even visible in the smoke that now swallowed it whole. In fact, True couldn't see farther than a hundred yards in that direction—to the east—and her way forward, eyes straining downriver, wasn't much better. *Shit.* Maybe Vivian *would* freak when she saw the apocalyptic world they'd inherited overnight. So far, she had defied stereotypes—a trait True tended to like in a woman—but surely any mother would balk at conditions like this.

She glanced toward the dry bag she knew contained the sat phone, nerves dancing in her gut. Now that she couldn't even lay eyes on the blaze to assess its strength, should she call Mel back? Or should she forget about Fallows and make an evac plan for the Wus?

*Get a grip, Truitt.* She'd push for Wonderland, just like Mel had urged, un-ideal as it was. For air-quality comfort, she'd tell the Wu family. To take care of business, she told herself. As long as she still arrived at Temple Bar on Friday, she'd be fine.

A hazy, oddly muted stream of sunlight filtered through Sam's bedroom window just past 6:00 a.m., accompanied by three sounds, all of which seemed out of place as he stirred under the cotton sheets. The first was Annie coughing in her bed in the apartment living room. The second was the low rumble of trucks—big ones—outside the Eddy, probably on the highway adjacent to the river, and the third was a muted but incessant pounding on the door leading to the stairwell and the Eddy bar.

He sat up quickly, his thoughts immediately on Fallows. Was he back to cause more trouble? But now that he was awake, his priorities reshuffled as he identified the reason for his daughter's intensified cough. The smell of smoke, not like a house fire—like a campfire—permeated his nostrils, despite the fact that Sam had gone through the building before going to bed last night, sealing all the windows they usually left open on summer nights in the mountains.

The pounding on the door continued, and he felt torn between going to Annie and answering it. He hurried down the hallway, tugging a Carbon Rural softball-team sweatshirt over his head as he walked. Whoever knocked so urgently on the other side of the door would just have to deal with his candy-cane-striped flannel pajama bottoms, gifted by Astor last Christmas.

He opened the door to Kim, a full five hours early for her shift, who rushed inside with a terse "You have your phone on you? I can't find jack shit on mine."

Sam trailed after her in his pajamas, scrambling to catch up in his groggy state. Astor, a light sleeper to a fault, emerged from her room, her expression as baffled as Sam's. Kim popping in wasn't unusual; her place was just down the street. He did, however, take issue with the early hour. "Find what on your phone, exactly?"

"Carbon Rural updates, county alerts, anything. The Outlaw County emergency app is a joke." Her eyes were glued to her own screen, one manicured finger flicking upward in search of information.

The smoke. The fire. The reason for Annie's coughing. "How bad is it?"

Sam moved automatically past her to the window on the landing and got his answer, which had adrenaline chasing any lingering desire for sleep from his head. The smoke was worse outside, far worse . . . He nearly choked on it as he craned his neck to the west in an attempt to get an unobstructed view of Flatiron. He covered his mouth with the neck of his sweatshirt to filter the air entering his lungs, but he shouldn't have bothered: when Sam finally made out the shape and scope of the mountain, he gasped out loud, the involuntary response leaving him sputtering.

The Flatiron Fire raged. No other word could describe what Sam saw to the west. What he had managed to convince himself was a tame show of nature last night now burned huge and hot, covering far more than the finger's breadth of forest he'd noted before bed.

He closed the window in a hurry; he couldn't have Annie subjected to this level of smoke. Not that it was much better inside the apartment. As he ushered Kim back in and shut the door behind them, her raspy cough still cut the air. He made a beeline toward the kitchen, where his own phone sat charging. Between Twitter, Facebook, and the county emergency-alert system, surely someone knew something. Or even better, maybe Mel had left him a text. Hearing her voice and confirming her own safety would be a balm to his already tattered nerves, and besides, Kim was right: they needed information, and fast.

"We need to pull back!" Mel yelled to José, spinning on her heel to retrace the path to camp. She didn't have to tell him twice, and they burst back into the circle of sleeping bags and trucks out of breath, where she gasped out an order to call for backup.

Doug White, with a talent for skeptical derision, looked up from brushing his teeth at the water station with a deliberate lack of haste. "Right now?"

"Affirmative." Mel ground her jaw, wishing the Red Book call had come in just a few minutes later last night, *after* White had finished clocking out. But until Hernandez himself showed his face, Mel was the second highest-ranking firefighter here, and she intended to hold her own. White's misogynism would simply have to wait. "And we need to get on the horn with any neighboring agencies we can. Eagle Valley

Fire Protection District, Outlaw County, even BLM, if they can send someone." They stood on Forest Service land but would take whatever help they could.

He complied, though perhaps not until taking his cue from Lewis, who jumped right on the horn. "I got Parker Pass Station 3 and 7, too," Lewis announced a minute later, head still bent toward his handheld. "And ODOT is on standby. How bad is it, Mel?"

Though she could no longer see the fire now that she was back in camp, that rolling lava still played behind Mel's eyes. "Bad. We're relocating," she announced to the crew at large, trying hard to keep the edge to her voice firmly planted in urgency, not panic. "Pack up and gear up."

Most of the young volunteers made short work of it, apart from Deklan, who wanted to know which agency would arrive first—*the county*—and which would be most effective—*probably Eagle Valley.*

"It takes a village, isn't that what you old-timers say?" he noted, while still trying to apply moleskin to his filthy feet, his dirty socks balled up on the ground next to his sleeping bag.

"Just pick your shit up," Mel ordered in response. She finished stuffing her down sleeping bag into its compression sack with more force than necessary, then called on Deklan to do the same. "Nobody has time to babysit you."

Deklan's ears turned the same shade as his fiery red hair at the reprimand, and Mel felt a swell of regret. As battalion chief, it was her duty to make sure the kids took this seriously, but that didn't mean she had to bark out orders like a drill sergeant. It hardly made her better than White. Besides, stressful situation notwithstanding, Mel was reasonably sure she was actually just projecting her own baggage onto the boy, trying to mother him while her own kids were out of sight and out of reach.

"I'm sorry," she told them. "Just . . . do your best to get loaded up. We need to pull back, stage further down-mountain while we wait for reinforcements."

Deklan finally complied in earnest, the first hint of fear in his eyes. *Good,* Mel thought, even while still feeling a bit mean. Fear was his friend. "And get yourselves fed," she added. She waved a packet of instant oatmeal at the kids, compliments of the Carbon Save Mart. They donated this stuff to the station firefighters by the caseload. "Looks like you'll get the action you've been waiting for sooner rather than later."

As José rushed to load the Gatorade water dispensers onto the supply rig and Lewis corralled the crew vehicles, Mel stepped away from the fray to check her phone for any messages. One had managed to get through sometime in the night from Sam. Seeing his name on her screen sent a jolt of gladness through her tired body.

"Will it ever stop?" she'd asked True once, in a low moment, when her love for Sam had, at least temporarily, overridden the stubborn resentment that clung like springtime algae to the boulders along the Outlaw's riverbanks.

True had only looked at her sadly, and Mel had read the answer in her face. *Did it matter?* Because love simply hadn't been enough. Finances aside, the stress inflicted by Annie's diagnosis had proven impossible to parse from the essence of them as a couple. *Collateral damage,* their therapist had said. *Friendly fire,* Mel had retorted.

But the text this morning gave her a welcome sense of relief: *Girls fine with me at the Eddy.*

Thank God. But what about True? The smoke could be funneling into the river valley by now, since the fire raged so hard here. Given the unprecedented speed of this fire, would she have to pivot from her usual course? Mel couldn't decide which was worse: True failing to carry out this week's handoff, crucial to keeping Annie's meds flowing, or getting stuck en route, putting herself, and her river clients, in danger. A quick swell of anger, not unlike the resentment that simmered persistently below it, arose in Mel. Just for once she'd love to have actual viable choices placed in front of her instead of the shit hand she and everyone she loved had been dealt.

*Get your head on straight.* Firefighters who had half their brains elsewhere made mistakes. Sometimes big ones. Occasionally fatal ones. She'd promised herself, from the start of this mess she'd gotten them into, that nothing like that would happen on her watch.

She only allowed herself to iMessage Sam back, cursing under her breath when she got a predictable *Text not sent* message. She tried again, sending the words as an iPhone text message instead. *Fire gaining. Annie ok?* When this attempt, too, resulted only in a scrolling wheel of death, she bit back another wave of worry—for Annie, for all of them—and simplified further, even though she knew this new message, in its succinctness, stripped down to only what mattered most, could alarm Sam. *Love to all. Kiss girls for me.* She hit Send three times before she heard her message sling through the ether with a *whoosh*.

# CHAPTER 6

Twenty minutes later, Mel and the rest of the Carbon Rural team had regrouped down-mountain. There they staged, once again fueled up, yellowed up, and ready with nothing to do but wait.

"All dressed up with nowhere to go," José noted, settling onto the running board of his truck.

"Like Deklan when he was *so* sure Hailey Myers was going to ask him to Homecoming," Ryan threw out, earning himself a smattering of laughs from the younger volunteers and a smack on the arm from Deklan. The rest of the crew found a seat on stumps or in vehicles to await the arrival of the additional muscle they'd requested.

The neighboring agencies made their appearance within minutes. First Eagle Valley, then the sheriff's department. Oregon Department of Transportation's larger rigs couldn't climb higher than the base of Flatiron, but even so, the sound of their additional trucks staging on the Forest Service roads below provided a sense of comfort. Some pulled tractors and bulldozers on flatbeds behind them, and the occasional screech of metal on metal as trailers were unhitched reassured the crew that the collective firefighting community was now behind them.

Everyone wore their Buffs over their mouths and noses now, and most of the men and women looked fidgety as they awaited orders from their respective superiors, packing and repacking their gear. Mel understood: everyone was anxious to either get started fighting this thing or get the hell out of here, one or the other. Her own muscles twitched as she shifted from boot to boot, her very cells seeming to hop around like electrons illustrated in a science movie shown in class. It was a feeling Mel listened to, a gut instinct if you will, a sixth sense. It was time for action.

"What do you think, Chief?" she asked the Eagle Valley officer standing closest. She reported only to her own superior officers, but she valued his opinion. "She look like she's gonna take a run to you?"

Because it sure did to her.

Before he could answer, Doug White chimed in.

"I don't think things could get too hairy." He threw an indulgent look toward the officer as if to say, *Leave it to a woman to overreact.*

"If the breeze picks up," Mel pressed, "we could see this fire make a play for the west, northwest." Even without wind to fuel it, the flickering swath of flame before them hadn't settled down since dawn.

The potential trajectory was obvious, at least to her, but White only offered a grunt that sounded a lot like a scoff. Mel refused to rise to the bait. If she planned to make fire captain before she turned forty-five, with the raise that would go along with it, she needed to exude confidence. When the Eagle Valley officer nodded, giving her words weight, Mel gave herself a mental pat on the back. Finally, they could see her point. But no: it was just that Chief Hernandez had arrived on scene, stepping up behind her.

"I'm thinking this blaze could run west, boss," White contributed immediately, as Mel's face heated with instant and righteous rage.

She couldn't help it, even knowing fighting her profession's built-in patriarchy would do her about as much good as Deklan trying to get out of cleanup duty. She knew the drill: no matter how hard she worked at every PT, no matter how well she scored on every training course, and no matter how many Coronas she drank with the guys off shift when she'd rather just be at home, she'd never be part of the boys' club. She suspected it had already cost her a fast-tracked promotion or two. If she failed to bite her tongue, it could cost her job. And Mel couldn't afford to lose even a day's pay.

Hernandez eyed the pine needles blanketing the dry dirt, the dense sage clinging to the slope of the west bank, carpeting Flatiron all the way to the peak, and nodded. "We'll stay on alert."

"Should we work to meet the dozers in the meantime?" Mel asked, because that uneasy feeling returned to her gut. "Start cutting containment between here and there?" Wind, ground fuel . . . either factor could change everything in an instant, sending their crew scattering, making retreat the only option again. She couldn't stomach the idea of putting her people at risk because the likes of Assistant Chief Doug White couldn't read a forest fire.

Hernandez gave her suggestion some thought but ultimately dismissed it. "We'll wait and see, as I said."

White did a poor job of trying to hide a condescending smile, and with a sigh, Mel settled uneasily back in to do as told. Prevailing fire-science wisdom did dictate that whenever possible, nature needed to run her course. Still, she wished the fire-science PhDs in Salem could stand in her crew's boots on the front line a few times.

As she breathed shallowly through the filter of her Buff, her mind flitted to Annie, down in town. Was she struggling for air, too, in the cramped apartment over the Eddy? Her asthma was always worse when the air quality dipped. What if her oximeter numbers made her ineligible for surgery?

Mel made a mental note to ask their pediatric team. It was the never knowing that was the hardest part of parenting Annie. The first time her daughter had experienced what the specialists called a "tet spell," she'd turned blue within seconds. When your baby couldn't breathe and you had to reach for the supply of *morphine*—of all things—that you always had to have on hand, you realized really quick: this was parenting at a whole new, terrifying level.

While other parents worried their kids might not get invited to the latest birthday party, or have trouble learning to read, or miss a field trip due to a head cold, Mel got to worry her daughter's blood would be suddenly denied oxygen. And a spell could hit anytime, anywhere, out of the clear blue sky, gray sky, and all skies in between.

Even when they had a good day, or a good week, Sam and Mel were left to wonder: How long would it last? Holding one's breath while your baby lost hers, waiting for the next downturn—which always came—was exhausting as hell.

"Bishop?"

She jumped, startled. Ryan had sidled up next to her, a frown on his soot-dusted face. "How long are we gonna be standing around?"

Mel looked for Hernandez, but he'd already left the scene, then sidelong at White, but he was staring at his phone, so she decided it was up to her to toe the company line. "As long as it takes for this fire to decide what she's gonna be." She sighed, wishing she could give him a different answer.

Ryan was a hard worker, eager to follow whatever order came down. She tried to keep the frustration out of her own voice. It wasn't Ryan's fault that White had undercut her, or that watching the Flatiron Fire felt a lot like watching Annie reach every infant milestone with bated breath. Would she roll over on time? Would she sit up? Would her breath be suddenly snatched from her lungs? Mel and Sam had scrutinized her for any and every slight change.

True had been nothing short of a lifesaver, Mel remembered as Ryan wandered away, digging a granola bar from his pack. Even if True didn't feel that same, awful constant tug between family and career that Mel felt every waking moment of her life, some of Mel's favorite family memories included her—scratch that, were *because* of her.

True offered a sense of relief that soothed the Bishop household like a balm. Just the presence of another adult hanging out on the deck at Highline, firing up the barbeque on a long weekend, kicking back with Astor, teaching her how to make hemp bracelets strung with scraps of river-polished rock, took the edge off in a way a glass or two of sauv blanc never could. Mel craved those evenings and lazy days when just a bit of the weight of being Astor and Annie's mom lifted from her shoulders, the heft of it temporarily shifted to True, who bounced Annie on her suntanned thighs and made her giggle.

It was this wish to dilute parenthood that cut deep and ragged, when she let herself dwell on it. How could Mel and Sam look to True to share all this responsibility with them, like Annie was a burden instead of the blessing and miracle everyone always reminded them she was? What no one pointed out: taking care of a child with a life-threatening, lifelong heart defect day in and day out wore a person *out*. Some days—no, *most* days—Mel felt fifty instead of thirty-eight, and some of those days, and not even the hardest ones, a little voice in her head whispered, *It's not fair.* On the hardest ones, the ones when they had to call 911, when even the morphine and beta-blockers couldn't touch the tet spells, Mel wondered . . . if God only gave people what they could handle, how had a deity who was supposed to be so damned perfect made such a serious fucking mistake?

Mel sighed and stood, the heat of her breath moistening her Buff. The flames licking at the ground cover before her still seemed docile enough, so why was she still feeling on edge? Was White right? Was she worried about nothing, or *was* the fire going to take a run?

She scanned the camp of crew members for Lewis again, spotting him refilling a collection of five-gallon Gatorade water dispensers. She walked over to make her case a second time.

"The crew's getting restless," she noted, then corrected herself, deciding to own it. "*I'm* getting restless. Something about this fire doesn't sit right with me."

Lewis hefted the last empty water dispenser toward the tap. "Then let's go with your gut. The wind direction has been nagging at you ever since we staged here."

Was this Lewis's way of acknowledging he knew it was *her* observation of the fire's behavior that had been snatched up and recycled by White? If so, it cost him nothing. No man working his way up the fire-station ladder had to worry as much as she did about stepping a toe out of line. But still, the surprise must have shown on her face. One of the first things you learned working for Uncle Sam was that you didn't shake rank, and Lewis was a by-the-book kind of guy.

"Just tell White it was your idea," she muttered.

Lew laughed but obeyed, and a minute later, Mel heard that self-important voice cut across the assemblage.

"New orders!"

Deklan and Ryan lifted their heads with interest, while others wandered toward White to hear the latest, including officers from additional stations. As first on scene, Carbon Rural retained seniority, at least for now. "While we wait to see what nature has in store for us," White bellowed, "we can be proactive. Starting with cutting some firebreaks, to meet the sheriff's department's bulldozer line between the base of Flatiron and town."

He nodded to Lew, who had the grace not to look Mel in the eye. She focused on Janet instead, who gave her a wink before waving her over and spreading out their Forest Service map on the hood of a water-tank truck.

"See here?" Janet said. "We can use FS 7312 as a starting point, curving the firebreak with the grain of the mountain."

Mel traced the route on the map with one finger, following the almost delicate topographical contours of the elevation lines. "If we get all our ground crews on it, we can have Flatiron encircled by midafternoon, evening at the latest."

Ryan tugged at his Buff, already dusted with the ash that fell from the sky to accumulate on their helmets and hats. "Ha, like a moat," he noted, leaning over Janet's shoulder, his voice muffled under the thin cotton.

Mel clapped a hand onto his shoulder, brushing off a layer of soot. "*Exactly* like a moat."

Each ranking officer dispersed to convey the new order to their respective teams, Mel following suit. Digging containment lines was grueling work, but at least now she could finally grant her crew their wish for something more to do than spend the night in the woods in their sleeping bags. She saw Deklan first and, noting that all his gear looked in order for a change, told him, "Go get first pick of the Pulaskis, kid."

It was gratifying to see his eyes light up. Over by the stack of gear off-loaded by another rookie, he tested the sharpness of the axe and adze heads of each Pulaski with a hesitant fingertip, weighing each heavy fire-line-breaking tool in his hand, deciding which one to wield. Soon enough, the sweat of manual labor would replace the pinch of pink excitement in his cheeks, but in this moment, his boyish optimism had her imagining Sam at that age, headed off to boot camp with only false bravado for company, and her heart constricted.

# CHAPTER 7

While Kim searched the radio channels for any useful information and Astor got herself Froot Loops from the kitchen, Sam used the time Annie still slept—albeit fitfully—to get the girls' go bags ready. Mobilizing Annie was no picnic, even in the best of times, and he went through the list of necessities now: oxygen tank (never stable in an environment like an evac), heart monitor (needing power), morphine, in case of the worst (must be temperature-controlled), and her portable heart monitor and the pulse oximeter they called her Pac-Man, for the way it clamped onto her finger as though taking a big bite.

He and Mel learned everything they could about tetralogy of Fallot starting the minute the diagnosis left their cardiologist's lips. The way the combination of four different defects—yes, four—prevented the blood leaving Annie's heart from delivering the oxygen needed by the tissues of her small body. The way this chronic lack of oxygen wore her down day by day, cyanosis tinging her lips and nose blue.

"We can repair it with patches, but only for now," Dr. Newman had told Sam and Mel, and Sam had leaned forward across the doctor's desk at Seattle Children's in utter disbelief.

But yeah, they'd heard that right. *Patches.*

Sam had immediately envisioned the rubber squares heat-ironed onto leaks in True's rafting boats. Eventually they peeled and water bubbled around them, causing a distressing little hissing sound. And then

True always said, "Well, that's that," and pried the patch off altogether and started over.

"Are you kidding me?" Mel had said, trying to rise out of her chair, letting out an involuntary moan when her C-section incision protested. "That's the best the collective medical community could do for a human being's *heart*?"

"No," Dr. Newman had said calmly. "She will need open-heart surgery. Most likely multiple surgeries, but for now—"

"*Multiple* surgeries'?" Sam had interjected. Because how could a baby be expected to go through that?

"*Open-heart*'?" Mel had echoed at the same time. That was how they'd been back then, tag-teaming each other's sentences.

Dr. Newman had explained with graphs and diagrams. Annie wasn't eligible for the less invasive catheter procedures she wished she could perform. The first surgery would repair what was possible now, and a second, probably around five years of life, would be needed to widen the arteries of Annie's heart.

Each to a tune of about $50,000. Annie's birth alone justified a bill of twenty-two grand, and apparently her stint in intensive care cost $3,500 per day. Plus meds. Plus oxygen. The only person Sam and Mel had seen more during their eighteen days in the NICU than the cardiologist was the rep from Seattle Children's billing department.

But at least they'd faced it together. At least Sam had had Mel's hand to grip at each meeting across the desk from Dr. Newman, and Mel had had Sam's shoulder for support on each slow but steady walk around the maternity wing.

True always told Sam to take a deep, long breath when he relived this stuff, reminding him that PTSD came in many forms.

"Guess I'm lucky to have hit the trifecta," he'd retorted once. Childhood trauma, military combat, and his daughter's birth, all contenders. True had told him she'd rather decline her invite to the pity party, but she'd laid a comforting hand on Sam's shoulder, just the same.

He refocused his mind, returning to evacuation protocol: Gas in the SUV? Check. Water in the portable can? Check. But where would they go? The most obvious answer flitted immediately into his mind, but he batted it back. Even though the smoke would be thinner at high elevation, the last thing he wanted to do was take Astor and Annie back up to Highline, to be reminded all over again of the end of their parents' marriage.

Never mind Sam's own reaction; he didn't need Astor acting out today, and couldn't stand the sight of the confusion on Annie's face. After almost a year at the rooms above the Eddy, his youngest daughter barely remembered Highline, which stung more than any barbed quip Astor could throw at him.

He knew what people around Carbon said, because they usually said it directly to his face: *Give yourself a break. Go easy . . . Few marriages could withstand the challenges you two faced.* But he could never seem to stop taking inventory of all the ways in which he'd failed Mel. Not able to shake the baggage of his childhood. Not providing enough for Annie. Not even knowing when Mel would call it quits. That shit day would be etched in his memory forever, when their creative math had stopped adding up and she'd thrown in the towel.

Now, navigating between the bedroom and kitchen of the little apartment over the Eddy to gather gear, all he could manage was a shallow inhale, which only made him feel worse. If it was this hard for him to draw breath, what must Annie be feeling? Every once in a while, she sat up in bed, hacking anew.

"She's a tough cookie," Kim said, attention split between looking after her and trying to locate the TV remote, having given up on finding valid info on the fire online. Apparently, social media searches were yielding very little so far in terms of useful information. Sam eyed Annie's struggle, counting all the ways in which she could relapse during this fire, their hard work at ensuring she was in as good of health as possible before surgery out the window.

"Asthma is common among children with congenital heart diseases," Dr. Newman always reminded them. As was the ultimate fear: complete heart failure.

Those three words always hit Sam like one of Chris Fallows's childhood punches to the gut he hadn't braced for. The doctors and hospital staff tried to counter the terror of them with words like *Affordable Care Act* and *covered costs*, but Sam spit back *premiums* and *out of pocket* and *prescriptions*.

When he next walked into the living room, Kim perched on the edge of the couch, coffee cup in hand, eyes on the screen. She'd found the remote but still struggled to navigate the unfamiliar menu. Sam took over, making just about as many missteps toggling from Disney+ to the local news. It had been getting darker by the minute in the apartment, and the TV screen cast an eerie glow, like it was dusk, not well after daybreak. How did this bode for Mel, out on the line? True, on the Outlaw? Sam just didn't know.

"Dad! Here. I'll do it!" Astor hijacked control of the remote, and Sam let her, one hand on his coffee cup to keep the hot liquid from splashing onto her pajama bottoms.

"There it is. Stop there, Astor."

She'd found their local news channel, where a ticker at the bottom of the screen listed Carbon's AQI zone—or level of air pollution—at red, a.k.a. "very unhealthy." *No shit.* Hopefully it was at least marginally better inside the apartment.

Annie gave up on trying to rest and decided she wanted Froot Loops, too, and while Astor climbed back onto the kitchen counter for a second bowl, Sam shifted Annie's weight on his knee, wrapping her Tinker Bell blanket more tightly around her shoulders before focusing back on the TV. In her polo shirt and overdone hairdo, the local newscaster for Channel 10, Madison something or other, looked out of place standing in the center of a dirt Forest Service road outside of town. "Thank you, Barry," she told her colleague at the desk, then glanced up from the notes clutched in her hand. "Caused by a lightning strike at 5:16 p.m. last night, July 10, the Flatiron Fire has burned 3,245 acres per last report, and is zero percent contained." Her eyes flicked down to the paper again. "Fire crews on-site are under BLM mandate to stand by—"

"Stand by? While the mountain burns? What is this shit?" Kim complained.

Sam shot her a look, but Annie wasn't listening, having snuggled deeper into her blanket, ear against Sam's chest. The sound of her cough still reverberated, shaking the blanket against Sam intermittently. Having prepared her sister's cereal, Astor now stood by absorbing the news and studying the adults stoically, but that was Astor. Sometimes it seemed to Sam that nothing fazed her.

". . . currently engaging in containment only," Madison continued, "as the blaze continues to burn on the west and southwest sides of Flatiron Peak. We're joined now by remote call with Carbon Rural District 1 Battalion Chief Melissa Bishop."

"They said Mom!" Astor contributed.

Sam nodded, feeling his first tentative smile all morning at the sound of her name. The camera angle went to split screen, a little phone icon springing to life on the right-hand side. He straightened at attention on the couch, the remote forgotten in his hand as, on the screen, Madison ran her hands awkwardly through her hair as she waited uncomfortably for the voice patch to go through. Then Mel's voice crackled across Sam's living room, the little phone graphic vibrating, and he found himself exhaling fully for the first time in over twelve hours. Annie looked up from her blanket, and Astor leaned in.

"Thanks, Madison," Mel said, from somewhere on the mountain. "Carbon Rural has been monitoring the fire since 6:00 p.m. last night, and as of this morning, we've been joined by the Bureau of Land Management, as well as county and Outlaw teams." Mel's voice, though clearly roughened by smoke, carried its usual smooth confidence that somehow reassured, even in an emergency. *Especially in an emergency,* Sam amended. She and True were strikingly similar in that way, ever tougher when the going got tough. "At this time," Mel assured them, "with an increasing wind factor and a predicted fire trajectory to the west-southwest, precautionary measures are being taken. The community of Carbon is advised to stay on alert for future instructions or evacuation orders."

"Stay on alert until *when*?" Kim questioned aloud.

"Until we know more," Sam shot back. He thought he'd done a decent job of keeping the fear and stress at bay until now, but hearing Mel's voice unraveled something inside of him he hadn't even realized was coiled so tightly. Because he hadn't had direct word from her in far too long. Which meant that for all her on-air confidence, it was bad enough out there that she didn't have time to run down the hill for a quick check-in.

Astor's solemn eyes moved from her father to Kim and back again. "I hate the weird smell in here. It's like burnt toast."

Kim glanced at Sam, worry in the fine lines around her eyes.

"Yeah, it's hard to think," he said to both of them, partially by way of apology, "with this stupid smoke going to our heads."

"Is Mom out there now?" Astor asked, eyes still on the little phone icon gracing the screen.

"Fighting the fire, sweetie, yes."

Mel had sounded tired, Sam thought, though she hid it well for the sound bite. He watched through the end of the news segment, hoping for a glimpse of her, but KBLS Channel 10 never got close enough for a face-to-face interview. There was a long aerial shot of the blaze, but Sam knew they had a better view right here, if they were to venture back onto the deck of the Eddy. If he were to brave the outdoors now, would he see the flames lick upward to disappear into the thick smoke above Flatiron?

Sam breathed deep, just to check: yes, Astor was right. The smoky smell still permeated, even inside, so he double-checked the locks on each window, making sure he had every one sealed. He pulled a Buff over his face and stepped out onto the landing, closing the apartment door resolutely behind him before Astor or Annie could follow. He trotted down the stairs and out the side door by the grill kitchen to the deck, and . . . shit! He could practically taste the smoke out here, the air thick on his tongue, making him cough again with just one breath. A layer of ash collected on the railing, reminding him of the snow that accumulated in winter; the girls liked to bring a plastic ruler from their school-supply desk out here, to make measurements. Today, Sam estimated that if he went inside to retrieve their Hello Kitty ruler, it would mark the ash as half an inch thick, at least.

God, could Sam even risk Annie in this air for the length of time it would take to buckle her into the SUV? And what about Mel, on the front lines? *Her* lungs couldn't exactly afford to be exposed to that level of smoke inhalation, either, given what she put them through on the regular.

He rubbed a hand down the rough stubble on his face, unsure of just about everything. Astor banged on the glass of the upstairs window, making him jump, and Sam came back inside, trying to pass his worry off as wonderment. "If it weren't summer, it'd be like a snow day today!" he said entirely too brightly.

Astor only frowned, shifting from foot to foot in her neon-dog-and-cat-print nightshirt. Sam wished the girls had been able to sleep in this morning, spared Sam's restless energy as he lapped the apartment. Like one of the opossums his old man used to trap under their house growing up, poor bastards.

When he came back into the kitchen, Kim had made a second carafe of coffee. He pulled her aside. "You got a plan for where to go, if they call for that evac?" he asked.

"My mom's in Portland. If Carbon gets to Level 2, I'll pick up Denise on the way." Her sister, Zack's mother. Sam nodded solemnly. Thinking of Zack served as a good reminder that life was unfair to more folks than just the Bishops.

"But you guys should go sooner, don't you think?" Kim jutted her chin in the direction of Annie in the living room.

"I'm not sure." Sam eyed the darkness outside the window, where the smoke seemed to collect against the glass like lead shavings to a magnet. Annie's small army of doctors had warned them against letting her O2 levels dip below 90, which was basically guaranteed if they got on the interstate, given the AQI. And while the idea of retreating to Highline still grated at his already raw nerves, there was also the Eddy's business to consider. Closing even one day would put Sam behind on his contributions to Annie's meds. "Hunkering down here is probably as good a place as any."

Kim gave him a doubtful look. "Unless the wind shifts, bringing this fire closer to town."

In which case the entirety of Carbon would be at Level 3. "Don't even put that shit out into the universe," he muttered.

"At least call Claude back and find out if the air quality is better up at Highline, like I suspect it is."

Sam felt the resistance pull from the very core of him, like the strain of muscle when lifting something far too heavy. "My Highline house is a mess," he said quietly. "You know that."

"Even if it is in a state of home improvement," Kim pressed, emphasizing her word choice, "it's got to be better than this." She gestured toward the window. "I'm sorry to be a pain in your ass, but it's true."

*Home. Improvement.* Basically Sam's life's goal, from the foundation up. He knew his inability to let that house go had broken Mel, but what she didn't understand: nothing had ever been gifted to Sam good enough as it was. His life had been littered with leftovers: the castoffs of other kids from their lunch boxes, the clothes from the closet discreetly situated in the middle school counselor's office, where he picked out jeans that didn't fit exactly right and shirts in styles he didn't like. Food from the church pantry, which consisted of everyone else's rejected canned goods: pureed pumpkin in April, pickled beets, groceries people had grabbed by accident, while not paying attention, like no-sugar-added peaches and lima beans when they'd meant to buy kidney beans. The secondhand furniture in his house growing up? Mark had sent Sam dumpster diving for that. Everything in Sam's life, when it came down to it, he'd had to work like hell to improve, fix, restore, or make better.

Mel had been the first thing in his life shiny and new, without strings attached. She'd come to him whole and healthy, with a sun-kissed river glow and a solid childhood upbringing behind her. Sometimes he sat back and marveled at her ability to walk through life carting so little baggage. And so he'd made sure: the things they'd bought together, they'd bought firsthand.

The dishes they'd picked out before their wedding still sat neatly stacked in the cupboard at Highline. The couch they'd selected on one of their many trips north to Annie's cardiologist in Portland still sat in the oversize living room, directly across from the partially rebuilt fireplace. It was why he was here above the Eddy, with the girls. Eating off paper plates and sleeping on sofa beds felt preferable to seeing half-finished failure at every turn. Returning to Highline, especially to ride out this fire? He didn't know if he could bear it.

Kim studied him, a frown tugging at her face, like she was trying to work out what exactly his hang-up was. He'd tell her, but who the hell knew where to start?

"As you're packing," she said at length, "don't forget the practical stuff, like shampoo and washcloths. That sort of thing. I can still remember the Carson Fire . . . back in '98? Five days straight, sleeping on a cot on the gym floor of Carbon High School, will instill in you a healthy respect for toothpaste and a hairbrush, let me tell you. Remember two pairs of shoes for the girls. Jackets in case the weather turns." She paused. "You'll tell me if you hear directly from Mel?"

Sam managed a tight smile. "Yes, mother hen."

As if on cue, his phone pinged in his back pocket, and he fished it out, surprised. "Speaking of whom . . ." He read the text, probably delayed between cell towers. A simple, succinct message sending love to him and their daughters. No updates or instructions. No reassurances.

He held it out for Kim to read, that damned knot settling in permanently in his throat.

"She's okay," Kim said immediately. "She's saying everything is fine, that's all." Though it didn't escape Sam's notice when she dug her phone out of her pocket, too, leaving a hasty message for her sister to start looking now for the crates for her cats. And to toss some bottles of water in the car for good measure, just in case this thing turned from bad to worse.

# CHAPTER 8

Following a rather somber breakfast in the smoke, True tackled the less-than-savory chore of repacking the groover—*we call it that because of the grooves the bucket seat leaves on your backside,* she'd told Emmett, to his delight—into the raft. She had just clicked the groover lid into place when Vivian approached her through the trees.

"So listen," she said, and True felt herself tense. Here it was, the moment Mel had predicted, right along with the ash and smoke.

"It's going to clear up," she said quickly, though the morning haze was definitely not dissipating. If anything, it had settled into the river valley even more stubbornly.

Vivian just lifted both eyebrows in silent protest. "I'm a straight shooter," she said, "and I need you to be the same."

True exhaled, setting the groover down and nodding. "All right. Yeah." She reminded herself that Vivian had entrusted her—*her*, True—with these precious four remaining days down the Outlaw. That trust felt sacred in a world where faith in people could be hard to come by. In their campfire circle, True had even found herself opening up about her own personal life—including how important her goddaughters were to her—in return. Maybe she'd felt comfortable knowing she was in like-minded company. Maybe it was seeing representation of gay family life, in contrast to the hetero one True was so acutely familiar with, that made her feel like opening up. Or maybe it was just Vivian. Either way, it was a first.

"How bad is this, really?" Vivian asked now. "What's the protocol?"

True wavered. Just like last night, the thought of letting Vivian down felt almost as unsettling to her as letting down Mel.

Almost.

She cared about Emmett. Liked him very much. And she was starting to like his mother even more.

But she loved Annie.

They had to get downriver to Temple Bar by Friday. There was just no way around it. When Mel had first come to her with this plan, she had looked the most desperate True had ever seen her, and she'd seen her trying to navigate Quartz Canyon with half of one broken paddle. Of *course* True would do anything for her and the Bishops. It was all just such a fucking foregone conclusion.

Anyway, there *was* no protocol, not when it came to wildfire smoke. "It's common for the AQ index to become poor when fires burn in the mountains around the Outlaw National Forest during the summers here," she told Vivian. It was why, when they'd first begun talking about this trip, she'd urged Vivian to book in July, not August.

"But this is early," Vivian countered, having apparently paid close attention to True's advice. "And this fire isn't just 'in the mountains.' It's on *the* mountain, the one right there." She hooked a thumb back behind her.

This, too, was true.

"I won't put Emmett at risk," Vivian said. A second look True recognized shone in her usually warm, dark eyes. The look was of a mother who was not to be messed with. True had seen that look in Mel's eyes more than once.

Which was what enabled her to meet her gaze head-on. "Of course not. Which is why I have a plan." *Stage at Wonderland. Rest a day, out of the smoke.* Would it work? It would have to.

She explained Mel's idea to Vivian, who absorbed this new itinerary in thoughtful silence before breaking it with one last question that managed to knock what little air True had in her lungs right out. "Would you try this with Astor and Annie?"

Would she?

*I am doing this for Astor and Annie,* True decided fiercely. It allowed her to look Vivian in the eyes as she answered. "I would have to."

Vivian nodded slowly. "Then our well-being is in your hands," she said softly, touching True's forearm lightly as she stepped back toward camp.

*Fuck* was all True could think, her limbs suddenly limp. Whose wasn't?

An hour later, she navigated the raft unceremoniously toward Cougar and Buckshot Falls, not stopping to play up the novelty of the Class III rapids for her clients. Usually she eddied out just above each landmark, hopping ashore to describe the whitewater they were about to tackle, showing clients which line they'd take by drawing a crude diagram of the rocks and falls in the sand at their feet. Today, she just wanted to get some miles under their belt.

"We'll start out left," she called out as they approached the roar of Cougar, drawing Vivian's attention immediately upon her. "And then we'll move to the middle after that first boulder, right where the water boils over that channel. See?" True released her grip on one oar to point, and Emmett swiveled on his tube seat to track the location. "Then row *right-right-right*, hard and fast, to avoid hitting the left bank by those blackberry bushes. Got it?"

Both faces registered bare panic. "Wait, left first?" Vivian shot at her. "Or right?"

"And then what, again?" Emmett added at a shout.

"Just follow my lead," True assured them, amused despite herself by the duo's unique "two against the world" dynamic.

"Toeholds, please," she called out as they took their first hard pull left, and Emmett and Vivian both scrambled to stick their sandaled feet deep in the crack of the inner tube at the interior base of the raft for stability. "Paddles in the water. And *row.*"

No matter how many times she ran these rapids, each plunge gave True a thrill, and she allowed herself to embrace the delicious drop of her stomach as Cougar spit them out at the bottom to drift toward the riffles at the next bend. She caught her breath, grinning despite the smoke, taking a break on the oars as the Wus recovered from the shock of the whitewater and took stock, wiping the spray from their faces. She rested her forearms for a moment, the burn slowly fading from her deltoids while the raft turned in a lazy half circle as it floated.

"That was cool," Emmett said, his smile a welcome break from the serious frown he'd worn since they'd hastily broken camp in the smoke of Fern Creek. True smiled back, always happy to make an ally in her love of adrenaline-inducing outdoor sports.

Vivian, too, was grinning, a sight that sent a little stab of unexpected joy through True's gut. Usually, it was easier to just paddle through rapids without client "assistance," but Vivian's toned biceps had been a welcome aid. True told her as much, enjoying the blush that touched upon her cheeks. Well, from that and the cold. Vivian shivered visibly following the waves of icy river water they'd taken onboard. True pulled them into an eddy long enough to ship her oars and tug a dry towel out of her dry bag and press it into Emmett's hands. "Give this to your mom, will you, kiddo?"

"Thanks, True."

Vivian looked suddenly vulnerable, clutching the towel to her chest, eyes stinging from the water and smoke, and True was startled to realize she nearly wanted to call off her revised itinerary right then and there, offering an evac instead. What if she was taking too big a risk, after all? *Looks can be deceiving,* she reminded herself. A woman didn't climb through the ranks at UCSF Medical Center as a single mother without being tougher than she appeared.

Still, worry clouded Vivian's face as Emmett cast an anxious glance back toward the silty air, one hand waving like a fan in front of his face. Despite True's reassurances, the sight of the smoke and ash continued to cast a pallor. True knew they all felt the weight of it, exhilarating rides through rapids notwithstanding, but so far, to True's relief, there had been no further talk of evacuating.

That relief came with a healthy dose of guilt. She looked again at Emmett. She was essentially putting this beautiful child at risk to save another, but what choice did she have?

"I've seen wildfires out here before," True assured them now as they all followed the path of Emmett's hand batting at the smoke. "Nothing we can't handle, right, E?"

Emmett looked dubious, and so she took up the oars again, rowing with long, deep strokes toward their next challenge, Buckshot Falls.

"That's right," Vivian contributed, squeezing Emmett's hand for reassurance. "Fifteen years' experience, kiddo," she declared, perhaps a tad too enthusiastically. "We're in good hands."

True managed a smile over the wooden handle of her oar, grateful for the endorsement even if it might have been forced. Even knowing she might not deserve it, not this trip. Apparently, Vivian hadn't become a respected lead RN without in turn recognizing and valuing fellow professional women as well, True decided as she rowed into the current. What was the saying? A high tide lifts all boats? It was refreshing to skip the part of the rafting trip where she had to prove herself double just because she lacked a Y chromosome.

She continued on steadily, letting the Wus go back to covering their mouths with the hems of their T-shirts to filter out the smoke that, while less thick here, downriver, still clung to the canyon walls they glided through. She focused on her stroke, knowing she'd need to row longer and stronger today than the day before. She let her thoughts turn inward, even as Vivian's vote of confidence echoed in her head.

Fifteen years . . . shit. True never loved the reminder that she was forty-two years old. She'd always thought she'd have years to figure out her future, plenty of time before societal norms would expect her to work a nine-to-five with benefits and a 401(k). But it couldn't be denied that everyone she'd started out rafting with had long since exited the industry, leaving the lifestyle for relationships, responsibility, "real jobs" that didn't take them away from their families for twelve weeks every summer. True had been the one to stubbornly remain, rising through the ranks of Paddle, Inc., each summer, welding in the offseason, before finally realizing that long-ago dream of embarking on her own guide business. She'd earned respect, sure, but also more than one nickname that hinted at her age and years of outdoor exposure. Sunbaked came to mind, a favorite of the college kids and single-seasoners thanks to her near-permanent tan lines, the skin across her shoulders a constant bronze tone against her blond hair. And, admittedly, probably also for that one night the newbies had discovered the stash of indica she enjoyed from time to time. She far preferred the other nickname, TrueBlue, which she liked to think she'd earned for her loyalty to the job and her love of the water she couldn't seem to leave.

Well, she had her own exit plan, she'd have them all know. And it had nothing to do with this fresh hell she and Mel had managed to get themselves into this summer. Automatically, she glanced back over her shoulder toward Flatiron, where, somewhere in the haze of the smoke upriver, her Pinterest-perfect yurt, with its rainwater-collection barrels and drought-resistant garden, sat at the end of her private, rough gravel drive just off the river road. She hadn't so much as unloaded her first load of solar panels before a caravan of trucks, *Don't Tread on Me* and MAGA flags billowing behind them in a wash of yellow, red, white, and blue, had churned up the dust around True's Chacos. Immediately, the hair on her arms had stood on end as intuition kicked into overdrive. At least ten men stared back at her through the dirty windshields of their rigs.

"Welcome to the hood," John Fallows had drawled, alighting from the last truck to spit on the ground at his feet. "We got our own little neighborhood watch out here, seeing as we're so far off the grid."

"All right," True had said carefully, looking from Fallows to his son, Chris, always in his shadow.

Additional men had emerged from their vehicles one by one, until a half circle of unwashed humanity framed her in. The closest guy offered her a wink. "So, you know, consider yourself . . . watched."

True had refused to be intimidated. At least, that was what she hoped she'd projected. She'd refused to run directly back to town and give up on homesteading, anyway. She'd known John and his crew grew illegal weed, under cover of their legal grow. Everyone knew. And a whole handful of property owners out here farmed similarly. Most kept to themselves. Most didn't mind a quiet, non-nosy neighbor. What she hadn't known—*Because you didn't ask*, Sam had pointed out later—was just what league she'd leveled up to.

She'd worked on the Outsider yurt in the following months with her head down, determination fueling her. Laying a foundation, wrapping the canvas around the frame, constructing the yurt's deck solo from a blueprint. Knowing that it would serve not only as her escape but as her professional art and welding studio for when she gave up the river for good. She could live out her days there, with very little overhead. She'd thought it all through. As a gay woman who wasn't the marrying type, she'd had to. No one else stood in the wings, waiting to take care of her in her old age.

She wouldn't let John Fallows, or anyone else, rob her of that.

She sighed, glancing away from the Wus and the nuclear-family coziness they represented. She'd almost convinced herself she didn't want that life by the time she'd seen the Outsider through Mel's eyes for the first time and had to admit that her subconscious, at least, felt differently. Showing off her homestead to the Bishops, she'd watched Mel's face slowly shift from admiration to confusion to realization. The river-rock fireplace she'd said she'd always wanted? Check. The herb garden out front, complete with a wraparound fence to keep out the deer? Yep. Shit. Even after working day after day in the Oregon sunshine, True hadn't realized she'd been building her retreat to Mel's exact specifications.

"You'll be set here for life," Sam had declared, startling True while she tried to wrap her head around her own self-sabotage, clapping a hand on her sun-warmed shoulder.

"You'll put your own spin on it," Mel had added softly before darting away to prevent Astor, just a toddler, from climbing up the deer fence.

True sighed at the memory, then glanced through the smoke again at Vivian, giving in to a moment of speculation before coming back down to earth. She should have named her yurt the Lost Cause.

"Ready?" she said, signaling to the Wus to begin rowing again as the hum of Buckshot Falls increased to a more insistent rumble from around the next bend.

Emmett lowered his Buff to flash a quick smile, but Vivian just lifted her eyebrows at True, as if to ask, *Are you?*

# CHAPTER 9

By 9:00 a.m., Mel worked alongside her Carbon Rural crew in a long line of ground pounders, all local agencies now on hand. A sense of urgency prevailed as Pulaskis bit into the parched dirt with muted thuds, the labored breathing of the crew's combined efforts the only sound not drowned out by the wildfire. They were as close to the flames as they could get, close enough to feel the heat through their flame-retardant shirts, close enough to stomp out embers that smoldered under their feet.

"At least we've got a breeze," Deklan called out from down the line, tugging his Buff back off his face for some relief.

A chorus of firefighters instantly gave him shit. "Yeah, *wind* is exactly what we need, dumbass," Ryan lobbed at him, while Lewis coughed out a bark of a laugh.

"Ow, what? At least I can breathe while I kill myself on this chain gang."

"Put your Buff back on," Mel called to him. "Your ears are already burning."

"What can I say, Chief? I'm a delicate flower."

More muted laughter. Deklan was good for breaking the tension, at least. Mel was glad he still had the energy to be cocky, which was more than she could say for herself. She bent back down to her task, feeling more like thirty-eight going on sixty, her Pulaski seeming to gain weight in her gloved palm with every upswing, the sweat that formed with alarming volume on her neck and head dripping between her shoulder blades to slide down her back and stick to her shirt on every chop through the dense underbrush.

Up and down the line, every other veteran firefighter bent equally to the task, knowing the stakes, understanding they all raced a clock. A secondary stopwatch ran in a blur of numbers in Mel's head, too. How long until the smoke in town proved too risky for Annie? How many hours could she breathe poor-quality air before she compromised her health too much for surgery? How many liters of oxygen did Sam have at his disposal in the portable tank at his place? Did Mel have time to break away to call him?

She refocused on the task at hand, the task she could actually tackle, or she risked going crazy with worry. Cutting this containment line was crucial; this "moat" would serve as a first defense between Carbon and the rapidly growing Flatiron Fire. They sure as hell didn't want it to reach all the way down to the rutted Forest Service roads at the lower mountain: while excellent firebreaks in their own right, roads came with a serious downfall . . . of the civilization sort. Mel had already taken inventory: along FS 7312 sat five houses, two small ranches, and a veterinary clinic. And just off FS 7312? The access road to True's place by the river.

If the Outsider was lost, what would that do to True? She'd done a lot to the place in the years since she'd erected it. Mel had been relieved to see it was no longer a placeholder for what could have been, in some alternate reality. True had made sure of that, adding an art studio off her welding workshop and building a little bunk setup for Astor and Annie, despite the fact that to date, Mel's younger daughter had been unable to spend a night away from her parents.

At least Sam's house still sat in safety. The wind whipped west, sparing his ridge, and Mel imagined the air quality had to be better at elevation. He should take the girls there now, she thought—the irony, given that she had wanted him to sell it, not lost on her.

With a determined grunt, she renewed her efforts with her axe. She worked steadily and slowly, ignoring the scream of her muscles, denying herself more than the occasional water break at the hasty rig staged on the road.

Every few minutes, White, accompanied by a supervisor from Outlaw County, swept the line, pointing out needs for improvement. "Let's double the width at the turn," he shouted at Janet and Lewis at one point. Then: "You call this containment?"

This criticism was directed at Ryan and Deklan, who'd left a layer of roots and pine scraps under their boots. Denying the blaze the fuel it needed meant scraping this stretch of forest clean, all the way down to mineral soil, at least two feet wide. The fire line had to be barren enough to prevent smoldering, burning, or spotting by embers blowing or rolling across the line. It had to suck the oxygen right out of this beast that breathed down their necks.

She heard Deklan mutter a curse as he tackled the shoddy stretch with renewed vigor.

True set her sights on Wonderland Lodge, twelve more miles ahead, nestled in the pines along the northern bank of the Outlaw River. She bit her lip in thought, fretting about asking for sanctuary there from the Martins, who'd owned Wonderland longer than True'd been alive. She doubted she'd receive their hospitality.

"Too long in the backcountry with no one but their dogs for company," she usually joked to her clients.

Typically, True and her party camped on the riverbank just past the Martins' property instead. Chances were good they'd be asked to do so again, no matter that the smoke now seemed here to stay in the river canyon.

But first things first. Lying between the Wonderland of Wonderland Lodge and True's current position on the river near Osprey Creek was

Quartz Canyon, 1.3 miles of tight, twisting turns through the narrow rocky channel of the Outlaw's most famous slot canyon carved out a millennia ago by the last ice age.

"Picture the log flume ride at Six Flags," she told Emmett, "then double the width of the slide, and multiply the strength of the current by about . . . oh, a hundred."

Usually, she enjoyed the look of wide-eyed trepidation this description earned her; she got to build up the anticipation, rev up the adrenaline, then distribute a generous number of high fives upon her clients' successful passage of the lengthy flume. Today, however, she was white-knuckling it as much as the Wus; more so, probably. Knowing what lay ahead sent a prickle of seldom-felt fear down her spine. Navigating Quartz was hard enough without the cover of smoke clouding her vision. She shuddered with a sudden chill.

She looked up from her oars to see Vivian studying her as they rowed across the flats following Osprey Creek. "What is it?" she asked, her pretty face arranged into a frown of concern.

True weighed her options—pretend everything was rosy, or come clean? She needed to continue to maintain what authority she'd earned from Vivian, but could use her muscle soon, it couldn't be denied. "It's not just the technical challenge of Quartz Canyon that makes it a Class IV," she admitted after a beat. She glanced at Emmett, at the bow. He had leaned far forward onto his stomach, out of earshot, fingers trailing in the foam. "It's the length of the rapids that gets to you. They just go on and on . . . over a mile of paddling—serious paddling—and we'll need to push hard from start to finish. There are obstacles to avoid at every turn; remember the boulder at Cougar?" Vivian nodded. "Imagine one of those every few meters, in a flume a quarter of the width we enjoyed at Cougar."

"But you do it every trip," Vivian pointed out. She didn't add, *Right?* But True heard it.

"Right," she supplied. "But we usually do it with more preparation, including plenty of scouting on foot before our attempt, not to mention visibility on the water." And ample rest. She didn't like the idea of heading into Quartz with her arms fatigued from rowing. They'd already pushed eight miles today, and had ten more to go before they even reached this biggest challenge of the Outlaw. By the time True heard the roar of Quartz, she knew her muscles would feel like Jell-O.

"I can help," Vivian promised, and while True might have been tempted to chalk up her offer to untested earnestness, there was a confidence on the woman's face that True was getting accustomed to. Who was discounting whom now? True wouldn't be *that* woman. Not in a million years.

"Thank you," she said, and Vivian literally rolled up the sleeves of her sun shirt. A moment later, her sleek black hair had been secured in a neat ponytail, and she'd pulled a trucker ballcap onto her head. *Hoo boy,* True thought. *That* look would definitely turn the heads of her fellow rafting guides, kid or no kid.

So True looked away. Ever since her realization about the Outsider and Mel, she was cognizant of her tendency to see things that just weren't there. What if this, too, was a mirage?

They ate a quick, unceremonious lunch on the small sandbar that split the river at Blackberry Bar, four miles out from Quartz Canyon. When she bent to haul their table and chairs out of the raft, Vivian laid an unexpected hand on True's arm. For the second time today, not that True was counting. *Careful,* she thought again.

"Save yourself the trouble," Vivian told her. *Spare your energy,* she heard. And as much as True hated seeming weak in front of a client, she was glad Vivian had absorbed her message earlier. She pulled out some beach towels, and they ate picnic-style in the gravelly sand amid the milk thistle and river weed, enjoying their cold cuts and hummus with organic rice crackers and homemade cookies with a generous side of ash.

Afterward, Emmett explored the shoreline while Vivian helped True pack up the cooler. The Yeti once again secured with tie-downs, the two of them sat on the sun-warmed rubber tube of the oar raft watching him pick his way between the rocks, stopping every few feet to crouch down into an eddy or under a boulder, peering at what lay underneath or within.

"He's still just a child," Vivian said softly. Almost to herself.

True watched Emmett's progress downriver, his white rash guard almost glowing in the hazy air. "I've got eyes on him," she said, realizing belatedly that wasn't the takeaway Vivian had intended.

"I had to buy him that sun shirt just before the trip," she said, still watching her child. "His old one was too tight. He insists that all his clothing be loose these days. Gets almost panicked about it if anything is too form-fitting." She was quiet for a moment, then added, so softly True had to strain to hear, "Emily."

True shifted her gaze from downriver to Vivian, a question on her face.

"That was her—is his—deadname." The final two words dropped from Vivian's lips with heavy finality, like bullets into a chamber.

"Emily," True echoed softly, sensing that Vivian needed to hear it aloud one more time.

"Am I a terrible person for missing her?" Pain lay transparent on Vivian's face now, fragile as a sheet of glass.

"Of course not."

Vivian exhaled long and low, as if she'd been holding her breath for the entirety of this quiet conversation. Perhaps she had been. "I love who Emmett is, I really do. I see how he has blossomed, has come into his own. God, before? He was dying inside, True. I can see that now, and I'm so glad—desperately glad—that he's found his way to becoming who he's meant to be. What is it you call it, on the river? A self-rescue. That's what Emmett is doing. But sometimes"—she looked up at True earnestly—"just sometimes, I mourn my daughter."

True nodded. "Of course you do." She thought again of her fierce love for Astor and Annie and mentally attempted to parse their identities as human beings from their birth-assigned gender, like peeling back shiny packaging to reveal what was really inside. It was harder to conceptualize than she might have expected. "I'm thinking of the god-daughters I mentioned," she told Vivian. "It's not the same," she added swiftly, "but I think I can understand. I do."

Vivian nodded. "Tell me more about them."

True didn't usually get personal with river clients, so it surprised her when she blurted, "Annie has tetralogy of Fallot. It's a heart condition. A serious one."

But she'd forgotten, momentarily, Vivian's medical training. "Very serious," she said with a frown. "How are you all doing with it?"

That small thoughtfulness—including True in this sentiment—touched upon something lying dormant in her she hadn't even known sought comfort. As interwoven into the Bishops' lives as she'd been from the start of their family, True had always felt like a rogue thread, an interesting side pattern at best, a snag at worst. But comfort was something she and the Bishops had in short supply these days, and she'd take it where she could get it. True thought of all the bills that piled up with absolutely no hope of repayment, of the shadows that lined the soft skin under Mel's eyes so often now, the look of tight worry always tugging at Sam's mouth.

"I've seen the medical bills; some have been twice my friend Mel's annual salary, even after making battalion chief at our local fire station. They're laughable . . . I mean, I literally laughed, trying to imagine Annie's parents paying those as a small-business owner and firefighter."

"Can they file for bankruptcy?" Vivian asked.

"They'd lose the house, I think, so Annie's dad—my friend Sam—won't go there."

That damned Bishop house was Sam's flag planted in the ground here in Carbon, his promise to his girls that their legacy in this town would be different from his own. Yeah, it was bass-ackward, but try telling Sam that.

"And their insurance plan basically flipped them the bird," she added.

Vivian nodded. "I know the feeling. It's why I took a job at the university hospital, even though the hours are horrendous. Better insurance." She let out a bitter laugh. "Slightly better, anyway."

"With Annie, if we—her parents, I mean—can't keep her on the . . . what are they?" She searched her brain for the terms and found them. "The ACE inhibitors and beta-blockers, her circulation will continue to worsen."

"Yes," Vivian said. She left it at that, but True knew the rest. Heart failure would follow. A perpetually cyanotic state.

*It's why I have to push us so hard,* True wanted to tell Vivian. *It's why we're muscling our way down this river instead of giving you and your child the trip you deserve.*

Because she couldn't, she turned to watch Emmett again, now making his way back to them. When he stumbled over a slippery rock, catching himself with a slender arm, Vivian tensed, but didn't rise to his aid. "I just hope he can pass, one day," she said quietly. "He's desperate to start hormone-replacement therapy, but it took two referrals to find a pediatrician, then a child psychologist, who would approve the paperwork for insurance. And that's in California. And with me working in the medical field, knowing every angle to pursue. And of course at any time, policies, laws even, could change, couldn't they?" Vivian took a breath. "I thank God for his genes. I keep promising him I developed late, so he will, too."

A ticking clock. It was all so unfair.

"It's the worst feeling in the world, knowing that I could be helpless to ensure my child has the care he needs."

Vivian's voice hitched on the last few words; even articulating this fear aloud seemed to snatch the air out of her lungs. True felt her own chest tighten painfully in response as she waited for Vivian to collect herself.

"I remind myself that there are plenty of shorter-statured Asian men," she said with a bracing smile. "And most don't have much facial hair." She offered True a shaky laugh. "But I can tell you: he was such a pretty baby."

True smiled. "I bet."

Vivian looked out over the river. "I had him alone, you know. Sperm donor. Back then, in the early aughts, adoption wasn't an option for those of us in the LGBTQ community. Not that it's exactly easy now, even with a partner, from what some of my patients say."

True could confirm. Her friends Alexa and Korey had been enrolled in the foster-to-adopt program for several years. It wasn't until they moved from Idaho to Massachusetts that they made any progress in the queue for a child to raise as their own.

"Emmett hit every milestone early," Vivian said. "Sitting up, walking . . . now, I keep trying to slow him down. Let him adjust to each step as it comes. Clothes shopping in the boys' section, like for the rash guard. Haircut at a barbershop. Baby steps. That's what he calls that."

Astor came to True's mind. Only eight years old and already desperate to be taken seriously. To be the superhero in her own story.

"I hope he realizes how heroic he is," True said. When Vivian smiled self-deprecatingly, True leaned forward in emphasis. "I'm serious. He's managed what plenty of adults have never figured out, at least the ones I know: how to self-rescue, like you said."

Vivian's slight shoulders straightened as she looked from True to Emmett, then back to True again. "You're right," she decided. "Thank you for the reminder. I think I needed that."

True gave the hand resting on the raft tube a brief squeeze—two could play at that game—as Emmett returned to the raft. "Hey bud," she said, clearing the emotion that had found its way to her throat with a gruff cough. "Find anything cool?"

"Nah. It's still so smoky," he observed, waving his hand in the air in front of his face like he might have some luck wafting it away. "I can't even see the trees anymore."

He was right: the smoke from the Flatiron Fire had settled into the river canyon so densely, True couldn't even make out the slopes of the mountains that rose just across the water. Flatiron itself was now completely shrouded, detectable only by the dark-gray, almost black clouds that continually blossomed and dissipated high in the sky.

"Do you think that mountain's still burning?" Emmett wondered, following True's line of sight toward the peak.

"Yes," she said tightly. Her normal flair for entertaining—and, let's face it, impressing—preteens seemed to have failed her.

"Maybe you should check that radio of yours again," Vivian suggested. "That woman you keep calling might know something more."

*That woman?* True lifted her eyebrows in Vivian's direction, a warning shot from the bow, before remembering herself. Vivian had no way of knowing who "that woman" was, and certainly wouldn't have guessed she'd stepped on a landmine by mentioning her. There was no reason her choice of phrasing should burn off the intimacy they'd enjoyed during their lunch break, at any rate.

"Funny story: that's Annie's mother, actually. My friend the fire battalion chief?"

Vivian's expression immediately relaxed, a sight True might have found amusing had she been one of the women True dated and then dropped once the river season got underway. Instead, it sent another jolt of the unsolicited possibility True had been feeling ever since they'd met through her. That jolt was dangerous, so she turned the conversation back to Mel.

"I can try to contact her," she assured her, "but I don't think it's necessary." True didn't need to make another sat call to know the Flatiron Fire continued to grow, complicating their already complicated plans to get to Temple Bar on time.

In the meantime, she tuned her radio dial to their emergency-dispatch call signal and listened in for a moment. No evacs yet, from the sound of it, beyond the few ranches that sat at the base of Flatiron, so that was good. But she still knew nothing about the other side of the slope, where her property sat. And what about Highline Road? What about the Bishops' place? True swallowed down a new rise of fear. What she wouldn't give for a little reassurance, Mel's familiar voice back on the line telling her everyone was fine. What she wouldn't give for a quick glimpse of her place today, tucked into the cedars hugging the southern bank of the Outlaw, under Flatiron's shadow.

*Shit,* True thought. She should have bulldozed that meadow into a firebreak when she'd had the chance.

# CHAPTER 10

*Frozen* now airing in the living room, Sam paced the apartment, cell phone in hand, wishing he could rub it like Aladdin's lamp and produce an update from Mel. Annie hadn't stopped coughing, so he'd given her a Benadryl to reduce strain on her lungs, but the smoke would only get worse. Resigned to taking Kim's advice, he called Claude, who confirmed that the air was indeed clearer up on Highline Road.

"Don't overthink it," Claude said. "Just come with the girls. I already gathered Ingrid's quilts, some of my papers on the house, my taxes. I'm go-ready, so I can help you when you get here."

Sam thought of Claude's late wife with a pang, swallowing a second lump that effortlessly arose in his throat. The kindest woman ever, Ingrid Schmidt. Her prizewinning quilts were a must to salvage; in fact, she'd made one for Astor before she passed . . . Sam made a mental note not to leave it behind, either. Right this minute, it sat folded on the edge of the couch.

"My River Eddy lease, property-insurance documents, the kids' birth certificates, that sort of thing are already in the Eddy safe, so I just need to get Annie ready," he told Claude. He hadn't been back to the Highline house for more than general upkeep or a quick hello to Claude since Mel had told him she was through. It had felt empty without her in it, even when he had his girls. But any emotional baggage he might harbor about returning now would just have to remain behind, here in Carbon.

He dialed the familiar number for Annie's pediatric cardiologist in Portland next, the receptionist patching him through to the lead RN right away when he explained the situation. Half an hour later, with the endorsement of Annie's medical team fueling him, he'd assembled everything the cardiologist insisted upon taking in addition to the kids' go bags: Annie's emergency oxygen cannula, her child-sized N95 mask, the ice packs necessary to keep her refrigerated meds cold. As he closed the fridge, Astor's school artwork caught his eye on the door, and there was Annie's clay handprint on display by the windowsill, by the Paddle, Inc., oar, a gift from True, whose home-decorating style admittedly left something to be desired.

He spun away from all of it, turning to unplug the medical-grade air purifier and set it next to the heart monitor and pulse oximeter by the door. None of this sentimental stuff could make the cut. Fitting the N95 over Annie's small face amid weak but futile protest—she wanted the one she'd stuck Hello Kitty stickers on—he rallied Astor, and the three of them made a break for the truck.

"This is cray-*zee*," Astor noted, waving her hand in front of her face when thick smoke met her at the River Eddy entrance. A brave front, or was she really feeling this cool under pressure? Sam never knew. She buckled herself into the truck before leaning across Annie's booster seat to buckle her, too, and he felt a swell of pride rise up, followed by a chase of regret. Astor was such a good kid, but she shouldn't have had to grow up as fast as she had.

"Eight going on thirty-eight," True liked to kid, but truth was, it was no joke, being the older sibling to a medically fragile child.

He turned on the windshield wipers to clear off enough ash to see properly, reminding himself he'd done the same half a dozen times during every smoke season; the river valley acted like a basin, collecting smoke, ash, and soot. It was no indication of the level of danger—or not—the mother of his children faced higher on Flatiron Peak.

They eased their way through town, which was oddly quiet for this hour, any folks not at work probably holed up around their TVs or radios for the time being, or else checking Twitter or Facebook for updates on the conditions outdoors. A few kids could be spotted in front yards—the smoke wasn't unbearable for those without compromised health—but bikes remained in yards and driveway basketball hoops looked abandoned. Even Astor turned pensive as she watched the road and the intermittent swipe of the wipers.

They turned up Highline Road as Annie continued to struggle with the N95, which, even at size XS, didn't cup her cheeks properly. "It's too hot in here, Daddy," she complained, tugging at the mask.

"I know, but you have to wear it, baby girl."

"But Astor doesn't have to!"

Sam ground his teeth as he felt her kick the back of his seat. He wasn't sure which was worse: dealing with a rare Annie-outburst while he was trying to keep his concentration on the road or witnessing her usual surrender to the inevitable.

"Astor will put one on when we get home," he heard himself say before flinching on the last word and instantly revising. "When we get to Highline, I mean."

As if he could sneak such a faux pas past Astor. "We haven't been home in a long while," she said solemnly.

Sam felt himself stiffen. Did she miss it? And if so, did that buoy Sam or dismay him? No one told him before he'd become a parent how fraught it would be with uncertainty. "You know it's easier to get you to school and meet up with your mom if we stay above the Eddy," he reminded her. He heard the false bravado in the uplift of his words and winced again.

Astor slid him a look. "I just meant . . . are you going to be okay with it?"

Sam exhaled. *Eight going on thirty-eight,* he reminded himself. Hell, no, he wasn't going to be okay with it, but the other thing about parenting? You found yourself doing a lot of things you didn't want to do. "Don't you worry about me. We're going to invite Claude over and have ourselves a little Bishop-Schmidt house party."

By the time they hit Highline Road mile marker six, however, where the dirt drive led to the Bishop property, Annie had succumbed to her mask in defeat, listless in her booster seat now that the allergy meds had kicked in. Sam had almost missed the turn, his gaze flicking to the rearview mirror after she'd given up on pummeling his seat to check on her. It was a constant dance: make sure Annie was calm, make sure she wasn't *too* calm. Ensure she wore a mask, ensure it wasn't depriving her of precious O2.

Astor, too, looked dour as she studied the gray gloom out her window. *So much for partying.* They parked the truck in front of the half-remodeled garage, and Sam hurried them into the house, shutting the front door—which he'd mercifully had the foresight to professionally replace and reseal last year—behind them. Annie clung to him, her arms around his neck and her legs clamped around his hip, but Astor moved into the open living space with cautious steps. She took one look toward the family room with its stone fireplace and cupboard for board games and puzzles—now relocated to the Eddy—and pivoted.

"I'm gonna check on my room."

Sam watched her go. Astor knew perfectly well that her personal effects had all been relocated to Mel's place in town and the Eddy, but maybe that was precisely the draw. With a sigh, he set Annie down in the old overstuffed armchair by the fireplace, then stood staring at the room himself for a long moment.

Folks in Carbon never understood why Sam had been so determined to keep the childhood home that had done him no favors, but renovating the space had felt like a way to rewrite Bishop history with his own young family. He'd knocked a wall out about ten years ago to achieve an open-concept look, and when Astor was tiny, he'd also redone the wood-plank floors. Time and money had disappeared after Annie was born, so the kitchen tile was not quite finished, and he'd yet to put the cabinet doors back on after painting. But he'd learned that it didn't take a lot of money to make a house look homey. Before Mel had left and he'd retreated to the Eddy, Sam had made sure to always have pillar candles on the end table, framed photos on the mantel, and photos on the walls.

He admired them one by one, taking heart in each one until his gaze snagged on Mel's fire-science degree certificate that still sat, framed, on the mantel of the fireplace. Suddenly his chest felt tight, and he knew Astor had been right to worry about him: being back "home" at Highline was every bit as fraught as he'd feared.

He counted backward from ten, finding a focus point directly across from him like he'd been taught—in this case, the bird feeder he could barely make out hanging from the eave outside the picture window. A lot of good it did; more and more often, domestic scenes like this one stirred up that damned PTSD worse than images of combat. Had he made a horrible mistake by coming back up here?

At least the sky did seem clearer. They hadn't lingered in their retreat from the truck, but the ash wasn't thick on the railing by the front steps yet, and though he couldn't see blue sky past the bird feeder, the pallor in the air was more milky than ashen. Annie's cough would lessen here, he told himself.

But not until he ensured all the windows were sealed, too, all the vents shut. Which would require him to shake off this melancholy and move from the doorway. He forced his limbs to comply, and once in motion, he managed to make quick work of it, only stopping once to tuck Ingrid's quilt from the Eddy around Annie's thin shoulders. She lifted her head to ask for his phone—she was a whiz at DoodleMath—and he handed it over at once in relief. "But stay here on the chair, all right, baby girl?"

She didn't answer, already absorbed in the game, her little fingers flying over the options in the app. It was just what he needed to break the spell the house had cast over him, and Sam actually chuckled as he got to work checking the windows. He even managed not to berate himself when he rediscovered more half-finished projects, more room for improvement.

"I think it looks just fine as it is," Mel had said more than once, and to her credit, she had looked truly baffled when Sam insisted the new decking wasn't weather-sealed enough or the new soaking tub not quite grand enough.

But Mel didn't have the "before" picture burning a hole in her brain. During Sam's childhood, the Highline house had been a shithole; there had really been no other way to describe it. Growing up piss poor under the harsh thumb of his own father, Mark Bishop hadn't sweated the small stuff, like trim or paint or front porch steps. He hadn't cared if the driveway had remained perpetually littered with junk cars, side jobs to his "business," an auto-body shop the entire town knew was just a front. The only thing he or John Fallows treated with any pride was their acreage on the Outlaw. They'd been growing there for as long as Sam could remember. Certainly longer than THC had been legal in Oregon.

Sam knew that acreage far better than he'd have liked, spending the summers of his youth out there with Chris. They'd combed the riverbank of the Outlaw for discarded fishing lures they could sell for a few cents in town while their fathers grew and sold the weed, ripped off customers at Mark's auto shop, liberated copper piping from construction sites, and supplied Carbon's residents with everything from Percocet to Dexedrine.

The most embarrassing part for Sam: everybody in Carbon knew exactly what was what, how you couldn't trust a Bishop or a Fallows farther than you could throw 'em, how those little shitheads Chris and Sam were no better, tooling around Carbon on their dirt bikes, shoplifting candy bars and telling dirty jokes. It hadn't even mattered if Sam hadn't been doing any of those things, save for the dirt biking. The BMX Mark had thrown into a pawn-shop trade had been Sam's only ride as he'd tried to separate himself from Chris with Boy Scouts, volunteering for the VFW, and, finally, joining the JROTC in high school.

All of which had been mercilessly mocked by Mark.

"What makes you think you're so much better than the rest of us, huh?" he had liked to lob at Sam, who'd had no answer. Who the hell knew why what was normal and natural to Chris felt so abhorrent to him. Certainly, his old man and the Fallowses hadn't given a shit.

The day Sam had helped line Main Street with flags for Memorial Day weekend, bursting with pride to have been entrusted with the task, his dad had laid on the horn as he'd driven past, making him jump, the edge of the flag he'd been lifting brushing the dirt. "Kiss-ass!" Mark had shouted, laughing. "My kid, the pussy!"

Sam clenched his hands into fists thinking about it, even now.

"Finally getting out of my way was the best thing he ever did for me," he'd told Mel, after his dad had taken the one-way ride up to Pendleton just after they'd met. "I should thank John Fallows for selling out his best friend for nothing more than a dime-bag deal gone sour."

Mel had found it hard to believe anyone could be glad to see his flesh and blood behind bars. She'd pressed the point, asking him a bit too often how he was dealing with it, *if* he was dealing with it, whether maybe it would help for him to talk with someone about it.

"What will help will be to see him there for myself," Sam decided, and so they'd taken the drive east together, the green forests of southern Oregon giving way to the stark beauty of the high desert. Bidding Mark good riddance though the grimy filter of the visitation Plexiglas, Sam had been determined to feel superior. After all, who was on the right side of that glass? Instead, he'd felt fourteen years old again, mocked for mounting those flags.

That kind of shame stuck to a person, like the secondhand smoke that had clung on Sam's clothes as a kid. Looking out the smoke-tinged window of his home knowing what he knew now, with his marriage in shambles and his kids at risk, he had to ask himself . . . *really* ask: Had his obsession—Mel's words—with keeping this house healed the past and elevated his family, or only opened up new wounds?

The latter, at least, was a certainty. And maybe he should have tried to sell the house, back when doing so would have taken the edge off what had been the sharpest point of his marriage. Back before chronic fire seasons had depreciated just about all the real estate in Carbon. But then where would he and his girls retreat to now?

He heaved a hard sigh, telling himself he wasn't doing himself or the girls any favors wallowing and what-if-ing. As Mel had put it, you couldn't coax a flame once it had been deprived of all fuel. Annie's medical needs, and the stress of paying for them, had sucked all the oxygen out of his marriage.

He texted Claude to let him know they'd made it to the house, then went through the rest of the place, plugging in Annie's air purifier and stashing her meds in the kitchen and fridge. There he found Astor scrounging the cupboards for a snack.

"I'm waiting for Claude," she declared in a huff, one knee braced on the counter, her nose in the top shelf of the pantry. "He'll have something other than this . . ." She slowed to sound out a label. "In-stant coffee and one min-ute stuff-ing."

"Good call," Sam conceded, his smile waning as his eye caught another collection of framed photos on the window ledge. Point for the open-wound column, he decided, as his gut felt the brunt of the blow.

Front and center sat the last photo Sam had taken of the four of them—his family right here on the deck, whole and intact. The next: taken two winters ago, while Christmas-tree hunting in the acreage behind Flatiron, then one of Astor and Annie on a trip to Yellowstone, arms wrapped around one another's shoulders in a rare moment of sisterly affection. Finally, an oldie but goodie: a young Mel and Sam toasting their purchase of the River Eddy Bar and Grill just after their wedding.

"I don't know whether you guys are hopeless romantics or hopeless fools for buying the place where you first laid eyes on one another," True had declared with a raise of her shot glass.

*Fools,* Sam supposed now, but not begrudgingly. Hindsight was twenty-twenty vision, and all that. Besides, True had only half the facts. Sam *had* met Mel at the Eddy, but that was mostly because he hung out there all the time. During Sam's teen years, and after, when he'd come back from the service, the Eddy had been a safe space when very few safe spaces existed for a Bishop. He'd suspected this meant the original proprietor, Edward Phillis, had made a deal or two with his father and Fallows over the years, but maybe not, because according to the wall of Little League and high school football-team photos gracing the walls, the man was a pillar of the community, his name, and the River Eddy's name, on all the jerseys. Gold sponsor. League sponsor. Team mascot. Hell, Sam couldn't remember now, but the idea had been planted. The owner of a place like the Eddy could contribute in a real way to his town.

Sam was not so sure it had worked out that way. Folks still looked at him sidelong, though Mel and True tried to tell him it was all in his head. Still, he and Mel had been closer to having that elusive "all" that day than they ever would be again: the chance for respect, Mel's job with its appealing retirement plan; they'd even been expecting Astor, though they hadn't known it yet. It all would have been enough, wouldn't it, if only Annie had been born whole. Instead, a hole had pierced her heart, leaving them all inadequate and empty . . . however fucking poetic that sounded.

Bless True's heart: in the years since, she'd never come back with an "I told you so." Which was why he'd returned the favor when she'd inadvertently bought the place next door to Fallows's operation. He'd warned her, though. Hell yeah, he had. And he'd flat-out banned her from bringing the kids out there, not even yielding when she'd shown him the little loft space she'd built with them in mind. No way were his girls getting anywhere near that wolf in his den.

He stashed the framed photos into his go bag, the Eddy one on top. That building, he *had* tried to sell. *Before this town suffers one too many smoke seasons,* he'd told his buddy Luke at Carbon Realty.

But investors had already become skittish. According to Luke, who heard it all the time: if their part of Oregon became a charred wasteland, the Eddy wouldn't be good for much more than the occasional stop on a dark-tourism tour. In the end, it had been more financially prudent to keep the place open to eke out what income he could than to shut it down and cut their losses.

*It is what it is,* he decided, just as Annie called to him from the couch. Her whiny voice, which meant she'd lost interest in math games. Sure enough, upon investigation, she now had a beef with Astor not sharing the bits of the Stouffer's cornbread-stuffing mix she'd stooped to eating out of the box like dry cereal.

He opened his mouth to order, *Share the stuffing mix with your sister!* before the sheer ridiculousness of such a command made him laugh instead. His hearty guffaw proved far more effective than any reprimand, anyway; both girls ceased their bickering to find out what was so funny. Then Astor quirked an eyebrow, looking so much like Mel in that moment, the mirth was instantly snatched from Sam's lungs.

*Joke's on me,* he thought, which only doubled the pain in his chest.

He tried not to let it show on his face, but no such luck. "Claude will be here soon," Astor told him, placing her young hand in Sam's and squeezing tight.

# CHAPTER 11

True heard the roar of Quartz Canyon well before she could make out its entrance through the haze. Even so, the sound came later than usual along the half-mile-long flat stretch that preceded it. Its low rumble usually began to make itself known to her slowly, joining the closer-at-hand cacophony of birdcalls and insects buzzing and oars slapping the water in a subtle snatch of sound here, a more insistent hum there, growing in intensity as she approached. Today, however, the birds had fallen silent or else had already fled the thick smoke on an exodus of feather and wing. She couldn't hear the mayflies or crickets, either, so the drum of the canyon's whitewater hit her in a sudden boom through the smoke that tightened her gut and had her sitting up straighter at the oars.

What if she couldn't see properly in the smoke? She swallowed down this worry even as it arose. Because what could she do about it? "There. You hear it?" she asked the Wus, who both nodded silently. "We'll eddy out at that next bend, where the reeds are growing along the shore. See?" Another set of nods.

"Do we scout this one?" Emmett's voice sounded small.

"Yep." True tried to counter his uncertainty with eager excitement, even as her stomach sank again. "We'll take a little hike up over that rock outcropping so we can get a good view of the entrance. We won't be able to see the whole thing, though, remember. This set of rapids is long."

At the bend, True dug in deep with the oars, turning the nose of the raft to shore. They had their pick of tie-off spots, which, while not unusual, made True wonder whether Mel had been right, and other stranglers had aborted their trips early.

Vivian and Emmett clambered out awkwardly to stand on the bank in their dripping water shoes, thumbs hooked into the straps of their life jackets as they waited on True. "Go ahead and start up the bank to those rocks," she called to them from the boat. "That'll be a good vantage point. I'll be right behind you." When Vivian looked hesitant, True added, "Nature calls."

She watched the Wus depart, trudging up the bank single file, then unearthed her small ammo box from its dedicated spot behind the Yeti. It looked just like the TP box, which wasn't a coincidence, but she sure as hell didn't want to mix them up. The last thing True needed was for one of the Wus to be on the groover, reach into the can for TP, and end up with Ben Franklins instead. Best to double-check, just for peace of mind. Subterfuge held even less appeal than ever after opening up to Vivian.

She strode off in long strides in the opposite direction from the Wus, making her way through the reeds along the riverbank to emerge onto a small, open lava bed, hidden from view from the river. She climbed up it easily—the bank was steep here, but the lava flow, so common here in southern Oregon, was only a few yards long. Once concealed from view, she popped the ammo box open at the edges—it was a simple two-sided clasp—breathing a sigh of relief that its contents still sat there as expected, waiting for her. She eyed the thick roll of bills wrapped in Saran wrap, bagged in a ziplock, before snapping the box shut again, her heart pounding even harder than it usually did when it came to this shit.

"You sure you gals got the cojones for this?" John Fallows had asked, a mean smile playing about his mouth, the day she and Mel met with him to seal the deal. "I hear little Zacky Murphy shit his Captain

Marvel Underoos when the Feds had him spread 'em across the back of their patrol car."

Mel had gone crimson and so True had risen to her feet in anger, and Fallows had reminded her in no uncertain terms that she wasn't even family, not like the Bishops, to whom he *might* consider throwing a bone, so she could go fuck off. "Unless Melissa here is batting for both teams," he'd added with a wink. "In which case, good on you, TrueBlue. Just watch out she isn't just using you for your connections." He'd laughed heartily, and Mel had been forced to yank True out of arm's reach. She'd already been winding up a swing.

True tried to shake the memory now, running her hands roughly through her hair, nails raking across her sunburned scalp. The sting of it helped, somehow, to take the pain out of it all.

She glanced back at the Wus, who stood at awkward attention in their PFDs, waiting for her as they eyed the whitewater churning downriver. True felt a deep pang of regret. They should be excited right now. True should be building them up, rallying them for the challenge of Quartz Canyon, not pushing all three of them far too hard.

She could still change plans. It was smoky, yes, but the fire remained a safe enough distance away. They could slow down, enjoy the journey. To get her head back in the game, she had to remind herself of the horrible weight of debt Mel and Sam always lived under. Of the way Annie's breathing became labored whenever she so much as played a game of hide-and-seek or tried to keep up with her big sister. She straightened her shoulders in resolution. What was a little bit of risk, a dash of danger, compared to that? She'd hated the sound of her favorite nickname on Fallows's tongue, but was she TrueBlue or wasn't she?

Besides, this would be the last time True climbed the riverbank and scrambled over lava and shale to check the contents of the ammo box, sweating through every minute of it. Stomach in knots.

*Only for Annie. Only until this final surgery.*

It was a mantra she repeated to herself over and over again, ignoring the question that persisted behind it. *You really think the Fallowses are just going to let you quit?* They had a good thing going with True, after all. What did they need the Bishops for?

True squared her shoulders, looking out over the Outlaw before navigating back over the shale and lava rock toward the Wus. In sickness and in health, right? An apt-enough comparison, she decided.

Throughout midmorning, Mel had swung her Pulaski with one part of her brain still perpetually back in Carbon, worrying over Annie's condition in this smoke. *Please,* she thought, *don't be too stubborn to take her to Highline.* Because she knew how Sam's emotional baggage could get in his own way.

"You're nothing like your father," she'd told him back when he'd been in the throes of his remodeling stage, trying to convince him that therefore, this house he'd moved his little family into was good enough as it was, just like Sam. "We are comfortable and happy, and you never have to deal with Mark ever again," she'd promised. "Him or Fallows."

To say the memory stung now would be an understatement, but she couldn't have known, back then, that it would be *she* who would cross back over the enemy line, doing business with the man he despised.

The welcome sound of the dozers coming in to cut a deeper, wider containment line in the wake of the ground pounders rumbled in Mel's ears by 1:00 p.m., shaking the ground under her boots and seeming to rattle even her brain matter in her skull. She looked up from her place on the line, glad for the welcome distraction from the mind-numbing task of manually clearing the brush. It wasn't every day—it wasn't every fire—that such measures were deemed necessary. Hernandez must have alerted the USFS that Carbon Rural had its hands full here on the wildland-urban interface, because they'd clearly decided to respect the hell out of this blaze.

She sent up a silent thanks for the support, because that dozer line was all that stood between this fire and potential civilian targets. If they couldn't contain the blaze here on Flatiron, the river canyon would be next. Her thoughts swung to True, floating through smoke that would only get thicker if they couldn't contain this thing. Her clients' health truly could become compromised. Or worse.

Mel tried to shake off the guilt this worry induced, if only to get her focus back on her job. True was her own woman. She'd made her own choices. But she had to call bullshit. The responsibility of this whole damn thing lay squarely on Mel. She'd known True would agree to running the money. She'd known why.

"Bishop," Lewis called from somewhere above her. "We taking five?"

Shit. "Negative, Captain. Sorry." She picked back up her Pulaski, her worry and the dozers' presence renewing her vigor. She swung the axe in faster and faster arcs, the blade sending little tufts of soil flying up around her with every bite into the dirt.

"Hey, Chief!" Janet complained, behind her. "Take it easy, will you? I'm breathing in enough shit as it is."

"Sorry," Mel muttered for the second time in as many minutes. She forced herself to settle back in, mimicking the steady rhythm of the Pulaskis ahead of her, her forearms burning satisfactorily with the effort. It wasn't more than a minute later, however, that she heard "Bishop!" again.

"All right, all right," she griped, but this time, no one was chastising her. Janet stood frozen, Pulaski limp at her side, staring west. Mel followed her gaze, and that was when she felt it: wind blowing from the east, cooling the sweat on the back of her neck.

What had been a light breeze had just kicked into high gear.

"Janet? Did you notice that? I think—"

But before she could finish her sentence, that gust of wind caught the fire at just the right angle, changing everything in a second. Mel watched in awestruck, almost inescapable resignation as the blaze, stable enough one minute, suddenly raged in an updraft, its flirtation with instability and power suddenly fully formed. This was the very scenario she'd been most afraid of. As the fire doubled in size before her eyes like a beast from hell, she shook herself loose from her shock with a yell.

"It's making its run!" she shouted in the direction of the Eagle Valley supervisor, her closest superior, who looked back at her with shock. Never had she been so sorry to have predicted a blaze correctly. In a flood of communal alarm, Pulaskis dropped to the dusty ground as the firefighters all around Mel abandoned them at a full sprint, heels digging into the dirt, knees bent in effort, screams drowned by the sudden roar of the Flatiron Fire.

Mel fell into pace amid the mass of dirty yellow shirts before pivoting to snag the back of Deklan's. The kid had veered off course in a blind panic, as if to outrun the fire on foot. She tugged him back.

"Here! C'mon!" Mel pushed him toward the road, nearly tripping him up when Deklan cast a frenzied glance behind them toward where the wall of fire literally loomed. "The trucks!" Mel ordered, waving one arm forward, her other palm pressed hard against Deklan's sweaty back.

They flung themselves into the back of one of the waiting water-tank trucks, a crew of Eagle Valley volunteers clamoring in after them, with a mere minute, maybe two, to spare. "Go, go, go!" Mel shouted to the driver, a fist on the glass between the tank and the cab. The man sat frozen in the cab, his fingers white-knuckling it on the wheel, watching the blaze approach as if in a trance. "Go, goddammit!"

The man snapped out of it and *went*, the heavy truck's massive tires grinding deep into the dirt as he slammed the gear into second, Mel still trying to count her men and women as the vehicle peeled out. What if Hernandez didn't have eyes on the ground?

"What's it gonna do?" Deklan sputtered, body craned backward toward the fire, arms taut as he gripped the roll bar of the back of the truck. He swung a look at Mel, eyes wild above his Buff, face marred by soot and ash. "Chief! What's it gonna do?"

His panic was visceral. The kind that broke out in a cold sweat across one's brow. The kind that made you shit your pants. "It won't jump our containment line between us and the river," Mel shouted back, a hand still braced on Deklan's shoulder. "Don't worry. It can't jump the bulldozed containment line."

And then, as if just to spite her, with a roar they could hear from the base of FS 7312 even over the clamor of the fire engine and the cries of the ground crews and the rush of this goddamned wind from hell, the Flatiron Fire jumped the dozer line.

# CHAPTER 12

The ring of fire spanning the length of the dozer line burned sharp and bright. To Mel, it looked like a coil set aflame in one of those gas firepits Sam had bought last summer for the back patio of the River Eddy. The flames rose in an almost orderly, defined strip, like the ground crew had laced the containment line with gasoline instead of digging, clearing, and cutting to bare dirt. She rubbed at the grit and sweat caked to her face and neck, one hand gripping a welded metal handhold in the truck bed for support. All that effort, for nothing. All the ground they'd hoped to hold, gone in a matter of seconds. Somewhere up there, in the blaze, her chief vehicle burned, along with dozens of jump kits, go bags, tents, and sleeping bags.

And below? The start of the urban interface—including Carbon's outlying communities and the recreational section of the river—waited in the late-morning haze of smoke like the proverbial sitting duck. The fire skirted the city limits for now, thank God, but for how long? Where were Sam and the girls? Had Sam abandoned his post at the Eddy yet?

It wasn't even mid-afternoon on their first day of firefighting, and already her crew was in full-on retreat. She tuned out White shouting into his handset as he radioed in this latest development to Eagle Valley and the county supervisor. The Flatiron Fire was officially out of control, and she already knew what came next: regrouping back in town for reassessment as experts better equipped to run point on a wildland fire converged on Carbon—Oregon wildland stations run by the USFS, Arden Aircrane, even the National Guard. The private wildland-firefighting operations would be called in, too, sending crews from as far away as Colorado, Nevada, and California. Helos would hit the air.

But for now, evacs needed to be ordered of the residents to the west of town, starting with the ranches and homesteads directly below Flatiron, and nobody knew the area better than Carbon Rural.

Mel looked over her shoulder as if she could actually see its progress below the mountain, on the wind. All she saw was smoke, of course, now thick black, billowing in the direction of the river.

*And True.* The thought caused her anxiety to spike further. At least Highline Road, nestled to the east of Flatiron, was, for the moment, out of the blaze's path. Mel's nerves threatened to positively flay her insides. If she had her own rig right now and could shed this shirt with her badge and Carbon Rural insignia tethering her here to duty and service, she would go find them this very moment.

At the base of the mountain, Hernandez ordered two USFS trucks to peel off from the group to drive up and down the small network of residential driveways off the Forest Service road, canvassing for the first, and most urgent, round of evacs. The last Mel glimpsed of them, an Outlaw National Forest employee braced himself at the back of a truck, bullhorn in hand. His order of immediate evacuation cut through the roar of the wind and the thick smoke and the sound of the fire, which, even here, a mile distant, hummed in Mel's ears like the crackle of a white-noise machine.

Back at the Carbon Rural Station, where the smoke was indeed thicker, Chief Hernandez, the Greater Outlaw Valley Fire Protection District, and the newly arrived USFS agent began their respective bids for authority, circling each other in a pissing match that Mel had no time for. She ducked away, finally able to dial Sam with the aid of a 5G network. When he answered on the second ring, the sheer sound of his voice had her nerves finally uncoiling in abject relief. At least momentarily.

He, Astor, and Annie were at Highline. An hour ago Mel would have cheered at this news, but now? Uncertainty slid effortlessly into the place fear had just vacated in her gut.

"The fire," she told him in a rush, "it jumped a line, Sam."

"Shit," he said. "But on Flatiron, right? Not near Highline? Because the smoke is much better up here, I promise it is."

Gripping the phone tightly to her ear, she pictured the girls safely ensconced inside the haven Sam had been so determined to create, sketching kitchen remodels and porch additions on the backs of resupply forms while deployed in Afghanistan, brushing the desert dirt off the paper every time the wind rose up. It had been cathartic, he had said. Or at least, that had been the word the Army chaplain had used, for Sam to restructure his life from afar, to redesign his childhood from the safety of seven thousand miles east.

"Not by Highline," she confirmed, but they both knew this could change in an instant. "Despite the smoke, if the order comes down, you'll evac with Claude, right? Even if it means returning to a shelter in town?"

*He'll leave it all behind for Astor and Annie,* she told herself firmly while waiting on confirmation. She forced herself to ignore the soft but persistent voice in her head that answered, *Like he gave it up to pay the medical bills? Like he gave it up for your marriage?*

"Of course," he answered, making her ashamed to have doubted him. Being buried under debt was one thing; the well-being of their girls was another. She knew this at the core of her being.

When she rejoined the group, representatives of the various agencies were still shouting over one another in the small conference room off the station kitchen. Had it really just been last night that Mel had sat right here, tossing fast-food wrappers at Deklan in retaliation for his smart mouth?

Hernandez stuck two fingers in his mouth and let fly a whistle that reverberated across the small room, shutting up everyone, even White, instantly. "First order of business," he barked, hanging onto first-on-scene authority by a thread, "is determining additional evacs."

Janet, still in her damp, ashy yellows like everyone else, unrolled the map of Carbon, spreading it out on the conference table, highlighters already in hand to mark Level 1 (*get your supplies and possessions in order*), Level 2 (*be set to go at a moment's notice*) and Level 3 (*go* now). With confident strokes of her pen, she marked the Flatiron Fire's current location and projected trajectory. Mel's eye instantly traveled to Highline Road, out of range from where the blaze currently consumed the mountain . . . at least for now. She pinched her eyes shut tightly for a moment, her eye sockets like sandpaper. *Please stay that way.*

"Start with Level 3, and work backward," she reminded Janet, who shot her a look as if to say, *This isn't your first forest fire . . . act like it,* before circling the circumference of Flatiron Peak plus the section below it already under evacuation order by the BLM in pink highlighter ink. With a softer glance at Mel—she'd probably just remembered that Annie was compromised by smoke—she wrote *LEVEL 3.*

The sheriff rep noted the locations on a yellow legal pad he retrieved from a nearby desk, then excused himself to start making calls. He'd alert his department in neighboring Outlaw first, then activate his crew of search-and-rescue volunteers, who would don their bright-orange uniforms to troll the roads in trucks, going door-to-door to ensure the evac notice reached every ear. Janet moved on to Level 2—*be set to go*—Mel's eyes still trained on her. This time, Janet used blue highlighter ink to circle the few roads on the far east side of Flatiron, its adjacent ridgelines, almost, but not quite, to the base of Highline Road.

She released an exhale she hadn't even realized she'd been holding, but still, the questions came to her mind unbidden. Had Sam packed Annie's inhaler when he left the Eddy? Had he convinced her to comply and wear the pink pediatric N95 mask critical to her breathing ability? Where was it? Mel couldn't remember. Probably forgotten under the back seat of Sam's car.

She pushed back from the table to confer with the sheriff rep, a guy she'd only met a handful of times, at mind-numbing training sessions and the occasional interagency picnic.

"My crew can start knocking on doors right now," she offered, "taking the roads west of Highline and that vicinity before your SAR crew can be mobilized." It wasn't normally her detail, but it would place her within a stone's throw of her daughters, should they need her. She'd take Lewis with her, maybe Deklan and his buddy Ryan. They seemed attached at the hip.

The man wavered, and Mel knew the word *protocol* screamed in his head like the siren every agency made it into, but then Hernandez nodded and he agreed.

"We'll take the two other sections, then. I want you on the road within minutes, though."

"Don't worry, she will be," Janet promised with a hint of a smile touching her lips, not bothering to look up from her map. The last thing Mel heard was her familiar voice calling the media to get the evac orders on the radio and TV news before she grabbed Deklan and Ryan, nodded at Lewis, and snagged a set of keys from the motor-pool board. "Let's go."

# CHAPTER 13

Sam paced the kitchen at Highline. Despite the digital clock on the microwave telling him it was only 3:15 p.m., it was dark as dusk thanks to the smoke. In the living room, he could hear Astor trying to remain patient as she helped Claude download the crappy Outlaw County emergency-information app on his phone. For some reason, Sam's hadn't updated the way it should have, and they needed to know: Were they at evacuation Level 1, 2, or 3?

"We can't get the blasted thing to work!" Claude called from Sam's living room.

"That's because you won't let me see it!" Astor protested.

Sam abandoned his search of the kitchen cupboards for Annie's backup inhaler and joined them in time to watch Astor take possession of the phone once again, swiping deftly across the surface. "Here, Uncle Claude."

Claude scrolled through a few pages, then sighed in relief. "Level 1," he announced. "Thank God."

"Does that mean we're safe enough to stay here?" Astor asked, brow furrowed.

"For now," Sam told her. And they were decidedly safer than if they'd stayed in the smoke in town. Still, he glanced out the window again at the deepening gloom, feeling like a sitting duck. It was all so overwhelming, and they'd just gotten here. It was times like this Annie could use both her parents working in tandem, but thinking that way only made Sam miss Mel more. And worry more for her safety, somewhere up at Flatiron.

Claude studied him, worry creasing his forehead just like Astor. "We'll get through this together, son," he said.

Sam looked up, trying to offer a shaky smile. "You've been babysitting us far too long, Claude. Take a few minutes to get your things in order, how about?"

Claude agreed, but the worry remained all over his face.

"I'll pop over in a bit to help you with Ingrid's quilts. We'll get your hoses ready, too." Sam nodded. Even at Level 1, it might become necessary to protect their rooftops from flying embers that might catch and take hold, and to water down their lawns and driveways, soaking the ground before it could spark.

Claude's face cleared somewhat. "That would be a lifesaver."

"What are *we* going to do?" Astor asked, once Claude's stooped back had disappeared back into the smoke at the end of the drive. "We already brought our go bags, and the rest of our stuff is at Mom's, or still at the Eddy."

Sam forced brightness into his voice. "That's right. We're already all set. Why don't you two play a game while I help Claude? Check the cabinet by the TV . . . I think we still have a deck of UNO! cards in there."

"Annie doesn't remember all the rules. She can't reverse."

"Candy Land, then. It should be there, too." The game had been rejected by Astor as too babyish during the move to town, but Sam didn't see the point in reminding any of them of that day. He'd been bereft. Astor sullen. Mel absent.

Astor took a few halfhearted steps toward the cabinet before turning back. "I'd rather help you and Claude."

Annie heard her sister and looked up from the episode of *PAW Patrol* Sam had cued up on his old iPad. "I wanna help, too. Astor! I wanna." She clamored to her feet clumsily, iPad cast aside amid the blankets on the couch.

For once, Astor exhibited patience, waiting for her sister. The sight brought a hard lump of pride, with a healthy helping of dismay, to Sam's throat. If Astor had decided she needed to be this nice to Annie, he had clearly done a piss-poor job of downplaying the gravity of the situation.

"I want you to stay in the house, but why don't you both fill up some water bottles," he offered. "And, Astor, you can put your watch on the charger in the kitchen. We'll want it fully juiced up."

He and Mel had bought her the Gizmo kids' smartwatch last year, when she'd found herself home with Annie alone when a tet spell had hit. Sam had only been greeting the UPS driver in the parking lot of the Eddy, but he was gone long enough for Astor to need a phone and come up empty. She'd worn it religiously ever since.

"Why does Astor get an Apple Watch but not me?" Annie had whined when Mel had presented the "present," which to Sam was nothing more than responsibility disguised in pretty gift wrap.

"It's not an Apple Watch, and it's just to use in emergencies," Mel had said. They'd shown Astor how to push the button for 911 and had disabled just about everything else.

"I should at least get to play *Plants vs. Zombies*," Astor had grumbled.

Sam smiled at the memory. Yanking his Buff high over his face and calling out to Astor that he'd be right back, he trotted the hundred yards or so up Highline to Claude's place. The smoke and ash raining from the sky brought an instant ache to his chest, and, not waiting for Claude to get to the door, he let himself in, surrendering to a coughing fit in the foyer. A pile of framed photos had already been stacked there: Claude and Ingrid on their wedding day, in . . . what? 1960? '65? Claude's framed diploma from Johns Hopkins, 1971. A portrait of their son, Peter, at a graduation ceremony, maybe college, maybe grad school. Peter and his wife and daughter on a beach. Sam thought he remembered they'd moved to Santa Rosa, or maybe Santa Cruz. So much for only packing the quilts.

"Hello!" he called once he'd caught his breath. "Claude?"

"In here!"

He was in Ingrid's old sewing room, which, Sam saw now, was still stacked with quilts, bolts of material, and batting on shelves that ran floor to ceiling. He managed to stifle a moan. No way they were going to salvage all of this.

"I've pared it down," Claude said, pointing at one large moving box stuffed with folded quilts. "Though it was damned difficult." He looked pained, the rare frown lines back, leaving deep creases on his tanned face.

Sam hoisted the box to his hip. It weighed an absolute ton, but he knew how hard it had been for Claude to resign himself to leaving the vast majority of Ingrid's creations behind. He didn't complain as he braved the smoke again to heft it into the back of Claude's ancient Ford pickup with a grunt. He made a second trip for the framed photos, then returned to the sewing room. "What else?" he asked.

Claude looked over the room, at a loss. He picked up a framed cross-stitch: *Home Is Where the Handkäse Is*. Ingrid had made the dish for the girls once, as a treat. To say sour-milk cheese had not become a Bishop family favorite would be the understatement of the year, but the gesture had touched Sam. He smiled sadly now as Claude returned the cross-stitch to its place on the wall. "Maybe Level 1 will hold," Claude said hollowly.

"Maybe." The fire was still traveling west, after all, away from their ridge.

Sam must not have sounded convincing, because Claude pressed, "What you said before . . . You're not planning to go sooner, are you?"

Sam stared down at his phone. He'd been trying to get ahold of Mel again, to no avail. "I don't know what to do," he admitted. He raked his hand through his hair. "You and I both know: Level 1 can turn into Level 2—even higher—just like that." He snapped his fingers in the air. "And if Level 3 is inevitable, I'd rather take my time about it, not have it catch me by surprise. But on the other hand . . ." He stared back out at the smoke, hands fisting at his sides in frustration at the lack of clarity, figuratively *and* literally.

"Annie can't risk the air quality outside," Claude finished for him. He sounded firm on this point.

Sam nodded. "If it weren't for that, we'd probably already be gone." All of them together, Mel included, like the family they used to be, if Sam had his way.

As if to punctuate this point, he stared out Claude's living room window at the sight of a small but steady trickle of family vehicles already on the road: their most proactive neighbors, *without* a medically compromised family member to consider. Soon enough, though, all but the most stubborn would follow suit, with cars stuffed to the gills with duffels and camping gear, dog kennels and crates.

"You've got all Annie's meds, right here," Claude reminded him. "Her oxygen, her canula, all that stuff needs power . . . another reason not to be on the road right now."

Sam nodded. He knew that was true.

"And if you do have to leave, you've got that portable power bank, that Goalie thing—"

"The Goal Zero," Sam corrected. He'd bought it to keep Annie's medical equipment juiced when they had appointments in Portland or Seattle. He needed to make sure it was charged, plus gather more portable water, and maybe pack the Yeti with ice. The Goal Zero was in the garage next to—

Sam's stomach dropped out from under him in a sudden realization. "Shit! Claude! I lent the Goal Zero to Kim last month, when her neighbor had that graduation party. She dropped it back off at the Eddy."

Claude's aura of comforting assurance slipped a bit upon hearing this. Actually, it fell off his face altogether. "You mean you have no way of keeping her equipment charged in case of evac?"

"I thought it was here!"

Claude gathered himself. "All right now, son, all right." He laid a hand on Sam's arm. "You just have to go get it, that's all."

He delivered this task like it was a routine run to the grocery store for a stick of butter, but that firm tone he sometimes adopted, especially when it came to Annie's medical needs, was back.

"How can I? I can't leave Annie!"

Claude turned from the window and took one more long look around his living room. He paused to straighten one of Ingrid's afghans where it rested, folded, on the arm of the couch and then exhaled a breath that sounded to Sam like he'd been holding it for a long while. "You can, if I'm here."

"Wait, what?"

But Claude was already yanking his Buff up over his face and tugging open the front door. "I'm gonna wait this out over at your place," he said. "You head into town." He held up a hand as Sam attempted to interrupt him. "Yes, I know . . . it's been a minute since I practiced medicine, but trust me, son. You don't forget forty years of ongoing training in a hurry. I know the drill . . . Pulmonary care, inhaler, the whole nine yards. Besides, while you're in town, you can assess the air quality in case it's gotten better for our little miss."

"Hold up, now," Sam called, trotting to catch up as Claude set off. They hadn't hauled Claude's hoses to the front porch yet, hadn't unkinked the coils and hooked them up to the water faucet. "Claude, we can't leave your house unprotected." When the older man didn't turn back, he added, "Can we at least discuss this?"

"Nothing more to discuss," Claude grunted, already starting up the truck. It took a couple tries, but he got it going. "I'm staying at your place with the little one. Dusting off my stethoscope and holding down the fort. You're retrieving the power bank and coming right back. That's all there is to it."

Sam searched his neighbor's age-worn face, looking for uncertainty. Regret. Misgiving. Finding none, he nodded tightly, wondering anew at Claude's sense of loyalty. His dedication to his neighbors. He felt a wash of gratitude, making it impossible to speak. He'd choke down all the *handkäse* in Bavaria for a friend like Claude.

They parked the pickup to the side of Sam's driveway, so he'd have plenty of room to pull out in his rig later. Back inside the house, they were met with an eerie quiet. Even the TV had been shut off. "Astor!" Sam called into the gloom. "Annie!"

"In here," Astor called.

He left Claude to seal up the doorway as best he could with damp beach towels and went in search of her. He found her with her sister in the living room: Annie propped on the couch, Astor on her knees on the floor, holding her sister's pulmonary-function machine to her face. "She said it was getting harder to breathe," Astor said, "so I went and got her inhaler and her tube."

Her sharp brown eyes sought her father's and held.

Sam stared back, communicating a silent gratitude for the second time in as many minutes. Astor acknowledged this with a solemn little nod.

"That's exactly right, young lady," Claude said, stepping into the room behind him. "Good on ya."

"Yes, thank you, Astor," Sam echoed, even while mourning Astor's innocence anew. Astor was a marvel. But she also deserved to be a kid. Not tethered to her emergency watch, burdened with listening closely for abnormalities in Annie's labored breathing. Watching the little plastic ball in her pulmonary tube rise pitifully before falling again.

He came to an instant decision. "We forgot something important back at the Eddy. Come along to keep me company?"

She blinked, a question in her eyes, but Sam didn't pause for her to ask it. "Your sister will be fine. Claude's going to stay here and take care of her until we get back."

Claude nodded his approval. Annie was already settled back into the confines of the couch, and so Sam grabbed the SUV keys and steered Astor toward the door before he could change his mind.

# CHAPTER 14

True made her way back along the rocky shore to Emmett and Vivian, directing them onto a boulder overlooking the river. From there, they eyed their biggest challenge of the Outlaw, or at least the part of it they could see. The Quartz ran the length of a mile, the narrow canyon walls closing in to form a fast-water flume.

"I'll be starting hard right, and then we'll need to merge into the center flow," True told them. It helped, she had learned, for clients to know what to expect . . . even if they promptly forgot it all. "Once we're in the canyon proper, the water will move hard and fast, and we'll basically just be along for the ride—oars in the water, of course—until we reach the Wash."

"What's the Wash?" Emmett asked, wide-eyed.

True made a circular pattern in the air with one finger. "Have you ever seen gold panning?" When Emmett nodded, she continued. "Imagine you're a fleck of gold being churned in a pan." When he blanched, she smiled. "It's like a funnel water slide . . . super fun."

"Super fun?" Vivian echoed skeptically, with a funny little quirk of one eyebrow, and True arranged her face into her most confident expression as she nodded enthusiastically. "And I bet even more fun in the smoke," she said, with a wink to Emmett. "No one else can say they've done *that*."

To Vivian, she added in an undertone, "We got this."

"Of course we do," Vivian agreed, though for the first time, True detected a note of hesitation in her tone. Her eyes watered as she peered out onto the challenge that awaited them on the Outlaw, then wrapped Emmett's Buff more securely around his face to filter out the worst of the smoke. Witnessing this gesture of care sent an answering pang through True, and it took her a moment to identify it as an echo of the maternal instinct displayed countless times by Mel. She wasn't sure how this startlingly unfamiliar feeling had snuck up on her, but since it threatened to shake the foundation of True's confidence in flinging the three of them down the flume of the canyon, she shut it down. Confidence was key when tackling Quartz. To get her head back on straight, True reminded herself that the Wus were among the most competent clients she'd guided.

Back in the oar raft, Quartz started out unassuming enough, though the din of the whitewater still out of sight promised otherwise. The canyon walls—lava rock stained in a white stripe at the high-water mark somewhere just over True's head as she bent into her oars—funneled their raft toward the first of many obstacles: a triangle-shaped boulder that sat in stubborn resistance directly in the middle of the water flow. She pulled hard right, knees bent, perched forward on her bench seat in the center of the oar raft, missing the boulder by a few generous inches.

The water speed picked up on the other side, just as she'd warned the Wus it would, and though both clients kept paddling as promised, the smoke obscured their vision, their paddles hitting the sides of the rock walls with a hollow thump on more than one forward stroke. Each time, this contact sent a tremor of shock through the already fatigued muscles of True's forearms and biceps as she made up the difference. She set her jaw in resolution—*Wonderland Lodge is the goal*—and dug into the whitewater again and again, shouting to the Wu family to keep paddling despite the challenges. *Always, always keep paddling.*

They'd reached the point of no return: the spot where the canyon turned into a full-fledged flume, where no matter what they did, no matter what strategy True implemented, they were one with the river, destined to rush downward on its back. The Outlaw's spray stung their faces, each wave of whitewater cresting and crashing onto the raft, into Emmett's lap, onto True's chest, causing Vivian to sputter and cough as she white-knuckled the handholds at the stern. There was no eddying out now. No pausing to take stock, and certainly no going back. Though this feeling of inevitability was par for the course, it felt otherworldly today to True, disembodied as they were lost in the fog of the smoke, blind to each dip and rapid of the river. She'd never felt so disoriented on the Outlaw, and her gut tightened in more than just the customary rush of adrenaline. For the first time she felt actual fear, compounded by the knowledge that it was far too late now to heed the warning of her earlier slip in confidence.

"Here it comes!" she shouted, sensing the final crescendo of Quartz was upon them. Just ahead, though she couldn't see it, True knew the Wash spiraled in an angry boil, dropping nearly seven feet in one fell swoop, waiting to deposit their raft into its vicious spiral. She dug deeper into the water than ever with her next stroke, even though her oar, too, hit rock as often as it hit water now. The canyon walls were so close now, True cried, "Duck!" several times as the raft spun and twisted and bumped its walls, bringing its passengers careening toward the jagged lava. Then they spun completely around, like riding an inner tube at a water park, just as True had promised, and she caught her breath and held it as her stomach dropped out from under her and they fell into the whitewater below.

She thought Emmett might have screamed; it was hard to be sure, with the reverberating slap of the raft onto the whitewater and the crash of the rapids. They spun two, three times in quick succession, giving True ample time to absorb the panicked faces of her clients as they clung to the raft ropes, toes digging into the toeholds. And then, almost as quickly as it had gripped them, the Wash spit them out, the raft shooting out the other side. They hit the last "train" of rapids, Emmett now riding the bow like a cowboy hanging onto a bronco as the inflated tubes crashed down two, three, four times. And then they were out, the raft eddying out in a shallow pocket of suddenly calm water.

"Well?" True gasped with a breathless laugh, uncharacteristically giddy now that they were out of it in one piece. "How did you like it?"

She peered into Vivian's and Emmett's faces through the haze of the smoke. As with every client, wildfire or no, each wore an expression of awestruck wonder mixed with acute relief. "We did it!" Emmett finally shouted, lifting one hand in triumph. His oar nearly hit his mother in her face.

"We did," Vivian agreed with a shaky laugh that echoed True's, and unlike every other time, with every other client, True reached across the middle tube to give her arm a reassuring squeeze.

By the time Wonderland Lodge emerged through the trees on the north side of the river, True's forearms screamed with every stroke, and the afternoon sun cast the smoky canyon into gloom instead of its usual harsh light. The adrenaline and worry from the adventure of the Wash had long burned off, and the Wus were quiet as they dipped their oars into the water obediently. True gave them the signal to let up and then turned the nose of the oar raft toward the small dock, navigating around the single aluminum Tracker boat the Martin family kept here, looking for a place to tie off.

"Stay put for now," she told the Wus, stifling a groan as her thighs cramped when she rose from the bench seat to step off the raft onto the floating dock.

Emmett made a low noise of protest. Vivian cleared her throat and said, "Listen, True, why don't you let me walk up there with you. I'd like to talk to the guy myself."

True wavered. That ammo box burned a metaphorical hole in her pocket. They *had* to spend another night out in the elements in order to stay on schedule, and staging a day here would keep them out of the worst of the smoke. They were at the mercy of the Martins' hospitality, and maybe Vivian's presence would smooth the way.

"All right," she decided, and all three of them trudged up the riverbank.

The grounds were quiet as she crossed the lawn, the motion-detector light over the deck snapping on in the gloom as she approached the back door. Henry Martin appeared on the deck in his signature Carhartt coveralls, a halfhearted nod his only acknowledgment of her arrival.

"Hey, Henry," True called once she was in earshot, forcing a light-hearted cheer to her voice. "Any room at the inn? We've had a long day of it." Hopefully he could identify her through the haze. Though she probably stood a better chance of accommodation if he didn't. True never sent business his way. She took away from it, really, floating guests right by his near-dilapidated lodge. But there was nothing she could do about this now. "I have two clients here who need to get out of the smoke."

"We're fixing to leave while we still got some light left in the day," he told her flatly. Guess he recognized his least-favorite rafting guide through the thick air after all. "You oughta do the same."

"Leave?" A quick flip of trepidation made itself known in True's gut. Did Henry know something she didn't? She hadn't had any sat updates from Mel, and last she'd checked her radio, the only evacs had been ordered directly under Flatiron. "Think that's necessary?" she asked. She tried to sound confident while checking that "bossy" tone he claimed grated so on his nerves.

"Wind is picking up," Henry said, leaning back on his heels as though to illustrate this point, hands stuffed into the front pockets of his Carhartts. "The other rafting groups, they've all come through," he added, even though he knew full well why True trailed last. "And like them, I'm not waiting around while this thing breathes down our necks."

True's mind spun through her options. "You taking the Tracker downriver, then?" It would hold six. Provided the Martins' guests had already departed of their own accord, there would be room for True and the Wus. The outboard motor would shorten the journey to under an hour, putting them ahead of schedule, but that was better than being behind.

"And get stuck at the coast when they close our road? No thanks. We'll drive."

That trepidation turned to lead in True's stomach. Next to her, Vivian seemed to tense as well. "Does he mean the road where we get picked up at the end?" she asked True.

She nodded, adding a muttered "But it's fine." Calling out to Henry, she said, "I haven't heard anything about anyone closing the river road." If they cut off access to the narrow, winding logging road that connected Carbon to Temple Bar, she could forget about her Friday handoff altogether. How would Fallows's contact meet her?

"Just a matter of time," Henry bellowed back. "Anyone with any sense in their head knows that."

Would *Fallows* know it, then? The man was many things, but stupid wasn't one of them.

Would he anticipate the closure of the road and have his contact planted at Temple early? Maybe True should do the same.

"Last I heard, they'd already ordered Level 3 evacs around Flatiron," Henry carried on, as True's mind spun, possibilities and contingencies leaving her dizzy. "Though nothing higher than a Level 2 anywhere around Carbon."

True grasped at this last bit of intel. "You're sure?" *Please let it be true, for the Bishops' sake.* Sam would make sure the girls got out, if it came to that, she told herself.

"That's right. Fire's headed west."

Vivian filled in the rest for him. "Toward us," she said, pivoting back toward True. She started to say something else, but Emmett cut her off.

"Do evacs mean evacuations? Does that mean we *have* to leave?"

They both waited for her answer, and when she couldn't come up with a damned thing, Vivian gave her a hard look before shouting up to Henry, "So you're driving out of here today?"

"Damned straight. And you should evac the river, too, lady."

Vivian spun back to True. "Should we?"

Her tone made it clear that this time she required an answer. "I don't . . . let me think." A low-grade panic had started to buzz in True's ears. Fallows had made it abundantly clear to both her and Mel when they took on this nightmare partnership: the ammo box—and the Fallowses' cash—was not to leave the Outlaw. Ever. But if what Henry was saying was true . . .

"You keep going downriver," Henry bellowed from the deck, finishing True's thoughts for her, "you'll be stranded at Temple Bar. No shuttles will be operating in this mess within a day, I can promise you that." When Vivian didn't answer, still looking to True instead, he shook a set of car keys in her direction. "You and the kid, you can follow us out in my old Ford. Bring Ms. Truitt, too, far as I care. But don't let her tell you it's all hunky-dory ahead. Not your problem if she'd rather string you along than return your deposit fee."

That was it. Fury surged in True, snapping her back to attention. "Keep your truck," she shouted, because she couldn't say *Fuck you, Martin*, not with Emmett within earshot. "It probably won't make it a mile anyway." How dare he imply that she'd put her clients at risk just to save a buck?

She turned and strode back toward the raft, Vivian on her heels, protesting, Emmett behind them and near tears, from the sound of it. By the time they'd reached the river, True was no calmer.

"I would *never* put you at risk," she insisted. Too hard. With entirely too much emotion lacing her voice.

Vivian remained silent, because she didn't have to say a word, did she? True, with all her protestations, was making it abundantly clear. Of *course* she had put them at risk . . . had been doing so since the moment of the lightning strike. She could argue that she had no choice. She could tell herself that the task that carried her down the Outlaw for the Bishops was a current she couldn't—wouldn't—fight. But now it had caught up with her; she'd let Vivian down, had lost her trust, and the level of distress this caused True caught her by surprise, just like that odd surge of maternal instinct.

"Do you want me to off-load your bags?" she asked softly. Defeat had taken the wind out of her sails.

Vivian swallowed but stood her ground. "I followed you down here because I want to know *your* plan, not that blowhard's."

True looked up. The betrayal she expected to see on Vivian's face was there all right, but something lay beneath it, underneath her concern for Emmett's safety. What, though, True couldn't quite put a finger on.

"I want my money's worth out of this trip as much as he thinks you do," Vivian continued, "but is he right about the shuttles? Will they stop coming?"

The handful of private operations that made a killing off the rafting companies, running shuttle vans back and forth from Carbon to Temple Bar on the very same road the Martins planned to navigate, were a no-nonsense, tough-as-nails crew, all ex-loggers and ballsy college kids not easily scared off. But even they would hang up their car keys if the river road closed and the canyon evacuated.

"Probably," True admitted. She forced herself to say the right thing. "You and Emmett should leave with the Martins."

Admitting this left her hollow inside, a sense of aloneness she usually didn't notice rattling around inside her, making her ache. The disappointment reached deep, but as loath as she was to see them go, getting them stranded would only make everything far worse.

"Leave without you? Why?" Vivian said sharply, a sentiment echoed immediately by Emmett.

"Yeah, why don't you come, too, True?"

*Because my loyalty lies elsewhere.* But God help True, this sentiment was feeling less true every hour she knew Vivian and Emmett. "There's one other option," she hedged, "but it's not much better." She waited for Vivian to nod her approval for her to continue. "We can push for Temple today, together, while the shuttles are still running."

Arriving three days early would be bad, but surely not as bad as not getting there at all. *Never return with the cash,* John had told her. He was always being watched. *Never bring it around Carbon.*

"Isn't that too far to go in one day?" Vivian asked, her brow knit in a concern True feared she didn't deserve.

Yes, but what choice did she have? "I can handle it," she answered, in the direction of the raft. Vivian was getting too good at reading the doubt on True's face.

"But wait, so it's still going to be over?" Emmett asked, his shoulders slumping. This touched True. And maybe she was wrong, but Vivian also had a look of disappointment about her, like she, too, was reluctant to cut their time short, prudent or no.

True got on the sat phone, placing a request for a late-evening shuttle pickup. The swing-shift operator at Rapid Shuttle, a college kid she didn't know as well as the old-timers, confirmed Henry's prediction. Tonight's run could be their last for the week.

"Good call, then," Vivian said, and a swell of gladness rose in True's gut at earning back at least a portion of the woman's respect in her leadership skills. *I'll keep working to earn back the rest,* she thought, surprising herself again. Could she? And did she really want to? She hadn't risked making this much effort with a woman since her Paddle, Inc., days with Mel.

*And look how that turned out,* her brain supplied.

She chastised herself for this thought, wondering when she'd become so bitter. Obviously, her feelings for Mel hadn't served her, but she had the most meaningful friendships of her life with the Bishops to show for it. But Astor and Annie were not True's kids, were they, no matter how involved she was in their lives. And Mel wasn't hers to love, no matter how loyal her devotion. True figured she'd made her peace regarding the former . . . Maybe kids just weren't in the cards. But the latter? Having a front-row seat to something just out of reach had made True feel frustratingly stuck, like when her raft got caught in a tributary stream parallel to, but not in, the flow of the rapids. She'd made it a point not to let it happen again.

Which had her looking at Vivian again, her thoughts stalled in this unfamiliar landscape, as she gathered her oars in her callused hands. The Wus assumed their positions on the oar raft, Emmett moving so reluctantly he lost his favored position next to True to his mother.

"At least you'll be sleeping in a bed tonight," True offered with a tight smile, pleased when Vivian didn't look cheered by this prospect.

"I was just getting used to those squeezy mummy bags," Emmett contributed.

Back on the water, True's heavy oar dipped and rose, dipped and rose in a steady rhythm, each slice into the slow-moving Outlaw cutting the flat water in time with the groan of the oars against the oar locks. Vivian napped at the stern, her mood still uncharacteristically low, her crisp white Columbia sun hat set atop her face as a makeshift smoke mask.

Lacking entertainment from the adults, Emmett absently picked through a baggie of trail mix, sorting out varying colors of M&M's. He lined up a row of them on the outer tube of the raft, the red and blue candy shells contrasting with the yellow of the thick vinyl. With one finger, he moved them along like cars, amusing himself when one slid off the side of the boat into the water.

"Buh-bye, fishy snack," he called after it, already moving the next M&M "car" up in line.

True stared beyond him at the water. Each rotation of her shoulders sent a burning sensation through her body, and with Wonderland Lodge now at their backs, it was better to focus on the pain than to think about what lay ahead. She wished once again that those damned nerves would settle in her stomach. Instead, they just kept arising with each oar stroke, mixing in a nauseating gut twist with her newfound desire to explore more with Vivian. Even if such a thing was still more of an abstract brain exercise than an actual possibility, it messed with her head.

But it was preferable to thinking about the roll of bills hidden in her steel ammo box under her seat. The parking lot, boat ramp, and pit toilet of Temple Bar—the extent of its nod to civilization—would be empty tonight, in the dark. Arriving so early, she couldn't hold out much hope that Fallows's contact would be there to relieve her of the illicit cash that still felt like it might burn a hole in the bottom of the boat. She nearly ran them all aground on an easy-to-read sandbar, trying to decide what the fuck she would do with this week's contraband delivery.

In her haste to course-correct, the raft jerked sideways, nearly taking Vivian into the water. *Shit!* She managed to right herself but lost her hat in the process. True turned to catch sight of her bent over the tube, trying to fish it out of the river, where it rapidly sank in a glowing disk of white canvas. Muttering a second curse under her breath, True dug in deep with her right oar, swiveling the nose of the raft 90 degrees before leaning forward and scooping up the soaked hat with the flat side of her oar.

"Thank you, True." Vivian smiled.

"No problem." *It's the least I can do, considering you're currently associating with what can only essentially be called a criminal.*

Their fingers touched as True handed back the hat, and Vivian didn't instantly pull away. But along with inciting a quick trill of attraction through her, the touch made True realize how thoroughly this fire and, even before that, True's errand for the Fallowses had robbed her of any real chance she had to share something meaningful with her. What happened to running the Outlaw for the sheer joy of making connections that could transcend the water and of introducing the wilderness she loved to new people? What happened to TrueBlue? It was stunning, she thought, how one could lose all sense of pride and purpose in one's work in just a single season. It left her with more respect for Emmett than ever, she decided, forced into an identity which hadn't served him. Her momentary disorientation was nothing compared to the incongruity he'd endured in his young life.

# CHAPTER 15

Sam had never seen Carbon so dense with smoke. As they came down Highline, they seemed to sink slowly into the abyss of it, their headlight beams barely illuminating five feet ahead of them.

"This is creepy," Astor said. "It's like . . . what do you call it? Like that machine Claude got to make the fog in his garage on Halloween."

Sam just grunted in answer, focused on straining to see through the dirty windshield and the gray pea soup outside. It *did* look ghostly out there. As agonizing as it had been to leave Annie at the house, Sam thanked God for Claude now, keeping her at higher elevation. They passed the grocery store, then Carbon Cuts Beauty Parlor, to merge onto the main drag in town that hugged the river on the right.

For a while they had the road to themselves, folks in Carbon hunkered down while awaiting further evac orders, Sam figured. He eased toward the River Eddy, noting a slight increase in traffic the closer he got. Several cars followed behind him on the highway, and just before the bridge, a Toyota Camry pulled out right in front of them, probably never even seeing Sam's vehicle through the smoke. Sam tapped the horn—just a warning—as Astor braced a hand against the dash.

"Sheesh, where's the fire?" she muttered, sliding a sly smile Sam's way.

His heart gave a little lurch even as he smiled back. When had his little girl become grown up enough to act like a smart-ass?

"Might be a tourist," he told her. Folks born and bred in Carbon didn't scare quite so easily after over a decade of regular forest fires. A duo of kayaks sat strapped on top of the Camry, listing alarmingly to one side as the driver hit the brakes again. Ah: a deer had dashed across the road in front of it, two fawns trotting in her wake.

On the other side of the bridge, Sam put his blinker on before the entrance to the River Eddy, only to be cut off again, this time by a Subaru pulling a pop-up camper. Three very excitable dogs sat in the front seat. Miniature Pomeranians, maybe? Astor smiled again, watching them leap onto the anxious-looking owner's lap as she attempted to drive.

"Maybe they know something we don't," she noted. "Animals sense things, you know."

For the second time in less than a minute, her astuteness struck Sam. "When'd you get so smart, hmm?"

Astor shrugged, then added with a low whistle, "So *here's* where everybody is."

The small parking lot of the River Eddy was packed with locals. Sam blinked in surprise, his theory that Carbon residents would take this fire in stride, same as the rest, instantly debunked. Some people stood by their cars, and others had gathered on the front patio, waiting, apparently, for the doors to open. The bandannas and ski masks covering most faces made them look like bandits conspiring together. A few chatted among themselves, probably comparing notes on fire preparedness, bitching about neighbors who didn't do their fair part to clear fields, and speculating on the fire's trajectory, but most looked concerned at best, alarmed at worst.

"It's like the whole town has shown up," Astor said as Sam found a spot between a Deschutes Brewery delivery truck—probably stuck here in the middle of his route—and Margo Hennings's Sprinter van, *Outlaw Rock Climbing Expeditions* wrapped across the sliding doors.

Sam nodded to Margo as he and Astor climbed out of the SUV. Was it really just last week he'd picked her brain about her van, pouring her a cup of coffee right here at the Eddy? Sam had been considering buying one himself, hoping to start a food-truck side hustle since the Airbnb idea had flopped—anything to generate another income stream for Annie. The bank had shot financing down fast.

"Ah, Bishop!" someone called out. "Glad to see your mug, man."

Sam squinted through the smoke. He made out the rig of Dan Jacobs, owner of Jacobs Hardware, the ACE location on Main Street.

"Hey there, Dan," he called back. "You all good? I heard what happened out by your place."

The Jacobs family had a few acres west of Carbon, right below Flatiron, and by the looks on the faces of Dan's wife and kids peering out at him through the windshield, they might have had to leave their property in a hurry after the fire had jumped the line.

"It was touch and go," Dan said, "Level 1 to Level 3, just like that." He snapped his fingers, and Sam flinched, thinking about Annie and Claude. Things could change so fast. Had it been a mistake to leave them? "I won't lie," Dan added, "we're glad to be ridin' this one out in town. You opening up? The kids could use a square meal."

Before Sam could answer, he spotted the distinct brown and yellow of a sheriff's department Chevy in the lot, lights flashing. "Hold that thought, Dan," he said as the sheriff's deputy, a fellow dad Sam recognized from Astor's class, waved him over.

"That's Kaylee Simpson's dad," Astor said, and Sam greeted him through the mist of smoke.

"Deputy Simpson, what's the word?"

Astor added, "Is Kaylee here?"

"Not just now, sweetie," Simpson told her with a smile, then looked back up at Sam. "But all these folks?" He thumbed in the direction of the parking lot behind them. "They've been caught flat-footed with a Level 3 order. The official announcement is coming soon, but your wife—uh, Battalion Chief Bishop probably told you about the fire jump?"

Sam nodded.

"Well, they've got nowhere to go until we set up an official shelter."

Nowhere to go. And they'd all come to the Eddy, like that was the most natural thing in the world. Sam took another look around at the sea of people who had assembled at his bar and grill. Dan Jacobs, hoping for a hot meal. Margo, charging her phone in the front seat of her van. Countless others, soot-smudged and miserable, hoping to get out of the smoke.

Sam's mind flashed suddenly on the rows of team photos still displayed in the bar. He'd sponsored his share of them after his predecessor's day, but he'd never quite achieved that elusive status of *upstanding citizen. Pillar of the community.* At least he didn't think he had. And yet . . . all these people, here at his bar, gathering at their local watering hole for shelter, camaraderie, information. It filled Sam with pride.

Deputy Simpson was still talking, something about temporary housing and a news team on its way. "And I imagine you could use the income, especially once reinforcements from out of town arrive."

"Wait, what?"

"Hotshots, smoke jumpers, contract workers, those types. They'll be arriving in droves, and if you can stay open, so long as it's safe, of course—"

"But I'm only here to grab something and go," Sam explained. "My daughter—" Simpson looked at Astor, so Sam clarified, "My younger one," and his face rearranged into an expression of concern. Everyone knew about Annie, and no doubt Simpson didn't want to stick his foot in his mouth twice. "She needs me up on Highline Road, so I'm just here for a minute."

Besides, he was no profiteer, even if one good day at the Eddy for a change *could* pay for Annie's next round of prescriptions. It might even pay off one of the smaller medical bills. He looked around again at the gathered assemblage. His neighbors. His customers.

"Maybe I could just open up, stay for a bit, until Kim can arrive," he decided. He'd call Claude the moment he got in the door and let him know.

Once he'd unlocked and disarmed the Eddy, people swarmed in behind him, the dining room packed in a matter of minutes. It was a better turnout than *Monday Night Football* or the annual Carbon High School alumni night combined.

He greeted a handful of additional familiar faces as he and Astor made their way toward the bar: a few were neighbors from below Highline who had felt twitchy about their Level 2 status, but most were residents from the base of Flatiron, like Simpson had said, already at Level 3, like the Jacobses. They wore expressions of stark disbelief over a heavy layer of fatigue and no small amount of soot and dirt, unsure if they'd have a home to go back to once they'd finished their burgers. Caroline Frenchman, the tough-as-nails owner of Carbon's only equine-therapy ranch, kept wiping tears with the cuff of her shirt. Matty Dillon, Carbon High's current quarterback, looked as haggard and lost as his dad, Dr. Dillon, holding a cat crate in each hand, which they must have liberated from their family vet clinic by Flatiron.

He called Claude, who assured him nothing had changed up on Highline, for better or for worse. "Just don't dally too long with that power pack, sound good?"

"Sounds good," Sam told him, then messaged Kim, who arrived not five minutes after getting Sam's text, wearing a stern expression. "I thought you'd promised to leave?"

"It's good to see you, too," he returned dryly before filling her in on Annie's whereabouts. And he *was* relieved to see her still in town as well; as validating as this full bar was, these customers weren't going to feed themselves. One look at her face, however, had him asking, "You okay? Everyone all right?"

"Yeah," Kim insisted, letting her purse and a backpack—probably her go bag—slide to the floor. "It's not like we're newbies to this, but . . . I don't know. Something feels off about this fire."

They both paused to observe Deputy Simpson milling about in his tan uniform, pausing at tables to check in with residents, assuring everyone of their safety here in town. *For the time being,* Kim's expression countered.

He slid behind the bar to get a pot of coffee on, Astor clambering up onto the counter to reach the industrial pods of Folgers. Kim clicked on the grill of the Viking stove to get it warmed up. As he was pouring water into the coffee carafe, Sam spotted the imposing figure of Fire Chief Gabe Hernandez, a.k.a. head honcho, entering the Eddy.

He started to wave him over, only to have someone else catch his eye. Chris Fallows, who, unlike his father, was permitted, if not exactly welcome, at the Eddy, though he hadn't darkened the door of this place in years. Sam hadn't spoken to Chris directly since high school, when he'd gone one way—JROTC—and Chris had gone another—juvenile detention. Last Sam had heard, Chris had been trying to make a go of it with a girlfriend a few towns over, but from the look of it, he was back on the payroll out at the grow. The farmer's tan and work boots gave him away.

Which just meant the two of them had even less to talk about now than ever. He turned his back to guide Astor through the process of adding the coffee to the machine and turning on the heat. Kim, bless her, was already making the rounds with a serving tray, handing out mugs and creamer packets to those who might want a cup of joe, and by the time Sam joined her with sugars, Chris had disappeared into the crowd. Which suited Sam just fine: the last thing he needed was to deal with a Fallows right now.

"Are they planning a press briefing?" Kim asked. She nodded toward Chief Hernandez, who had now been joined by the NewsWatch 10 crew, busy setting up beside him near the bar.

Simpson, overhearing, told them, "Sorry, I wanted to run it by you folks, but . . . he's supposed to go live in a few minutes."

Sam wove through the crowd to get back to the bar. "Hernandez!" he called, waving an arm to get the chief's attention. When he didn't glance up, he added a louder, "Hey, Gabe!"

The fire chief turned, as did that same young reporter who'd reported on the fire earlier—Madison something or other, who gestured excitedly to her one-man camera crew as Hernandez waved Sam over.

"What's the status of Mel and her crew?" Sam asked Hernandez. "Were they anywhere near the action when the fire broke through the line?" He knew he wasn't supposed to be privy to this information, but Hernandez, like Simpson, knew that small-town familiarity tended to blur such lines.

Madison sidled closer, happy enough to take advantage. "Mr. Bishop? Can we have a word? Just a few minutes of your time."

Sam shook his head at Madison, focusing on Hernandez. "Any update on the Highline area?" If the head-of-command showed any concern at all for that area, he would make a beeline back with Astor and the Goal Zero right this minute, press conference or no.

"It'll only take a sec," Madison persisted.

Hernandez waved at her in annoyance, telling Sam, "Level 1 is holding steady up there," he said, while Sam exhaled a sigh of relief. He'd give Claude another update and let him know he'd be just a bit longer. "And if it stays that way," Hernandez continued, "the higher ground up there could provide a good vantage point for fighting the fire, should it continue to creep west."

"Creep west?" Madison interjected.

Hernandez's lips pressed closed in a tight line. Clearly, he'd already said more than he should, as a favor to his crew member's ex.

"We heard they're currently holding the line at the bottom of Forest Service Road 7312," Madison pressed.

*Near True's property,* Sam thought with a start. As well as the Fallowses'. He knew what that acreage meant to both of them—a sanctuary for the former, a business asset, and a lucrative one at that, for the latter. He darted a glance to where he'd last clocked Chris but still couldn't spot him in the crowd.

Kim materialized, sweat beading on her brow. "We're out of buns, and I don't know what to do about the salads . . . no one prepped them."

147

"Shit, I'm sorry." He should be helping her, not trying to pry information out of the fire department. "Listen, let's just limit the menu, all right? Appetizers, soups, and chili, that's it. Plus drinks!" he called after her. Now that the Eddy was open and he was here, he might as well make it worth Claude's time. And Kim's.

She smiled gratefully and disappeared back behind the bar as Hernandez began to address the crowd, distracting everyone from the poor service provided today by the River Eddy.

"Hey, folks. I'm here with Deputy Wilkins of Carbon Police and Jason Carrs of Eagle Valley Fire"—each man stepped forward in turn with a raised hand—"and we have an official update, if you're ready?" This last part was delivered to the news crew. The cameraman nodded gravely.

"As most of you know, the Flatiron Fire officially ignited at 5:16 p.m. last night, the, uh, tenth of July. It's burned 8,234 acres at last estimate, moving more rapidly than we'd anticipated from the south slope of Flatiron to the west, down to Forest Service Road 3370, where, unfortunately, it jumped our firebreak."

Though the chief had clearly tried to slip this last bit of information in without fanfare, an audible gasp sounded through the quieted crowd as this news caught and flared. Some people nodded, their evacuation orders suddenly making more sense, some clutched one another, their food orders momentary forgotten, and still others placed calls and sent texts.

Chris was back, having planted himself by the front door, and for a guy who liked to claim he'd seen it all, Sam noticed he listened as raptly as the rest. Sam frowned, his presence here still needling him. For the most part, the bad blood between him and Chris was a byproduct of their fathers'. Sam had less beef with him, so why the cold stare from across the room? He had to force his attention back on Hernandez when he began to speak again.

"Now listen," the chief continued, one palm up to regain the attention of the crowd. "Your concerns are valid, and I'm glad to see so many of you folks here, taking the evac orders seriously. This fire is moving in unprecedented ways."

"In what ways, exactly?" Madison asked, thrusting her News 10 mic closer.

"Well, for one thing, the wind has been unpredictable, and it picked up in the night. This fire burned hotter and bigger all night long, which, in twenty years serving this town, I've never seen. For another thing, the humidity is still higher than usual, which could mean—"

"More lightning?" someone called from the crowd.

"Or rain!" a glass-half-full type contributed.

Hernandez called for order, then consulted his notes again. "In addition to the mandatory evacuation protocol this morning for the Flatiron and Buck Peak area," he announced, back on track, "we also issued Level 1—be prepared—via radio, TV, and Outlaw Alert for Highline Road and Carbon city limits residents, respectively."

Some folks grumbled at the mention of the optional emergency-text-alert system put in place last fire season; to say it hadn't been well received among the "don't tread on me" crowd would be an understatement. But Sam noticed that plenty more people than not reached for their phones again to open or install the app.

Hernandez continued, listing agencies working with Carbon Rural as well as staging headquarters at several strategic locations on and near the mountain, where crews were, as they spoke, holding the fire from encroaching on Carbon. Sam instantly thought of Claude and Annie again. Then Hernandez opened the floor for questions. The whole statement had only taken about three minutes.

"What are you all gonna do to keep the roads clear?" someone shouted out.

A very valid question, now that everyone knew the fire had jumped a line. The police representative fielded it. "We have traffic controllers at the intersection, and we're asking residents to evacuate only when advised for their section of town, so that—"

"When we wanna leave, we will!" someone else interjected, to a chorus of agreement. Sam caught Astor's frown at the sudden anger projected across the room and was glad anew that at least Annie had been spared this scene.

"All right, all right! You all are free to do so, of course!" the rep backpedaled. "But for best traffic control, just use discretion. For starters, stay here awhile." He nodded in Sam's direction, many eyes following the gesture of solidarity, and despite his thoughts on Annie, Sam's chest swelled a bit. He doubted anyone would blame him; he was a Bishop, and as such, he still had plenty to prove to this town.

"What was the response time for Carbon Rural?" someone else called out from the crowd. "Last night, at the onset?"

Another resident echoed, "'Cause I heard they waited at least twelve hours, and now look!"

Hernandez reached for the portable mic. The police rep seemed happy to hand it over. Hernandez hardly needed the amplification, however, determined, it seemed to Sam, to set the record straight on this count emphatically. "Carbon Rural was on scene within twenty minutes, well within wildland response protocol. We followed standard Red Book interagency procedure," he told the guy who'd shouted out the question, "which, yes, Randy, calls for an overnight monitor status before taking action."

"Some good that does!" someone else shouted, to echoed agreement from Randy, Dan, and several others across the room. Hernandez held up a hand again. Sam felt for him, the bearer of all this news. He bet the chief wished Carbon Rural had the budget for a media liaison right about now. "You all can be assured that all agencies are actively combating the Flatiron Fire," he called out. "You can report *that*," he told the news crew, knowing full well they planned to broadcast it all. "First priority, folks? Keeping this blaze as far from the wildland-urban interface as possible, and certainly from the Carbon city line."

"Are you bringing in a hotshot crew?" someone else called.

This question was lobbed by Leslie Pearson, city-council secretary and Carbon High booster president standing toward the back, her hands framed around her mouth like a cone in order to be heard.

"That'll be up to the wildland teams, but I'm sure we'll be calling in additional resources on an as-needed basis," Hernandez hedged. "Hand crews, first." Less flashy than hotshots, Sam knew these private contractors—usually consisting of college kids peppered with a smattering of out-of-work lumberjacks and railroad guys—extracted exorbitant hourly rates. *Mercenaries,* Mel always called them, though not in civilians' hearing.

"And where exactly are we putting up all these teams?" someone called out.

Hand-crew teams were twenty strong, and depending on budget restraints, the USFS might see fit to send more than one of the 110 at their disposal. Sam thought Carbon could use forty firefighters for sure. Maybe sixty.

The police deputy fielded this one. "Carbon High School will serve as a primary shelter for any evacuated citizens," he told the room, "just as soon as we can get it set up. Any out-of-district fire crews we call in will utilize the football field and county fairgrounds."

Folks nodded. This, at least, was standard protocol during Carbon's summer wildfire season. Crews came and went from the greater Outlaw region every summer; Carbon High had served as a shelter in the past, and Sam remembered the hand crews who'd come through town every day in big caravans of trucks and engines from their nearby tent cities. Like the folks at his bar tonight, they, too, made for good customers . . . or rather, Sam's *other* customers made for good customers, the locals always trying to one-up one another as they bought the out-of-state fire crews' coffees and pancake breakfasts day after day. It was even more lucrative when the hotshots showed up in town; then, the Jameson and Crown Royal flew off the shelves, too.

Deputy Simpson hadn't been wrong: if Sam was looking for a silver lining in addition to serving his community, he could find it in a much-needed uptick of business in the following weeks it would take for crews to fully contain and put out this unprecedented fire. Assuming, of course, that it didn't consume the River Eddy first.

# CHAPTER 16

Little more than twenty-four hours since standing with Emmett on the shore of the Outlaw to bear witness to the ignition of the Flatiron Fire, True glimpsed Temple Bar emerging from the gloom of late twilight and smoke. The ramp was usually a hub of activity as shuttle vans came and went, boat trailers maneuvering for position and clients and crew hauling piles of gear and coolers, but right now, Temple's single boat ramp and small parking lot sat empty. No contact from Fallows's operation loitered in the usual place by the concrete maintenance building. No surprise, given the lack of traffic at the ramp that served as their cover, but True felt a lurch of disappointment all the same. Now that she'd already cut her time short with the Wus, she'd hoped to just get this over with. She could at least get back to Carbon, help Sam with the kids. Worry her pretty head about Mel again for a change.

She stifled another bitter laugh and navigated to the ramp in an eerie silence, the slap of her oars on the still water loud in her ears. A single light shone over the pit-toilet bathroom, orange in the smoky air, and True flipped on her headlamp to guide their nose up onto the sloping concrete of the ramp.

"As soon as we're grounded, you both can hop out," she told the Wus, who clambered out the sides of the raft clumsily, their sudden splashing jarring in the gathering dark.

She followed suit—more gracefully, she'd like to think—water to her knees at the back of the boat, pushing the stern up the ramp with a grunt of breath. Her biceps were so spent, the damned thing barely moved. Vivian turned immediately to help, and Emmett gamely grabbed the tie-off rope at the bow, tugging. Together, they got the loaded-down raft out of the water, True leaning forward, hands on her knees, to catch her breath in the thick air.

"Thanks," she told them. "You all can grab your dry bags and change out of your wet clothes, if you like." She pointed toward the bathroom. "There's space to change behind it, too," she added. "Benefit of having this place to ourselves . . . total privacy."

"When will the van be here?" Emmett asked, eyeing the darkening sky.

True consulted her watch. "About ten minutes, I'd guess." She'd been promised a shuttle driven by one of the old-timers least likely to be spooked by the smoke.

Emmett set out with his gear, but Vivian hung back, offering to help with the Yeti cooler, which was a two-person job even mostly empty. True took her up on it, heaving her end out of the boat while thinking ruefully of the steaks still thawing inside, ready for tonight's dinner. They'd skipped it, opting for trail mix and granola bars as True continued to row, and row, and row.

"I really am sorry to be ending early," Vivian said once they'd set the Yeti down on the concrete.

And she sounded it, too, but True was tired and miserable and feeling a bit too sorry for herself, so instead of "Me, too," what came out of her mouth was "I'll give you a refund, so don't worry about that."

She felt the backlash of Vivian's hurt even before she registered it on her face. It reverberated from her very being. "No, thank you," she said tightly. But then she seemed to recover herself. "You know, True, I have a sense that you wish this trip had gone very differently, and so do I. I know we're rookies when it comes to this rafting stuff, Emmett and me, but this was an act of nature, and—"

True couldn't do it. She couldn't let Vivian think she, or Emmett, had done anything wrong. "It's my fault." She took a step toward

Vivian, noted her crossed arms and braced stance, and thought better of it. "I did want things to go differently," she told her. "But you didn't do anything wrong."

"Obviously," Vivian shot back. "What I was going to say," she continued, "is that I understand we're not exactly assets, but we're not liabilities, either."

At True's baffled expression, Vivian blurted, "Why were you so quick to pawn us off?"

Wait. Was Vivian hurt because True had told her to go with the Martins? She just barely managed to mask a very small, very cautious smile. She *did* risk a cautious step forward. "I didn't want you to go with the Martins," she said, relishing every word for how true each one was. "But I couldn't in good conscience advise you not to. This is getting real," she said, indicating the smoke around them. "As much as I want to spend more time with you"—she deliberately emphasized the single word, even feeling a pang of betrayal to Emmett as she did so—"I had to think of your safety."

Vivian made a face of frustration. "But you wouldn't come, too. Why?"

Why. True just looked at her, feeling once again caught in that distributary, as good as a million miles away from where she wanted to be. *I can't tell you why.* She just shook her head, the weariness and misery from moments before coming back to claim her.

How to fix this? How to explain? True was still wrestling with this, and Vivian was still waiting, when Emmett returned, emerging back through the gloom to startle them both.

"Mom, there's a moth in the bathroom *this big*," he told her, hands spanned at least six inches apart. "So, you know, be careful."

As far as dismissals went, it sufficed. Vivian picked up her gear bag and turned heel, leaving Emmett to help True with the rest of the gear. They hauled out the table and tents, then the dry bags containing the sleeping bags and pillows, the tarp, the stove, and the fuel canisters. True set them all in orderly file on the ramp by the boat, a creature of habit even though tonight she certainly had ample space available to spread out. Her thoughts were racing the whole while, everything she should have said to Vivian instead of what she had said running in a loop in her head.

*I got into something over my head.*

*My problems tonight do not define me, I promise.*

*I am a woman you can trust, and trust me, I want to see you again.*

Emmett helped more than his share, hauling out the awkward, bulky Paco Pads they slept on despite the fact that they were taller than he was, then the chairs, and finally the ammo boxes . . . one, two, three . . . and four.

True grabbed the last one from him, *the* ammo box, the smallest one that meant everything and that had ruined everything. She clutched it tight against her sweat- and river-water-soaked tank top, ignoring Emmett's protests that it wasn't too much for him, that he could carry it. As he set back out toward the bathrooms to check on his mom, she flicked a glance toward the road where she expected the shuttle to emerge soon in a flash of headlight beams; daylight faded fast here in the river canyon. She couldn't quite let go of a lingering hope that a truck with the ridiculous *Fallows, Inc.* wrap around the door would suddenly show first. Imagine actually wishing those guys anywhere. No, True was on her own, for better or worse, that concept of *aloneness* stirring something restless and discontented in her again.

Though she was normally in a hurry to part ways with this ammo box by this point in her weekly river journey, tonight, her first instinct was to not let it out of her sight. But that meant bringing it back in the shuttle with them, and Fallows's words echoed in her head: *Never, ever let me catch you with my cash off the river.* She decided she should stick to Plan A, as best she could, glancing around her at a loss. *Stash it somewhere here?* Usually, it was so easy. Fallows's contacts rotated between the lanky young guy with long hair—usually up in a sloppy man bun—and the wiry old guy always wearing a sweat-stained Mariners ball cap and carrying his tackle box and rod. Both blended in with every rafting dude and loner fisherman True had ever met, fixtures of the dock every Friday. The shuttle drivers all knew them. The guides all tolerated them, apart from when they tried to bum a beer. The clients were oblivious, unless they had teenage girls, in which case they found themselves tugging their daughters away in a hurry from unwanted attention.

Old Dude never failed to hit on all the other female river guides, too, and when True warned Fallows that every single one of her river sisters was well and over it, he'd only smirked.

"You're a solid nine yourself, you know. With a little effort, you probably don't even have to date chicks, honey." She'd caught sight of Fallows's hand snaking around to the hollow of her lower back and pivoted away with an angry curse.

"Put your hand on me and you'll lose it," she'd hissed.

"Chill, neighbor." His eyes on her were small and mean. She'd felt naked in her tank top and river shorts. "Just thought we could break the ice with a little foreplay. But we can be strictly business. Fine by me."

True had spent her entire adult life avoiding guys like this, and now look at her. Cowering here as twilight descended, trying her damnedest to do his bidding. She looked at the bright side: at least she didn't have to interact with either of his sleazy friends tonight. Young Dude's meth rot wasn't on display as he slid her a smile from the parking lot. Old Dude wasn't here trying to hit on a fifteen-year-old in a bikini top. But that meant it was up to True to decide what to do now with her contraband. And time was wasting.

Should she stash it in the bathroom? Such a high-traffic area seemed like a bad hiding place. The boat ramp offered a few ledges and shelves of concrete where it had crumbled over the years at the edges; maybe she could leave the box to one side, hidden from view from the water.

*To potentially be swept into the Outlaw? No.* But on the other side of the ramp, at the end of the parking lot, stood a big spruce. It was the bane of the shuttle drivers' existence; they had to navigate around it as they made their three-point turns pulling their flatbed trailers stacked with rafts. True knew a couple drivers who hadn't lasted a season they'd hit it so many times, knocking off side mirrors and nicking rafts. Anyone would know that spruce, should someone ask about it, like where precisely it was, perhaps because they needed to find it.

She crossed the parking lot to it in quick steps, casting a glance to her left as she passed the bathroom. The Wus would be out soon. Right before the tree, she paused midstride, feeling the crunch of glass and plastic under her sandals. Taillight shards from last week; someone had probably been fired for that one. Flipping her headlamp on, she surveyed the tree. It had a gargantuan trunk, but it was visible from all sides, of course, plus people poked around it regularly to survey damage. But about three feet up, she saw her salvation: a little burrow in the tree trunk, almost two feet wide, dark and crumbling on the inside. The result of some sort of bug or beetle infestation? A parasitic fungus? Either way, it would suffice. She slid the small ammo box inside, shoving it to fit. Once pushed in as far as it would go, what was left of the thin layer of paint covering the lid was only visible if you were looking for it.

She took a step back, circling the spruce, second-guessing herself. *It's like I'm Gollum with the goddamned ring.* Maybe she *should* just keep the cash with her. The idea made her squirm, but so did walking away from it here, unattended and exposed at Temple Bar. She needed a second opinion. She had no way of contacting Fallows or his henchmen, a deliberate move on both his part and hers, but she could dial up Mel. She turned back toward their pile of gear to unearth her sat phone, only to bump headlong into Vivian, who let out a startled "Oof."

"Shit! You scared me," True told her. She peered at her more carefully in the dark. How long had she been standing there? Uncertainty sat tight in her gut, a rubber band stretched taut.

"What were you doing just now? With that box?"

*Snap.* Shit, shit, shit. "Nothing, it's . . ." True felt herself unraveling. "I—"

Headlights cut through the trunks of the trees, making her jump again.

"I came down here to tell you the shuttle's here," Vivian said, but her eyes were still on the tree. "Does whatever that is have something to do with why you wouldn't accept the ride with the Martins?"

True tried to study her face in the dark, her eyes now blinded by the headlights. She couldn't see much: only any hope of earning this woman's faith in her draining away. God, Vivian probably thought she had a stash of something here. Needed a hit or something. "It's not what you think—"

A honk sounded; then True heard the backup sensors of the shuttle, easing down to the ramp to where their gear lay in wait.

Vivian turned. "We have to go." She spun back. "You know, True, I also came down here because I felt I owed you an apology. And I guess I still do. It was none of my business why you turned down the Martins, just like it's none of my business what you're up to now. Let me be clear: if we were still on the river, and you still had my child's life in your care, it damned well would be, but now? I guess I'm just glad it's all over."

She turned and strode toward the pile of gear, hefting a duffel far too heavy for her and flinging it toward where the shuttle van had come to a stop in the loading zone. True stood in place a moment longer, alone by the tree and the ammo box, fighting a harsh onslaught of tears, Vivian's words still ringing in her ears. *Glad it's all over.* She swallowed the hard lump in her throat, blinking hard in the smoke to stem the flood. Vivian and Emmett would be gone from her life in a matter of hours. And Vivian was right. They'd be better off for it.

# CHAPTER 17

Sam's office at the back of the River Eddy felt like a sanctuary after the chaos at the bar. With the press statement over, he retreated there to check in with Claude again, tugging a reluctant Astor along with him. She was loath to miss any of the action in the grill.

"What if they say something about Mom?" she protested, dragging her feet after Sam.

"We'll be the first to know," Sam said, setting a plate of grilled-cheese sandwiches Kim had produced on the desk. "Eat some dinner, honey," he said, adding, "Chief Hernandez will update us."

She flopped into his desk chair—she usually smiled at the way it swiveled, but not today—and he sank a hip into the edge of the desk with a sigh, relishing the relative quiet of the office. He pushed a triangle of sandwich toward Astor again, who swiveled away with a face.

"I'm not hungry."

Sam helped himself to his own triangle, biting into it without tasting it.

"Dad? What does Claude say about Annie?" *A little mother,* Kim called Astor. Had Sam and Mel somehow done that to their older daughter, making her grow up too fast once Annie had been born? Had this been inevitable? "What's happening at home?"

"Honey, just . . ." *Just let me stand here, not making decisions, not dealing with crisis, just for a second.* "Just let me think." Sam rubbed roughly at his face with the heel of his palm, trying to clear his head. He could swear he still felt smoke stinging his eyes, now that he'd stopped for half a second. *What is happening at the house?*

He looked around the messy office for his phone, taking in the invoices piled up on his desk, the orders awaiting their suppliers, and the tower of boxes leaning up against one wall . . . Kim's over-order of water glasses he had to hope their warehouse supplier would take back. The purchase had been an honest mistake, but Sam had still barely managed to curb the harsh admonishment—fueled by too little sleep and too much stress—that had risen within him. What if they were stuck eating the cost?

They'd lost money the last two summers in a row at the Eddy, smoke season socking in their little canyon by the river with oppressive air quality. Retail sales from local businesses across the Outlaw Basin went down 20 percent, according to their small-business association. And now with this new fire? If the blaze continued in its current trajectory, it was only a matter of time before the river corridor was consumed, and rafting tourism along with it. And then what? No out-of-town customers in the River Eddy, buying burgers and beer after a day on the Outlaw. And with evacuations and fire right here in Carbon? No locals, either, after they'd all been forced to shelter at the high school or had fled town altogether to bunk with relatives and friends. What would they lose this year—thirty percent? Forty?

He thought again of the framed photo of him and Mel at the bar celebrating their impulsive purchase just after tying the knot, then glanced across the office toward the open door. He'd been right out there at the bar when they'd snapped that pic, Sam remembered, his newly minted wedding band still feeling foreign on his finger.

He and Mel had both been so impossibly young. So incredibly confident and naive. Was that part of him still somewhere inside him? Or had that fierce optimism been buried under too many unpaid bills as they had sunk deeper and deeper in debt, two stones tied to the same cord of shared parenthood? One thing was certain: the River Eddy fell ever deeper from the black to the red with every month Sam couldn't seem to break even.

He sighed, reaching out to lay a hand atop Astor's head. Still curled up in the office chair, she swiveled gently back and forth now, unenthusiastically chewing a bite of grilled cheese. Now that she'd moved the plate of sandwiches, Sam spied his phone on the desk, and he punched in Claude's number.

"How's she holding up?" he said without preamble as Astor glanced up, alert. Sam put the call on speaker.

"Oh, all right, I suppose," Claude tells them. "Had a bit of a coughing fit, but the inhaler worked well enough. I gave her one of her fruit pops."

Sucking on the cherry-flavored lollipops helped calm Annie's ragged breathing when nothing else worked. "Good, good."

Sam took heart, knowing that Claude knew his daughter so well. Their dentist threatened that the habit would lead to problems down the line, but today, much like the Bishops' finances, Sam and Mel had to triage that shit. Inability to breathe now, or cavities later? No parent would pick the former. Besides, the sad truth was, Annie only had so many comfort mechanisms at her disposal, and so many times she needed comfort.

"Whatever it takes to keep her calm," Sam told Claude now.

"She's a trooper," Claude said.

She had to be.

When she'd been born, Annie had been so small. Five pounds, eight ounces, even though she'd been full term. Common for tet babies, the NICU staff had said. The image of Annie's newborn self, her skin the dusty gray-blue of smoke, of the churning, angry water in True's favorite rapids after a hard rain, of the nurse's faded scrubs run too many times through the washer, had been seared into Sam's memory forever. Fear always flooded Sam when that image surfaced in his brain.

Yet another manifestation of PTSD, he'd been told.

Eager to change the subject, he filled Claude in on the briefing Hernandez had given, and then asked, "How's the smoke up there?"

"'Bout the same, although . . ." He hesitated.

"What?"

"I don't know if I like the way the wind's picking up."

Was it? Sam turned to the window, but he couldn't see far enough through the haze to notice if the trees outside were bending one way or the other. He and Astor should head back up with the Goal Zero, help Claude pack up Annie.

"I'll get an update from the chief," Sam promised, "and be on the road in ten."

Mel patrolled the roads with Janet as day turned to dusk, the bloodred sun sinking over the horizon like a fiery crimson coin, flat and thin as pressed copper against the ugly gray of the sky. The measure of a full day away from her kids, knowing her daughter struggled in the haze. The rookies and volunteers had all gone home for the night, White and even Lewis had clocked out hours ago, but it was full black by the time she could do the same, the stars and moon scrubbed out by the smoke. She headed directly for the River Eddy, the closest place to get answers; Hernandez had told her she'd find Sam there. In her haste, she crossed right over the outdoor patio overlooking the river, normally her favorite spot to grab a beer. *You want to sit inside and catch the game or watch the fish jump?* Sam usually asked patrons.

Pushing open the door to a sea of locals, she caught sight of Astor, en route from the office, immediately.

"Mom!" They collided with an "Oof" that sent Mel staggering a step backward, the crown of Astor's head hitting Mel's stomach.

"Hey, honey. Hey, you're okay."

Because much to Mel's surprise—and probably Astor's—her stalwart older daughter had burst into tears upon contact with her. She squeezed her tight as Astor held on, crying softly, the stiff uniform jacket of Mel's yellows rough against her face, a brass snap pressed to her cheek. The jacket had to reek of smoke. "You're good, kiddo. It's all good."

And it *was*, at least for this one instant, when she could cradle her firstborn close.

"You're here," she heard, and raised her head to see Sam, who had already crossed from behind the bar. He enfolded her wordlessly in an embrace. Consoling one another was still embedded in their relationship, like muscle memory. Sometimes Mel almost forgot they weren't together anymore; in each other's presence they always seemed to pick up right where they'd left off, like Sam had just been on a short deployment, or Mel had simply been in the field. Sometimes, like right now, she wondered what they were even doing apart. But then her thoughts swung to their daughter's health, and the instant pressure that wrapped around her made Sam's arms feel more like a vise. She pulled back.

"How's Annie?" she asked immediately. "Have you talked to Claude?"

"Just a few minutes ago. They're hunkered down."

Mel frowned. "Shouldn't you be there?"

He bristled. "I was just trying to figure out how to cut out when you showed up. I only came down here for the Goal Zero, but all these people . . ."

He trailed off as Mel felt that pressure cinch tighter. She didn't want to argue with Sam, certainly not tonight. But still: "Annie's more important than anyone here at the Eddy," she reminded him.

"I know that," he shot back. "Can you just trust me?" He didn't add *For once*, but Mel heard it. She held up both hands in surrender.

"How was the press conference?" she said. "Did Hernandez say anything about road closures?"

Sam frowned. "No, why?"

It didn't hurt to be honest. "I'm worried about True."

"Did you raise her on the sat phone?"

Mel nodded. "Last I heard, she hoped to shelter with her clients at Wonderland Lodge." She bit her lip. "That was before the wind picked up, though."

"Raise her again," he said. "Even if the blaze gets stopped short of the Wild and Scenic river corridor, the smoke'll be hell."

"It's hell everywhere," she told him ruefully. "Which is why I'm worried about Annie."

Sam's shoulders straightened, like he was trying to ready himself for round two. "I told you I called Claude and—"

Mel silenced him with an uplifted hand. She had only mentioned her worry as an explanation, not as a criticism. Together or not, they still had to see eye to eye, tethered as partners in parenthood. No one told you about that part of post-separation life. How no one could just walk away, dusting their hands of it all. Sam's mantra echoed back to her, as it always did during moments like this. *We're a team.* It took both of them to take care of Annie, and that was truer now than ever. But Sam was right. Mel's trouble was with trusting.

"Listen," Sam said, "I think . . ." He trailed off midsentence, his face a scowl. "What's he still doing here?" he asked, presumably more to himself than to her.

Mel still turned to follow his stare across the Eddy. Though not as chilling as the idea of John Fallows in the flesh, the sight of Chris standing there by the dartboards like he owned the place was still decidedly unsettling. He was, after all, only a small step removed from the one person Mel absolutely, without question, didn't want to deal with today. Besides, even looking at Chris Fallows made her feel dirty.

A quick sidelong glance at Sam confirmed that he seemed as wary as she felt. Her irritation with him burned off like alcohol under fire.

"He's definitely on my last nerve today," he told her.

"He was in earlier, too?"

At Sam's curt nod, Mel fought back a new wash of trepidation. Was Chris here on behalf of his father? Was Fallows worried True wouldn't stay the course on the river? Or, and this possibility appealed even less, had he decided the situation was dire enough to warrant his presence at Temple Bar himself? Every scenario made the nerves dance a staccato beat along Mel's spine. Fallows had warned her and True from the start: he didn't want to hear excuses. Problems weren't a part of their agreement. The Fallowses flat-out didn't tolerate them. Just look at young Zack, serving time. Take the trimmers roughed up or robbed or both by the competition. Consider Mark Bishop himself to be a cautionary tale; not even the best friend of Fallows was safe from persecution.

Mel forced herself to ignore Chris, which normally would have been highly satisfying. Hell, any other night she'd have done it for sport. Now it took everything in her to shrug carelessly at Sam. Code for *Let it go.*

She redirected her attention to Astor, who wanted to know if she was going to take a shower now that she was off duty for a few hours. "You're smelly." She laughed.

Mel pinched her arm lightly. "What, you don't like eau de woodsmoke? It's this season's hit fragrance."

Astor rolled her eyes with dramatic flair worthy of the teenager she would one day become. "You tell dad jokes worse than, you know, an *actual* dad."

Mel tried not to read too much into Astor's observation. The truth was, she and Sam *had* traded roles to some extent since the separation and Mel's promotion to battalion chief. Would she lose her feminist card for letting her new role as chief breadwinner instead of chief nurturer feel like a demotion of some sort? She had to admit: Sam had come a long way from the moment she'd shown him the plus sign on their first pregnancy test.

"What if I'm as bad at it as my own dad?" he'd managed to voice. "What do I know about being a father?"

Mel had tucked herself under the crook of his arm, so that her body fit snugly against his side. She'd hoped the heat of her would be a comfort, a reminder of how well they fit together. "You know plenty about being my husband," she'd reminded him. "Fatherhood will feel just as natural."

She had been right, she thought now, watching Sam coax Astor into finishing her grilled-cheese sandwich. And they'd been happy, absorbing the implications of that pregnancy test together. Sam had taken on the challenge of fatherhood with the same fierce determination with which he took on everything else. Top grades in high school, just to prove he couldn't be lumped in with the likes of Chris. The best scores on the Army physical the recruiter had ever seen. He'd felt a bit panicky, he'd told Mel, signing his life away, hurtling himself toward two tours in Afghanistan, but who the hell other than Uncle Sam was lining up to support him?

Sam had returned home to Carbon a decorated veteran. "And after all that, you're going to let an embryo the size of a pea unnerve you?" Mel had joked on that inaugural day of fatherhood. She smiled now at the memory, only to sober again quickly. One thing she knew with near certainty: they would still be together, she and Sam, had Annie's health not brought them to their knees. What was harder to determine: whether this fact was a crack of light in the darkness, or simply proof of a breach too severe to weather.

"Mom," Astor whispered now, "is the fire out yet?"

Her heart did that thing it did these days, whenever her children needed her and she could not deliver. She'd be at the station and not able to lend a hand with Astor's homework. Or in her sparse apartment without the DVD the girls had requested for that night. Or far worse: right next to Annie and still powerless to help her breathe. She swallowed, trying to dislodge the horrible lump that swelled in her chest.

"Not yet, kiddo."

Her mind skidded to Chris Fallows waiting for her, just steps away in the grill. Because that had to be why he was here. She thought of the houses that had already burned below Flatiron, right down to the framework, still steaming where streams of water hit glowing embers.

She thought of the stacks of medical bills that *hadn't* burned, in Sam's home office on Highline. And she swallowed again.

"But we're on it, Carbon Rural and all the other teams," she told Astor, purposely ignoring the quick stab of worry she felt for Annie as she said so. Claude had things under control, and Sam would be back with her soon. He'd as good as promised, hadn't he? "It's only a matter of time before we have a handle on this thing."

She let herself absorb these words, willing herself to believe them.

# CHAPTER 18

To say it was a tense ride back to Carbon would be an understatement. Only Emmett seemed oblivious to the tension in the air between Vivian and True; several times during the winding journey through the mountains, their driver, Don, a retired trucker from Carbon, caught True's gaze in the rearview mirror and lifted his eyebrows as if to ask, *What the fuck?*

True just shrugged at him, hoping he'd assume the out-of-town mom was just stressed about the fire and smoke. It would certainly be warranted. She leaned back against the seat of the shuttle van, trying to keep her eyes open in the dark. Usually, once the sun went down in the mountains, the summer heat disappeared with it, but tonight it was still unusually hot, the interior of the van stuffy and unforgiving.

She dug into one of the coolers at her feet and offered the two cans she grabbed at random to Emmett and Vivian: a Dr Pepper and a Sprite, respectively. Vivian had informed True of a strict no-high-fructose-corn-syrup-or-caffeine rule for Emmett at the start of their trip, but tonight she handed over the Dr Pepper with a quiet sigh. The sound of Emmett popping the top sounded unnaturally loud in the van.

She refused the Sprite, and True handed it up to Don. "I hope you folks will come back," he said toward the back seat. "I'm not sure our little slice of paradise showed you her best side this week."

True appreciated the attempt to win her back some business but knew Don shouldn't bother.

"Can we, Mom?" Emmett asked, slurping at his can of soda as it foamed out of the opening. "Come back?"

"We'll see," Vivian said quietly, mom-speak for *Not a chance, but we're not talking about this right now*, and Emmett slumped in his seat. True smiled at him. It was either that or give in to the lump in her throat again. "If she says no, I just might have to put you to work as my rafting employee," she threatened. "You're a natural river rafter, bud."

"Really?" Emmett asked, lowering his soda. "You think so?"

True nodded, and even Vivian's expression softened at the look of cautious pride on his face. His mother had been right: bringing Emmett out into the wilderness had been exactly what he'd needed to help him find his stride, and True was honored to have played a role in it, no matter how things had ended up.

Don glanced back again and gave Emmett a thumbs-up. He was driving uncharacteristically cautiously tonight, wiping his brow repeatedly as the flatbed trailer pulling their raft bounced behind them along the ruts of the road, and though it would further lengthen what was already destined to feel like an interminable drive, True was grateful. With one hand, he played with the dial of the radio, tuning it to a fire update, and, resting her head back against the seat, she listened in.

"This is bullshit," Don said as the DJ reported a 12 percent containment rate. "What were we doing watching it grow? We shoulda started fighting it sooner, you know?"

"Why didn't they?" Emmett asked, leaning forward again across the middle row.

"The forests need to burn every once in a while, Emmett," True told him. "It's good for the undergrowth to get cleared away, so we don't have bigger fires, with lots more fuel, later."

"But this *is* a big fire."

*Yes, they all are now, aren't they?*

Don grunted again in agreement. "Damn straight. It's *the* big one. You watch."

Vivian shot True another look, the warmth from earlier gone again in an instant. True frowned at Don, hoping he'd get the hint and stop with the alarming talk. But she knew what he meant: over 60 percent of their national forest lands in the Outlaw Basin were overgrown to the point of irresponsibility. They were due for a big one, no doubt about it, their wildlands a perfect tinderbox primed for what forest-management professionals called a megafire. True had sat in a conference room at the Outlaw Motor Inn just this past spring, surrounded by fellow outdoor industry leaders and business owners, listening to a panel of experts, Sam included, explain to them how their livelihoods could so easily disappear in a puff of smoke.

It had been a packed house, even the climate-change deniers among them drawn to attend the forum thanks to the very *un*deniable decline of their bottom line as the tourist season shortened by a few more weeks each year. Her favorite fishing guide had sat next to her, sharing his notes, and she'd spent the first fifteen-minute break trying to avoid an ex-girlfriend who now worked for the Pacific Crest Trail Association. Tension and emotions had run high, even without adding personal drama to the mix. One big fire—*the* big one, as Don called it—so early in the summer season could be the final nail in the coffin for most of them. And the solution, outlined by the BLM rep who'd come down from Portland, had caused the room to erupt in uproar: setting 60 percent of their forest ablaze in a series of controlled burns, intended to get the undergrowth back to a manageable level, would produce ten times the amount of smoke from an average fire, spread out over the entirety of a summer. No one could afford to close shop for an entire May–September season.

"What about selective logging?" someone had yelled over the din. "We need to bring it back!"

"You wanna do it, Bart?" someone had shot back.

A colleague of Sam's from the Forest Service had raised his hands, standing up from his place at the panel table to interject. "Yeah, clearing the undergrowth by hand would work," he shouted, and the room had quieted by degrees. "But two problems." He'd ticked them off on his fingers. "First, it's not profitable. No logging company is coming in here to clear your kindling. Big trees sell, and big trees are not what we want gone, guys. Our spruce, our Jeffrey pine, our ponderosa? Even our madrone and oaks? They're not falling in a forest fire. It's the sage, the scrub oak, the saplings that are choking out the forest floor, and guess what, geniuses? Simpson Lumber, out of Roseburg? Even the biggies, Columbia Lumber? Puget? They're not buying scrub-oak logs."

A muttering had broken out across the crowd as this truth sank in, but the rep wasn't done. "And reason number two," he continued. "You know how many boots on the ground we'd need for a forest cleanup like that? Shit, I can't even get enough hires for trail cutting and mainte- nance, and that's a national database of good-paying, government jobs."

"We need to reimplement the CCC!" someone yelled.

"We need government aid, FEMA or something," someone else suggested.

True remembered how Sam had scoffed, sitting up there on the panel, and she'd known what he was thinking, but in the end, the meeting had gone like all the others True had attended over the past few years, with no solutions and only increased frustration. They'd all filed out of the conference room in the same way: with their heads down and their fingers crossed that this, at least, wouldn't be the year. That they'd all get at least one more during which to make profit, save up, increase their insurance, and pray.

So much for prayers, and so much for crossed fingers. "You can say you were here when it happened," True told Emmett now with a sigh, turning in her seat to smile tiredly at the kid. "Just think," she added, trying desperately not to think about Annie, or Mel, or her Outsider yurt sitting like the proverbial duck on the urban-wildland interface. "You saw the big one ignite."

He nodded solemnly while Don huffed again, and True swiveled back in her seat to stare out the windshield at the black, smoky night, their headlights reaching only a matter of yards to illuminate the thick forest on either side of them.

Despite trying to convince Astor otherwise, Mel was starting to think she didn't have a handle on anything at all. The atmosphere in the bar had grown heavier by the minute, and not just because so many warm, sweaty bodies pressed in close. It was nearly 8:00 p.m., but no one was leaving, including her. She itched to take the drive up Highline to check on Annie before getting a few precious hours of shut-eye, but Chris Fallows still loitered by the bar, pinning her in place. Why was he here? He sat with several of his father's seasonal workers, presumably to get the latest updates like everyone else, but what if he was really serving as his father's eyes and ears? What if his presence had less to do with the Flatiron Fire and more to do with her and True?

Mel swallowed tightly, wishing she could glean whatever intel Chris hid behind his poker face. Had Fallows decided to get his own hands dirty for a change, risking the river road? For that matter, was True still on the Outlaw, as planned? She'd tried to call her, to no avail. Which had made her wonder: Was she off course? The reception, even via satellite, was usually fine by Wonderland Lodge, but notoriously bad at Temple Bar.

Mel couldn't decide which location would be better: current radio chatter informed her that the Flatiron Fire had been contained at the Forest Service road at the base of its namesake peak, but it could be only a matter of time before wind pushed the blaze further to the southwest.

*Leaving the fire with nowhere to go but the river valley.*

The young media liaison for Outlaw County, Keith Bonaparte, must have gotten the same update on his cell phone, because he rose from his seat, where he'd been nursing a beer now that the press conference was over, gesturing to Sam to quiet the crowd.

He started with the good news. "Word just in, people. We have containment on the urban interface line."

A thunder of applause accompanied this announcement, but underneath it, Mel heard the low rumble of murmuring from the more fire-science-savvy of the community.

"If it's not heading Carbon and Highline way, what's that mean for the Outlaw?" someone called out.

Mel pinched her eyes shut as her prediction of a moment before was confirmed. "I'm told efforts will need to be redirected there," Keith admitted as the clapping died down to a smattering. It ceased altogether as the prospect of the Outlaw—Carbon's prime recreational hot spot and tourism draw—becoming a ravaged wasteland sank in. If the worst came to pass and the river corridor was consumed, a full-on public outcry would follow in its wake, drawing complaints from locals and environmentalists alike.

"At least the Wild and Scenic Act will kick in some federal funds," Sam reminded the crowd. Mel nodded. Saving the protected river would take higher priority to the federal government than saving dot-on-the-map Carbon. And that boded well for True.

But before Mel could parse the nuances of environmentalism versus local jobs, Keith had a second announcement, one that was news to Mel. "As a result, as of twenty-one hundred this evening, ODOT has ordered the Outlaw River Road from Carbon all the way to the coast officially closed."

*River. Road. Closed.* In less than an hour's time. The words detonated in Mel's brain like shards of shrapnel. Forget the uproar forthcoming from those who relied on the river to fund their outdoor recreation businesses. Forget even the generalized fear of the flames progressing west. The closing of the river road would seal off Temple Bar completely. To *everyone.* And seal *in* anyone who hadn't gotten out already. Her thoughts swung wildly back to True, somewhere in the wilderness with her clients, undoubtedly unaware of this update. They could become stuck, put in the path of the fire. Put at risk, all because of Mel.

*Don't. Fucking. Panic.* With the fire on a new trajectory, Highline Road would almost certainly remain at Level 1. She heard the liaison: the firefighting focus would now shift, Mel's team along with it. She could focus almost entirely on helping True. New assignments would come down the line, and she'd be back out in the field, able to be proactive, by morning.

Which seemed impossibly far away.

So when she saw Chris Fallows slip through the crowd and out of the Eddy, several but not all of his cronies on his heels, it was all she could do to keep from leaping up from her chair immediately to follow him. Were they headed west to Temple Bar before the closure became official? The timing of their exit couldn't be coincidence. Did they think True might use the river-road closure as a way to disappear with their cash? And what would they do to her if so?

*Think,* she ordered herself instead. *Be smart.* Surely the sheriff's department personnel tasked with enforcing the road closure would turn Chris and his friends around if they attempted to travel west, though the Department of Transportation *did* always give rafting traffic the courtesy of a couple hours, at the very least, in which to pull stakes and get folks off the water.

Which only opened her mind up to further threats. If True secured one of these last-minute rides for her clients, her absence on the river would only confirm Chris's suspicions. Or worse, she could arrive at Temple Bar only to be met by someone in Fallows's back pocket. A local or even a Fish and Wildlife employee, ready to hold her for questioning, just for being in the wrong place at the wrong time. *Fallows knows people everywhere,* Sam had always told Mel. He'd set up Zack Murphy to take the fall for him for far less. God, if True was arrested, if the truth came out . . . Mel couldn't even go there. Money-laundering and drug-smuggling charges would ruin far more than just Annie's chance at surgery.

She was still turning over each awful possibility in her mind when the only one she *hadn't* allowed herself to conjure suddenly presented itself: True herself, walking right into the Eddy, cool as anything.

Mel nearly spilled the water glass she'd been gripping too tightly. "True!"

She looked exhausted, her damp tank top hanging limply on her muscular frame, her trucker cap low over her tanned but drawn face. She hadn't changed out of her board shorts and Chacos, and Mel could smell the smoke and dried sweat from here, but none of this stopped Mel from practically flinging herself at her as she walked through the door.

"Thank God," she breathed. "What happened at Temple?" she whispered.

The crowd jostled them, a local or two angling to greet True, too, and Mel caught a barely discernible shake of her head as she released her. They had an audience.

"You're ripe," True joked loudly, brushing soot off her torso after contact with Mel's stained shirt.

"*I'm* ripe? Well, you weren't the only one out in the smoke all day, sleeping on the ground last night."

"Auntie True!" Astor wormed her way through the crowd, not satisfied until she was pressed close to True's side, regaling her with the tale of barricading the house from smoke. Sam trailed behind with a gruff "Glad to see you back in one piece."

Mel wasn't sure if it was the feeling of being watched or women's intuition that had her and True glancing up at the same time, but they both caught sight of Chris Fallows's return to the Eddy in the same instant. And behind him, framing the doorway, stood his father.

*Guess his purpose at the bar had been to gather intel, after all.*

And by the looks of it, Fallows hadn't liked what he'd heard. He stared Mel and True down stonily, his eyes hard, and then very deliberately rubbed the fingers of one raised hand together in a gesture for cash. There was really no mistaking his meaning, but he mouthed his message anyway: *Where the fuck is my money?*

But Mel was still staring at his face. Sam had told her more than once: When John Fallows gets scared, he's a mean motherfucker.

Which invited the question: *What are you so afraid of, John?*

# The Flame

# CHAPTER 19

"I should have brought the cash back to Carbon," True confided to Mel in a hoarse whisper after filling her in on the past few hours in a rush, "protocol be damned."

Mel shook her head swiftly, her ponytail flying back and forth. "You couldn't have known."

True weighed the validity of this statement against the shitstorm she'd found herself in twenty-five miles downriver from anyone who could have helped her, and nodded slowly. As a river guide, she had to make decisions on the fly, and she always stuck by them. She'd do the same now.

She glanced back at Fallows. "Then what's our next move?"

Mel pulled back, allowing True the chance to assess her closely for the first time. Mel looked utterly exhausted, but True's heart still caught for a beat in her throat, even with Vivian and the tense way they'd left things still at the back of her mind. Perhaps precisely *because* of that. Unrequited love was, by definition, no one's fault, but sometimes, even after all these years, it still stung.

Standing outside the shuttle van at the drop-off point in Carbon, waiting for Don to liberate the Wus' duffels from the back, True had searched her brain for something—anything—she could say to Vivian to make their parting better. But there had been nothing, of course. It was done. They were probably already on the interstate by now, all this drama in their rearview mirror. Regret still sat like a stone in her stomach, unmoved by the worry and stress all around her.

Mel offered a wan smile, brushing her hair out of her eyes, and as True stepped back, she noticed the Eddy had begun to clear out. As Sam shouted, "Last call!" those with homes to go to slowly filed out, the evacuated residents from Forest Service Road 7312 at the base of Flatiron last to leave, having only cots awaiting them at the temporary shelter in the Carbon High School gym.

When True glanced back across the Eddy, Fallows hadn't budged, however. She made eye contact and made a beeline for him. She couldn't afford to wait for him to cause a scene in the empty bar, in front of Sam.

She wove through several families gathering their gear, Mel on her heels, but by the time they had sidled past all the suitcases and duffels to confront Fallows, Sam had somehow beaten them there.

"Last call for *you* was about a decade ago," he said, a thumb pointing in the direction of the door.

Fallows stood his ground by the door, evacuees squeezing around him like debris through river rocks. "I guess we'll clear out when we're good and ready," he told Sam as several of his crew members gathered around him.

In other words, *I still call the shots, kid.*

They stood toe to toe for a long moment, and though Fallows was several inches shorter than Sam, it didn't seem it, despite the gleam of something vulnerable around the whites of his eyes. Could it be fear?

A flush of red crept up Sam's neck, reminding True that no matter how much she loathed dealing with this man, Sam couldn't even be in the same room with him without having a visceral reaction. What must it have been like, growing up as a Bishop in Carbon, having to prove yourself to every adult, having to shake labels like *white trash* and *redneck* and *criminal* at every turn? Her protective instinct kicked into gear, and True stepped in front of Sam.

He didn't appear to appreciate the gesture. "Everything's under control," he told her, frowning at her as if to say, *What's wrong with you? Get yourself and Mel out of here.* Fat chance.

"That's right," True tagged on. For the benefit of the remaining customers at the bar, she attempted a bored scoff, adding in a raised voice, "Carbon, we've seen forest fires before, haven't we?"

Fallows only smiled coldly. "Not like this one, sweetheart." He pressed a finger into Sam's chest, then flicked it up to flip the bill of his ball cap off his head. When Sam flailed to grab his hat before it flew to the ground, Fallows laughed loudly. "Jesus, junior, how are you still falling for that one?"

He kicked it across the bar floor for good measure. When Sam turned to retrieve it, Mel on his heels, Fallows rounded again on True. "Where the hell is it?"

"At Temple," she hissed, with a sidelong look toward Sam to ensure he hadn't heard. "Same as always."

Now she was sure Fallows looked scared, for the first time True had ever seen, anyway. "Then you get that we're *fucked*, right?"

True forced herself to remain calm. Icy calm. "Like Sam said, everything is under control."

"Sam doesn't know shit. And clearly neither do you, given that *I* am *here* and my *delivery* is *not.*"

"I don't know shit about what?" Sam's tone was hard as he returned, cap clenched tightly in one hand, the other in a fist against his thigh. True flinched. She was standing at Temple Bar with Vivian all over again, her reputation on the line.

Fallows attempted a hearty, cold laugh. "Take your pick, son."

Sam lunged at him. "How many times do I have to tell you to leave?"

True piled on, hoping to continue the redirect of Sam's focus. "And what exactly is your problem with me, anyway?"

"This asshole's always a problem," Sam answered.

Fallows reserved his smirk for True this time. "But I'm never too much for *you* to handle, right, honey?"

"That's it." Sam lunged, dropping his hat again to snag a handful of Fallows's shirt.

"Stop it," Mel said from behind True. She tugged Sam away, muttering something about Fallows not being worth Sam's time or the energy it would require to mop his blood from the Eddy floor. True was only half listening, eyes still trained on Fallows like he might dart away any minute, snake in the grass, one of the rattlers that disappeared into the granite lining Whiskey Creek.

Fallows broke eye contact first, a significant victory, True decided, with a grunted order to his men to stay put. "We'll finish this outside," he told True, then sauntered out of the Eddy without a backward glance.

She didn't follow him, not with Sam's eyes burning a hole in her back. She waited until Mel could draw his gaze back to her face, as only Mel could, imploring him to give his attention to what mattered. "Our daughters," she heard Mel say, then, "Highline" and "time to go." True chanced a glance back toward the bar to see Sam nod, turning to finish closing up, and only then did she slip out the Eddy door to continue what she'd started with Fallows.

Once outside, she faced him square on, feet planted firmly, just like when riding out Quartz Canyon from her perch at the bow, ready to take a hit against a river rock, a wall of water, or both.

"Knew I never should've given a chick a man's job," Fallows threw at her.

"At least *I* anticipated the river road closing in the smoke, genius."

Fallows stepped forward, bringing them chest to chest, his breath hot on her face. "I don't have to do a goddamned thing but sit on my ass and wait for my fucking will to be done. You should know by now: my operation does *not* have a cleanup crew. There is no Plan B. Ever. So I'm only going to ask this one more time. Where? Is it? Exactly."

True forced herself to stand her ground. If she acquiesced to every dude who wanted to claim her personal space in this world, where would she be?

Fallows gripped her arm. Hard. "Spill, sister."

True bit down a cry of surprise as her eyes smarted. The fucker was shockingly strong for a man in his late sixties. All that weed trimming, she supposed. It toned the biceps. Through clenched teeth she described the spruce tree in the Temple Bar parking lot. "No one can see it; no one will go looking there."

"You better hope you're right," Fallows told her, bumping her shoulder roughly as he strode toward his truck. "Because the way I see it? Your job's only half finished."

Sam never thought he'd live to see the day when Kristina Truitt possessed the look of a cornered animal. But by the time he caught up with her on the Eddy deck, she was braced against the railing, staring out across the darkened parking lot and rubbing her left bicep.

"What the hell did he want with you tonight, True?"

True lifted her head and shrugged in what she was clearly trying to pass off as a lack of concern. She didn't have to feign the fatigue that radiated from her, though. "I'm a grown woman, Sam," she said tiredly. *In other words, my business is my business.*

He lifted a hand in acknowledgment. Yes, True demanded respect and positively radiated badassery, and no, she didn't need him to sweep in and save the day. But this was his damned bar, was it not? And for a moment there, Sam had felt sure there was something more going on here than just a scuffle between very opposite-minded people on a bad day. Something that *did* concern him. Fallows never could resist reminding Sam when he was not in on the joke.

He tried a different tack. "You know I don't associate with that man," he said, just as Mel rejoined them on the deck. Because maybe

True needed the reminder. Fallows hadn't darkened the door of the Eddy in ages before this week.

Neither woman argued with him, and maybe he'd imagined it, but had he just caught a quick glance between them? Despite the sticky heat that still clung after the sun had disappeared over the horizon in a fiery show of crimson, something icy slid under his skin. A prickle of foreboding.

He hadn't imagined it. A sheen of fear hung in the air between the two women he cared about most in this world. Was it just the fire? Their worry about Annie? Doubt sluiced through him. PTSD could make him paranoid, he knew this. His childhood could cause him to second-guess the motives of others. He'd spent the better part of his boyhood fighting this feeling, the one that had him cowering in the dark of his bedroom closet as his dad and John hit the lights to duck from the cops, that had him evading teachers' inquisitiveness when he'd shown up at school without sleep, circles of fatigue under his eyes. From the time of his earliest memories, Sam had been the only one, it seemed, waiting perpetually for the other shoe to drop, anxiously listening for the knock on the door, or the phone call that would give bad news, for CPS or the sheriff or the principal. And he was beyond done with all that.

"You'd tell me," he said to them both, hating the weakness he heard in his voice and the vulnerability he felt, "if something was truly wrong here? With . . . him?" Feeling impotent like this always caused shame to burn through him like oil slicking the streets of Kabul.

True shook her head, but didn't glance at Mel again. It felt like a deliberate choice. The sense of foreboding positively ballooned in Sam, prickling every nerve ending. And to think that Mel had just been second-guessing *his* decisions.

"Mel?" Was she protecting True? If so, from what?

He wouldn't be cast back into that place he hated, playing the victim, too weak and small to stand up and walk out of the dark closet that was his childhood. After a decade of trying to make a new name for himself in Carbon, he was finally making some headway. No way was he going to let anyone—even Truitt—drag the Bishop name back into the dirt.

He told himself it couldn't even be a possibility, but that didn't stop the invasive feelings of disloyalty from coming. He was still wrestling with them when Mel's radio on her hip squawked to life.

"Hernandez," she said after glancing at the receiver. A second later, her phone was at her ear. When she lowered it, she looked between True and Sam, anguish written all over her face. "Briefing ASAP at the station. I need to go directly."

Which meant she'd run out of time to see Annie, all because of this mess with Fallows. More confusion wound its way around an echoing regret in Sam. How had she allowed that to happen? How could *he* have? As always, it was hard to know who had dropped the ball, him or Mel. "I'll lock up right now," he told her. "Grab the Goal Zero, and Astor and I will head back."

The lack of smoke shocked his senses as they reentered the now empty Eddy, the tightness in his lungs giving way to an almost painful sense of release.

True cleared her throat loudly. "Listen, you should know, I hate that creep every bit as much as you do." She looked like she meant it. She looked outright miserable, now that Sam really took notice.

"That may not be possible," Mel said quietly.

Sam turned to study her, too. Maybe they were right and it wasn't his place, maybe he was just overreacting again, but something still nagged at him about tonight, and protectiveness prevailed. "You know that old saying 'Keep your friends close, and your enemies closer'?" he asked True earnestly.

She nodded.

"Well, Fallows has no friends."

"I have *no* interest in being his friend."

The solemn promise in her tone settled some of the turmoil in Sam's belly. Still. "The only way to keep your hands clean is to stay far away from that man, True. Mel." Another idiom surfaced. *Lie down with dogs, get up with fleas.*

Before he could recite it, Hernandez interrupted again on the walkie, his voice cutting back through the bar against a background of heavy static. Mel reached quickly to turn down the volume on her radio. She depressed her speak button, requesting a reconfirmation of the latest order.

"I've really got to leave," she said. "I'll just say goodbye to Astor."

But a minute later, when the two of them entered the office, Astor lay curled into Sam's desk chair like a snail in its shell, fast asleep. Her cheek pressed awkwardly into the armrest, puckering her lips into an open-mouthed *O*, and a soft little snore escaped on every exhale. For the first time in days, she looked so childlike, so at peace, that Sam had to stifle a pained sigh.

Mel came to a halt just shy of rousing her. "She never falls asleep this easily."

Sam agreed. It could take Astor hours to settle down on a bad night, and how was tonight anything but? "We should let her rest."

They locked eyes, for the moment in sync again. The nagging doubt faded, and Sam felt just as he had when Mel stepped through the door of the Eddy this evening, enfolded in the comfort of their partnership. It felt right, but . . . "I guess we do have to—"

"I'll stay with her." They both turned at the sound of True's voice; she shifted from foot to foot in her grimy river sandals. "That way you can get back to Annie, Sam." She turned to Mel. "And you can get to the station."

The gesture, so typical of True, snuffed out the lingering uncertainty Sam had felt earlier. He'd been wrong, of course he had. True was as TrueBlue as always. Stepping up once again as a crucial part of their family's team. He nodded as Mel did the same. "If you're sure you'll be okay?"

True's eyes flicked to his, and she didn't reprimand him for trying to play the "knight in shining armor" card this time. On the contrary, her gaze entreated him ever so briefly before flicking away again. For a moment, he thought she was about to ask him something. But then the stalwart woman-against-the-world confidence that he'd learned to expect from her since their Forest Service days returned, and she straightened her shoulders. "Yeah, of course. Just need some shut eye, same as the rest of us."

Near 10:00 p.m., he finally made his way back up Highline through the dark, the flow of traffic that had been trickling down in the afternoon now eerily absent. Anyone who'd planned to leave already had, and anyone remaining would be settling in for the duration, taking comfort in the Level 1 order. All *Sam* wanted to do was to get home now to his younger daughter.

He walked in the door and set down the heavy power cube to see Annie still on the couch, cradled by Claude.

The old man held out a hand in greeting. Or maybe in supplication. "Now, don't worry," he said, "but our *kleines fräulein* isn't doing all that well."

*The little miss.* Sam's heart always gave a little lurch of tenderness at Claude's use of his favorite nickname for Annie, but now it walloped with instantly ramped-up anxiety. He should have been home hours ago. He shouldn't have allowed himself to get distracted, not even by Mel. Because Annie looked an ashen shade of pale blue . . . the telltale sign of an impending tet spell.

He rushed over despite Claude's continued assurances, tugging Ingrid's homemade quilt down from her body to assess her. She protested weakly, popping her thumb out long enough to ask, "Where is Astor, Daddy?"

"She's with True, peanut."

"But *I* wanna be with True," Annie protested.

Of course she did. And thinking of True made Sam's heart lurch again, though it was hard to tell in which direction. That happened to him sometimes; familial obligations and promises entangling hopelessly. He leaned in to kiss Annie's forehead, stealthily attempting to listen for any rasp to her breathing at the same time. Rapid.

She was coughing, too. He did his damnedest to not flinch every time, but it was a losing battle. Had been, actually, from the very first time poor air quality had wreaked havoc on his daughter's fragile respiratory system, several years ago during the Briggs Fire. Watching a three-year-old nearly hack up a lung wasn't a sight Sam wished on anybody, and that fire hadn't gotten within fifty miles of Highline. Tonight was worse. Far worse.

"Maybe we should get the hell out of here," he said to Claude in an undertone. Because doubt gripped him, per usual when it came to this parenting gig. Should he evacuate? Had he made a mistake leaving Astor at the Eddy? At what point did the risk of lung damage outweigh the risk of travel?

"Maybe tomorrow," Claude countered softly, with a pointed look at Annie's pulse oximeter on the side table. His message was clear: Annie's vitals did not warrant a road trip. At least not tonight.

But Sam had to see for himself. How else could he possibly make the impossible decisions that were thrust at him every waking moment during this fire? With a nod of understanding, Claude turned the oximeter on and waited for the beep that would indicate it was ready to measure Annie's oxygen levels again. Opening and closing its little jaws, he made a path through the air toward Annie's finger while Sam paced the living room, trying to peer out the windows.

"What do you think? Should we let Pac-Man gobble you up again?"

Annie giggled, a weak little sound. When the oximeter beeped again, he turned around.

Claude shook his head. "As I said."

*Please,* Sam thought, *don't let this turn into a tet spell.* Though if it did, they had power to run her O2 here at the house, he reminded himself. They still had refrigerated meds and syringes. And now they had the Goal Zero. Claude was right. Keeping Annie here, where all her medical gear stood at the ready, remained the right move.

Annie coughed again, right on cue, and Claude retrieved the N95 mask she hated so from the table. "When she's not on the O2, this should help some," he said, still frowning.

After he fit it on her little face, Annie stared back at them with wide brown eyes—her mother's eyes.

"Better, right?" Sam asked, and Annie nodded gamely enough, offering a clumsy thumbs-up. She was such an obedient, optimistic kid. Even while fighting for breath. Even at midnight. Did all the surgeries and doctor's visits instinctively cause his younger daughter to be more pliant, Sam wondered? Take the smoother path? Choose the least resistance? Sam scoffed at himself—what a bunch of psychobabble—but still, overhearing so much gloom and doom, even though he and Mel tried to keep it from her, had to impact a five-year-old's malleable psyche.

Claude doled out Annie's prescriptions and helped her swallow the syrupy liquid while Sam eyed the remaining medication left in each plastic bottle. They were due for a refill, but when he'd noticed earlier this week, he hadn't called it in. No point in asking for refills when you couldn't pay.

"Cuddle with me, Daddy," Annie interrupted, offering him a corner of her quilt.

Sam exchanged one last pointed look with Claude, then leaned down to scoop her up.

"I'll do you one better," he told her as Claude saw himself out with a promise to return at first light. "How about you sleep with me in Daddy's big bed tonight?"

"Like . . . a slumber party?"

"Exactly."

Setting her onto the king bed, Sam lay down on top of the comforter Mel had bought half a decade ago, trying to allow Annie's presence to ground him. His daughters were his stability, as crazy as that sounded, given Annie's condition. His magnetic north, pointing him toward a sense of purpose. And knowing his purpose usually calmed Sam.

Tonight, this calm was short-lived, as Annie tugged away her O2 mask and succumbed to another fit of coughing. Sam patted her back softly, just as he'd done for her as an infant and as a toddler. Just as he'd seen Claude do. It never got easier.

It would forever feel unnervingly unnatural to him, watching a small child catch her breath after only a few minutes of play, watching her seek out a seat to sit quietly while the world spun along without her participation.

"It's to be expected, nothing out of the ordinary in her condition," all the specialists told them. They educated the Bishops with graphs and maps of the human heart, illustrated the path of oxygenated blood through the network of arteries and veins spanning throughout Annie's body. "You see how much more effort it takes?" they all pointed out. "You see how much harder her heart has to work? Normal for her. All normal."

Yes, Sam saw. And there was nothing normal about it. Becoming educated on the anatomy of the human heart made it intrinsically worse, somehow, knowing exactly why Annie felt so winded. Knowing exactly what was broken inside her.

Only True seemed immune from coddling Annie. Picking her up without a care in the world, she tossed her on her back like a sack of potatoes, not like the fragile specimen everyone else saw, and gave her a piggyback ride to whatever next activity eluded her. She said things like "C'mon, kid, let's go," not "Do you need another rest, Annie?" She expected her to keep up with Astor, to take on both hiding *and* seeking when they played, to get her oar in the water whenever she took them out on the river for a day trip. If anyone was pampered by True, it was Mel, not Annie. Oh, Sam suspected why, but not a day went by that True didn't act classy about it. Besides, could Sam blame her?

Was Mel finally getting some sleep at the station tonight? As Annie's breathing grew more rhythmic, he checked his phone. Two missed calls. He texted Mel back with a thumbs-up and an *Annie okay for the night*, too tired and frustrated to do more before falling into a dreamless sleep.

# CHAPTER 20

*July 12*
*6:00 a.m.*

Thirty-six hours after the spark that ignited the Flatiron Fire set the week on an entirely new trajectory, True woke to a radio report citing that the blaze still raged at under 20 percent containment, with weather that continued to defy normal heat and humidity levels.

*Just rain already,* she thought fervently, rising from her Paco Pad next to Astor in the Eddy office to peer out through the gloom of the deck. They'd been too exhausted last night to even make their way to Sam's apartment upstairs. The events of the evening came back to her like a bad dream. Fallows, threatening them. Sam . . . God, the look of suspicion on Sam's face, the potential for outright disappointment waiting in the wings behind it, had cast her right back to the bank of the Outlaw, seeing that same expression on Vivian. Was she destined to let down everyone she cared about in the same twenty-four hours? If so, she guessed she could count on wronging Mel next.

Which had her staring out in the direction of the river corridor again, trying to read the weather. Was it a trick of the low, hazy light, or had the sky grown overcast somewhere above the smoke? Rain could be a blessing, but it could also come with lightning, and more lightning was the last thing Carbon needed right now.

She'd promised Astor her famous river pancakes, complete with Nutella, so she returned to the kitchen to hunt up ingredients, determined to stay in the good graces of at least one Bishop, trying hard not to think about making these for Emmett and Vivian just days before. She'd volunteered to stay over with Astor because she loved the kid and wanted to help Sam and Mel, but also because she'd dreaded the idea of being left alone to ruminate on what couldn't be.

She'd just dumped the Bisquick into a bowl when the Eddy door creaked open, the unexpected intrusion causing the box to slip from her fingers. Pancake powder puffed in a cloud around her face.

"It's just me."

"Shit. Mel. You scared me."

But the fear only settled in more adamantly when True turned to face her. Mel had bad news. She just knew it. "What?"

"I just came from my morning briefing. As the Flatiron Fire spreads, it looks like it's heading south by southwest, as I feared, which means—"

"The Outlaw," True supplied in a resigned whisper, the name of her beloved river tight in her throat. "God, Mel, it's bad enough for the river road to close, but if firefighters are actively—"

"I know," Mel hissed. "I know." Her voice was even tighter than True's, maybe even close to tears. The stress was consuming both of them, and Mel probably wouldn't admit it, but the loss of Sam's trust had to be eating away at her, too.

True rounded the corner of the bar to place her hands on Mel's shoulders. She was back in fresh yellows, the heavy fabric rough under True's palms. "Just breathe. We'll think of a plan."

Mel shook her head wildly. "You heard Fallows." She mimicked his crude drawl. "There is no Plan B." She looked up at True. "If the ammo box fails to show, we'll never see this last payoff needed to keep Annie current with her meds. She needs refills as it is."

Closure or no closure, fire or no fire, True would not let that scenario come to pass. Even if her hands were as tied as everyone else's. "Then we'll come up with a Plan B of our own."

"I don't see how."

"If the fire's actively threatening the river corridor, maybe I can get a rapid tag for my place. Access the river that way." The county-issued tags allowed evacuated homeowners back onto restricted roads and property to retrieve possessions and assess damage. Of course—

"You know those are only for use *after* a fire," Mel said, shaking her head again. "Not to go *into* one."

True laid her eyes on Mel unflinchingly as she repeated herself. "Still. Maybe I can get a rapid tag *now*."

Mel stared back at her, her expression uncomprehending. Was her sense of protocol so entrenched she couldn't make the leap? When comprehension did dawn, Mel didn't look pleased. "I can't possibly," she snapped. "It's a danger to you, True." She swallowed. "There has to be another way."

If there was, True sure as hell didn't see it. Even when Mel left again for the station after rousing Astor to say good morning, True couldn't figure any other way to get to Temple Bar to retrieve the ammo box before the fire—or anyone else for that matter—beat her to it. She called Sam to assure him all was well, got an update on Annie—holding steady, though last night was touch and go—and settled Astor in front of *Jurassic Park*, the only DVD stuck in Sam's ancient office TV/DVD combo. She set back to work on the pancakes, her mind still churning through—and discarding—options. She was busy beating the batter within an inch of its life when she heard Astor's voice rising over the sound of the TV in the office. A sound of surprise, followed by the quieter murmuring of conversation.

Had Mel returned? Maybe she'd rethought the rapid tag.

True dropped the first batch of pancakes on the griddle and hurried to the office, her heart already warming to the thought. Instead, the sight that met her at the doorway made her blood run cold.

John Fallows, in the flesh. But all True could focus on was the fact that he was touching *Astor's* flesh, his arms encircling her as he playfully covered her eyes as a raptor attack played out on the TV.

"Get the hell away from her!"

Though forceful, True's voice sounded oddly distant to her ears. Detached from her body somehow. Her limbs were stiff, too, like she suddenly couldn't move. But she would, oh yes she would, if she had to. *When* she had to.

"Tsk, tsk. You'll scare the girl," Fallows drawled.

But Astor was already scared. Astor, whom True had taught to sit tall and take no prisoners, had shrunken in on herself, shoulders curled forward as if to put as many inches between her body and this man's—this adult man's—as she could.

True's sudden presence seemed to give Astor the permission she'd been waiting for. She shrugged out from Fallows's arms with a little yelp of relief, then scurried over to press herself against True's side as though she hoped to infuse herself there.

*Oh, Astor.* True put an arm around her but didn't take her eyes off Fallows. "What do you think you're doing? How did you get in here?"

She wasn't sure which question she wanted answered first, but it didn't matter; Fallows was in no hurry to fill her in. He barely turned his gaze from the TV as the raptor attack faded out. "Honey. Like I was telling Mini-Mel here, Uncle John just wanted to check in."

"Is he really my uncle?" Astor asked in a whisper from under True's armpit.

True's gaze remained laser-focused on Fallows. "No. He's nothing to you."

"Semantics," Fallows chuckled; then he coughed. From the kitchen, a strong smell of burning hit True's nose, accompanied by a waft of smoke.

The pancakes.

As if cued to action, the shriek of the smoke detector sounded from the hallway.

"I'll go," Astor said instantly, already turning heel and sprinting for the kitchen. True knew she knew the drill, thanks to hours at the grill with her dad. Turn off the burner, grab a dishcloth, and start fanning the smoke for all she was worth.

Which left True alone with Fallows. "I already told you everything I know last night," she shouted over the incessant sound of the alarm. "So I'll only ask you one more time. Why are you here?"

Fallows smiled, displaying a mouthful of dental neglect. "Because I can be." He rose and crossed the room, not stopping until he stood just inches from True's face. It took everything in her to resist being the one to step back and concede space. Even when Fallows leaned in and whispered in her ear, his lips brushing her lobe, she stood her ground, feet planted. "I can be anywhere I want to be. At any time. Here. At your cute little abode on the river." He jutted his chin back toward the Paco Pad, where Astor had settled in to watch the movie minutes before. "Even in a Bishop baby's sleeping bag."

"You fucker, I'll—"

"True!" a new voice called out over the continued wail of the stubborn smoke-detector alarm, accompanied by a pounding at the front Eddy door. "Sam? Anyone in there?"

Kim. She'd probably heard the alarm from her place next door.

"Right in here!" True yelled, with some relish, right in Fallows's face.

He finally took a step back. From the kitchen, she heard a few harried words between Kim and Astor, and the alarm went abruptly silent.

Knowing that Kim was now at Astor's side gave True a boost of confidence. "I will call the cops—"

He laughed, the sound mean and tight. "No, you won't."

Confidence dashed. "I'll get your damned money," she whispered.

"Bingo." He tapped her nose with one finger, none too softly, either. "You catch on pretty quick for washed-up river trash."

True didn't have time to react before Kim was in the doorway, brow furrowed, the scowl on her face punctuating her deep dislike of Fallows. "What's going on here? Astor said something was wrong."

With one arm, she barred Astor entry back into the office. "No, hon, you stay back."

Fallows finally slunk around True, patting Astor on the head as he slipped through the door. Kim pulled her back to give him a wide berth.

"Keep your panties on, ladies. I was just leaving."

Ten minutes later, the griddle still smoldering, the remaining pancake mix now concrete in the bowl, the image of Fallows looming over Astor still played across True's brain.

"I'm okay," Astor promised for the third time. "Pinkie swear." Her proud chin tilt was back, an encouraging sign. "I'm tough, like you."

"I know you are." True looked her goddaughter in the eye. "But, Astor, you shouldn't always have to be." And neither should she, fear and guilt for having left Astor alone for even a second, susceptible to being cornered by Fallows, notwithstanding.

Astor considered this. "Well, I know how to turn off the smoke alarm, but this time I decided it was maybe juuust too high for me to reach," she added slyly, with a trace of ego.

True laughed shakily, despite herself. "You clever girl, you."

As soon as enough of the fear and adrenaline had drained from her body for righteous anger to set in, she called Mel from the smoky Eddy deck.

"I still think the rapid-tag idea is too risky," Mel said immediately upon picking up.

True didn't waste time arguing with her. "Fallows was here," she told her. "He threatened Astor."

Mel's tone shifted in an instant, the effect reminding True of a false bottom suddenly falling out of a floor. "*What?* Did he hurt her? Is she all right?"

"She's all right, but Mel?" True waited until she had her full attention. "This is bigger than just getting paid for the delivery now. It's even bigger than helping Annie. We have to protect *both* the girls. And to do that, it's time to go on the offensive."

"What is that supposed to mean?"

"Just that we stop reacting to every move Fallows makes, and start making a few ourselves."

Silence stretched on the other end of the line for what felt like a full ten seconds before Mel said in a rush, "I left a rapid tag under the napkin dispensers by the cash register. It was supposed to be just in case."

But True was already on the hunt, tilting dispensers until she felt the hard cardstock of the tag beneath her fingers. "I got this, Mel. I'll get the ammo box, and I'll get Fallows off our backs."

And away from anyone with the last name of Bishop.

# CHAPTER 21

Mel disconnected the call with shaky fingers, True's words ringing in her ears. *Go on the offensive.* With True, that could mean anything, and Mel's nerves were already shot: Fallows's relentlessness at the Eddy last night had put her out of sync with Sam again just when she'd been rediscovering the groove of their partnership, punctuating her disloyalty in a way that made her loathe what she needed to do all the more. And now, outside the station window at Carbon Rural, a seemingly endless line of trucks bore down the highway into Carbon. Reinforcements in the form of privatized hand crews.

Local traffic had given way, and despite the uncomfortable cocktail of heat, smoke, and humidity, people in N95 masks or handkerchiefs watched the progression of the out-of-town crews from the sidewalk. Cutting through the sound of the engines, car horns honked in support.

*Bring in the cavalry,* Mel thought ruefully. She always had to work to not resent crews like this for their abundant overpay and bonuses she could only dream of. It wasn't like she could apply to join them as they hopped from state to state, playing the hero; she was away from Astor and Annie enough as it was. Besides, Carbon Rural couldn't exactly afford to turn down the help.

"Best for all just to try to get along," Hernandez told the Carbon crew over a hasty breakfast, confirming that the wildland experts with the USFS and Oregon Wildfire Response and Recovery had officially taken over command. Hand-crew teams from Dust Busters, Firestorm, and Flashback Fire had reported for duty, along with the first hotshot crew, arriving from as far as Flagstaff. "But Carbon Rural has been invaluable," Hernandez said. "With the help of the Outlaw and Eagle Valley crews, we've contained what we can close to town."

"Which means it's time to take the fight to the river corridor," Mel interjected.

White didn't miss the chance to shoot Hernandez a look, and Mel bit her lip. True was rubbing off on her. "Sir," she added weakly.

Hernandez sighed. "Your sense of urgency is valid, Bishop." He looked around the table. "And I doubt you're the only one sick of playing defense."

"Up against the ropes, more like," Deklan mumbled.

Hernandez actually chuckled as he checked his watch and rose from his chair, probably already due at another interagency meeting or press release. "You'll be happy to hear, then, that I've been ordered to send a team down the river road today," he said.

Mel sat up straighter. "The full length of the road?" If she could get downriver, maybe True wouldn't have to mess with the rapid tag after all.

"At least the section that runs parallel to the south bank of the Outlaw, opposite the fire. Maybe even on the north bank when the road crosses Wonderland Bridge. That a problem?"

"Not at all." A bit of the extra weight that had settled onto her shoulders lifted. One fewer person in danger meant one fewer complication, not to mention one less way she'd let Sam down this week.

"We'll knock on doors, encourage proactive evacs, and help the hand crews hold the line." Hernandez turned to his second-in-command. "White? I'll leave it to you to assign duties; then FEMA has requested we set up a remote command near the closure area."

White started making noise about being so far from the action as Mel felt herself deflate. With her least-favorite superior in charge, she'd never get the assignment she asked for.

Ryan held up his hand. "Wait. So closing the river road wasn't just a precaution? My folks are gonna freak."

Lewis gave Ryan a sympathetic nod as Hernandez left the room. It was every local's worst fear during smoke season, especially those with small businesses, like the Sloans, who were hoping their son would follow them into the fly-fishing game after he got this firefighting thing out of his system.

Or like Sam. Or True.

Mel glimpsed a rare, shared look of maturity pass between Ryan and Deklan. They were starting to get it: forest fires made far more lasting impressions than simply a scarred land and inspired far more sobering anecdotes than the boastings of rookie ground pounders.

"So where will we be assigned?" Deklan asked White cautiously.

"I'd love to help mobilize the crews from the command center," Mel cut in carefully. Because if she knew White . . .

White's head swiveled to her. "You're next-in-command, Bishop. I need you to head up the crew in the field while I man the command center."

*Well, that was easy.*

"You'll take Lewis and the volunteers," White continued. Under his breath, as they all pushed out from the table, he added, "You can babysit our rookies."

She called True back as they loaded up. "Don't use the tag," she told her. "I can get the ammo box."

"What? How?"

"We're rolling out now. River road. It will place me closer than I think your rapid tag can."

"But how will you . . . ?" True trailed off.

"I'll find a way."

They departed Carbon at 0700 in a small convoy, keeping parallel to the fire while the hotshots from Arizona utilized whatever resources were at their disposal (a.k.a. whichever they damn well pleased, Janet muttered) to attack the blaze from the air before it hit the federally protected Wild and Scenic section of the Outlaw. They'd already commissioned a water tanker from the Outlaw airport and planned to scoop water from the ranches and properties with ponds.

Like Claude's, Mel thought, picturing the old man's acreage on Highline adjacent to Sam's, with its carefully tended garden and duck pond used for irrigation. She imagined the boots that would soon trample down the marsh surrounding the pretty little pond, the hotshots tossing their packs and mud-caked gear on the oak bench on which Claude had hand-carved a memorial for Ingrid.

She redirected her focus from the hotshots to her own assignment. The sooner she completed her task, the sooner she could detour to Temple Bar to retrieve the ammo box, and the sooner she could get Fallows's boot off the backs of their necks. At least while the fight, as she'd put it, was here in the river corridor, it was not up on Highline. Level 1 status there would hold.

She gripped the wheel of the command truck she'd been assigned and leaned forward into the next curve as her volunteer riding shotgun, an old-timer everyone just called Sly, braced a hand on the dash. He'd signed on with Carbon Rural after his wife told him he was driving her crazy in retirement, underfoot all the time. Deklan and Ryan rode in the back bench seat. A wildland fire engine followed; in a rare show of generosity, White had assigned them one of the good ones, she'd noticed, the West-Mark that had just come out of the shop last week. Lewis rode shotgun in it, their driver engineer—Carlos today—at the wheel. One of the two hand crews trailed about an hour behind them, tasked with burning more backfires closest to where the blaze edged toward the river. Mel's crew's containment lines further downriver would serve as insurance, hopefully never needed.

A stack of rapid tags sat in Deklan's lap, ready to be delivered to the often antisocial and sometimes downright hostile residents of the off-the-grid homes out here, their green cardboard practically glowing after her debate with True. As a last resort, the tags would be affixed to the front doors, and Deklan shuffled them absently like a deck of cards as they bumped along the rural road. The rhythmic slap of them against his leg echoed in the quiet cab, playing on Mel's nerves. She'd assured them all this mission would run like clockwork. *So much so that their battalion chief can slip away for about an hour to run a personal errand at Temple Bar?* She sure as hell hoped so.

"You get enough sleep, kiddo?" Mel asked, tossing Deklan a backward glance. With the river road officially closed, she didn't have to check her speed as she would normally; no opposing traffic should surprise them on the hairpin turns.

"I dunno. I guess."

"After he finally got to call his mommy," Ryan supplied with an elbow into Deklan's rib cage.

"She was worried, okay? The wildland volunteer website never gets updated. Sheesh. Sorry someone loves me."

"Someone loves me, too," Ryan shot back with a dumb grin. "My girlfriend. She loves me so good, I—"

"We all know there's no girlfriend," Mel interjected, earning her a chuckle of amusement from Sly. He hadn't been subjected to the Deklan-Ryan show much yet and was in for a treat.

Luckily, *she* could tune them out, because even without traffic on the river road, driving now demanded her full attention. Just ten miles into the thirty that led to Temple Bar, the smoke had thickened, funneled as it was into the narrowing river canyon. This road—originally intended only for loggers—proved dangerous in good conditions, the way it wove right to the edge of the river in some places, crazily climbing in elevation to return to the ridgeline in others. The last time they'd driven a wildland rig out here, the heavy-duty tires and weighty engine had sent scree tumbling down the embankment toward the river on the tightest of the turns, the near nonexistent shoulder of the road providing little to no room for error. She was sure that behind them, the West-Mark engine was sending even more debris downhill today, Lewis navigating less cautiously than on a training run. Mel tempered her own speed, hoping it would encourage prudence.

They drove another mile or so at a crawl before starting another downhill descent as the road eased closer to the river bottom.

"Ah, shiiit," Deklan said.

Now that they were well below town, they could follow the Flatiron Fire's progress; it burned bright over their right shoulder as they drove, on the slope on the far side of the river. Just like at Highline, ash spun in the wind, obscuring their view out the windshield if the wipers weren't on full blast. Mel experimented with the headlights: Full brightness? Or dimmed as in a snowstorm, so as not to reflect the flakes of ash, turning them from sooty gray to bright white?

"At least it can't jump the Outlaw," Deklan noted as they approached the first of the many mountain streams that fed into the river. They'd arrived at one of True's favorite first-night camping spots, Antelope Creek. The fire burned on both sides of the creek on the north bank with effortless abandon, but Deklan was right: the wide Outlaw indeed stopped the path from reaching the south shore.

"But there's plenty of reason to stop it on the north bank, too," Mel let him know. Wonderland Lodge sat on that bank. More than a few fishing cabins. And after the river road crossed from the south side of the Outlaw to the north at Wonderland Bridge, it led directly to the take-out area at Temple Bar.

"When are we gonna cross over and fight it?" Ryan wanted to know. Mel noted he sounded less eager than he and his rookie friends had two days ago.

"Not until evacs are completed over here on *this* side," Mel said. "The hotshot teams are already on it, as well as several hand crews. We're going to follow the orders we were given." *At least, you boys are.*

"Wait, so we're gonna drive right past the fire, over here on the south bank?" Deklan wanted to know.

Mel nodded. "We'll eventually get out ahead of it so we can cut a containment near Wonderland, but we'll be knocking on doors first."

"Perfectly safe," Sly grunted. He turned to Mel. "That's what I told Doris, and that's what it'll be, right?"

"Right," she promised, even while inwardly flinching.

"Like we were perfectly safe cutting that containment on the slope of Flatiron?" Deklan noted dryly.

His observation was spot-on, of course. Every firefighter knew not to promise anything to anyone. Caution kept you alive. Assuming the worst worked in your favor. No one answered for a beat. "You're right to keep your guard up," Mel conceded to Deklan. She hoped Ryan was listening, too. "Never know what the wind will bring, right?"

She chanced another glance in the rearview mirror to see Deklan swallow and Ryan's cocky grin fully disappear. "Right," they echoed.

For the majority of the morning, they kept abreast of the fire, driving parallel to the blaze along the river road all the way to Devil's Drop, the last of the smaller rapids before Quartz Canyon. It took them far longer than Mel had anticipated to veer onto every private dirt road, ignoring the *Private Property, No Trespassing,* and *No Hunting* signs posted on trees and stakes at each long dirt driveway to knock on doors. Had there always been so many folks living out here?

"Halllooo?" Mel called out at each property, running her siren in one quick bleep of warning before allowing Deklan and Ryan to exit the truck to approach the houses. These were precisely the type of homesteaders most likely to shoot first and ask questions later if a couple of teens crossed to their door without invitation. Their homesteads were mainly comprised of double-wides littered with junk cars, very few of them resembling anything close to True's carefully curated yurt studio.

Of course, Mel doubted *anyone* put such deliberate care into their home, except maybe Sam. The first time Mel had seen True's place, the vulnerability laid bare on her face, watching Mel take it all in, had almost been too damned hard to look at, like squinting into direct sunlight. *The Outsider.* Mel hated that name. It made her ache for that tender part of True, the part that, no matter what True said to the contrary, no matter what brave front she put up, wanted it all. Mel wished she could tell her the same thing she told Sam: it wasn't a "build it and

Amy Hagstrom

they will come" situation. Life threw curveballs, and no amount of river rock or solar panels could change that.

"Clear, Chief!" Deklan called out now, and Mel let the sight of the front porch of yet another dilapidated homestead wash the image of True's yurt from her consciousness. Deklan affixed a green rapid tag and descended the sagging porch steps, leaping much like a monkey himself as he returned to the truck.

All of these properties sat empty, thank goodness, save for a few animals. While Deklan and Ryan continued to affix tags to each door, Sly and Mel called in a few to Animal Control—livestock still contained in barns and stalls, mostly—knowing the department would be making rounds as soon as they were cleared to drive the river road. Deklan attempted to chase down a few panicked dogs, all of whom escaped capture.

"They'll be fine," Mel assured the boys, even while swallowing her own misgivings. What could she do? She had to keep her priorities straight. Animals tended to flee; the dogs would undoubtedly find a drainage pipe or irrigation ditch to cower in, where they had as good a chance as most.

"These all pot farms?" Deklan asked, climbing back into the battalion chief truck after clearing a ramshackle cabin deep in a tangle of overgrown forest.

Mel eyed the dense vegetation, excellent camouflage back in the day when the Feds combed these woods looking for hidden grow sites. "Must be." It explained the increase in farms out here, off the grid. "At least, this place probably is." She wondered how often search and rescue and the sheriff's department had been here in the past few years, checking on compliance with state regulation.

"Wouldn't kill 'em to clear the ground of undergrowth," Deklan observed, kicking at the layer of brittle pine needles blanketing the dirt drive.

"Bad for business," Mel told him tightly, "once upon a time. Now, these farmers are just lazy." *Or growing far more than is legal, in order to*

210

*sell commercially to the cartels on the I-5 corridor.* The Fallowses being the worst offenders, of course.

"Oh yeah," Deklan said. "I forgot weed didn't used to be legal and stuff."

"Whelp," Sly grunted from the front seat, as mention of illegal grow caused Mel's mind to flit to Fallows, and then to Astor and the fear she must have felt this morning. She shut that thought right back down. If she fixated on that now, Mel would be unable to do her job. And if she couldn't do her job, she wouldn't collect the ammo box. She wouldn't get her payout. Annie wouldn't get her prescription. Every terrible thread of Mel's reality was knotted to the next, in a seemingly endless tangle.

They continued to pick their way along the river road, listening, over the sound of their own engines, to the intermittent buzz of chain saws across the water—one of the hand crews at work on firebreaks closer to the blaze—and watching the regular rain of Phos-Chek falling from the sky from the planes that circled the air, releasing the rust-colored fire retardant onto the flames like that saffron-tinted powder thrown at the Holi festival True had taken her to in Portland once. They were making good use of the daylight, but the task seemed never-ending. So much for Mel's optimistic promise to retrieve the ammo box from Temple Bar today. At this rate, she'd be lucky to make it that far southwest by this time tomorrow.

They made it another five miles downriver over the afternoon, and when the persistent flicker of flame over their right shoulders finally dipped out of sight in a cloud of smoke, leaving them with a view of only ash-gray forest instead, Deklan sighed in relief.

"And . . . we're officially ahead of the Flatiron Fire. About time, too."

"This means Wonderland Lodge is still standing over on the north bank?" Ryan asked, peering through the windshield in an attempt to spot it.

He wouldn't. Not in this smoke. "Yes, it's there," Mel told him, "and should remain standing, after we cut a containment line." They'd set up camp here on the south side of the narrow, one-lane Wonderland Bridge, built to last from the CCC days, where it was safest.

Mel eyed the bloodred sun, angry against a dark sky, and thought of True, standing not far from here across the river only the day before, asking for Henry Martin's mercy. She thought next of Astor, braving this disaster without her mother. Of Annie, with her father.

Never since her separation had Mel wanted to be with them more, all together at the house on Highline, its weather-sealed windows keeping the wolves—in all forms—at bay.

# CHAPTER 22

*July 13*
*5:00 a.m.*

True got up with the sun, or what she could see of it, which was essentially zero. The rapid tag had been burning a hole in her pocket all night. Longer, really . . . ever since Mel had assured her that she could gain access to Temple Bar herself.

She'd delivered Astor back to Sam at Highline yesterday afternoon; as True expected, Sam had gone white as she'd described what she could of their interaction with Fallows at the Eddy.

"I don't understand," he said, peppering Astor with questions. "Are you hurt? What did he say to you? Why was he back there? None of this makes sense."

True shot him a look. "Don't interrogate her, Sam," she said in an undertone. With every word, she could see Astor reliving the ugly encounter. And it was *True's* fault the animosity had been stirred back up between the Bishops and Fallows. True's and Mel's. The guilt felt thick enough to reach up through her gut and choke her. What if Astor internalized blame, too?

But before she departed, Sam pulled True aside again by the door. "That confrontation last night, and now this . . . Fallows has never shown the least interest in my kids. Thank God," he added. "So why now?" His expression clouded just as it had at the Eddy,

Sam sensing something didn't add up. She'd been privy to the same look whenever Sam confided in her about his marriage. Why wasn't it working? What had he done wrong? Why did two and two never add up to four?

It wrenched at her gut. "Stop it," she begged him. "You'll never make sense of Fallows, Sam." It was true, just not as true as her own culpability. "I should have been more diligent with Astor," she added. "It's unforgivable, and I'm so sorry, Sam."

She squared her shoulders, preparing herself for more blame, but instead, Sam palmed his own skull, raking his fingers roughly through his hair. "I should have known he'd slink back around. I should never have left." He looked over at True, and she sensed him wrestling with something again. She feared more questions, but in the end, he said, "Just . . . stay away from that man, True," his voice thick with defeat. "Please."

Instead, True had entertained every fantasy she could dream up for how to get to Fallows and make him suffer for what he'd done to Astor while Mel took care of the ammo box. The problem was, no matter how inventive her imagined revenge, it didn't change the fact that she and Mel were still puppets on a string. A warning of Sam's echoed in True's brain. *Fallows would sacrifice anyone.*

But what had Fallows himself told her? *I protect my assets.* True would bet money someone was still holed up at his property, tasked with defending it from fire. Even more than a few someones . . . seasonal trimmers, undocumented ag workers . . . maybe even Fallows himself.

While Mel retrieved the ammo box, True could utilize her rapid tag to gain entry to the river and the Outsider, positioning herself perfectly for a faster, and hopefully final, handoff.

With any luck, she told herself this could all be over today. Not that luck had exactly been flowing down the river corridor this week.

Mel eased out of her sleeping bag on the hard ground across the Outlaw from Wonderland Lodge. She was instantly alert, her priorities already splintered cleanly in two: today, her crew could finally tackle this blaze in earnest, now that evacs had been issued, and *she* could finally find a way to continue down the river road to Temple Bar.

She stood and shook out her sleeping bag, a sprawl of firefighting humanity at her feet: dirt and soot-encrusted, mustard-yellow-shirted bodies lying prone atop unzipped bags on the dewy ground. Her own crew members lay sprawled next to private Dust Busters and Firestorm crews; only the hotshots, Mel knew, would have segregated from the rest. She could glimpse their neatly rolled bags about fifty yards away, already strapped to their packs in anticipation of another strenuous day with their own specialized agendas.

She nudged Lewis gently with the heel of her boot as she rose, just to make sure he got up to help her unearth the MREs from the truck cab, then made her way between sleeping bags to the back of an outbuilding. Squatting behind cover, she relieved herself.

When the rest of the crew began to stir as the sun made a weak attempt to show between the hazy pine boughs over the river, Mel tossed her own share of the morning rations toward Deklan and Ryan, who accepted the unexpected generosity with twin whoops. Teenagers were always hungry, even when faced with ravaging wildfire. Mel, however, seemed to have lost her appetite.

At 0600, they got an update from the overnight hand crew: *She's keeping us busy on the west side. Gonna finish this line, then move toward you as conditions permit.* Mel read the update aloud to Lewis, then waved her crew in for a morning debriefing. Giving her next orders was easy: they needed to cut an insurance line here at Wonderland, then make sure the access road stayed clear of debris, so the hand crews and hotshots could move their way downriver. At the mention of clearing the road, Deklan cast an eager eye toward the truck panel storing their power saws. "Not so fast. The line, remember? You'll need your Pulaski first, kid."

"Yeah, yeah," he muttered, already rubbing at his sore biceps. He tugged his Buff up over his face to block both the smoke and his sour expression.

They'd cross as a unit back over the bridge to the fire-plagued north bank to cut the containment line needed just east of Wonderland Lodge, for the purpose of protecting the building listed on the National Registry of Historic Places. If time permitted, White informed them via radio from his position at the command station closer to town, they could work their way back upriver until they met the hand crew, which Mel estimated should be somewhere near True's property in the acreage between Buck Peak and the river. Mel hoped to God she wasn't there, utilizing the rapid tag she had been assured she didn't need, but knowing True . . . Mel pushed back the thought. Busy as they were with all hands on, and this deep in the river corridor, she had no way of knowing. Just as she had no way of knowing how Annie was faring this morning up on the hill at Highline, where Astor even was at this point, any of it.

*Trust Sam,* she told herself. Whenever her work had to take over—to pay the bills, to have insurance—she'd always had to, hadn't she? Even when they'd been at their worst. What were they now?

"What do we think of this weather?" Lewis asked, cutting in and saving her from rhetorical—not to mention redundant—thoughts as they all filled their canteens and loaded their packs. He frowned as he glanced upward at the dense smoke.

Mel looked up at the sky. Lost in her own agenda, she hadn't paid the weather any attention. It had to already be at least eighty degrees, and even more humid than the night before. Sure, humidity in and of itself could help their cause, but . . .

"You thinking fireclouds, Lewis?" Hernandez asked, confirming Mel's worry.

"What's a firecloud?" Ryan asked, his skeptical tone suggesting he figured Lewis was pulling his leg. Of course, that was José's MO, but their driver engineer's duties lay elsewhere today.

"It's what you fart after eating all those MREs," Deklan guffawed, subbing in.

"It's when smoke rises, then condenses in the upper atmosphere," Mel supplied. "The water already in the atmosphere combines with water evaporating from the burning trees and brush, forming a dense cloud called a pyrocumulus, or firecloud."

"In other words, a hot mess . . . literally," Lewis supplied.

"But not, like, made of fire . . ." Ryan's sentence trailed off, doubt adding an upward lilt to his voice that probably hadn't been heard since puberty.

"'Course not, dumbass," Deklan said. "This isn't World of Warcraft." But he turned to Lewis all the same. "Right?"

He made it a point to keep his own tone even, but everyone could hear the trepidation that crept around the corner of his question.

Sly slapped him on the back. "Hey now, since when has a cloud ever hurt anybody?" he said with obvious false cheer. "It may lead to rain."

*Or more lightning.* Mel clamped her mouth shut hard on the word.

"Plus," Sly continued, "those hotshots are pros. They'll have things under control." More baloney he'd promised Doris to set her mind at ease, no doubt, but Mel let it go.

Lewis snagged the water bottle midair to drop it back into Deklan's hands. "So stop fooling around and get ready to roll out."

Mel's own mission would be harder to accomplish. And she was acutely aware that if everything didn't go exactly right, it could compromise her team. Even cost her her job. She swallowed hard. Even when it was hell, even when she felt pulled impossibly far away from her kids, she *needed* this job. Her whole family did.

But then she thought of True, risking exposure and even arrest out on the river each week, and her resolve strengthened, even if her nerves still churned as she ran her toothbrush under a conservative stream of water from their Gatorade jug mounted on the side of the engine. She dipped her head under the flow next, for only the count of three seconds before hastily shutting it off and running her hands through her hair, slicking back strands still stiff with dust-caked sweat. And to think she'd just had a shower yesterday morning at the station.

She sat down heavily in the passenger seat of the truck cab, toying with the radio, worrying the thick cord between her fingers. Thinking. *Scheming, more like.* She slammed one hand down hard on the dash in a sudden burst of frustration, making herself jump at the violent yet satisfying crack. *Dammit.* Mel hated what she had to do.

There was no way around it, far as she could see: getting away from her team would require a lie. Two lies, she forced herself to amend, one outright to Lewis, her second-in-command out here, when she told him Hernandez had called her away on a side job, and another of omission to whoever Lew told her to take with her, enabling her to disregard Carbon Rural's buddy system. She'd never thought she'd see the day.

*I'm doing this for my family,* she reminded herself fiercely as she dug into the MRE stash to count out rations. Out of the corner of her eye, she could see Lewis refilling the water jugs. Doing his duty, unaware that his colleague, his comrade in arms, planned to shirk hers. Mel forced herself to think of Annie at her worst: hooked up to machines, disappearing on a rolling gurney down long, shiny hospital corridors, her body impossibly tiny under a thin sheet. *I'm doing this to protect the girls and True.* Because where would her best friend be if Mel failed to retrieve the ammo box and its contents? She thought of Fallows's ominous presence at the bar and doubled down on her resolve.

They rolled out on foot, Mel leading her crew over the bridge and up the embankment on the slope adjacent to the lodge. When she looked back, the tired-looking souls trudging after her in a stoic line made for a sorry sight. "Here's good," she called out eventually, after the last of the rookies had crossed the dirt access road leading into Wonderland. They'd use this road as a launching point for the containment line that would protect the lodge. From this vantage point on the ridge, Mel gauged the distance to be about 200 yards to the riverbank. Doable, though brutal, even with power tools at their disposal.

She waited for Deklan and Ryan to lift their axes and begin to stab unenthusiastically at the earth before doing what she knew she had to do.

"Be right back," she told Lewis, who worked his side at the front of the line, feigning a bleep from the radio on her chest that hadn't made so much as a squawk. She walked exactly five steps, turned her back, unstrapped the walkie like she meant to speak into it, waited another count of five, restrapped it, then walked back. To Lewis, she said, "Gotta move downriver, do a sweep."

"What? Why?" His confused expression made Mel's stomach lurch.

"Hernandez is on my ass again. Whataya gonna do." She couldn't look Lewis in the eye, so she settled for staring down at his dirt-encrusted boots.

"Take one of the kids, hmm? Deklan, how about?"

"You just want him outa your hair," Mel accused, trying for a laugh. She managed a wan smile, which Lewis had a hard time returning. And no wonder: Who found things funny forty-eight hours into a fire? Containment was barely at 20 percent. They'd slept on the damned ground. Ain't nobody happy, least of all the battalion chief and her first assistant. "Sure," she told him. "I'll grab him as I leave."

But she waited for Lewis to disappear along the line, up and over the top of the hill, then strode toward her truck without pausing as she passed Deklan and Ryan. She didn't need the deadweight. She certainly didn't need to answer Deklan's persistent questions. Both boys were bent to their task, finally working without whining, as Mel turned the key in the ignition, feeling her truck roar to life underneath her.

She pointed the nose of the truck west, putting the fire at her back, lurching along the river road from Wonderland toward Temple. Other than river shuttles, hardly anyone drove this route save for the Martins, dropping off guests to fish at the boat ramp, or the few Carbon folks with fishing cabins out here. Like Fallows's contacts, whom True had to deal with. But also like Colby Phick, who had water rights out this way, and the Wrights . . . good people, if determined to keep to themselves. Mel hoped they'd evacuated by now. She had forgotten how severely this route twisted and turned as it sought out the path of least resistance amid the ridgelines and cliffsides, and she found herself fighting a sense of misplacement, like she was going in the wrong direction. Probably because she *was*. Firefighter training, like Sam's Army training, was harder than one would think to shake off, even to save one's own skin, and it felt horrible to be driving *away* from her crew instead of toward it. Just like being away from her daughters felt horrible, and working with Fallows felt horrible. Yes, every move she made this summer took her one step closer to Annie's final surgery and health—but simultaneously one step farther from herself.

The smoke lay as dense here on this road as everywhere else, and Mel's headlights shone through the gray-black trees with an eerie lack of impact, even in daytime. The wind had picked up, too, blowing the boughs of the trees. She swallowed another rush of nerves and uncertainty. *You've come this far,* she told herself firmly. Because she couldn't forget what else the academy had taught her: *You never, ever abandon a mission.* And certainly not one this important.

The closer she got to Temple Bar, the heavier the sense of wrongness lay on Mel's conscience. She was taking this risk for her family, but where would they be if something happened to her out here? Something worse than risking her job? The catch-22s just kept coming.

It didn't help that the electricity in the air now felt like a living, breathing thing, charging every move she made. She envisioned the usual chaos of the boat launch in daylight, then adjusted the picture in her head. Today, the morning light was nonexistent. The launch would be a ghost town. She didn't like being alone, which was rich, considering the lengths she had gone to to evade having company on this mission. At least with the boat ramp deserted, no one would bear witness to her playing hooky from her team. From her carrying out her little errand. At least she was still heading away from the blaze, not toward it.

She made the turn at the dirt junction between the river road and the spur to Temple and was straining forward at the wheel, trying to discern the parking lot through the smoke, when she heard it: the telltale *crack!* of wildfire. At first, she thought she had imagined it, she was so jumpy out here on her own. Because this crack was not at a distance, as she'd heard droning on all morning. This deafening roar reverberated off the nearest ridgeline; the Flatiron Fire proper, crashing through forest. Jumping a line.

Impossible! She'd just heard the hotshots, working with the hand crews on the ground, report they had this all in hand not even an hour ago. And yet this sound was unmistakable, even if it was indescribable to anyone who hadn't heard it, especially to anyone who hadn't heard it in the field, in the expanse of the wilderness. Hearing it alone, shaking the cab of the truck, was nothing short of terrifying.

The roar felt so close by, the sound and vibrations hit Mel before the smell and sight. When she did see it, the wall of fire looked angrier than ever, and her terror doubled. Her heart hammering so hard in her chest she could feel the pounding in her pulse in her neck and head, she watched as ponderosa trunks broke like twigs; she could glimpse their flaming tops falling to the forest floor somewhere in front of her. Had the fire jumped further west, into the path of the road? She had no way of knowing until she came upon it, swerving this way and that. Had all her deep misgivings about this mission been on point? Was she going to die out here, her truck crashed into a tree trunk or over the riverbank? Would her remains be identified in a burned-out rig, with no one, other than True, to explain why she'd been here, on her own, betraying her team, in the first place? The thought of that very viable reality was almost more than Mel could bear.

On the ridge above her at her two o'clock, the underbrush and madrone trees and sage were ablaze in a blanket of red. Somehow, impossibly, the Flatiron Fire had burned right past the line created by her crew to beat her here.

Skidding to a halt, she cast a desperate glance toward the road in front of her—the path to Temple Bar—and then behind her, where smoke billowed and tree trunks cracked parallel to her under the pressure of two-thousand-degree heat. Mel found herself smack in the middle, in the worst game of pickle ever played. The ammo box lay just before her, not a quarter mile further down the road. And True was counting on her. True, who might be in danger right this minute as well, thanks to Mel, who should never have given her that rapid tag. But closest to this blaze was her crew, her Carbon Rural *family*. Had they been caught by surprise at Wonderland? Were they scrambling, right this very moment, to fight this new breach?

Thinking of them shifted something vital in her brain, and her training kicked in. She reached for the radio on her hip, just to come up empty. Fuck! She must have forgotten it back at Wonderland Lodge after her mock call.

Never had Mel felt so alone. So untethered. So out of control. Her brain spun through all the bad options at her disposal in a blur. Should she turn back? Push for Temple anyway? She'd already sacrificed so much, putting herself in such danger. This road would not remain passable for long, and she was so close to achieving her mission, she could practically taste it in the ashy air. She shifted the truck back into drive and was just preparing to floor it when the handheld on the dash screeched to life. She'd forgotten it even existed in this old truck.

Relief sluiced through her. "Bishop here!"

Lewis's voice crackled through the speaker, the poor connection scrambling every other word. "Mel. Thank God. You accounted for?"

"Affirmative. What happened?"

"Heard . . . break . . . as we cut containment . . . rendezvousing with . . . crew 8 at . . ."

Mel gripped the handheld harder, as if she could force the words to emit more clearly. "Lewis! Rendezvousing where?"

". . . cross river at . . . bridge."

Mel nodded. Her team wouldn't have tried to combat this blaze without backup. They'd have recrossed the Outlaw, escaping to the south bank. To safety. Which meant she could still make a run for Temple. She eyed the road in front of her, willing it to stay clear enough to see.

"What's . . . yo . . . ETA?" Lewis asked.

She glanced automatically at her odometer, which she belatedly realized she'd forgotten to set before departing Wonderland, another standard protocol. "I'm fifteen out, at least," she told him. "Near the end of the line at Temple."

"Temple?" Lewis repeated the word like he assumed he'd misheard. "What's happening out there?"

She squeezed her eyes tight, wishing she could drown out the sound of cracking trees and the roar of the blaze. "I have eyes on her," she admitted, willing back a fresh wash of fear and nerves. Because she did. The fire was *right there*. But the ammo box was also right there, just around the corner.

"Circle back!" Lewis shouted, and that never-ceasing tension between loyalties in Mel ripped further at the seams. To follow orders again would be a relief in this free fall she was in, but how could she let down Annie?

Lewis misread her hesitation. "I got 'em," he added, his voice still cutting out intermittently. "Did . . . count three times. We're at eighteen . . . cluding . . . self."

Eighteen? Mel sat up straighter in her seat. Lewis knew they ran a crew of twenty. Always twenty. "Who's missing?"

"What? No one!" Lewis's voice raised as the sound of a siren cut through the speaker on his end. "I've counted . . . eighteen, minus you and the rook. Deklan."

*Deklan.* Mel's heart seemed to stall in her chest before lurching like a transmission stuck in the wrong gear. God, why hadn't she thought of Deklan sooner? Her stomach lurched next: had she eaten an MRE this morning, she would have lost it.

"Bishop?" Lewis shouted. "Bishop, come in!"

But Mel had dropped the handheld. It dangled from the dash by its cord like a live wire, and she fished it back out of the air numbly. "I'm coming," she said, though not to Lewis, who had clearly lost connection. Every fiber in her being spoke to Deklan, somewhere out by Wonderland, abandoned by his crew. Neglected by his chief. All thought of making a dash for the ammo box evaporated from her mind like Phos-Chek gel in one-hundred-degree heat. "I'm on my way."

With a cry of frustration and a slam of her palms on the wheel, she swung a wild U-ey right there on the dirt. She pressed harder on the accelerator, focusing her full attention on keeping the wheels out of the ruts of the road. In the smoke, the lack of landmarks disoriented her. What would she find there when she did arrive at Wonderland? Had the crew's containment line held well enough to protect the lodge like a storm jetty from a tsunami? Certainly, this demon of a fire was already eating its way through any fishing cabins or storage structures that might be unfortunate enough to stand in the wilderness in between. She visualized Deklan stranded in the parking area, trying to hide his fear behind teenage machismo and a fiery attitude. *Please, please let him be there.*

She strained to see whatever else she could through the windshield, though she shouldn't have bothered. Sparks poured down on her from the fire burning above. On the other side of Wonderland Lodge, the trees would be burning, blocking the road where they fell. Mel could still hear the crash of conifers as they surrendered like dominos, some having stood hundreds of years.

She gunned the engine of the truck, trying to outrace the destruction, intent on her goal of reaching the Wonderland parking lot before the fire consumed it. The singular mission put everything else momentarily on hold, clearing her head somewhat even as her heart continued to pound and she breathed like she was running a race, not driving a vehicle.

Her brain leaped to her personal emergency shelter, stashed in the cargo compartment of the truck, within reach near the dash, ready to deploy at a moment's notice, and she tightened her jaw. After undergoing hours upon hours of wildland training with that thing—the Shake 'n Bake, they called it—Mel hoped to God she'd never need to use it. She wasn't going to die like that, cooking from the inside out.

And then suddenly she was there, peeling out on the dirt as her tires skidded along the last turn into Wonderland. Which still stood, she registered with a jolt of relief, whole and untouched. The team's efforts at cutting a line must have paid off.

But the parking area sat empty. Tire tracks crisscrossed the dirt, evidence that the heavy Carbon Rural rigs had bailed out of the parking lot at sudden speed, but though Mel scanned the area frantically, no rookie, face bright red with indignation, waited ready to give his chief hell. She leaped out of the truck anyway, just to be sure, coughing as she ran blindly through the dense smoke. "Hallo! Deklan!"

Why yell, when there was clearly no one there to hear? Maybe this was just what humans did, Mel figured, when faced with potential tragedy alone in the world. Even a firefighter trained and ready for such incidents needed to bounce disaster off someone else.

"Dek!"

Visibility was gone. Sound was gone. All Mel heard was the incessant roar. All she saw was smoke. *Think!* She forced herself to draw a ragged breath through her Buff and pause long enough to allow a fragile trail of logic to catch up with her frantic mind. The ridge where she'd last seen her crew cutting the containment line had been abandoned, as best she could tell. But the flames had spread east—she could testify to that thanks to her harrowing drive. It was possible the fire had already consumed what it could below the ridge. Which meant patches of "cold black" might remain, smoldering in its wake.

Seasoned wildland fighters knew to seek out these patches of already burned-out brush in the forest. Little safety zones, the black's barrenness promised life to the fire crews instead of death. Mel had always found the dichotomy poetic, but now, she just hoped to God Deklan had remembered enough of his training to utilize this resource. If not . . . if he had panicked and the unthinkable had happened, it would be her fault. All her fault.

She looked back at her truck, still idling. Looked toward the bridge over which her crew had fled, still passable. *Retreat,* the echo of Lewis's order shouted in her mind. She was solo. She lacked assistance. She had no business doing anything else. But with Deklan in the wind, retreat wasn't an option.

# CHAPTER 23

Mel deployed the latch on the storage compartment on the truck's dash and snagged her day bag, groping into the cavernous space once more for the damned Shake 'n Bake. Shouldering the bag and bivvy shelter, she abandoned the truck, the heat and wind hitting her with blunt force. She pushed onward anyway. Her vehicle would be useless where she was going: in the direction she'd last seen Deklan and the crew, up on the ridgeline—in the previously burned cold black.

She'd follow the containment line that seemed to still hold the flames at bay, and make sure Deklan hadn't decided to keep battling the blaze on the other side of the ridge. Somehow he'd become separated from the others, and she had to cross at least this sobering possibility off the list of horrors in her head.

She scrambled up the embankment, hands grasping fistfuls of dirt, feet skidding out on the uneven terrain, blindly gasping thick, ash-filled air. The smoke caked her lungs, her Buff a sieve doing her little good. She thought of Annie; was this how breathing felt to her when her symptoms acted up? She flashed upon a story Sam had told her of being a kid here in Carbon, stuck in the truck cab of his dad's Chevy while Mark chain-smoked Marlboros. He must have felt as helpless and trapped as Mel did right now.

She felt her way along, keeping the recently cut containment line on her right shoulder like both a safety net and a guideline—the encroaching fire just beyond—until she crested the ridgeline. No

Deklan. Standing, she spun in a circle, eyes smarting, tears streaming as she wiped at them angrily, trying to see through the smoke. Instead, she saw only flames where the Flatiron Fire consumed the narrow canyon on the downhill side of the slope—a pocket, they called it—between the ridgelines. She shivered, despite the sweat that poured down her back and along her neck. If any member of her crew had descended into that pocket, they weren't returning.

Lewis would never direct them there, but again, Lewis hadn't known he was responsible for her rookie. The real question was: Would *Deklan* have attempted the pocket? And even if so, what the hell had happened that he'd ended up alone? Guilt churned with the sharp fear in her belly, bringing nausea with it. She forced herself to pause and steady herself. Shielding her eyes with soot-covered hands, she scanned the terrain as best she could and got her answer. Or at least, a clue: about thirty yards down, she could make out a scab of cleared earth, a swath of containment dismayingly similar to Deklan's mediocre work.

Deklan could be somewhere in the thick of all this, belly to the searing ground as the fire ate up everything in its path below him, bivvy shelter melting into his standard-issue yellows. Praying? Swearing? Crying out for the comfort of his mother?

Gasping, Mel fought back another wave of helplessness and self-loathing. She wanted to yell out again, but there was no point. The sound of the fire still drowned out all else, rushing with an angry hiss of wind through pines; it didn't help that the pitch sounded reminiscent of a human cry. That injured wind screamed and screamed over the top of a deeper growl in the undergrowth, almost in the earth itself, like whitewater over the stones of the Outlaw. Every few seconds, an urgent *pop!* sounded as sap burst from the burnt, cracked trunks of pines, leaving the trees to bleed out in inky, ghoulish streams. Continuing down into the pocket would be even more dangerous than her fire-and-adrenaline-fueled drive back on the river road, an even greater risk for her, for her family, for Annie. But what else could Mel do?

She made her way down gingerly, sidestepping debris and skidding through brush. The fire hadn't consumed the undergrowth here yet, but it would be here within minutes, relishing the new fuel. The smoke was the thickest she'd experienced yet, and even through her Buff, her lungs screamed. She considered her emergency oxygen canister in her pack and decided to hold off. She might need it more on the ascent back up, especially if she was running by then.

Ten yards down, she could make out Deklan's Pulaski, left behind in the dirt. Fifteen yards and she caught a flash of silver, which confirmed her fears. "Deklan!" she yelled, as loudly as her lungs would allow. "Dek!"

She came upon his prone form, wrapped like a burrito in his metallic Shake 'n Bake, the very second she saw the hired hand crew approaching from the other side of the ridge, the fire to their left flank, their mustard-yellow coats a filtered, almost surreal sight. Her senses all went on overdrive with the roar of chain saws biting into bark, the wind whipping embers and ash. The screaming static of radios at full decibel, the rasp of lungs, the shouts of men and women swallowed whole by the cacophony of sound.

"Dek!" She gasped, sinking to her knees in the dirt. The flames might not have gotten here yet, but that didn't mean he was unharmed. Prematurely sheltering could lead to asphyxiation.

*You should know that!* she wanted to yell at him, but she also knew that panic and fear could chase even the best training out of a rookie's head. She reached for his bivvy and shook hard, connecting with a shoulder or maybe a hip. With a cry, he responded, flailing out of his bivvy, sucking in smoky air and coughing.

"Deklan, stay still. Calm down."

"Chief?"

Crying and shaking, he reached out his arms to her, and she pulled him out of the suffocatingly hot bivvy with an awkward grunt. He was just a child. A child. And she'd sacrificed his safety for what? An ammo box? Cash for the Fallowses? Even Annie's chance at surgery did not restore the balance.

All because Mel hadn't been there with him to warn him away from the pocket. To ensure he retreated to the cold black and then across the river with the others.

"You're alone?" she confirmed, hands gripping his shoulders. Because what if Lewis had miscounted? What if Ryan, or one of the others, had followed his lead?

Deklan nodded his head, though more like his vision was foggy than in certainty. "Ryan . . . Lewis . . . they all went up, but by the time I saw, I was down here, too far . . ." He gasped. "Are they okay?"

"They are," she told him, even while yanking him back uphill. "Everyone's all right."

"I didn't think I could retreat," he said. "I didn't know where the fire was."

"It's easy to get disoriented," she agreed. *Fighting wildland fire is like scuba diving,* Hernandez had once said, which had struck Mel as ridiculous at the time. Fire and water? But he'd been right: up looked like down in this level of smoke. It was easy to swim toward danger instead of away from it.

Deklan reached blindly for his Pulaski.

"Leave it," she commanded.

She half pulled, half pushed him back up the hill until a trio of hand-crew members appeared through the haze to assist, one pressing an oxygen mask to Deklan's face, holding the canister while they climbed to the ridge. Mel thought about her own O2 again, but without a free hand there was hardly any point. She gripped Deklan's coat arm instead.

At the top of the ridge, Deklan bent at the waist, hands on his knees, and vomited into the dirt. One of the hand-crew kids nodded, like he understood all too well what Deklan grappled with.

"He saw it hit," he said. "I mean, *we* heard it, you probably heard it, but his team? They got the full fire show." He slapped Deklan on the back. "And we all knew: once the Flatiron blaze hits the pocket? It consumes everything in its path. You're lucky, kid, that you have a chief to come save your ass."

Deklan looked up, wiping his mouth with the back of one filthy hand. "You . . . you came back for me?" He stared at Mel in horror between gasping sobs. "I put you in danger. I'm such an idiot. A fucking idiot. Lewis always says so."

He absolutely did not, but Mel's guilt swelled tenfold anyway, threatening to bring her to her knees as well. "Listen to me, Deklan. When something goes sideways in the field, the blame is always on the leadership. Always. You got that?"

Deklan stared at her and nodded as the crew members murmured their agreement.

"My fault," Mel repeated for good measure. "All mine."

The appearance of the wildland engine, lights, and siren running just over the bridge in safety might have been the most beautiful sight Mel had ever seen. Beyond it, she glimpsed the remaining truck and her crew, some members pacing in agitation, some leaning against the hood of the engine, eyes on the blaze across the water. When she hit the brakes, slamming the vehicle into park, she heard Lewis's whoop even over the din of the fire and the whine of the siren.

"Thank God!" he laugh-yelled. Mel could feel the relief his entire being seemed to dispel in waves. He looked shell-shocked, coated in soot and sweat, but beautifully whole. "Figured you'd find us if we kept the lights going."

He greeted her with an arm thrown tight around her shoulder, describing the way the wind had changed direction, turning back on the crew at forty-five miles per hour as they cut containment in the canyon, out of sight of the flames. "It reached the trigger point so fast, you woulda gotten whiplash," he said numbly, eyes pinched closed, hands cradling his skull. "Still, I called for evac, but with rookies on the comms, it was chaos. We scrambled to the ridge before we could be caught in no-man's land, forced to deploy shelters."

It must have been the haunted look shining in Mel's eyes that had him adding, "What took you so long to get here, anyway?"

"I'm sorry," Mel managed. "I was . . . I checked the ridge first."

"Shit." His tone fell flat. "Why on earth would you do that?" He finally looked beyond Mel to see Deklan climb out of the truck cab on shaky legs and added with a frown, "What's got the kid ready to soil his yellows?"

How badly did Mel want to answer with a *Rookies will be rookies* quip? How easy would that be to sell? Instead, she squared her shoulders and said, "I went back because you said you were eighteen, and I knew that meant Deklan wasn't with you. And that meant I had to go back because, Lew, he wasn't with me, either."

"What do you mean, he wasn't with you?" Lewis's face had gone white.

How could Mel explain herself? She couldn't. "I found him about halfway down the pocket. He'd deployed his Shake 'n Bake, like you said you might, and was sheltered in place."

"Bishop," Lewis said. "I don't understand."

"I was on the ridge," Deklan answered, "with you all." He trailed off, his eyes still glassy, his face still flushed from a lack of oxygen.

Lewis looked like he wanted to shake him by the shoulders until whatever the hell played behind his eyes came pouring out of his mouth. "Talk, son."

"I knew we were trying to connect with the hand crew, so I kept moving forward. Downhill. I couldn't hear a damned thing out there, and then . . . and then . . . you all were gone."

Lewis couldn't seem to decide whether to yell or soothe. "I do remember you there now, cutting a shit containment line. With Ryan. But then . . ." He pivoted toward Mel, his face a study in agony. "Then the shit hit the fan, and when I saw Ryan return, my brain only seemed to recall you taking Deklan with you."

"I was all right, Chief," Deklan said robotically. "I sheltered in the scrub." But he sounded as though he were still there, on the slope, caught in that fold in the earth, now smoke-choked, that wedge of flame yawning.

What was it they said about the chaos of war? Being in the midst of it made you crave all you stood to lose. But what if it wasn't war? What if the chaos had been of your own making? Orchestrated by your own selfish agenda? Mel deserved to lose her career and more.

"I made a grave error in judgment," she told Lewis, choking, even before the sentence was fully out of her mouth, on the inadequacy of these words.

At first, Lewis just stared at her, uncomprehending. "Meaning . . . what? You didn't update me, give me an accurate count?" He spoke slowly, as though walking them both through a stubborn but solvable logic problem, coaching Mel toward the answer they both wanted to hear: Deklan had been accounted for by someone. His crew's leadership hadn't put a young life at risk. This was the only formula that made sense, after all. "Bishop, did you lose track of him?"

"No, no, no, no," she muttered, rubbing at her eyes, which were stinging from the smoke. From ash. "Listen, I can't explain it," she said, while watching Lewis's respect for her slide off his face. Worse: watching pity take its place.

"I know it can get tough out here," he said carefully. "Confusing and chaotic."

God, now she was being patronized. Which was still nothing, *nothing*, compared to how she'd compromised her crew. Compromised Deklan.

"But you're the battalion chief, Bishop," Lewis said. "You'll *have* to explain it, eventually, before the safety board if not to me. If not now."

"I know. And I will."

Mel turned away, stumbling on the uneven ground of the gravel staging area, unable to mount any further defense. A rush of tears rose so fast, they ran unchecked down her filthy face. She felt her stomach heave once more as she retched, vomiting what little water she hadn't sweated out onto the brittle bushes along the side of the road.

# CHAPTER 24

True turned off the highway onto the river road, flashing the rapid tag at the surprised search-and-rescue volunteer assigned as gatekeeper at the junction. Not waiting for his official permission to proceed—probably a relief to them both—she now strained through the windshield in an attempt to make out the elbow-bend turn that indicated she was within yards of her own long driveway. The usually familiar route swam before her eyes like a moonscape today; she could barely make out her neighbors' properties, the familiar sight of the Joneses' weathered barn completely obscured, the Juarezes' horse pasture a flat gray expanse. As anticipated, the river road was barred entirely to traffic beyond, and as she made the turn toward her property instead, she tried Mel on her phone while she still had a signal. She doubted she'd pick up while in the field, but the sat phone was a luxury True only had on the river, and once she passed the final cell tower near Buck Peak, service would be nonexistent. When her call went to voicemail after the first ring, she told herself she'd worry about trying to rendezvous with Mel after getting to the Outsider.

The first raindrops hit her windshield just as she made her way up her drive, and the sound of them on the glass left her suddenly giddy with relief. By the time she was in sight of the canvas-dome rooftop of her yurt, however, the rain had already ceased, and a much less welcome sound boomed in the distance: thunder.

Why couldn't they catch a break? She was closer to the base of Flatiron than she'd been in two days, and the smoke mushroomed here, just over the ridgeline, below which a ring of flame glowed orange. Gone was the murky ambiguity of a hazy sky or even thick-as-soup smoke. True was now treated to a clarity she'd never asked for.

She wrenched open her truck door and leaped into forward motion, any intention to check out the situation at the Fallows property taking a back seat to preserving her own place. Douse the roof, she told herself. Mow the field. She wouldn't waste time attempting the latter, not if she hoped to somehow connect with Mel, but she made her way blindly to the only spigot she'd already installed next to her herb and vegetable garden and cranked the water on. Squinting into the bright demarcation between flame and cloud, she directed the hose onto her roof and sprayed full blast.

*Lightning.*

Just as Mel had feared. And only two seconds later came the answering rumble of thunder. She craned her neck to scan the sky, but where she should have seen the quick, telltale flash, she glimpsed only a brief, dull glow of white light.

Which meant one thing.

"Shit," Lewis said, confirming her fears. He threw his gloves to the ground in frustration and fear and probably half a dozen other emotions he couldn't name. "Are you fucking kidding me right now?" he asked in the direction of the sky.

"What?" Ryan asked hollowly from the water station, his Dixie cup pausing halfway to his lips.

Sly answered him. "We're in for that firestorm, kid."

Ryan's jaw dropped, though Deklan didn't even lift his head from where he'd been sitting, uncharacteristically quiet, in the background. Mel waved him over, offering him a wet Buff for his head.

"Because of those pyro-whatever clouds?" Ryan asked. "What does that mean?"

"It means this motherfucker has just created its own wind system," Lewis said, bending and swiping his gloves back out of the dirt.

"Which will produce more lightning, which in turn could set additional fires," Mel added flatly. The desperate roller coaster of events in the Wonderland pocket, followed by the sharp drop of horror upon realizing just how close she'd come to losing a crew member, let alone her professional reputation, left her every bit as wrung out, emotionally and physically, as Deklan.

And the hits just kept coming. This weather system would almost certainly generate stronger winds, which would only fan the fires and make them hotter, though she saw no point in saying so. But because Ryan still looked lost, she added, "Nature hates a vacuum." She looked out over the untouched forest to the northeast. "Empty spaces don't stay empty for long."

They all seemed to take a moment of silence as if by mutual agreement, or simply shell-shocked numbness, and more than one of them jumped when one of the vehicle radios crackled to life. "Trailblazers to Carbon Rural 1, come in."

One of the hand crews. Lewis answered, but they were all privy to the update transferred over the airwaves.

The horrible *pop* Mel had heard over an hour ago from the road? It had been the sound of a back swell. The fire that had been steadily consuming its way west down the river corridor had doubled back on itself in a sudden shift of wind, and like a sucking tide, it now gained volume as it licked its way right back in the direction it had come.

"Could this shitty day get any worse?" Lewis growled.

It seemed it could. Lacking fuel in the acreage it had just consumed, the hotshot crew reported, the fire slowed briefly where the blackened forest floor still glowed orange, but had quickly found new ground, where it now threatened, impossible though it seemed, the Outlaw's southern bank. Closer to all the crisscrossing Forest Service roads and homesteads in the Wild and Scenic section between here and town. *Home to True. Please,* Mel thought again. *Don't let her be at the Outsider.*

It was already her fault Deklan had been placed in danger, and it would be her fault if True was out here somewhere, exposed to this fire that was now out of control. Mel longed to confirm her location, but there was no time to dig her personal cell phone out of her pack. No time to process what she should do next, no time for anything.

"We're at mayday level here in the Wild and Scenic," the Trailblazer rep told them.

In other words, give up the ghost. The various interagency and independent ground-pounder crews loaded up all around Mel in a mad scramble, sirens on a low pulse, lights already flashing. Their orders: beat the blaze back to town to join the hand crews in holding the line. *So much for going on the offense.* Everyone was behind the curve now. It wasn't just Mel chasing the tail end of an agenda that had run away from her.

The orders for her own Carbon Rural team came in from White, though on the shared radio line instead of to Mel's walkie directly: retreat and oversee search and rescue in doubling the efforts on evacs and traffic control.

Such as it was. Mel knew firsthand: the sight of flames plus an all-out evac order almost always equaled large-scale panic, even in a community used to brushing ash off their cars every morning of every August. She rallied to carry out the order, only to see Deklan still by the water dispenser, trying to refill his bottle. His movements were at half speed, his fingers clumsy. Still in shock.

"Hey, Lew?" she called out, startling when he answered from directly behind her. "We need to assign Deklan a ride out of the field to be checked out by a medic."

Lewis nodded. "He can come with us."

"Us? What do you mean?" Mel had been partnered with Sly on the way out. Lewis had his own vehicle.

Lewis shifted uncomfortably, clearly anxious to get moving and to not have this confrontation, but he looked her in the eye as he said, "White is taking you off active duty."

"What? Right now?"

Lewis looked apologetic, but also resolute. "Effective immediately."

Panic seized Mel. She expected fallout following her rogue actions; she deserved nothing less. She knew she would be made accountable, and even welcomed the chance to do so, with an incident report back at the station. Hell, with a full investigation if Hernandez ordered it, when this was all over. But *now*?

She still needed to be out here. She needed to be sure True was safe.

"I had to report what happened," Lewis told her. "You heard Hernandez. White's field lead, even if he's remote."

Mel nodded numbly. This explained White's use of the shared line. Technically, Lewis was her inferior, but Mel had flipped the script on them both back at Wonderland. He held out his hand for the keys to her rig, and she handed them over on autopilot, amazed at how, even when everything around her was falling utterly apart, small muscle memory remained intact.

Because what recourse remained to her now?

The shame of her actions at Wonderland had soured her stomach for any further attempts at an ammo-can grab, but it didn't protect her from the full impact of the blow of her defeat at Temple Bar. Without their cut of that cash, Annie's prescription would run out before her surgery, compromising her eligibility. And of even more imminent concern, Fallows could become violent. She'd failed her daughter, and now she'd fail True. Mel gripped her middle, sure she was about to be sick again.

Lewis drove fast, trying to paint the lines between the shoulders of the road while squinting through the gloom. Mel rode shotgun, trying *not* to count the continual—if intermittent—flares of lightning or the number of misguided choices she'd made today. Hell, all summer.

She had no cell service right now, but back in town, Mel would head directly up the hill to Highline, just about the only place this fire still *wasn't*, and connect with True to warn her off her property. Once she was safely out of the river corridor, they'd make a new plan, Plan C, if they had to. And Plan D after that. She'd tell Sam to pack the SUV, power everything up, and drive Annie all the way up to Seattle, if needed.

She formed her plans without interruption, Lewis's mouth set in stony determination to carry out his directive to deliver Mel to Carbon. And in a last-minute changeup, Deklan had departed with a hotshot with an ankle injury headed directly for the closest health clinic in Eagle Valley. They passed first one Forest Service road, then another, the silence in the cab unbroken until they passed near the cell tower by Buck Peak and both reached for their phones. Mel didn't dare try True, not with an audience, and her call to Sam failed. She reminded herself the connection was always spotty on Highline, swallowing a fresh wave of nerves.

Lewis's call to his family went through on his second try, and the relief in his voice was palpable. The conversation was short.

"Susan okay?" Mel asked, when it ended.

"She made it to her sister's house in Eugene," he said curtly. "Jacob will meet her there."

Their college-aged son. Mel nodded. "Good. Good."

They were still a good ten miles from town and achingly, frustratingly close to the turn to True's place when something caught their eye: a solid form emerging from the smoke. Lewis hit the brakes and let loose an expletive: a woman ran along the side of the road, waving at them to stop in a frantic sweep of her arms. Lewis yanked the wheel to skid out into the gravel of the shoulder.

Mel's seat belt bit into her clavicle at the sudden stop, and the woman was at her window before she could even roll it down. "What's happening?" the woman shouted. "Is it close?"

"Level 3," Lewis shouted at her. "Didn't you get the alerts?"

The woman shook her head and said, "Not out here. Just have a landline."

"Do you have a vehicle ready to go?" Lewis asked her, and the woman nodded. "Follow behind then!"

"But my neighbors," she shouted back. "They're trying to round up their horses. And the farms further back . . . I don't even know if they realize . . ." She trailed off, her face contorted in a show of anxiety.

"We'll get 'em," Lewis told her, already on his radio. He waved down a Forest Service truck that had splintered off from the rest of the fire convoy, directing the driver to hang back to guide the woman and her car out. She ran back up the long driveway she'd emerged from, barreling down the road a minute later, her Subaru loaded to the gills, a frantically barking Chihuahua making itself known in the back seat.

Lewis waited until the truck had swung out ahead of the Subaru, lights now flashing at top visibility, then nosed down the dirt road to warn the woman's neighbors. Mel leaned forward in her seat, not daring to voice her approval for fear that Lewis would second-guess himself and resume their direct course for Carbon.

They crossed paths with two additional families already evacuating, and Lewis gave each a short blip on the siren, an auditory thumbs-up. A third neighbor refused to leave his home—or even open his front door to "the Feds" to discuss the matter when Mel ran up the steps—and a fourth needed help coaxing a wild-eyed mare into a stock trailer before departing in a cloud of dust and smoke.

When they eased back out onto the road, Lewis paused, then swung into the next Forest Service road over with a muttered, "We can't just *not* help."

They swept the road, then the next one over as well, continuing until the occasional rows of mailboxes—sure signs of inhabitance—became fewer and farther between; this deep into the wilderness, the maintained Forest Service roads faded into overgrown logging roads that spiderwebbed into the trees. Before Mel quite realized it, they were just yards from the back acre of True's place, somewhere through the haze.

"One more detour," Mel said as they approached an unmarked Y in the road that she recognized. "Please, Lew. It's my friend's place. I just need to make sure she's not there."

He looked like he might argue, but he swung the wheel anyway, and they lurched to the right, bumping over potholes the size of small boulders. A moment later, the forest opened up onto a small clearing, True's yurt in the forefront flanked by carefully fenced-in gardens and her pretty stone walkway. As Mel feared it might be, True's truck idled beside the road, and True herself wielded a hose aimed at the canvas stretched tight over her dwelling. She cursed under her breath, then called out to her.

"True!"

When she turned, the relief on her face slid right into Mel's soul, washing away her frustration. "I've been trying to call your cell!" True said. "Do you have the—" She shut her mouth midsentence, spotting Lewis in the driver's seat of Mel's rig. Only the heavy smoke in the air saved her from telegraphing far too much.

"C'mon," Mel yelled. "Leave the place. It's time to go!"

True hesitated only a moment more, then cranked off the water. She made to follow them in her truck, but Lewis objected.

"Just jump in with us! Too many evacuees on the road as it is."

She turned off the engine and pocketed the keys, and they took True's private drive back to the Y, where Lewis turned back toward the river road and Carbon. Apparently, he was done delaying the inevitable. But before he could make the turn, True stopped him.

"I'm worried there may be some seasonal workers stranded at Fallows's place," she said, pointing, as Lewis made a noise of protest. "You know how he can be."

She looked at Mel, as if still trying to glean the information she needed from her. Mel shook her head, trying to convey that there was no longer any point in trying to connect with Fallows or anyone on his payroll. Now that she'd found True, all she wanted was to get back to Carbon to her family.

But Lewis knew how the Fallowses could be, too; everyone associated with emergency services in Carbon did. "One last sweep," he decided with a low curse before Mel could argue.

They bumped down the dirt drive to the Fallows property, a drive Mel had never taken. She knew True had been warned away as well. It narrowed rapidly, the overgrown branches of pines and madrones brushing against the truck's windows as they drove. Brittle leaves made a whooshing noise against the glass. Clearly, the inhabited part of Fallows's place lay elsewhere on his acreage. She was about to instruct Lewis to execute an awkward three-point-turn just past a dilapidated barn when a flash of metal caught her eye through the grime of the windshield.

Sweat beaded and dripped under the N95 mask she'd yanked on about five miles back as she strained to look closer. It flashed again, and her eye followed the movement to a loose line of barbed wire lifting in the wind. A tangle of blackberry bushes mostly obscured it, and Mel would have dismissed the fence line as abandoned if it wasn't for the roll of green camouflage netting—the type sold at an Army Navy surplus store—half covering the wire, half in a heap on the ground at its base, clearly blown off by the gusts of hot wind.

"See that?" She pointed, and Lewis nodded.

"Well, I'll be damned."

They all knew what that camo netting meant: concealment. And concealment could only mean one thing this deep in the Oregon woods: an illegal grow. They'd found the heart of Fallows's operation.

True hopped out of the truck, so Mel followed her, peering over the half-obscured fence to make out the row of hoop-style greenhouses behind it. Had the smell of smoke not been nearly permanently embedded in her nostrils, she knew that this close to harvest time, the telltale skunky scent of weed would have led her here, if nothing else.

They both paused, surveying the property as thunder continued to rumble in the background of their consciousness. A sagging double-wide trailer sat at the far end of the acreage, at least a couple hundred yards away. Closer, cheap plastic sheeting billowed in the hot wind, and the tromped grass path between them and a dilapidated toolshed suggested frequent use.

"Doubt anyone's around though," Lewis said, eyeing the trailer skeptically. He hit the sirens anyway. Grabbing the bullhorn mounted on the passenger side, he bellowed, "Helllooo! Carbon Rural Fire Department! We have evac orders for this residence!"

Nothing.

"Helllooo!" Lewis called again. "Anyone need assistance?"

Only the rush of wind and the routine pop and snap of fire, still just over the ridge, answered his call. "Should we hit the road, then?" he asked.

"I'm just going to check the outbuildings," True said, already ducking gingerly through the barbed wire, never one to wait for group consensus.

"Hold up!" Mel called. Because what if the property line was booby-trapped? The characters who worked these grows were known for it.

But True was already making her way to the shed, and Lewis still waited by the rig, and so Mel followed with a small wail of frustration, picking each step with care. The outbuilding was closed tight, but one swift kick from Mel's boot pulled the simple hook-and-eye lock loose from the aging boards of the door with a sharp crack.

"Impressive," True muttered, blinking into the gloom of the interior.

Mel smelled weed first, the potency in the closed-in space practically knocking her on her ass. It hung from the rafters, out to dry, in large clumps, not yet trimmed. Her first thought: *This is a shit ton of dope.* Even more than she'd suspected Fallows grew here.

Her second: no one would leave this stash voluntarily.

"Hello?" she called out, as loudly as she could in the smoky air. True echoed her. "Anyone still here?"

Silence greeted them. Hopefully, whoever had been tasked with guarding this grow had decided their life was worth more than the thousands of cannabis plants the rows of greenhouses must contain, in addition to the endless rows drying in this shed.

Mel turned to leave, only to practically fall on her face as her boot came down hard on a loose floorboard.

True reached for her immediately. "You all right?"

"Yeah, the floor's just seen better days." She crouched down, investigating further. "Actually, this board's not loose. It's completely unattached." She tugged.

There was a space below about the size of a manhole. What if someone was hiding down here, afraid to be caught on this acreage? Mel remembered a case just last year when an undocumented immigrant suffocated in a trimming shed not unlike this one when a gas leak brought the fire department to a grow site in the next county over.

True returned to her side, fumbling with her flashlight and pointing it into the darkness below. "Hello!" she called out again.

Silence. But something else, too. A metallic glint in the darkness, revealing the steely gray of a gun shaft. Double shit. Mel sank to her knees, pulling out a 12-gauge, a .22, and a Smith & Wesson rifle . . . she wasn't sure what caliber. Sweeping the light across the dirt below the floor, she checked for anything else and, easing to her belly to reach the floor of the hole, yanked an REI duffel out next. Its navy-blue canvas looked almost new.

"Isn't that just like the duffel Kim described? That her nephew Zack got caught with by that state trooper?" True's breath tickled the back of Mel's neck, shallow and a bit panicked, raising goose bumps on Mel's sweaty skin.

Fuck, it *did* remind her of that duffel. And along with that reminder came another: Fallows could pin all of this on them just as he had on Zack, if they weren't careful.

"Mel?" Lewis's voice cut through her racing thoughts, sending them scattering and bringing both her and True scrambling back to their feet.

"Coming!" Mel yelled.

"Find anything?"

She looked down at the duffel, then at True, then back at the duffel, her gaze narrowing through the smoke until it seemed all she saw was the zipper pull, inviting her to tug it.

She did.

No glint of metal this time. No guns. Just stacks and stacks of green.

And not of the herbal variety.

Cold, hard cash. And far more of it than she and True ever ran on the river.

Mel actually stumbled back from it, like the currency might leap out of the duffel and bite her.

"Oh my God," True said beside her. "Grab it!" she whispered, then, just as quickly: "No! Don't touch it! Shit, I don't know! What should we do?"

Mel had no fucking idea. But she thought of the ammo box still waiting for retrieval at Temple Bar, a lost cause. She thought of Annie, coughing in the smoke. She thought of her best friend, still half hyperventilating beside her, and what it could cost them if they came back to Carbon empty-handed for the second time in two days.

"We'll bring it to Fallows," she said.

"As what?" True shook her head emphatically. "Penance or something? We can't replace what we've lost with his own damned stash!"

Shit. That was true. Fuck.

"Hey, guys?" Lewis called again. "Let's roll out!" He still sounded distant. Hopefully he'd been unwilling to break protocol and leave the fire vehicle.

"We can't come back empty-handed, either," Mel whispered to True. Annie couldn't afford it.

True nodded.

They both looked back down at that money, just sitting there in the open duffel bag.

Fallows's money, which could very easily replace what they'd lost on the river, becoming presurgical-prescription money in a serendipitous act of alchemy.

"What should we do?"

Once, during fire-science training, Mel's supervisor had said there would come a time in every firefighter's career when training protocols took a back seat to good old-fashioned survival instinct.

"We do what we have to do," she decided, reaching into the duffel and stuffing two thick stacks of bills into her go bag, and tossing the duffel back into the hole. True looked like she might have more to say, but after just a moment's beat of hesitation, she nodded, kicking the floorboard back into place.

They slid back out between the shed doors and hurried past the greenhouses, trying to see through the sudden onslaught of tears at the backs of their eyes. Mel's stomach was in knots, her brain blaring a warning of *Bad idea, bad idea, bad idea.* Had she learned nothing in the past twenty-four hours? She already faced disciplinary review for lives she had put at stake. How many more laws was she going to break, trying to cover her own mistakes?

But another, more visceral voice drowned out the litany of these thoughts.

*Woman up,* she told herself harshly.

This was for Annie.

# CHAPTER 25

True's pulse pounded in her ears as she and Mel reached the barbed-wire fence bordering the grow site. Something didn't feel right about this, and it had nothing to do with her conscience.

"Wait. What do we tell Lewis?" she asked. Mel was a public servant. Would she really risk tampering with evidence?

"We tell him nothing," Mel panted. "We saw nothing. We found nothing."

True bit back a frustrated sound. She should have known there was nothing Mel would not do for Annie, but grabbing this money was a mother's desperate move, and what they needed right now was a calculated one.

"But think, Mel! Where does that leave us with Fallows?" If they gave him the wads currently burning a hole in Mel's bag, he'd eventually realize they'd robbed Peter to pay Paul. Keep it for themselves and Annie, and they'd face his wrath immediately.

"We . . . we tell Fallows we know about the stash," Mel reasoned. "We bring him the stacks we grabbed as proof, and we tell him we'll go to the Feds with the information if he doesn't drop the Temple Bar thing."

True shook her head. "It's no good," she shot back. "He still has our involvement in his business to leverage, not to mention sabotaging my place, ruining life for Sam again, threatening the kids . . ." She swallowed the hard lump that arose instantly, thinking of what had already happened to Astor. "He has far too much on us, and always will."

If there was one thing True always prided herself on, it was living her life on her own terms, and the thought of Fallows trapping them like this infuriated her.

Suddenly, she was filled with a fury akin to the one she'd experienced in the office with Astor, fury right up to the brim of her being. Fury at the fire, fury at Fallows, fury at the universe for Annie's damaged, punctured heart. Fury at the fact that she and Mel were caught here, in this impossible vise that only tightened and tightened, no matter which way they pivoted or how they squirmed.

Goddamn Fallows. Goddamn small towns with long memories. She braced her hands on her knees, shallow breaths drawing in more smoke than oxygen, trying to think of a way out—any way out. Maybe this place would burn to the ground in the Flatiron Fire. That wasn't out of the realm of possibility, though True wasn't accustomed to getting that lucky.

What if she told Lewis that she and Fallows were in on this together? He'd believe it, given how close she lived to the skunk smell of all this weed. And Fallows wouldn't be able to deny it without admitting his role in their cozy little arrangement with the Bishops. His hands would be tied—tied to True's, yes—but tied all the same. And Mel's name—Sam's, too—would be clear if True took the fall. There had never been a time when True wouldn't do anything for the Bishops, and that included all four. Right?

But the instant she opened her mouth to suggest this, crazy as it sounded, her mind swung back to her beloved Outsider. Clear as day, she could see her front gate, welcoming guests down a path of river rocks, the design flowing like a wave of water tumbling over a river boulder, edged by moss and lichen.

But for the first time it wasn't Mel she envisioned walking down them in some alternate, impossible future. Startlingly, it was Vivian. Vivian, who might never want to speak to True again. It was so clear in her mind: Vivian in her little yurt. Vivian on the water with her, the Outlaw River at sunset putting on a dazzling show. And despite the fact that this reality felt nearly as improbable as a future with Mel, True suddenly felt that feeling she got in her chest, like air and wind and light all combined, whenever she put her back to the sun and began to row. And she found herself doing something *truly* crazy: prioritizing her own well-being as high as any Bishop's.

She gripped Mel's arm more urgently. "I have a better idea."

"What?"

Instead of answering, she spun back to retrieve the duffel, then threw one tanned leg over a coil of barbed wire and hopped the fence, lithe as a cat. "Lewis!" she called. "We got something!"

"Are you crazy?" Mel gasped, right behind her. "True! Talk to me!"

True was already on the other side of the fence, holding it open for Mel. "I'm sick of being caught flat-footed," she told her over the peals of thunder. "Sick of waiting for his next move. We're going to nail this asshole."

"But how—"

True caught Mel by both shoulders and forced her to stop. To look at her. "Do you trust me?"

The question seemed to jar Mel out of her panic. "That's a stupid question," she said, and True nodded, equal parts grateful and validated.

She retrieved Lewis without another word, and a moment later the three of them were recrossing the open space with the greenhouses, Lewis peppering them with questions.

In the shed, his eyes widened at the sight of the cash and the guns. "Holy shit," he practically whistled. He looked at the radio on Mel's hip. "You call this in yet?"

"I wanted you to see it first," she said carefully. True knew what she was thinking: Could the solution to their problems really be this simple?

It was beginning to look like it. On this second assessment, they discovered a high tower of ammo boxes stacked under the floor as well as a stash of sawed-off shotguns. Lewis gave a low whistle, muttering something about evidence that would allow Carbon to be finally rid of this blight on their county, and True shot Mel a look of cautious victory. Fallows couldn't come after them for the missing cash *or* prey upon their devotion to Annie or Astor if he was busy dodging firearms charges that had absolutely nothing to do with them. Or better yet, incarcerated.

It was risky, yes, but on the river and in the field, *risk* was something Mel and True were both intimately familiar with. They could finally make something stick, True knew they could. These guns would tip the scales.

"We'll call it into ATF and DEA right now," Lewis decided, "even if they won't be able to dispatch any resources to act on it immediately." He glanced back outside the shed door toward the billowing smoke. "In the meantime, we'll document everything as best we can."

They took dozens of photos with their phones, and then Lewis sent Mel back to the rig for several of the large evidence bags always stored in their glove box. He deposited the duffel in one and several guns in another and was busy securing the shed with yellow hazard tape when Mel discreetly dropped the stacks of bills she'd taken into an open evidence bag. It made a very anticlimactic, soft *thunk* as it landed amid the rest.

"Are you sure?" True whispered. "What if we need that for Annie?"

"Annie will get her surgery," Mel whispered as Lewis finished securing the scene, "somehow." Her brows knitted in worry, but she seemed resolute. "What you said before? About getting caught flat-footed? I'm sick of it, too. I'm tired of breaking rules. It's not me. I can't keep risking innocent people."

True frowned, because yeah, they had been breaking the law all summer, but Fallows sure as hell wasn't innocent. Mel's tone led her to believe she referred to something new, something fresh, and she wanted to know more, but there was no time.

Nothing new there.

Back near their vehicle, the wind whipped harder and hotter than ever.

"It's getting worse," Lewis said, squinting in the direction of Carbon. Even more alarming: the radio in the fire vehicle buzzed non-stop. Chatter from half a dozen agencies filled the cab, and the sat phone was lit up like a Christmas tree. A fresh swell of fear rose in True's throat, stinging with the acidity of bile.

Lewis leaned into the open window of the truck to jump on the radio and give their status and coordinates. "Returning to town with one additional evacuee," he told dispatch.

The voice on the radio was terse. "Coordinates and ETA?"

Lewis looked over at True, who said, "Two hundred block of Forest Service Road 440."

Lewis relayed the address, adding, "We can be back to the station ASAP."

"Negative, Lewis," the voice on the dispatch returned. "Report directly to Carbon High to stage there for further orders. And avoid the highway at all costs."

Lewis frowned. "Avoid southbound?" he confirmed.

"Southbound *and* northbound," dispatch returned. "We're at a standstill both directions after an all-out Level 3 evac."

Lewis released a soft expletive. "Level 3?" he confirmed. "Where? Last we heard, the fire was still west of town."

"Negative," dispatch repeated. "All points east of the river have upgraded to Level 3, from Flatiron to Carbon urban, which is at 2."

"All points?" Mel gasped.

They all swiveled their heads toward Carbon with one accord; in the hour or so they'd taken to clear the Forest Service roads and discover the Fallowses' grow, all hell had broken loose to the east. The demarcation line of the Flatiron Fire glowed orange through the smoke on the ridgeline like a smudged sunset. But it was no longer the only show in town. While it continued to lap at the forest below the peak, a new, dense black cloud of smoke now plumed directly over Carbon, where additional flames now blazed out of control on the slope above the highway.

"Holy shit," True said. "Is that . . ."

"Yes," Mel confirmed, eyes squinting in the haze. "A second fire." Splotches of pink rose on her cheeks, always a sign of high stress. Astor got them, too.

"Almost certainly ignited from one of the lightning strikes in this fucking firestorm," Lewis agreed. He fumbled with the handheld, his fingers suddenly shaking as he attempted to nest it back on its holder on the dash of the truck.

True stood frozen in place, limbs locked, unable to take her eyes off this new blaze. It looked like the plume originated at elevation, on a ridge just east of the original ignition site. The bottom went out from her stomach as she realized how close it looked to Sam's place.

This occurred to Mel at the same time. "Do you think that could hit Highline?" she cried. Her face had gone from red to white.

"No," True answered swiftly. But her grip on Mel's knee gave away her fear. Because just like the base of Flatiron, Highline could jump from Level 1 to Level 3 *just like that.* "We need to stay calm," she said, then immediately ignored her own advice. "Lewis! Let's get moving!" She pulled herself into the Carbon Rural vehicle and tugged Mel up into the cab beside her.

Lewis complied, and Mel had just shouted, "Go!" when the truck backfired. Illegal firearms on her mind, True automatically ducked. It only took a moment for reason to prevail, but when she lifted her head, she saw that the three of them in the truck hadn't been the only ones startled by the sudden blast. A handful of people burst out of the adjacent trailer like a flock of jays flushed from the brush.

Surprised, Lewis laid on the horn, trying to get the people's attention, but most of them sprinted across the pot grow in the opposite direction.

"Growers?" Mel asked.

"More likely ill-fated bodyguards for whatever they've got running out here," Lewis cursed, siren and lights now going. "But are they really too stupid to seek safety when their lives are on the line?"

*Or too afraid,* True thought, thinking of Fallows. After all, their grow had just been breached. Only one straggler headed toward the sirens and horn instead of away, staggering up to the truck, breathless.

"Get in, kid," Lewis said without hesitation, and the boy—because he couldn't have been older than a teen—reluctantly but gratefully obeyed.

# Megafire

# CHAPTER 26

The Flatiron Fire was officially promoted to megafire status at hour 1500. Sam heard the announcement over the radio from Chief Hernandez himself, and like every longtime resident of Carbon, he knew what it meant: the original fire had not only gained ground and size in the hot wind but had now merged with the new, smaller fire he could see burning just shy of his ridge on Highline.

"At least one hundred thousand acres so far," he repeated hollowly, listening to the PSA. "My God."

And with no meaningful containment in sight. His first thought went to Annie as the public-announcement warning on the radio screeched its awful *EEEEEEK EE EE EE* that always made your stomach flip and your heart rate spike, even when it was just a test of the broadcasting system. But upon hearing the words *Level 3* spoken by the radio DJ in the same sentence as *Highline Road*, that spike became his new baseline, and for the first time since this nightmare had begun, Sam's fear expanded to the physical safety of his entire family. Astor was at risk. Claude. Sam himself. Mel, somewhere out there. He squinted through the kitchen window into the abyss of heat that was now Flatiron, absorbing the reality that this fire actually could, with reasonable probability, even take the house.

No longer would it provide them with even inadequate shelter from the smoke. He looked automatically at his watch. 15:40. He hadn't been a firefighter's spouse for nothing: Level 3 meant he had thirty minutes, tops. Sure, he'd been Level 2 ready for two days now, but actually mobilizing was another thing, requiring a shift of mental and physical gears that wouldn't be easy with two small kids. Hell, he could barely manage the task on the average school morning. He calculated what needed doing in one part of his brain while counting minutes on one hand. He could have the girls ready by 15:50, if he hustled. He'd want the car loaded by 1600, giving him five minutes to double-check they had everything and another five for a buffer.

Which he'd need, because already Astor was upon him, worry pitching her face. She pointed to the radio. "That means we have to go, right, Dad? Do we have to go?"

Her voice quavered, and behind her, Annie cried softly, her hands clamped over her ears.

"Make that noise stop, Daddy."

God, if only he could. *You can do this,* he told himself firmly. *Stay calm, work through it, and just get it done.*

He turned down the volume on the radio, scooped up Annie under her armpits, and deposited her on the couch. Trusting the TV remote control into Astor's hands, he said, "Find something for her." She opened her mouth to protest, and he silenced her with a rare "Stop!" He sucked in a breath. "Find something for her, then come find me. You can help."

He consulted the handwritten list on the Post-it note he'd already stuck on their primary go bag, a rare thankfulness for their complicated custody schedule rushing through him. Handing Astor and Annie off every week *did* keep them organized. He and Mel always kept a written record of Annie's most essential medications, just to make sure nothing fell through the cracks.

God, Mel. He wasted precious seconds peering out the window again, fear for her churning in his gut. Where was she? Whom was she with? Lewis? He was good . . . that made Sam feel the tiniest bit better. But what if she was with the rookie teens? A volunteer? That asshole

Doug White, who couldn't stand her? The fear in Sam swelled, lurching him forward again. *Astor. Annie.*

The former was back at his side, and he tasked her with piling ice into the cooler, which sat by the Goal Zero by the door. Meanwhile he found the backup heart monitor in the top cabinet over the dishwasher, and even though Sam tried his best to work methodically and calmly, he pinched his finger on the stupid plastic child lock on the cabinet door as he reached for it too quickly. Next, he fished in their kitchen fridge for the meds that had to remain cold until the last minute, then scooped up the emergency vials of morphine, which he'd stashed out of reach in the cupboard. The hour, unfortunately, was upon them.

As Astor dripped water all over and Annie continued to cry and cough from the couch, her "Ingrid blankie" wrapped around her like a tortilla, Sam reached for the overdue and outdated stack of insurance paperwork and medical bills next, then hesitated. What exactly happened next if the entire pile burned to ash? He kind of wanted to find out.

What else? What else? Besides the scrapbooks and framed photos that already sat by the door with Annie's go bag, was there anything else he couldn't live without? What about all the tools he'd inherited from his old man? They were worth a ton, which was more than he could say for Mark Bishop himself. What about his fly-fishing gear or his bow? It was time to make those final decisions about what came with them on the ride down Highline and what he could be prepared to lose forever.

Everything, as it turned out. Sam took full stock, from the comfortably cluttered living room with its windows that still awaited curtains to the exposed drywall of the half-finished addition he'd insisted on building as a one-day sunroom. His eye lingered on the entryway through which he'd ushered first Mel, then both Astor and Annie from Carbon General Hospital as newborns—well, Astor as a newborn, Annie as a three-month-old graduate of the NICU—and Sam knew with a sense of certainty that had eluded him his entire adulthood that he was prepared to lose everything if only he could keep his girls safe. It was so obvious to him now. His family made Sam the man he was, just as it had made Mark Bishop the man he wasn't, not a house. Not even this house.

Thinking of family shifted his thoughts back to Claude. He lacked a radio, so Sam needed to let him know about the evac order, too, a task he hadn't factored into his time frame.

"Astor?" he called, and she was right there, right away, her face pink, color high on her cheeks from her exertion in the increasing smoke. *Eight going on thirty-eight* . . . another of True's quips, and she wasn't wrong, as sorry as Sam was for it.

"I need to go talk to Claude again," he told her.

"Leaving me alone?" Her lips quivered in a rare show of childlike vulnerability, which only made Sam feel worse.

"I'll be right back, I promise. Everything will be fine."

Because this had to be true. It had to be.

He couldn't tell if Astor believed it. She was still watching him carefully as he took a deep breath before opening the door—the smoke was worse than ever—then ran up the driveway at as fast a jog as he dared, one hand over his mouth. Breathing in this air was dangerous for everyone now, respiratory compromise or no.

Crossing the newly mowed field, he kept his eyes on his feet; he could see the uneven terrain under the Muck boots he'd tossed on, for lack of a more readily available choice by the door, but if he glanced up, the smoke had already obscured his usual view of Buck Peak to the north and looming, imposing Mt. Shasta, situated behind Flatiron. He could only make out the shape of the latter because the fire cast a glow that burned through the dark, choking haze.

*Mel is somewhere out in that haze.* He knew he had to stop fixating on this fact, but he couldn't shake it. She should be here. They were a family, and Mel walking out the door and Sam failing to bring her back didn't change that. None of that mattered right now.

This thought carried him to Claude's door, and he pounded on it, relaying his evacuation message in a coughing fit. "Just loading up, and then I'll be at your door with my truck," Claude called back. "We can fit more into it."

Sam didn't take the time to do more than acknowledge this before sprinting back across the field, tripping once in the uneven terrain, hardly able to see even his hand in front of his face. The wind whipped hot on the back of his neck, but at least the lightning strikes from the earlier afternoon had ceased. Now there was only ash and smoke and heat. So much heat.

Back through his own front door, he sputtered as he yanked the Buff from his face and yelled out his return to Astor, his mind already casting around for something more adequate to cover Annie's face with when the time came to move her. *We have more N95 face masks stashed somewhere.* Could he double hers up? Another quick glance at his watch told him there was only time for the priorities, but Annie? In this smoke?

He heard Astor answer him, but her voice was mostly drowned out by the still-wailing radio on low, and besides, the N95-mask search had gone straight to the top of Sam's to-do list. He rummaged like a crazy person through his bathroom drawer, then tried the medicine cabinet in the kitchen, pushing aside plastic bottles of children's Tylenol (sometimes Annie's fevers got stubborn) and Ace bandages and Band-Aids to finally unearth the extra N95s at the back of the shelf.

Astor appeared back in the kitchen. "Dad!"

The radio continued to screech on the kitchen counter—he wanted to turn it all the way off but didn't dare, in case he missed any new updates—and outside, they could hear the increase of traffic on Highline. The last of their neighbors, better prepared than the battalion chief's husband for an evac notice? Firefighters, en route to Flatiron from the south? Dare he hope . . . *Mel?*

Sam threw a glance out the window, remembered he couldn't see farther than the end of his own nose out there, and rechanneled his energy. "This fire is close enough that we're going to go into town right now, sound good, Astor?"

"Yeah, but, Dad! Listen to me!" She waved him over. "You need to check Annie."

"Why?" Sam shot back. But then he stopped, and really looked at her. Astor's expression edged closer to panic than he had ever seen from his competent, ice-water-in-her-veins firstborn. Even closer than earlier, first hearing the siren. "What is it? What's wrong?"

Astor's voice quavered. "One of her spells."

*Fuck, no.* Sam was already halfway into the living room before the expletive had fully formed in his brain, and at Annie's side before he could yell back to Astor, "Her med bag! I just put it next to the cooler!"

Annie's cheeks were blue, her lips were blue, her nose was blue. Her constant coughs now racked her small body so hard, her chest and abdomen bucked with the effort of each one. She cried hysterically, or would, if she could draw breath, panic causing her eyes to widen at Sam in terror as her hands clawed at his shirt, at her blanket, at the couch.

"Baby, baby, okay," Sam tried to soothe. "You're okay, you're okay," he chanted numbly as his brain screamed, *Help! Help! Help!* Because he knew: it was Annie's panic that threatened his daughter most. It was her panic that was going to force him to sink the morphine into her arm, just as soon as Astor brought the goddamned vial back to his side.

He had to stay calm for his child's sake, but at the sight of Annie's cyanotic state, her agony became his agony, her desperation to draw a breath his desperation. Annie's needs folded into his own right at the seams, her comfort sewn directly into the sinew of his bones. If he could, he would drain all his pumping blood into her waiting veins.

"Here!" Astor thrust the little glass vial of morphine and the already prepped syringe at him; she'd even torn open the plastic at the top of the syringe, so all he had to do was extract it, stab it into the top of the morphine vial, and sink it into Annie's flesh.

She screamed as he did it—she always screamed—but within seconds, her body stopped spasming as the meds hit her blood system and her lungs relaxed. As her face went slack. As her shoulders slumped.

Astor, too, had sunk to her knees at the side of the couch, quietly crying.

"I always hate this part," she said.

Sam did, too. It was even worse than the screaming. Sometimes, just to ease them all through it, he would try to joke with Annie, once the sting of the needle was past them.

"Where's Wonder Woman?" he'd asked her gently, leaning in to coax her up like the doctors instructed. The low dose should never knock her out completely. "I only see Slug Girl."

"I like being Slug Girl," Annie usually murmured.

Thank God for Astor, Wonder Woman from day one, though she should never have to be. As Sam eased Annie into his arms, he waved Astor over as well, enfolding her into his embrace for a brief second before having to ask her to repack the meds and drag the cooler to the front door.

It was a good thing they'd still been here when the tet spell hit, in the house where Sam could access the meds so easily, but it also punctuated anew just how fragile Sam's tenuous hold on his family was. His house still stood, for now, but he could lose Annie anyway. It had served as a sanctuary during the tet spell, but it wasn't the magical "safety" in the game of life Sam had tried to make it be. They were now precious minutes behind schedule, the buffer Sam had built into their evac eaten away by the medical emergency.

He consulted his watch. 16:22. They'd lost ten minutes.

Claude pounded on the door, and Annie whimpered against Sam's shoulder as Astor let him in. He looked ragged, mud staining his jeans where he must have fallen, but immediately, he noted Annie's condition and crossed the room to assess her. Sam saw what he saw: lips still tinged blue, but not the indigo they'd been moments ago. And Annie's fingers were pink again, against his arm.

Claude nodded gravely. "Let's go."

"To the Eddy?" Astor asked.

"I don't know," Sam told her. "Let's just go, okay? We gotta go."

A sudden noise sounded again outside, but instead of a pounding, this was a crunch of metal, accompanied by the shatter of glass. Sam flung back open the door.

"My SUV . . ." Sam gasped. The cedar tree in the driveway had fallen directly on top of it in the wind and heat. "How . . ."

But Claude didn't waste a second's time analyzing. He'd already turned back toward his truck with a load of gear. "We'll take my truck! Keys are in it. I'm going to start your water out front," he said.

It was standard Level 3 preventive protocol to assist the eventual first responders by soaking the roof and grounds before an evac, but at Claude's age, he shouldn't be outside at all, let alone running hoses. And there wasn't time: Sam's watch now said 16:32.

"Forget it!" he yelled. "Take Annie so I can load everything up!" She was crying softly again against his shoulder, stabilized enough to leave her uncomfortable but still too listless to walk on her own. Thanks to the tet spell, someone would have to carry her from here on out, and she was too heavy for Astor, who was already sprinting back and forth from the SUV to Claude's truck, tossing in duffels and boxes with rapid speed despite the heat, wind, and smoke.

Claude turned back, tripped on the loose stones of the walkway, staggered, and fell.

"Claude! Are you—"

But then Astor was there, helping him up, and Claude was reaching for Annie. "Give her here! I got her, I promise."

"Astor! Go to the truck with them," he ordered, grabbing more boxes himself. One held the extra N95s, which he pressed into Astor's free hand. "You put one of these on, too."

Astor didn't need to be told why: she tugged it over her ears and onto her face between coughing fits and immediately got back to work. Sam didn't notice the tears still in her eyes until they'd both stooped to pick up the last of the gear at the same time. "It'll be okay, honey," he managed.

By the time they had everything—*did* they have everything?—
Highline Road was eerily quiet, save for the wind. Even the heartiest,
most stoic of Sam's neighbors had already rolled down in a caravan of
trucks, minivans, and cars. Everyone else had mobilized faster than
him. *They don't have two kids—one with medical needs—and an elderly
man to assist.*

He ran to the truck to check on him and Annie, but Claude waved
him away, his eyes shadowed by soot and worry and dirt smudges.
Under his Buff, his face must be doing that worried quiver Sam always
hated to see in his aged expression. Which he hadn't seen much since
Ingrid had died, actually.

"You go take a final check," Claude said, his breath labored, nodding toward the house, "and then let's go!"

But Sam shook his head. He didn't need a last glance inside to
know his revelation from earlier still held. Everything that mattered was
already in Claude's truck.

Gasping and coughing, he eased himself in next to his girls and
Claude, all of them squeezed onto the single bench seat. It wasn't until
he had groped in the dark and smoke for his seat belt that he looked up
through the windshield and saw what had struck new fear into Claude:
the Flatiron Fire. Not on the ridge. Not on the slope on the other side
of the road.

*Right here.* Upon them.

# CHAPTER 27

Mel had never seen Carbon in such chaos. Even the old highway, usually underutilized as a bypass for the new interstate, was choked with oncoming cars. Vehicles made use of both lanes, north and south, in their exodus, and Lewis veered to the shoulder of the road and eased to a crawl, churning up dust along with the smoke.

"They're gonna kill me," the boy they'd picked up at the grow kept repeating as cars honked, people yelled, and arms flung out of windows, sometimes to wave others forward in an act of cooperation but more often in a show of anger or frustration as motorists cut in front of one another in an attempt to merge.

"I would worry more about *that*, if I were you," Lewis said, pointing at the billowing smoke toward the north, and at the sight, Mel tapped down a rise of bile in her throat. What did this second fire mean for Sam's place, a.k.a. her daughters' current sanctuary?

*We'll know when we know,* she told herself in a desperate mantra. First, though, they had to get back to Carbon. *Get there, get there, get there.* She leaned forward against the dash, trying to see past the ash raining down, as if thrusting herself forward could urge their vehicle faster.

Lewis's knuckles were white on the wheel. "You will be helping me record a report," he informed the boy tightly, who hugged his scrawny knees to his chest, hunched between Mel and True. "And you'll be talking to the DEA."

"They'll kill me," he repeated. Mel wasn't sure if he meant the Feds or Fallows, but he looked like he might puke, so probably the latter.

"We'll get you somewhere safe," Lewis told him, his mouth set in a grim line, "and go from there."

But the closer they got to town, the closer they got to the fires, and the worse the congestion and panic became. Several cars were now driving on the soft shoulder like Lewis, careening in their direction in a confusing game of chicken.

"Watch out!" True yelled as Lewis slammed on the brakes to avoid hitting a deer leaping out in front of the vehicle, the animal intent on its own exodus. Mel glimpsed a raccoon running parallel to the road, loping in pace with the cars, a sight she'd never seen in daylight. Dogs barked, children cried, and people shouted.

"This is insane," True said as a delivery truck laid on its horn and just wouldn't stop. "Do they really think anyone can go any faster?"

But Mel only heard *faster*. She nodded urgently. Yes. *Faster. Faster, faster, faster.* Her family depended on it. With a tiny register of surprise, Mel realized this title didn't only mean her children. She needed to lay eyes on Sam, too.

At the Carbon city limits sign, several additional roads merged, and cars became bumper-to-bumper. One Carbon Rural truck had been haphazardly parked in the turnout by the sign, lights and siren going. Two firefighters attempted to direct traffic through the dense smoke. Mel didn't recognize either of them in their full jumpsuits and N95s, but Lewis hit the brakes.

"Janet!" he called out the window, and one of the firefighters turned toward them, her expression glassy. "What's the latest status?" he asked her. "Where's this new fire burning?"

Janet shook her head and pointed to her ear, indicating that she couldn't hear the question.

"Just . . . report to White and Hernandez at the school," she said, "if you can. They're evacuating it."

"The school?" Lewis shouted. "We thought that *was* the evacuation site!"

Why were they quibbling over evac sites? Mel shook Lewis's shoulder. "We have to go directly up Highline!"

But Janet shook her head fervently before hopping out of the way of a rogue Chevy pickup, and when Lewis hit the gas, navigating another block past the Quik Save, Mel understood why: the Flatiron Fire was a wall of flame directly across the road, fanning east.

The heat of it hit Mel's skin even through the truck cab. Next to her, True's face had gone white, and their Fallows grow passenger cried out and attempted to yank his door open; Lewis hit the child-lock button just in time.

"Knock it off!"

Where was the kid planning to go, anyway? People still trying to escape this block had fully panicked; abandoned cars had been left directly in the roadway, their inhabitants fleeing on foot, their vehicles immediately becoming obstacles to others. Horns continued to blare as people attempted insane maneuvers to get around the abandoned vehicles, bumping over curbs and onto sidewalks. More animals ran wild here in town: dogs clawing their way out of opened and abandoned crates, cats dashing between cars, more raccoons coexisting with the domestic pets, all driven to flee.

A half dozen additional fire rigs faced off with the wall of fire on the east side of town, where the combined efforts of multiple agencies seemed to be making slow but steady progress. Still, the fire had completely swallowed the East Carbon Apartments, and Happy Daze mobile-home park appeared to be next. Teams of hand crews dashed back and forth between vehicles, grabbing gear and assisting with hoses. It was terrifying to see the coveted privatized crews, so highly trained in wildland fighting, now scrambling to be of any use in the urban setting.

Lewis swung a left at the next intersection, his destination clearly Carbon High, and Mel let out a sharp yell of disapproval. "What about Highline?"

"You heard Janet," he snapped back, his jaw set, his face dripping sweat.

"Lewis! Please!" She made a mad grab for the wheel.

True pulled Mel back from trying to overpower him in her panic. "The girls are probably already there, at the school," she shouted. "We should go there first."

Mel shook off her arm. Because what if they weren't?

They crossed the bridge over the Outlaw, and she spotted the River Eddy through the smoke, its usual picturesque backdrop with the river below now a hellscape in varying shades of angry red.

At Carbon High, chaos reigned. It seemed no one knew whether to stay or go. Multiple fire vehicles staged, at the ready to load passengers. Refugees from the fire who had either abandoned or lost their cars queued in the parking lot, adding to the fray. Lewis struggled to find a place to pull off the road, but Mel flung herself out of the truck before he'd even come to a complete stop.

"Astor! Annie!"

She and True wove between shell-shocked citizens and fully suited-up firefighters, but within minutes, she knew her family wasn't among the refugees. "True! They're not here!"

"Then we're going to them!"

Back at the truck, however, Lewis shook his head emphatically. "I won't do it, Mel. I can't abandon my crew, and neither can you." The word *again* echoed between them, despite being unsaid.

"Lewis! This is my *family*! My girls! What if it was Susan or Jacob?"

"Dammit!" he cursed, kicking at the tires in frustration and fear. Tears mixed with the sweat that dripped from his face. He took a deep, bracing breath, coughed up a storm, and then very deliberately hefted the bags of evidence to his shoulder and laid the keys on the bench seat. "Junior here and I are going to check in with White," he said, a hitch in his voice as he nodded in the direction of the assembled fire engines. A command tent had been hastily erected in their midst. "We'll only be gone a minute."

He yanked the kid out of the cab and, turning his back to Mel and True, walked him resolutely toward the fray. The second they'd disappeared into the crowd, True and Mel both pounced on the keys as one. True snagged them first, and had already slid into the driver's seat and hit the gas by the time Mel slammed shut the passenger-side door.

True fought her way toward Highline at a reckless pace. Past the sheriff's department personnel stationed at the junction, ineffectively barring traffic. Past the houses along the lower end of the road. Even with the windshield wipers going a mile a minute, she could barely see a thing, ash and sparks raining down on the glass as she took the turns by memory, or instinct, or something in between.

Could this fire-department vehicle even make the drive? Could anything less than a wildland engine at this point? True cast a sidelong glance at Mel, but if she was wondering the same thing, she wasn't voicing her concerns, her mouth moving in an endless whispered mantra of *Go, go, go.*

She hit a pothole head-on, and the truck lurched. "Shit. Sorry." She gripped the wheel tighter, reestablishing them on the road. She tried to make out the status of the houses they passed along the lower part of Highline, trying to gauge from them how Sam's might be faring; were they smoldering? Burning outright? Escaping the worst of the carnage? But visibility was at about two feet, max, so she strained to see forward instead. Only forward. It was the only way she'd get to Sam and the kids with herself, this vehicle, and Mel all in one piece.

A sudden impact to the back side of the truck sent them abruptly skidding again. True's seat belt bit into her shoulder as she was thrown forward.

"True!" Mel yelled, bracing an arm against the dash.

"Sorry! I don't know what that was." Had they hit something? God, some*one*? True strained to see behind her in the rearview mirror and thought she could make out two orbs . . . headlights milky in the smoke. Another vehicle?

"Is it Lewis?" Mel shouted, twisting in her seat for a better look. "Rogue Rural?"

But this vehicle was so close, so—*bam!*

Another impact, this one accompanied by the unmistakable sound of crunching metal and glass. Someone had crashed into them from behind. True laid on the horn. Could they not see their truck through the smoke?

"They're coming up alongside us!" Mel yelled.

True veered left, trying in vain to avoid a third impact, which sent the truck into a tight tailspin. The fourth spun them into a dough-nut pattern, the resulting cloud of smoke, dust, and ash leaving them blinded. True had the impulsive thought that they'd traded one natural disaster for another, entering inexplicably into the eye of a tornado. "What the fuck!"

The other vehicle had slammed on their brakes and now blocked Highline at a perpendicular angle. Several figures piled out of the rig as True threw the truck into reverse.

"Can you get around them?" Mel shouted, but no, she couldn't. She couldn't even maneuver around one of them . . . and at least five men now blocked the road. Who? Why? And then the weak beam of their headlights finally illuminated the vehicle that had slammed into them, and the adrenaline tightened into a leaden ball of fear in True's gut. The familiar *Fallows, Inc.* wrap peeling on the driver's-side door told them all they needed to know.

"Mel. Oh my God."

Pounding on the windows elicited a cry of alarm from Mel, who shouted again for True to "Hurry! Go!" but the men had already yanked open their doors, and strong arms already pulled at True, jerking her roughly out of the truck.

"Mel!"

Fallows himself gripped Mel by the shoulders, shaking her. "Give it up!" he yelled at her.

"What?" Mel gasped, her voice tightened in shock and fear.

"My guys saw you at the site." He continued to yell over the constant roar of the wind and fire. Fallows's men tightened their circle around Mel and True, expressionless in their Buffs and bandannas to ward off the smoke, sidearms on every hip. "Saw you go in my shed and take what you wanted. You think I don't have surveillance? You think you two can stiff me what you owe me, and then rob me blind, all at once? You're stupider than you look!"

He jerked Mel's shoulders with every sentence, practically throwing her to the ground, and True shook her own captor and launched herself at him, managing to slam a shoulder into his side before three guys pulled her away. A sharp stab of pain shot down her arm as her hand was yanked behind her back, and then her head hit something hard. A side window or maybe a door. She tasted metal as her mouth filled with blood.

She fought to keep consciousness as Fallows shoved Mel toward one of his goons and then pivoted to spit at True's feet before frisking her with rough, callused hands. "Give it up. The cash you snatched. Where is it?" When she shook her head, still seeing spots, he fisted his hand and sent it into her gut. Then again. "You wanna be treated like one of the guys? You will be." A third blow sent her knees into the dirt, and a fourth brought her face to the ground, where she had a hazy, horizontal view of their go bags and gear being tossed from the inside of the truck cab, ripped open, and searched.

"Please," she heard Mel beg, and True tried to lift her head to see her. "We don't have it! We just need to get to my kids. I'll do anything. Please." The desperation in her voice landed harder than Fallows's fists. True knew she meant it.

She managed to find her feet again in time to see Fallows yank Mel up against him, laughing when her head jerked awkwardly at the sudden impact. True bit back a sob, her own impotence the hardest gut punch of all. A scathing look contorted Fallows's face above his bandanna as he pressed his face right up to Mel's. "You can see your precious children when I have what's mine."

Nausea roiled in True's gut, and she spit out more blood as an ugly realization dawned in her clouded head. Fallows had blocked their path, right here, right now, for this exact purpose. He'd stooped even lower than True had imagined he could go, exploiting a mother's primal need for her kids in hopes of wringing something out of her that she couldn't even give.

Mel continued to claw at Fallows in an effort to escape, and True knew if she found a way to slip free of the vise grip that held her, she would run the rest of the way up Highline on foot if she had to. And she'd only get more desperate the closer the fire crept.

True tried to call out to her, her voice snatched by the howl of the wind. She took a staggered step in her direction, the need to get to her, to help her, burning through some of the pain. Vision still blurring, she homed in on the sight of Fallows's sidearm. Could she grab it while his attention was on Mel? Or would his men be on True within one step? It was a risk, but True had just decided it was riskier not to when—sirens! Cutting through even the roar of the fire. At the sight of a sheriff's department Suburban, Fallows's men scattered as if on instinct, making a leap for their truck, and Fallows released Mel. But not fast enough.

"They rammed us off the road!" True shouted as the deputy who had been stationed at the base of Highline leaped out of his vehicle, his hand already on the service revolver on his belt. His partner took Fallows by force and cuffed him deftly as Mel sank to her knees in the dirt.

Relief washed through True to see her freed, only to feel another clutch of panic as Fallows's getaway vehicle peeled out, nearly hitting her. It left their boss in the dust, however, just as another car, this one a civilian sedan of some sort, skidded to a stop. Lewis alighted from the driver's seat, swearing loudly.

"Got about halfway across the parking lot to White before realizing there was no way in hell I wasn't coming up here to back you up," he told Mel, who had scrambled to her feet in relief at the sight of him. "When the sheriff detail said they'd just seen Fallows screaming up here in your wake, I knew that meant trouble."

He turned toward the deputies. "He's threatening them for what we discovered at the Fallows property," he shouted as they shoved Fallows into the patrol rig.

"You can't prove that!" Fallows bellowed back.

"Two full evidence bags of guns, ammo, and cash say otherwise," Lewis told him, "all to be processed by the DEA ASAP."

"Fine, fine," the deputy shouted, coughing on each word. "In the meantime, you're under arrest for assault and reckless driving," he told Fallows. "Not to mention obstructing an emergency-evacuation route."

True heard this from what felt like very far away, hands braced on her knees, still trying to fully come to. Her head rang from her impact with the car. She managed to lift her head and confirm that Fallows was really in cuffs, that Mel was still here, trying to shake off Lewis's concern for her. It was so hard to see anything in these conditions.

The deputy also eyed the billowing smoke, all that obscured the red wall of Flatiron somewhere behind it, and turned to his partner. "We'd better get downhill."

At this, Mel grabbed Lewis's arm. "The kids!" she shouted. "The house! We've wasted too much time already!"

Lewis nodded. "I know, I know, but this is all I could get my hands on." He gestured frantically toward the Honda Civic he'd commandeered. The tire rubber was already melting off the axles.

"We can get the rest of the way up in the department rig," Mel insisted, gesturing toward the truck she and True had hijacked, which still sat at a haphazard angle on the road where Fallows had hit it. "It's made it this far."

One deputy shouted to them, waving them back, and True caught the words *restricted* and *hazardous* and *no time* before his partner urged him, "Forget it, just go!" and then they were gone, peeling out in the dirt back in the direction of Carbon, Fallows in the rear seat.

Lewis looked like he might want to follow suit, but he, too, could see there was no stopping Mel.

"We can try," he shouted, "but we stay only long enough to hold off the fire until an EMS vehicle can get up here for Annie." He waved Mel toward the department rig. "Load up. True, you head down in the Honda."

True just shot him a look while hefting herself back up into the battered truck behind Mel. She swiped roughly at the sweat pouring off her face. "When hell freezes over, Lewis."

"Wouldn't *that* be a welcome development right about now," he shot back, sliding into the driver's seat and hitting the gas.

# CHAPTER 28

The heat in the cab of Claude's truck was now nothing less than an oppressive physical force, pinning Sam in place with the unrelenting strength of a gravitational centrifuge.

"Dad!" Astor screamed in an octave Sam had never heard from her, straining against her seat belt in fear, but he barely registered the sound over his own terror. They hadn't even left the driveway, and yet directly in front of them, visibility had horribly, terrifyingly improved: the Flatiron Fire burned hot in a dramatic billow of red and pink and black, the wind sending a huge flume of smoke toward the east, illuminating the entire upper road.

"It looks like the . . . poster from . . . school," Astor gasped, her words oddly muffled by her mask. They'd had a contest at the elementary; the winner of the best fire-safety poster had been a sixth grader with a penchant for dramatic watercolor strokes. He'd won a trip to the fire station, where he'd allegedly sprayed Dave Lewis with a fire hose. Sam let his eyes rest on Astor's face for just a fraction of a moment, even her scared expression preferable to the sight of the blaze out the windshield.

He wrapped an arm around her, and she shrank into him, her face pressed close to his armpit.

"Claude!" he prompted, because the old man seemed to have frozen in place in the driver's seat. "Go!"

Claude sort of jumped in his seat, like Sam's cry had activated him, turning the key aggressively in the ignition. Nothing.

"Claude!" Sam shouted again, because *why* were they not *moving*?

"I know, I know!" He cranked the key again; this time the truck gave a screech of protest, but the engine still refused to roll over. "It's overheated!" Claude yelled, pointing one thick finger at the heat gauge on the dash. "Grab the hose! We gotta cool it!"

Sam wrenched open the door, only to emit a curse before flinging it shut again on base instinct. Because the second he'd exposed them to the outside air, a new, unprecedented heat had hit them all with full force against the wall of wind. It was as though they'd suddenly tumbled straight into an industrial clothes dryer.

"Dad!" Astor yelled again, and despite her morphined state, Annie began to cry again, a high-pitched, raspy wail. Even with the truck door closed again, the heat in the cab had risen. Surely, it had not been this hot in here three minutes ago. Even one minute ago.

"What-are-we-gonna-do?" Astor cried, eyes huge as she stared forward, watching the fire approach. She gasped a breath, her eyes streaming tears, strands of hair stuck to her sweaty cheeks. "What's happening?"

Somehow, impossibly, this newly merged fire had beaten them, meeting them at Highline before they could flee. It had gobbled right through Sam's precious timeline, his carefully laid-out evacuation plan, his and Claude's cautious efforts. It had caught them flat-footed, sitting in a Ford that simply wouldn't run.

"I don't know," he shouted. Outside, all he saw was black and red and sparks in the air. Inside this metal shell, he felt only increasing heat.

"Are we burning?" Annie mumbled. "Daddy, are we gonna burn up?"

"No!" he yelled, looking swiftly at Claude, which did nothing to reassure him. Claude's eyes remained forward, his full focus on the fire, his hands now oddly braced on the steering wheel. Sam watched as the glass of the truck windshield steamed with this new, intense heat slowly, like a defroster working in reverse. "No, Annie, no," he managed more calmly. They all needed to remain calm. "Claude?" he said. Then, "Claude! We need to move!"

In answer, he turned the key in the ignition again. Not even a sputter answered from the engine.

"Do we go back inside?" Astor yelled.

"Daddy," Annie cried again.

"Let me think!" Sam shouted. They couldn't just sit here in the truck.

Claude tried the ignition yet again, cursing at the truck, his stooped shoulders angled toward the steering wheel as if he'd decided that putting his full weight behind the task would urge the old beast into gear. Nothing this time, either. Not even a click. Sam's stomach dropped out from under him in a sickening lurch.

He must have said something, though he didn't fully comprehend what, because Claude looked at him directly for the first time in minutes, his face a mask of something Sam had never, in all his years living next door to him on Highline, seen in the old German man: stark fear. "It'll only get hotter in here," he said, his voice, always so stalwart and steady, unnervingly shaky. "It'll catch us in the car."

"Dad?" Astor cried again. She clutched at his sleeve. "Claude!"

Sam cast an automatic glance back in the direction the mass exodus of evacuees had taken, though the last of the cars had long ago been swallowed in the haze of black, brake lights no longer visible. Every cell in his body told him to follow them, to get out and run if they had to. But then he looked forward again, and he knew instinctively they could not outrun what was coming for them.

Astor followed Sam's gaze. "The fire's *everywhere* now!"

She was right. After merging with the new lightning fire, the Flatiron Fire had split somewhere on Buck Peak, one side burning faster than the other through the dry undergrowth of Highline. It now consumed both sides of the road, down Highline *and* up, threatening to meet in the middle, like two forks of a river, Claude's truck and the

Bishops' house forming a sort of sandbar between the blazes. No, they wouldn't escape it on foot any better than in this coffin of a car.

Was this it, then? Were Sam's mistakes going to cost his children their very lives? Were they all going to perish here, depriving the woman he loved of her family, if Mel was even . . . hadn't already . . . Sam couldn't go there. All he knew: he and his kids were paying far, far too high a price for his wanting to keep his family whole and happy on this hill.

Claude looked once more at the blaze, then seemed to snap back into action, thank God. "Get back in the house!" he decided, suddenly loosening his vise grip on the wheel to hastily unbuckle Annie next to him. The leather steering wheel cover remained indented when he released it, softened in the heat. "All of you! Now! Take a deep breath! Brace yourselves! But get back in the house!"

"Shouldn't we—Claude, what about your pond?" It was a desperately flung suggestion, the words literally stolen from him in the oppressive heat now that Claude had reopened his door.

"What? No! Look!"

Sam did, only to see flames billowing on all sides of Claude's property.

The heat smothered them like a blanket, and he heard Annie cry out again, only to have her voice nearly instantly stolen from her by a fit of coughing. Sam, too, suddenly couldn't breathe—actually couldn't breathe; for the first time, the density of smoke that wafted in now was enough to choke them all. Taking as shallow of breaths as he could, he thought of that airline regulation, the one where you put your air mask on first, before your kids', and decided that was both the best and the most useless advice ever. As if he wouldn't die trying to loosen Astor's seat belt. As if he wouldn't drown in this smoke trying to ensure Annie got back through the front door. It was the way he felt about tet spells times one thousand.

Still in the truck, Astor had gone uncharacteristically quiet, her eyes wide as she watched the angry flames out the window get closer and closer, the wind spurring them on. Sam yanked on her hand, his other arm loaded with only what he deemed most essential, with what he always wrote at the top of his priority list: Annie's cooler and oxygen. Even the medical bag proved secondary right now. Claude had already scooped up Annie and was making an awkward, unsteady sprint toward the front door, her small body wrapped around his midsection like a baby monkey. When Sam put his hand back on the door handle to make a similar exit with Astor, the metal burned his palm; he yelped in surprise at the unexpected, searing pain.

In the driveway, the smoke instantly rendered him blind. Now he understood Claude's weaving, stumbling gait. He kept his hand tight in Astor's and made what he hoped was a beeline for the porch steps, pushing through the front door just after Claude.

It felt better in here, just slightly—he could breathe, he could see Annie and Astor breathing, though Annie coughed and sputtered again after being exposed to the air, to a point that had Sam digging blindly through his pockets for her emergency inhaler. He could see Claude struggling to make a sprint for the kitchen.

It was a hazy gray inside, the smoke thicker than in a casino lounge, but Sam could choke out, "Claude! I don't know if we should stay!" He cast about through the chaos that reigned in his brain for hard facts he might have gleaned through the years: wildfires had an uncanny habit of sweeping right past or over some buildings, even while consuming others. Their mowed field might provide protection, but it just as easily might not. He was certain now that had they stayed in the truck, they'd be dead already. Did the same fate await them here in the house?

Mel's words rushed in to haunt him. *Is this really the hill you want to die on?* No, no, no. Never.

But now it was too late. Leaving would be suicide.

But if this house *was* to be his last stand, Highline serving as the only sanctuary left to them, running the hoses and soaking the roof jumped in priority. Braving the elements one more time, he flung back open the door, running, near bent double, to the closest outside spigot and cranking it all the way open. Would it be enough to keep the lick of the flames from jumping from the field and neighboring rooftops? He just didn't know, but he ran to the next one, and then the last, ensuring all hoses were flowing.

Claude yelled something just as Sam ran back inside, though he could hardly hear him over the sound of the wind and, now, more water running in the kitchen sink. Claude bent over the tap, stoppering the drain with the little rubber piece Astor usually dropped behind the counter when she was on dish duty. "Get me towels . . . all the towels!"

Sam ran for the guest bathroom, on this floor just off the living room, pulling hand towels off the rack and thrusting them at Astor, who'd followed him, crying. "Give these to Claude," he ordered, refusing to allow himself to stop and comfort his daughter, refusing himself even one stingy glance at the familiar determination in Astor's young eyes, fearful that right now he wouldn't find it.

Claude soaked a towel and wrapped it around Annie, who in her drug-induced disorientation tried to yank it back off, sputtering on the cold, wet terry cloth. He ignored her, which was saying something. Annie had had Claude wrapped around her little finger from the day she'd come home from the hospital, already battle-worn from multiple surgeries.

The next time she flung off the towel, Sam urged the inhaler on her, demanding her to breathe on cue, yelling at her really, as she sobbed, eyes bleary and body limp, depressing the plastic button and blindly hoping the medication made its way into her lungs.

He ran up the stairs to the girls' bathroom next, yanking Astor's octopus-print terry robe off its hanger and dousing it in water from the tub. His eyes streamed tears: fear, smoke, adrenaline—somehow it had all become the same thing, one chemically driven, emotional ball of synergy that kept Sam moving forward, kept him soaking towels, gave him the strength to stagger back down the stairs under the dripping weight of them.

All the while, his brain played on a loop: *How is this happening?* They should have had time. He had his go bags. He had his list. He had his timeline. He'd waited for the evac order. Where had he gone astray? He'd never seen a fire do this. In all his years living in wildfire country, he'd never seen anything move this fast.

The wind rattled the windows now, smoke pouring in from even the best-sealed panes, the ones Sam had actually outsourced to a construction crew. He had no idea what was happening outside, only that it was angry and loud. He hadn't realized fire could carry such noise, but thundering cracks cut the air amid bursts of hissing steam over a never-ending roar like the sound of hydraulic power coursing over a dam. The emergency broadcast still blared its warning, background noise to intermittent *BOOMs* of his neighbors' propane tanks blowing up, the fire consuming houses one by one. If he counted booms, would Sam know when they were next? The morbidity of this thought would have shocked him, had any shock value remained possible. But Sam had gone numb inside. Fighting for his life, fighting for his children's lives, while knowing they were all at the absolute mercy of the elements, shut something down inside him. It was like Sam was back in Afghanistan, where he'd somehow removed his heart from his body, his soul from his actions, to get through a day of combat. And this was worse. So much worse.

Claude, however, seemed to thrive in battle. He worked with singular purpose, stuffing towels everywhere he could at the cracks, along window ledges and under doorways, while Sam continued wrapping the girls like sopping mummies, ignoring their cries and screams and coughs.

"Take them into the primary bathroom. The one on this floor, that has the bigger soaker tub," Claude ordered, and Sam obeyed blindly—literally, for the most part—even as his mind spun, and he tried to determine whether they should still make a run for it instead or whether hunkering down was truly the smartest choice now. It always seemed so clear when he watched stories like this on the news. It always seemed so obvious, what people should do. He rubbed at his eyes blindly, attempting to see. *Nothing is obvious. Nothing is clear.*

In the primary bathroom, he spun in an aimless circle. Wait . . . did Claude mean put the girls in the tub in the water? Or in the dry tub? What would Mel do? Again, he wondered wildly: Were he and Claude destined to be lambasted in the news media, those people everyone talked about who'd done the wrong thing, walked through the wrong door, put these children at risk for nothing? If so, it was Sam's fault. All Sam's fault.

He ushered the girls unceremoniously into the dry tub, layering wet towels and blankets over them. A compromise. Faintly, over the sound of the fire, he still heard the warning siren blaring, but it no longer came from the kitchen, through the radio. What he heard, Sam realized, came from outside, down Highline, and after a moment of letting it register, he identified it as the siren from one of the smaller fire rigs used by ground crews. *Like Mel drives.* He'd know it anywhere. How many times had he heard its surprisingly loud wail as he visited the station with the girls? How many times had Dave Lewis, or the new kid, Deklan, let Astor and Annie climb into the cab and push the button, running the lights simultaneously? Annie had delighted in it, clapping her hands at the *bleep-bleep-bleep reeeeeer* coming from the tinny speakers, and all those burly firefighters had gamely clapped hands over their ears and gone about their chores, happy to let the little Bishop girl with the heart condition have her fun.

He ran to the window, remembering belatedly that, just like before, it would be too smoky to see a thing. Wind rattling everything. Rushing smoke into the bathroom like some valve somewhere had been released, opening up the floodgates of a hell Sam had thought existed only in the movies. He squinted: lights filtered weakly through the haze on the road. The sirens grew louder and louder. The girls sobbed, curled up in the tub with towels over their heads, no longer yanking them off, no longer needing to be told to cooperate. Surely they could barely breathe through the towels, but they didn't squirm under the sopping pile, their little sides rising and falling in a sad, weak sort of obedience. Astor's arms wrapped around Annie's stomach, Annie's face smushed into Astor's armpit. The heat bore down, worsening by the second now, not by the minute.

# CHAPTER 29

It felt like both five seconds and five hours had passed when Sam heard the crash of the front door and then, impossibly, miraculously, Mel's voice cutting through the never-ending noise. "Sam!" she screamed, the sound of her footfalls—heavy in her boots—already on the hardwood. "SAM!"

Relief sluiced through him, thick and hot, feeling every bit as intense as the heat and the smoke.

"Is that . . . Mom?" he heard Astor yell, her voice muffled by terry cloth and wind and booms.

"Yes, but stay where you are!"

If he knew Mel, which Sam most certainly did, she would come to them.

"In here!" Sam yelled, torn between running to meet Mel and remaining here with the girls, still huddled in the tub. Her boots thundered down the hall, and the bathroom door he'd wedged closed shook. He leaped toward it, yanking it open against the resistance put up by the soaked towels lining the crack at the bottom of the door.

"Mel!" He collided with her, the solid bulk of her radio unit strapped to her chest momentarily robbing him of what little air was in his lungs. He didn't care, holding her tight, inhaling the strong scent of smoke and dirt and sweat on her yellow shirt.

Her arms wrapped around him, too, but only briefly, before she lunged toward the girls. True stood behind Mel; Sam only just then registered her presence.

"Mom," Astor cried, trying to rid herself of the towels to get to her mother.

"No, no," Mel rasped. "Stay down. Stay there." Her voice sounded tighter and higher than Sam was used to, the urgency there impossible to miss. It sent a new wave of alarm through him. If Mel and True were here, so was Mel's crew, right? They'd have engines that could stand the heat. That could carry them down Highline. "Why don't you want us to go?"

"We can't transport Annie until we get an EMS rig up here," Mel said. She tugged Sam back toward the little bathroom window, gesturing for him to look. He did, and *holy shit*. Where smoke had obscured his view just moments ago, visibility had been oddly restored. It took Sam a second to understand why: direct flames now lit up the street. The wind had driven the Flatiron Fire back up their hill, just as Claude predicted. Had it essentially encircled the house? Yes, it burned right there, ringing around the field and on both sides of Highline, having left the near slope of Buck Peak aflame in its wake. Sam knew in this moment he and Claude had made the right call: had they set out on foot, or even if the truck had cooperated, they would have been caught on the road when the fire made this turn. Trailing so far behind the other evacuees, and without the protection of a fire engine, they would have been consumed whole.

The reality of this was so sobering, he swallowed impulsively, his throat burning. Instinctively, he staggered back toward the girls. Astor and Annie looked like small, poorly costumed ghosts slumped in the tub, adding a macabre twist to what was already a scene of doom.

"Stay here with the girls," Mel ordered, turning for the door, True, as always, on her heels.

"You stay, too!" Sam shouted back at Mel, grabbing her by the shirt sleeve.

She shook herself free. "Sam, I can't!"

The sudden sense of abandonment as his fingers grasped empty air brought another question to Sam's lips. "Where's Claude?" he asked in a panic.

As Mel wedged the door open just enough to slide back through it, they all glimpsed the answer to this question at the same time. Claude had fallen again between the hallway and living room and was now trying to ease himself back on all fours.

*Oh, Claude.*

Mel reached him first, pulling him to his feet with one shaky arm and turning him back in the direction in which she'd come. "Go!" she told him. "You're halfway out already! You, too!" she told True. "Go with him!"

The tone of her voice had Astor lifting her head. "Mom? Don't you leave, too!" she cried in panic, looking up through the haze of smoke. "What are we going to do?"

Mel crouched down to meet Astor at eye level. She touched Astor's quaking shoulder briefly, then Annie's, in a trail of a caress, like she was both loath to leave and loath to stay, where she would be as impotent as the rest of them. Sam understood completely.

"True and I are going to keep the house wet," she told her. "Claude, too. Dad already started the lines. We'll keep the house wet, and that will help."

"It will keep the fire outside?"

Mel hesitated, her jaw doing that thing it did when she couldn't quite stomach what she had to say next. Sam had seen it often enough. "It will help," she repeated.

"But when will this be over?" Astor cried, as unsatisfied with this answer as Sam. She looked frantically from Mel to Sam to Mel again.

Again, Mel struggled for an answer. Finally, she said, "Soon." Her throat worked as she swallowed hard. "It will be over soon, baby."

A hitch in her voice made this even harder to hear. Tears from the smoke and so much more bled a trail down the dirt and grime on Mel's cheeks as she rose from her crouched position to leave.

Sam wanted to stop her again. Wanted it as much as Astor. Instead, he locked eyes with her one last time, hoping he could ensure her safety by sheer willpower alone.

She sensed it. "Don't worry. We've got Lewis outside as well," she told him. "And Sam?" She returned his gaze. "That was a good call, turning on the water. A great call."

The gratitude Sam saw in her eyes burned away the edges of the fear for just an instant, but then she was on the move again.

He crawled into the soaker tub with his girls, feeling through the smoke for Astor's hand, for Annie's. "Okay," he whispered—or cried, he wasn't sure which—into their ears, brushing their wet hair back from their sweat- and water-soaked heads, letting them bury their small faces into his chest. "Okay, babies. It's okay."

He curled his body around them, and the three of them huddled there, in the tub, Sam reminding himself over and over that he didn't need to play the hero. The mother of his children more than filled that role.

Mel knew the impossibility of fighting a wildland fire with a garden hose. But here she stood, legs braced against the wind and the heat and the flames that literally licked her boots, her face wrapped in her Buff, shoulder to shoulder with True, Lewis, and Claude, who looked, the few times Mel risked a glance, like he might topple with fatigue into the fire at any moment.

Before them, across their field, somewhere in the midst of this angry, churning blaze, Claude's house already burned, Mel was sure of that, each wall and window and warm memory of his late wife adding fuel to the fire as it fell. They could hear the intermittent crashes and booms as drywall dropped as though detonated, as glass shattered, as wood cracked. Most people didn't realize how loud it could be in the presence of a burning building. When you saw it on the news, every-thing was muted by audio and voiceovers. They all got the full experience now, in surround sound, the noise deafening. Next to Mel, Claude cried openly as he aimed his hose at the burning ground, but he didn't retreat, and he didn't complain.

The mowed field between the houses proved to be their salvation. It slowed the progress of the blaze from Claude's property to Sam's, buying them time—buying Annie time—so that instead of a wall of flame, they faced a carpet. But still it crept, this fiery carpet, low and thin, like a predatory animal slinking toward them through the dense smoke. In a moment of inspiration, Mel handed True her garden hose, opting to add Sam's pressure washer to the mix, which she attached to the only water hookup in the garage, unscrewing the thick rubber hose to the washing machine in the mudroom with clumsy hands. She ran the pressure washer at full capacity in wide arcs across the ground at her feet, but even so, it only delayed the inevitable, pushing back the crawling fire less than an inch at a time.

It was at least ten more minutes before she heard a new, much more welcome sound through the din. She paused, pressure-washer hose in hand, trying to listen. Yes . . . that was the promised EMS rig, and a big one. Probably a Type 3 engine, as well, from the magnitude of the rumble at Mel's feet.

She felt a tentative smile crack her dry, burnt lips as beside her, Claude let out a hoarse whoop of gladness. They'd done it . . . They'd held the blaze at bay long enough for help to arrive. The sight of Mel's crew spilling out of the second engine brought a sudden rush of tears to her eyes . . . She hadn't thought she had any moisture left in her body. She caught a glimpse of Janet's silent nod in her direction as she hopped down from the running board, her careworn face still smudged with soot. Men and women shouted orders over the noise, their voices disembodied through the thick smoke. From the EMS rig, an entire ground team from Eagle Valley piled out in full structural gear, wasting no time unwrapping hoses in the driveway. They must have off-roaded the last few hundred yards, where the fire burned on both sides of the road.

"In the house!" Mel shouted to them, dropping the sprayer end of the pressure washer onto the smoldering, wet ground to rush over. "Please! Get my girls!"

Two men wearing Dust Busters jackets entered the front door, while Claude said, "Go, go!" and Mel went, sprinting back across the grass to make sure Sam and the kids made it out to the trucks.

She should have known it couldn't be that easy. First, the only medic qualified to supply Annie with the extra oxygen she needed to make the journey down the hill had just passed his EMT-Intermediate level last week, which led to a lot of panicked floundering with the tubes and tank in the doorway. Mel's attention divided; half the time, she focused on continuing to fight the blaze in front of the house, but the other half, she was craning her neck to watch for Annie's evacuation from Highline.

"They'll get her to the rig," True kept saying, but *when*?

When Annie finally emerged in Sam's arms, she made for a pathetic picture, still wrapped in wet towels, her face obscured by a pediatric oxygen mask and nasal canula. Astor ran behind, an N95 pressed to her face with one hand—they simply couldn't be adjusted to fit properly—and Annie's medical supply bag in the other. On her back she'd strapped her own go bag, as well as several of Claude's prized quilts that had never made it out to his truck.

"That girl is a freakin' marvel," True declared. But behind the pride, her voice shook with worry and fear and entirely too much smoke inhalation.

Sam pressed Annie back into the arms of the EMT, who climbed into the cab of the EMS rig. Janet followed; then Lewis held a hand out for Astor, who swung up behind him. Mel lifted a hand in farewell, finally understanding the sentiment *godspeed*, expecting Sam to heft himself up into the vehicle behind the girls. Instead, he pushed off the running board at the last moment, hopping back onto the dirt of the driveway.

At least three people yelled his name, and he ignored all three, running back to the house and grabbing the hose from a barely standing Claude. "Go. Now!" he told him, shoving the old man in the direction of the EMS rig in his place.

Claude attempted a protest, but his words were lost, stolen from his throat by the cloying smoke. Sputtering and coughing, he pulled Sam into a swift embrace and then launched himself toward the engine. Shoulders hunched, head down, he made his way to the safety of the rig on shaky legs. As Lewis lifted him up, Sam swung around to True.

"You, too!" he shouted, completely ignoring the stunned *Who, me?* look she flung his way. He grabbed at her, practically pulling her toward the rig. "Please, True. My girls need you. Because what if . . ." He cast a look back over his shoulder toward the blaze, where debris from neighboring roofs flew through the wind, where the flames licked in an angry roar. "Just—please!"

True looked between him and Mel and back again, as if unsure from whom she took orders these days, then came to her own conclusion.

"Hold up!" she yelled toward the rig, jumping into the back just as it began to move, managing a tight maneuver in the drive before pointing its nose toward town.

"They'll make it," Mel told Sam, whose hands were now braced on his knees as he coughed in the direction of the dirt. The EMS rig, like the Engine 3, was built to withstand the heat and debris that Claude's truck simply couldn't.

"Good," he managed. "Thank God."

As Mel redirected her hose toward the fire, part of her wanted to take Sam by the shirt and shake him for giving up his space beside their girls, but the other part had never been more grateful. Having him by her side in this moment felt so right, it made the entire past year feel like a stupid, pointless detour. How had it taken their literal feet to the literal fire for her to see it?

The righteous anger that usually burned hot and bright in her being melted into the marrow of her bones, and the fact that this revelation came as they fought for *this* house, the house that had broken them in the first place, was an irony she would have to unpack later.

If later ever came.

She expected Sam to pick up Claude's hose and use every remaining second to combat the blaze, but instead, as the Dust Busters piled into the engine, he reached for her hose and dropped it to the ground. "Annie is safe," he said, tugging her toward their last chance at a ride out of the inferno. "Which means it's time to go."

From the back of the Type 3, Sam watched as a Douglas fir, lit up like a torch, toppled onto the roof of his deck with a loud crack, just to join the cedar that had flattened his SUV. For an instant, a shower of sparks impeded his vision, and then he saw the flames begin to lick the roof.

This structure, in its current state, represented every toxic family pattern Sam had been determined to break since he'd left for his first deployment. The sense of purpose that reimagining it for his own family had given Sam a visceral feeling, like every ounce of parental responsibility his old man had lacked had skipped a generation and landed squarely in Sam's gut. And maybe he'd needed that. Maybe fixing what was broken in this house had been essential, even, but that purpose had been served. His girls were safe. Mel was at his side, pressed in close on the jump seat of the engine.

The only thing left was to let it burn.

Once the thought landed, it burrowed itself directly into Sam's frontal cortex, igniting into something akin to hope. Was this how ancient peoples had felt, watching the pyres of their ancestors burn in fiery surrender? He remembered something Mel had told him after she'd finished her fire-science training. *Ash is the purest of elements.* It mixes with the earth and helps create new growth.

It was time to be reborn. He tore his watering eyes away from the house and onto the road ahead of them as the engine eased out of the driveway, not looking back even as he heard the fire find its way from the porch roof to a second-story window in an explosion of glass and heat.

One of the firefighters clapped a hand on his shoulder in sympathy. "Hey, now, this is what insurance is for," he shouted over the noise of the fire and the engine.

Money for Annie. Money for what mattered. *Yes,* Sam thought, egging the fire on with a fervent prayer of thanks. *Let it burn.*

# CHAPTER 30

The ride back down Highline was like driving through a hellscape. The Type 3 carried them down the hill at a speed Mel wouldn't dare; dust flew up in their wake to mingle with the burning ash they now had to clear from the windshield, the wipers flicking across the grimy glass in quick arcs. Even so, visibility was more of a pipe dream than a reality; embers flew up across the glass like sparks flying from a welder's grinder, showering down on them in a hailstorm of fire. Their driver, a man Mel didn't know, swore under his breath, swerving to stay on course. If this vehicle didn't weigh whatever it did, they'd be squirreling out on the road like teenagers on a joyride. Luckily, it drove like a tank, tearing through the dirt, leaving new ruts in its wake.

They swerved often to avoid the worst of the smoldering hot spots where the fire had breached Highline, the flames still licking their way across. Despite the fact that it was not yet nightfall, Mel reached over and flipped the headlights on, and the light from the beams shone orange instead of yellow, bouncing around through the flames on every rut and pothole they hit. It reminded her of a flashlight in the hands of a toddler. Next to her, Sam pressed in close, sitting tall and straight, his eyes on the road.

The fire burned hotly on both sides, a red carpet the truck plowed through like a field of poppies.

"No way Claude's truck could have made it," Sam said, an observation echoed from the driver's seat. Even if it had started properly, even in four-wheel drive, Claude's truck tires had been in danger of losing traction or popping altogether in the heat of the burning underbrush and sage, leaving him, Sam, and the girls stranded like sitting ducks.

Mel kept reliving the moment when she'd found her daughters in the bathroom, then witnessed their evacuation, Annie burdened with medical paraphernalia, Astor crying out at the sight of the fire lapping at the house and road. On the EMS rig ahead of them, they must have witnessed the same terrifying scene Mel was subjected to now, and imagining their abject fear left a dull feeling of despair in the pit of her stomach. Thank God they had True.

On the right-hand side of the road, all Sam's neighbors' homes burned. It was like a movie; they were on a set, Mel would have told Astor and Annie, tearing along the road past balls of fire and thick billows of smoke, just waiting for a director to yell, *Cut!* It actually helped to tell herself this as well, because this couldn't be real. This couldn't be happening.

On the left, the houses down near the bottom of Highline remained standing. Apart from the red haze in the air, they looked normal. And then Mel nearly laughed out loud at the absurdity of this thought. They'd left "normal" behind hours ago.

They finally reached the base of Highline Road, where hazard tape restricted entry coming from the direction of town. The going was slower here, and their driver made his way more carefully, lights flashing, until finally they were at the entrance to Carbon High, where evacuees still streamed out of the gym doors, piling into the remaining cars and trucks.

"They've decided to open up the county fairgrounds," a woman suited up in Outlaw County Search and Rescue orange told them. A good twenty miles south. Out of the path of disaster.

"My girls?" Mel pressed. "They were just ahead of us."

The woman nodded toward the gym. "Just waiting on their mama." She gave Mel a sympathetic smile. "Your friend is with them, and your neighbor, sitting with your youngest."

At the door, they met with yet another gatekeeper, this one checking evacuees off a list. Mel gave their names—Sam Bishop, Melissa Bishop—and the man wrote them down on the clipboard. Mel barely registered any of it, focused on how nice it felt to say their names in tandem again, her mind, now that they were out of the worst of it, having room for only what felt most essential.

But then the man looked back up, a frown on his face.

"Did you say Bishop?"

"That's right," Sam supplied.

"There's been a request that you report to Sheriff Paulson just as soon as you get to the shelter," he said.

Sam looked confused. "Me?"

"No, her. Her, and a . . ." The guy looked at his clipboard again. "A Kristina Truitt. Paulson needs a statement regarding John Fallows's arrest."

Mel's gut instantly tightened, but she tried to press forward again with a vague nod to acknowledge she'd heard. This man and his requests did not constitute essential in Mel's book. Not right this second, anyway. She needed to get to her girls. And she needed to keep Sam by her side.

But he'd stopped. "What arrest?" he asked. "What about Fallows?" His eyes narrowed as he glanced from Mel to out across the chaos of the room, seeking True, the look of suspicion on his face eerily similar to the one she'd caught the other night in the Eddy. "What on earth could be important enough for the sheriff to request a statement in the midst of this insanity?"

When she didn't answer him immediately, she felt that suspicion slide toward anger. Justified as it was, it made Mel's stomach constrict again.

"I have the right to know what's going on," he told her through a clenched jaw.

Of course he did, but their girls were waiting for them. Astor was upon them already, launching herself at them from a cot near the door.

"Mommy!" she yelled, and Mel didn't miss the significance of the extra syllable, which she had been adamantly declaring babyish for months now, rolling right off her tongue. The sound of it threatened to undo her the moment she laid eyes on her.

She assessed Annie next, who still appeared listless but otherwise unscathed, hugging her tightly as Sam relieved Claude so the old man could ride out with the other evacuees. The second she released Annie, Sam's eyes were on her again, seeking answers.

But could she give him what he needed? The chaos of the past three days made it impossibly difficult to determine just where she'd gone wrong and he'd gone right, and vice versa. Health decisions, money, property . . . it had all combined and combusted in her head somehow, fueled by their decisions during this fire.

She managed a nod, and, catching her intent, True ushered both girls out of earshot with a murmured "We'll get everything all organized to go."

Once they were alone, or as close as they were going to get, with volunteers and public-service personnel still dashing here and there, herding people toward the door, Sam said firmly, "Start at the beginning."

And so, with her heart still in her throat, Mel cast her mind back to the initial spark that had spurred her and True to action so many months ago, with Kim's nephew's arrest. At the end of this sordid tale, would he still have any respect for her?

"The opportunity just opened up, right before my eyes," Mel told him, beseeching him with her eyes to try to understand. She explained the symbiotic timing of True's rafting trips with Fallows's trafficking needs, the relief that had washed over her each week as she'd deposited the cash that would fund Annie's next round of prescriptions. "I thought I'd found a solution after so many setbacks."

"But you kept me in the dark," Sam said, betrayal in his eyes. Mel had to look past it to answer him.

"I had to."

Her meaning simmered in the air between them. Any firefighter worth her salt knew that every spark needed an ignition factor, and Fallows's nefarious business operation hadn't been the sole element involved. *Oxygen, heat, fuel.* All three were necessary to ignite a fire such as the one she and True had stoked. The whole thing had gotten completely out of control, yes, but it hadn't happened in a vacuum.

Sam had a blind spot when it came to Fallows, and in his attempt to course-correct and find his own path, his pride got smack in the way, placing obstacles in Mel's path, too. Obstacles she'd had to make her own way around.

Sam didn't contest the point. "But how did all this lead to an arrest tonight?"

Mel exhaled. This would be the hardest part. She picked her way carefully as she told him about finding the stash at the grow site and the confrontation on Highline Road, but Sam's agitation grew with every word anyway.

"I *told* you to never have anything to do with that man," he interrupted, color rising hotly in his cheeks as it always did when he felt the threat Fallows posed to his family. Mel didn't argue. Here it came, the moment when Sam lost trust in her altogether, just when she'd learned to trust *him*. "I *knew* something was going on," he continued, and then his voice broke as something else occurred to him and he asked, "Was Chris . . ."

"Chris wasn't there," Mel told him. This, at least, would bring Sam a small measure of relief.

Instead, he spun the wheel of blame to point the needle at himself . . . so characteristic of Sam, Mel could have cried. "I should have trusted what my gut has been telling me for days," he told her. He took a step toward her. "But you're all right? Tell me you're all right."

The distressed little boy he had once been stood right in front of her, the decorated veteran of two deployments smaller, somehow, than Mel had ever seen him as he scanned her up and down, taking full measure of her battle-worn self. Mel knew he couldn't possibly distinguish between the bruises Fallows and his men had placed there and the soot and grime that had preceded them, but that didn't seem to matter.

"Oh, Mel," he said. "I get how you would be willing to do anything for Annie." His voice sounded striated, like something vital had been excavated from somewhere deep within him. "God knows I get *that*. But what if I had lost you, too?"

Hope flickered in Mel. "You didn't think you had already?"

"Had I?" He was studying her again, but this time, Mel didn't think he was trying to identify bruising. At least not the ones evident on her skin.

"No," she said softly. "You hadn't. You still haven't." The moment she had watched him let the house on Highline burn to the ground, the last of that chip on her shoulder, the one that had weighed her down for far too long, had lifted.

A breath Sam must have been holding came out in a choked sort of sob, and he pulled her to him tightly. "I know I haven't always done right by you," he said into her ear. "By you or by Annie."

Mel shook her head against his chest. "Working for Fallows—even for Annie's sake—kept me tied to that man every bit as much—more, maybe—than you hanging onto the house ever did."

Sam embraced her tighter in response, and in that touch, she felt a sort of release, a deflating of the pressure that had lived in her body for so long. After clawing her way through motherhood from the moment Annie had been born, she, like Sam, now had to let go of the fear of not being enough, providing enough, giving enough, for the people who mattered most.

She pulled back to look at him, an almost forgotten but much more welcome heat stirring within her as their shared culpability of impossible choices burned off in the air between them.

"Let's get the girls and get out of here," she said. "Together."

They found True by the door, Annie on one hip, no easy load to cart around, Mel knew. As she relieved her of the burden, True's eyes flitted from Mel to Sam with caution. "We all good?"

"All good," Sam said, laying a hand on her shoulder as Mel added, "No more secrets," with a sigh of relief.

Annie's eyes flitted closed against the crook of Mel's neck. "Mommy, I just want to sleep now. Can we go home?"

Mel pushed that problematic word—home—stubbornly aside and focused only on the *sleep* part. She and Sam had been trained by proxy by the best pediatric-cardiology team in the Pacific Northwest. Tired equaled low O2, and low O2 could almost always be attributed to sub-par circulation. What caused subpar circulation? A weak heart. It always came back around to Annie's heart. She studied Annie more closely. They couldn't risk another tet spell.

She addressed Sam over the top of Annie's head. "Forget the shelter. We need to get her out of this smoke *now*, before she worsens again."

He didn't hesitate for a moment. "Directly to Portland, then, where she's closer to her cardio team."

"Where's her medical bag?" True asked.

"Astor managed to bring it with her, though not all the medications made it along for the ride. At last it's not charred to bits, still in the cab of Claude's truck."

True's face fell. "Maybe we should have stashed away some of Fallows's cash after all. We didn't know you'd need it to replace the prescriptions."

Mel gripped her hand. "We needed Fallows put away more."

"And if that money had been on you when he ran you off the road, he would have jumped you for it in about thirty seconds," Sam muttered. "And be in the wind about five minutes after that."

Mel's steps faltered, the implication of what this meant hitting her full force. "Evading the arrest that was crucial to silencing his threats," she said.

True smiled at her. "Well done. I would have rather that money burn to ashes than end up back in Fallows's grubby hands."

"We're not criminals," Mel agreed. She glanced at Sam. "This whole summer, it's felt like . . ." She searched for just the right term. "Bad juju."

"Bad karma," True said.

"Bad blood," Sam added darkly.

"Besides," True said with a slight upturn of her lips. "Photos can get erased, or photoshopped. Without that physical evidence—all of it—it would have just been Fallows's word against ours."

"Which is hopefully still at least slightly more respected in this town," Sam said. He added a soft, if slight, smile to punctuate this, and when Mel smiled back, True caught the look between them and grinned, too.

"About damned time," she said as they made the dash through the parking lot to get Annie into a car and out of the smoke of Carbon.

# Mop-Up

# CHAPTER 31

*July 15*
*11:00 a.m.*

A steady rain—sans lightning—began to fall on July 14, and the Flatiron Fire became officially 100 percent contained at 10:00 a.m. on July 15, opening up the river road and clearing the sheriff's department and ATF to follow up on the search warrant they had now served to John Fallows. According to Mel, who had heard it from Lewis, Fallows still sat in county lockup, unable to make bail.

True was thankful; the reprieve from worry of retaliation had given the Bishops time to access emergency funding provided to Carbon fire victims, which enabled them to replace Annie's lost prescriptions and pay for the upcoming trip to Seattle for surgery. Holding that voucher in her hands had felt a whole hell of a lot better, Mel had told True, than depositing Fallows's payments ever had. And if Mel had felt any prickling of doubt over handing over perfectly functional cash, True was certain it was easily offset by the relief at knowing Annie's breathing became steadier each day, her energy returning in the fresh air as she awaited surgery in the city. According to Sam, she had even taken to jumping on the bed in the hotel.

True had been there in person to witness the ATF raid of Fallows's property, rolling up to the Outsider the moment she was granted official access, her rapid tag finally put to legitimate use. To say it was a satisfying moment would be the understatement of the year. Just as Fallows hadn't been able to get at them in the past two days, he certainly couldn't touch them now. He couldn't even get his grubby grip on his son; according to Sam, who'd heard it at the Eddy, Chris Fallows had fled north to the Alberta oil fields before the smoldered remains from the Flatiron Fire had even cooled, and could any of them blame him? Sam said he just wondered if it was even far enough . . . After all, he himself had to put more than one international border between himself and trouble back in the day.

Mel always found it strangely poetic that mop-up—the practice of ensuring every ember was out—could prove as taxing and as tedious as fire containment in the earliest stage. A fire was handled with pains-taking, tender care at its conception and at its death, with a desperate pummeling in between.

As a result of her pending disciplinary review and potential inves-tigation after the events on the river road, she'd been assigned to cold trailing, a tedious task that had her guiding the rookies over every square inch of the fire perimeter on foot, putting out every live ember along the western slope of Flatiron Peak. It also kept her from her family, but only for the short term. She'd join Sam and the girls in time for Annie's surgery.

"We have to make sure there is absolutely no heat left to escape," she told Deklan, who had regained most of his previous swagger, con-fidently stomping out hot spots again. The sight was a balm to Mel's tender, singed soul.

As they traversed the mountain, they rehabilitated fire lines, labo-riously shoveling and raking back the soil they had displaced only days ago in order to offset the risk of erosion in the coming weeks and months. The ash mixed with the mud from the rain to produce a thick, heavy sludge that resembled brown-gray cement.

"This is bullshit," Deklan declared, newly released back to fieldwork by Carbon General, and while Mel agreed wholeheartedly, she threw herself into the backbreaking task, relishing each protest of her muscles. She'd probably be pulling this grunt-work duty for a long time to come, but it beat losing her job by a mile. And it was the least she could do after putting Deklan's life at risk. After abandoning her crew.

The drizzle finally let up as demobilization began, the sky a stark slate of gray that blended with the still ever-present smoke as each interstate agency, private hand crew, and celebrated hotshot crew rolled out of Carbon one by one to the waves and cheers of the community. Most residents who had sheltered at the high school and then at the fairgrounds had spent their idle time making posters on sheets of cardboard repurposed from emergency food shipments, which they now displayed proudly. *Thank you, firefighters!* read most of them, with a smattering of *Keep Oregon Green!* (double meaning implied) and *We love you, hotshots!*

The ammo box of money True had stashed in the crook of the tree at Temple Bar was never found. Mel went down to the raft take-out at her first opportunity, only to find the tree hollow empty. Maybe Fallows had sent one of his crew members down to retrieve what was his, or maybe one of the first responders to clear the river road had spotted it first. Mel didn't care which. She, and Annie, had what they needed.

At the Outsider, True turned from the sight of the red and blue lights still pulsing over at the Fallows property and looked northeast, where she could already make out a swath of charred forest through the haze of the smoke. It still smoldered, gaping like an open wound, and she knew it would hurt like one, too, at least until the earth began to heal itself.

Her property was intact, right down to the chicken wire lining her garden fence and her welcome mat at her yurt door. Just a half mile down the road, the Eldersons' place had been wholly consumed, while next door to them, the Chandlers' home still stood. What stroke of luck spared some Carbon residents but not others? She worried the green rapid tag in her hands. So many folks had never been able to use them, Sam included. It gave True an idea, just a little sprout of one, but that was enough to give her a sense of *doing*. Of helping, in some small way.

Retreating to her neglected art studio, she pawed through her many half-welded metal pieces, trying to find just the right ones. It felt weird to fire up her welding torch, the heat and the fire feeling altogether *too soon*, but the end result proved worth it. Wiping the sweat from her face as she lifted her welding mask, she surveyed the 3D iron sculpture of a mountain she'd created. It stood taller than her.

She carefully separated the ends of the cheap twine attached to her rapid tag and affixed the tag to one of the interconnected bars of iron that formed the mountain. Stepping back to survey her work, she smiled, then hopped back into her truck to drive into town.

At the River Eddy, as she'd predicted, residents filled the bar on this first day back to business as usual in Carbon, mostly just trading war stories and commiserating with one another. True explained her idea to Kim, who silenced the crowd with one of her earsplitting wolf whistles.

"Any of you all who have rapid tags you couldn't use, give them here," she announced. "Truitt is collecting them for a . . . What is it for?" she asked True.

"An art installation," True said. "A memorial of sorts . . . to acknowledge all the town lost."

Some residents looked skeptical, most just looked battle-worn, but many dug into their pockets or went out to their cars to retrieve their sheriff's-department-issued rapid tags. Most were wrinkled, soot- and ash-stained from being pressed into use at road junctions, allowing residents reentry to their homes, but some still looked painfully brand-new, the shiny green cardstock stiff. Those, True knew, belonged to residents who never used them, their homes taken completely by the blaze.

Back at the Outsider, she affixed all these rapid tags to the mountain sculpture, until the peak, previously a cold metallic gray, looked alive with fluttering green paper. If only Flatiron's rebirth would be as swift, True thought. She added Sam's rapid tag last, at the very tip of the metal peak, the name *Bishop, 2303 Highline Road* still visible in smudged Sharpie ink.

She'd just finished when she heard the crunch of tires on her drive, and she tensed before remembering that it couldn't be Fallows. Still, she couldn't have been more surprised to see who *did* roll down her drive. Emmett bounded out of the passenger side of the rental car first, followed by his mother, alighting onto the gravel with more restraint.

"True!" Emmett had crossed the tiny yard, leaped up the steps to the deck, and flung his arms around True's torso before she could even brace herself for the tackle. They both stumbled a step or two, Emmett laughing, True clutching him so they wouldn't fall, before she could recover enough to look over his head at Vivian.

"What are you guys doing here?" She hoped her surprise didn't sound like a lack of hospitality. How had they even found the place?

Vivian stepped up onto the deck of the yurt to join them. "I'm sorry to just show up like this," she said. "We asked around in town, and I wanted to call first, but, well . . . cell service doesn't seem to work out here."

True nodded. It most certainly didn't.

"We've been in a hotel," Emmett offered.

"We got as far as Ashland," Vivian filled in, "before I-5 closed due to the secondary fire."

True felt a lurch of misgiving. With all that had been going on, it hadn't occurred to her that the Wus might have gotten caught in the clutches of Carbon's emergency as well. But the highway was open now, and they could have gone home. Yet they were here. Why?

"We've been watching all the news," Emmett said, spinning away from True to gaze out over the property. Smoke still lingered in the air, but she could tell when he spotted the river by his quick smile of recognition. He raised his gaze to study the blackened mountainsides next, parts of Flatiron Peak still smoldering, and when he twisted back around to address True again, his face was solemn. "It was a megafire, just like you said."

Vivian took a step closer, joining them on the deck. "I was so scared, True."

"I'm sure," True agreed. "You must have been terrified, waylaid like that."

Vivian gave a breathy little laugh, like she was slightly embarrassed, but held True's gaze as she said, "I wasn't scared for *us*, True."

It took a second for her implication to sink in. "Oh." Vivian still wore a self-conscious smile, and True glanced down first, because what if she was misreading this whole thing? She addressed Emmett again. "Oh, well, I'm just fine, as you can see." She wiggled her feet at him. "Even my river-sandal tan remains intact."

Emmett smiled, then peered curiously around her toward the yurt. True remembered her manners. "Come on in."

Emmett didn't need to be asked twice, taking in the circular room, from the pine lattice work around the canvas to the river rock and the ladder to the small loft space. "Go ahead and explore," she told him as she held the door open for Vivian.

"We saw other news reports, too," Vivian said more quietly, once Emmett had begun the climb up to the loft. "A big illegal marijuana bust was made not far from here. Arms, cash, and ammo, too."

True's gut tightened, and she took a step back without quite realizing it. What was Vivian implying now?

But she laid a hand on True's arm, and that subtle but unmistakable current of electricity flew between them again. "You were credited by name as crucial to the success of the arrest," she continued, then took a breath like she needed to get out whatever else she had to say before True could interrupt, or maybe even Emmett. "And I don't know the details, and I'm not asking for them, but I want to tell you how sorry I am. For how I acted, that last day on the river. I shouldn't have doubted you. You gave me no reason to."

"Well, that's debatable," True joked-not-really-joked, because relief was rolling from her in waves. Vivian didn't blame her. Vivian didn't see her in the same light she must see people like John Fallows, and True hadn't even realized quite how devastated she'd been to think otherwise until right now, with these two people in her Outsider.

Maybe that vision she'd had at the Fallowses' fence line hadn't been just a smoke-induced dream. Maybe the spark she felt with Vivian was real, and the connection she had with Emmett could last. Just maybe, she could have what Sam and Mel had, her yurt retreat serving as more than just a backup plan for when she hung up her river sandals for good. Stranger things happened.

The Wus spent the rest of the afternoon at the Outsider, Emmett most enamored with the path to the river, Vivian lingering in the welding and art studio, admiring True's rapid-tag sculpture with such genuine amazement that True's heart nearly burst from her chest. When the sun set, a vibrant red in the still-hazy sky, they walked back to the rental car, Emmett dragging his heels at the prospect of being stuck in his seat for the six hours back to Marin County.

"I really am sorry you and Emmett had to experience what you did on the river," True told Vivian, dragging her heels herself. "It wasn't exactly the Oregon I wanted to show you."

"Well, about that," Vivian answered. "I was hoping I could give you a deposit for next season."

"What . . . now?"

Because Vivian already had her phone open to True's rafting website, the payment tab displayed. "Well, yeah. I don't want to lose my spot."

True smiled. "Let's aim for June next year," she told her. "Much better weather forecasts in June." She went to remove her hand from where it rested on the open car window, then paused. "Of course, autumn here in Oregon is pretty nice, too. Winter as well, when the snow falls."

Vivian laughed. "It's a date," she told her.

In spring, the morels emerged. Outside Carbon, they popped right up out of the ash between the scars of the firebreaks and the blackened Douglas fir trunks still oozing their bloodred-hued sap. Even as the trees wept for what they'd lost, the soil looked forward, with spiraled, tightly furled sprouts nodding toward the sun.

The ferns and mosses had recolonized the ground first, some as early as two weeks after the Flatiron Fire stopped smoldering, the species with rhizomes—horizontal stems tucked away under the earth—poised to repopulate in the rich post-fire soil earliest. The aptly named fireweed followed, then stubborn milk thistle, peppering the barren ground with pops of color.

Mel took measure of the regrowth every time she and Sam visited True at her Outsider, which was often, now that Fallows no longer cast his shadow over the place. True seemed less guarded these days in every regard, actually, opening her door wide for the first time. Maybe, Mel thought with a smile, it had something to do with the frequent visits from Vivian Wu and her son, despite the fact that their next rafting trip wasn't for another month.

The girls loved it there. Astor had become a regular apprentice in True's art studio, helping her create the miniature fire sculptures it seemed every Carbon resident now wanted for their mantel or front yard. What had started as a fundraiser for the fire victims had exploded; word of True's mountain sculptures had spread and were now in demand all over the West.

"I wish they 'spoke to' *fewer* people," True said often, a sentiment Mel certainly shared.

"Fire season isn't going away anytime soon," she had to admit.

Which was why it was probably just as well that she and Sam couldn't afford to rebuild on Highline after using the entirety of their home-insurance payout to settle Annie's medical debt, including the deductible and out-of-pocket costs following her final successful surgery. But he'd just shrugged when Mel had voiced her regret over his lost home.

"Nothing to regret," he'd said, giving Annie an extra squeeze. "Maybe we should follow Claude's lead and rent a little place on the Oregon coast." He'd lobbed this suggestion lightly, but the meaningful glance he sent Mel's way had her giving the idea serious consideration; a transfer to a less tinder-dry county might just offer the family-work balance she'd been craving for far too long. He turned to the girls. "You kids want to take a break from morel hunting and learn how to go crabbing?"

"Yes!" Astor and Annie had chorused.

"'Course you do. You're Oregonians," he'd said. "Born and bred."

For now, he chased them—yes, Annie included—around True's yard, leaping over logs and sliding around garden fencing.

"Hey! Watch my herbs!" True yelled, laughing with a lightness to her tone Mel hadn't heard in . . . actually, she couldn't remember the last time she'd heard True sounding so free.

"You seem really good," she told her, because one thing Mel had learned in the last six months: You never knew when flames would lick at your door. Best to say things to people you loved when you could.

"I *am* really good," True told her, smiling at her in a way that made Mel suspect she was thinking of Vivian again. It made Mel smile, too. Perhaps, just like her, True had let go of something that she had been holding for far too long, and that had not been serving her.

The community of Carbon was also trying to learn the art of liberation. Gone was the high school; it would be two years before the Carbon High kids could return, bused an hour each way to schools out of district in the meantime. Gone was most of the west side of downtown. After the mop-up, Mel hadn't been sure what she'd been expecting, but it hadn't been *nothing*. But for almost six straight months in the downtown sector, blackened foundations sat abandoned and exposed to the elements while insurance companies haggled with business owners, the process to make good on their claims proving even more arduous than for private homeowners.

The charred framework of the grocery store, the Quik Save, the pharmacy, and so many other businesses stood waiting, their foundations littered with random remains: a half-melted plastic pink-glazed doughnut the size of a horse outside what used to be the local Winchell's, the metal safe in what used to be the center floor of the Chase Bank, a stone chimney all that was left of the Log Cabin restaurant.

The Eddy still stood miraculously intact, nestled between the charred remains of the gas station and the previous site of the East Carbon Apartments, which now housed FEMA trailers. A blessing, Sam had said, that he intended to pay forward, selling half the business to Kim so they could both continue to profit from it, wherever the Bishops decided to settle.

"It will all come back," he reminded Mel, gesturing out over the cauterized foundations of Carbon businesses and homes between swings of a hammer as he helped neighbors and friends of the Eddy. Beyond the back deck, the Outlaw weaved between charred trees, bare and brittle as blackened toothpicks. Across the street, new cars sat parked beside burned-out shells, and children played along the fluttering remains of hazard tape warning residents away from eroded creek beds and ravines.

She knew he was right. In addition to the morels and weeds poking their way up through the ashen soil, a surprise harvest of blueberries emerged as if overnight in the cold black that continued to scar the land, carpeting the ground in between knobs of charred madrone and tree trunks, flourishing in the lack of competition on the forest floor. The girls combed the hillsides beside True's property, once even accompanied by Emmett, buckets in hand, their mouths stained blue after only a few minutes of picking, their shoes immediately dusted in dark black ash.

If Mel knew True, pancakes would be on the menu the next morning, and next week blueberry pie. By next month, True would be back on the river with the Wus, and by next fall, Annie would be healthy enough to start kindergarten. Whether the Bishops were still here or on the rugged coast, the scouting troops and elementary school kids would take field trips to Flatiron, planting seedlings to prevent rivulets of erosion, and those small trees would entice back the smaller forest-floor inhabitants, the burrowers and the nesters, which in turn would bring back the hawks. Within a year, tender new shoots of sage and madrone would follow, and with them, the deer and the larger predators. Nature would reset itself in this blank slate of burned land, and so would Mel and Sam. Mel as a woman who needed to prove herself a little less. Sam trusting in his family and in the universe a little more.

Today, however, the front-facing slope of Flatiron Peak was still an ugly slash of blackened earth, and Mel allowed herself a moment to remember the heat. The chaos. The all-consuming fear. She always would. But she also remembered that scars—on the earth, on one's psyche, on one's skin—did not represent weakness. Like the fresh ones on Annie's slight chest, scars on this land represented survival. And survival meant life.

Mel stood in the cool, clean air, looked up at a perfectly blue sky, and breathed it all in. They wouldn't just survive, she corrected. Like the new growth finding a foothold in the scarred soil, she, True, Sam, and her girls would thrive.

# Author's Note

This is a work of fiction. While I worked to remain true to wildland science, liberties were taken for the sake of the story. And while based in southern Oregon, the Outlaw River, Carbon, and its residents are fictitious. Any resemblance to any real or actual locations or persons, living or dead, is coincidental.

# ACKNOWLEDGMENTS

I could not have conceptualized this story had I not been fortunate enough to call the wilderness and communities of southern Oregon my home for over two decades. Yes, every summer brought smoke season, but first, it brought sun-soaked river and lake days, star-studded skies, and clear, high-elevation air. The residents of this region feel a tangible loss, sometimes one entirely too close to home, when megafires strike. *Smoke Season* was inspired in part by the wildfires that raged in southern Oregon and Northern California during my residency, the Almeda Fire in Talent, Oregon, and the Camp Fire in Paradise, California, in particular. I want to acknowledge the residents who lost homes, businesses, and even lives during these fires.

*Smoke Season* would also not be in existence without my literary team. A huge thank-you goes to my agent, Abby Saul of the Lark Group, for believing in my work from the very beginning. And of course to my Lake Union team, starting with my editor, Chantelle Aimée Osman, who took on this project with such enthusiasm, as well as the copyediting and proofreading team who always take such good care of my work. I am also extremely fortunate to have a developmental editor as talented as Tiffany Yates Martin, who I am convinced is a magician; her intuitive reading allows me to pull the best of a scene or character out of the proverbial hat and put it on the page.

I would also like to thank the wildland and firefighting experts who proved so patient with my questions regarding protocol, ranking, and interagency collaboration: most notably Reuben Harrell, for sharing his experience as an engineer paramedic for Colorado municipal fire departments, as well as the folks at the Bureau of Land Management, National Park Service, and US Fish and Wildlife Service who allowed me to pick through their many resources available to the public. Any technical errors that remain within these pages are my own. I also want to give a special shout-out to the teens from my community, including my son, who spent their summers on ground crews all across the American West: if there is a more grueling way to earn college-tuition money, I don't know what it could be.

My education for this novel also would not have been complete without the multiple trips I spent with the OARS rafting company during my years as an outdoor-adventure travel writer. The leadership displayed by the rafting captains on these trips along the rivers of Oregon, California, Wyoming, and Idaho, and the many hours of adventure and camaraderie spent with my sons in this capacity, inspired the character of True and her rafting business.

I also could not have conceptualized the character of Emmett Wu without the honor of knowing trans children and their parents. Thank you for sharing a glimpse of your lives with me. You know who you are, and you set an example I hope many families will follow.

And of course, I am indebted to my amazing writing-critique group: Kathleen Basi, Brian Katcher, Heidi Stallman, Joseph Marshall, and Kelsey Simon. I would be lost without your careful critique and encouragement during every Zoom meeting.

Most of all, however, I thank my family. At times, I know it is not easy to live with a writer. Nate, Calvin, and Tobias you spent your entire childhoods with one. Erika, you become a temporary widow with every round of edits. Thank you also to my parents, a.k.a. the best cheerleading squad a person could ask for, to my in-laws and extended family, and to my closest and dearest friends, who have been so loyal in their encouragement of my work. You are all appreciated beyond measure.

# BOOK CLUB QUESTIONS

1.  A multilayered moral dilemma lies at the center of *Smoke Season*, with Melissa Bishop and Kristina Truitt blurring lines for the sake of young Annie's health. Were all their actions justified? If not, at what point or points did they cross that moral line, and at what consequence?

2.  The concept of "family" is presented in several forms in the novel. How does True define family? Sam? Mel? Vivian? How does each character's relationship with "family" influence their actions throughout the novel?

3.  How does Sam's past define his present and threaten to define his future? What does he sacrifice and what does he gain in his attempts to prove himself to his family and his community?

4.  What is the significance of Sam's house on Highline Road? In what ways does that significance differ from True's yurt retreat on the river? In what ways are the two properties similar?

5.  *Smoke Season* includes three point-of-view characters, and throughout a large portion of the book, these three characters are placed in three distinct settings. In what ways did Sam's storyline caring for the girls, Mel's storyline fighting the fire, and True's storyline rafting with the Wus parallel one another? In what ways did they diverge?

6. The Flatiron Fire added fuel to events already set in motion that summer by True and Mel. Had that unlucky lightning strike not occurred, increasing the urgency and danger of what was already a tense situation on the river, what would the end of that summer have looked like? Would Mel have come clean about her involvement with the Fallowses, and if so, would Sam have forgiven her? Would True have found her way to Vivian? Why or why not?

# About the Author

*Photo © 2022 Erika Balbier Photography*

Amy Hagstrom is a writer, travel industry editor, and author of *The Wild Between Us*. Her work has appeared in *U.S. News & World Report*, *OutdoorsNW* magazine, Travel Oregon, and *Huffington Post*, among others. A lifelong outdoors enthusiast, she served as a volunteer EMT with her local county search-and-rescue unit before launching her writing career. After raising three children in the Pacific Northwest, Amy traded the Cascade, Siskiyou, and Sierra Nevada mountain ranges for the Sierra Madre mountains, making her home in central Mexico with her wife. For more information, visit www.amyhagstrom.com.